"Bill ... I've never done this before. Could ...?"

Chandra spoke hesitantly, her voice tremulous with unspoken doubt and desire.

"Ain't done what, hon?"

His hand reached across to cover hers where it fidgeted nervously with a damp paper napkin on the table top. It was a big, warm, strong hand.

"You want us to go some place else together?" Bill asked softly, and held her eyes for a moment before she could look away.

Chandra felt herself flushing, then the blood seemed to drain from her face.

"I—don't know," she said barely audibly. "I want to, but I—have to think about it."

"It don't do to think too much," he said gently, and she shivered...

*Other Books
by Frances Casey Kerns*

Cana and Wine**
A Cold, Wild Wind
The Errand**
The Stinsons
The Winter Heart**
This Land Is Mine**

*available from WARNER BOOKS

ATTENTION: SCHOOLS AND CORPORATIONS

WARNER books are available at quantity discounts with bulk purchase for educational, business, or sales promotional use. For information, please write to: SPECIAL SALES DEPARTMENT, WARNER BOOKS, 75 ROCKEFELLER PLAZA, NEW YORK, N.Y. 10019

**ARE THERE WARNER BOOKS
YOU WANT BUT CANNOT FIND IN YOUR LOCAL STORES?**

You can get any WARNER BOOKS title in print. Simply send title and retail price, plus 50¢ per order and 20¢ per copy to cover mailing and handling costs for each book desired. New York State and California residents add applicable sales tax. Enclose check or money order only, no cash please, to: WARNER BOOKS, P.O. BOX 690, NEW YORK, N.Y. 10019

The Edges of Love

a novel by

Frances Casey Kerns

WARNER BOOKS

A Warner Communications Company

All names, characters, and events in this book are fictional, and any resemblance which may seem to exist to real persons is purely coincidental.

WARNER BOOKS EDITION

Copyright © 1980 by Frances Casey Kerns
All rights reserved.

ISBN: 0-446-91093-7

Cover art by Elaine Duillo

Warner Books, Inc., 75 Rockefeller Plaza, New York, N.Y. 10019

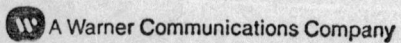 A Warner Communications Company

Printed in the United States of America

First Printing: February, 1980

10 9 8 7 6 5 4 3 2 1

Dedication

Let it be known that I am very well aware of the existence of some very fine people who are literary agents and editors—David Hull and Kathy Malley, to name only two.

Writing for publication is often a frustrating thing—for the writer—and writing is sometimes a painful and often a very lonely endeavor. One has—if fortunate—a loving, supportive family and a few priceless friends, but when he begins to write, actually to set typewriter to paper, he is alone, and that solitariness goes on at least until there is some substantial feedback, coming from disinterested people—which pretty well disqualifies family and friends.

So, basically, this book is dedicated to readers, and particularly to those readers who take the time to write letters. They can never know how much their comments, consideration and support are valued and cherished by writers. These are the people who keep us—*make* us—go on trying to "hold up the mirror."

Tuesday

1

Chandra Whitman put records on the stereo, new ones to which she had not yet had time to listen, flipped on the kitchen speakers and went to work there. In a little less than an hour she would wake Thegn, they would pick up Bruce and Gail at the high school, then they would be on their way to meet Grandma at the airport. Chandra's mother had not spent Christmas with the Whitman family for a long time. But why did they pick a plane due to arrive at three forty-eight, Chandra wondered harriedly. We'll be leaving the airport at the height of afternoon rush hour. She chopped boiled eggs for the chicken casserole and chided herself wearily for this constant impatience and dissatisfaction and criticism. Her sister Dorothy had, of course, chosen the flight for her own convenience, leaving San Antonio as it did just after lunch time. It would never occur to Mama, Ethel Barrie, to think of arranging schedules around Denver traffic. Around Chelsea, Texas, where

Ethel had lived all her life, city rush hours were not a factor. But Dorothy might have thought of the problem. Dorothy and her husband, Tom, lived only a few miles from the San Antonio airport, whereas it was a thirty-mile drive from the Whitman house on Clover Hill west of Denver.

Being honest, Chandra knew that any time of day would have been inconvenient somehow. She was so busy. She had little but contempt for those women who always made a major production of all they had to do but, still being honest, her life was fearfully crowded and complicated while, she suspected, her family, and particularly her mother, believed her to be a lady of leisure since they had bought the "big, fine house" seven years ago and she had stopped going out to work for the ad agency. There was, after all, proof of her status, wasn't there? She and Eric had had a baby, hadn't they? And she managed to have the time to do all that writing.

Still, she was glad her mother was coming. Wearing and difficult as Ethel could be, she was still Mama. Her love for all of them was real, tiring sometimes, demanding, even unacceptable, but real. The fact that Chandra often could not like her mother was no reason to detract from Ethel's love, a love which had lasted through situations almost incomprehensible to Ethel before they came up, and which had expanded readily to include Eric and Gail. In fact Eric, Chandra's second husband, not Bruce's father, and Gail, Eric's daughter from his own first marriage, were terrific favorites with Grandma. She wanted so much to be "fair," taking Eric's or Gail's part in any discussion far more readily than Bruce's or Chandra's. And Thegn, Ethel's youngest grandchild by many years, was Grandma's darling. This did not mean Grandma was in any way willing to see the five-year-old "ruined." To expedite a non-ruination policy, she would put on a critical, often disapproving face for the little boy. Didn't it say in the Bible, "Whom he loves, he chastises," or something to that effect? Why did all Chandra's family, particularly Ethel, have to be so indirect about their feelings, their good, positive feelings, at any rate? Still, Christmas was a time when a grandma was especially dear, rounding out the celebration so warmly. Christmas was a time for grandparents almost as much as for grandchildren. Chandra yearned wistfully for those few days when all the outside things would be done, Grandma fetched home, shopping over, the tree up, school and Eric's work temporarily in abeyance, when they would all be here at home, enjoying the holidays. What a shame there was always so much to go through first, so that the really good part was often so nearly spoiled by weariness and commercialism and the rest of it.

So far as Chandra's own work was concerned, housework aside, of course, she had been desperately busy, trying to get everything caught up, or at least to reach some plateau with it. Grandma didn't want to be entertained, she always said, but she did expect, and always manage to get, a great deal of attention. She would be helpful, in her way, with the household holiday doings, the cleaning, cooking, gift wrapping and the rest of it, but she would insist relentlessly on togetherness, particularly with her daughter, and on a great deal of palpable appreciation.

Chandra smiled a small grim smile. What her mother was least willing to give openly was the thing she most persistently demanded from others. All right, she thought, trying for firmness. I can do those things for Mama, for the two or three weeks she'll be here with us. Why not make another person feel needed and happy, if you know what that takes? Mama stopped her emotional growth some time way back. She doesn't even know the word reciprocate. She's getting on for eighty and she isn't going to learn the word, or the action, at this late date. I can give her some of what she wants because I'm more aware of it. It's just her way, getting along with, showing open approval of Eric. One's own child is supposed to know it's loved, right? What are daughters for, in her books, but to be criticized and counseled and kept in their places? While a son-in-law, an outsider, needs to be admired and made the most of.

Suppose they hated each other, couldn't get along? How would I feel then? She grinned tiredly at the cake batter she was mixing. Well, then I'd be feeling sorry for myself, left out, pressured, pretty much the way I'm feeling anyway. It's not jealousy; well, not much. It's just that Eric doesn't see how hard she is on me, or maybe that he doesn't understand it. He can just say something like "Don't let her get to you," and think that can be the end of it. He won't see that Mama has the ability, the power, to regress me to childhood where I have to keep trying to prove myself—look at me; I am a worthy person in my own right—of whatever the hell I should be worthy of: your approval, love, respect, just positive notice? I'm *not* just the little crippled girl, your baby who was hurt in that accident where Glen was killed. That was so long ago, thirty-six years. See me *now*, know who I really am.

Chandra's eyes burned and she rubbed them irritably with her knuckles. She *was* that little girl to Mama, grown big, maybe, and with a family of her own, but still just as much in need of guidance and correction. Mama had stopped growing, but she couldn't stop Chandra—could she?

She poured the cake batter into its pan, scraping the bowl with unnecessary noise. She had wanted to listen with care to the new records and she was missing everything about them.

The answer to her difficulties with Mama was, of course, that she, Chandra, was thirty-eight years old and the fact that the difficulties existed was ridiculous. She had nothing to "make up for" to anyone. Her brother, the only son's being killed was none of her doing, nor had she had any choice about her own permanent injury in that long-ago accident. Certainly it had not been her decision that she be born to Ethel and Luther Barrie years later than their other three children, or that Luther had died when she was eight. Why did she always feel indebted, as if she had to go on compensating, ashamed, responsible for her crippled leg and . . . ?

She slammed the oven door. More ridiculousness. Knowing those things, knowing she was an adult, with different standards, a different life style from Mama's, more intelligence, perception and other good things, didn't enable her simply to *be* those things, calmly and coolly, not in Mama's presence, or even in the thought of it. If she could leave me alone, be my friend as I'd like to be hers, not always radiate censure, just let me *be*. But to be is up to me. Isn't it? I'm the one who's letting myself feel these things . . .

Determinedly, she snapped her mind away from the endless circling and went to put a load of laundry into the dryer. Returning to the kitchen, she was aware of the dull permeating pain in her leg, and that she was limping badly. Already, this had been a very full day, and it was not half over. Her leg, despite the medical advice, surgery and exercise, just would never be strong. She had been a normal enough child—at least her parents had let her have that—running, climbing trees, riding other kids' bicycles, all of it, but the injured leg remained weak, slightly smaller than the right one, slightly twisted, with the ugly, puckered scars running almost from knee to hip. The leg had been almost severed in the smashed pickup truck. Merely saving it, not having to amputate, had been a small miracle for the doctors. And, if there had to be an accident, she was lucky that it had happened when she was a resilient, blindly determined two, rather than a crushable, stoppable, more advanced age. The doctors—several had consulted—assured her parents that she was a little remarkable, that, had she been older or less determined, she would almost certainly have spent the rest of her life in a wheelchair.

Chandra poured herself a cup of coffee and carried

it, with a plate of cookies, to the table, trying abstractedly to remember if she'd eaten anything else today. She was often careless about meals for herself, always had been, indifferent, resentful at times of other people's regular, relentless need for meals when she had so many other, more interesting or exigent things to do. This was one of the things about which she and Eric had a mild, running disagreement. She saw to it that meals were there, regularly, for the family, but sometimes skipped one herself, did not fret if one of the children did so. Eric was convinced that a good and sufficient diet, the proper amounts of sleep, were the solution to a multitude of problems, all that was needed. Since they had first met, almost eleven years ago now, it seemed that Eric had been pressing her to eat. She appreciated the concern, though it had come to be an irritant, like so many other things. It seemed he had a tendency to stress what, to her, was unimportant, and not even to be aware of ...

Well, somewhere along the way, just in the past few years, food had become more important to her, to the extent that she was now fifteen or twenty pounds overweight. She still skipped other meals, but made up for it with little snacks like these cookies at odd moments. She wanted to lose weight. This was the first time in her life she had ever had even to consider dieting. She wanted to want to stop smoking, to make the effort and find the time for more physical exercise. So many things ... These lacks, the lessening of self-discipline, the physical failings, were they indications of imminent middle age? How could she be so near to forty? Inside, she felt almost the same girl who had run away from Les and Mama and come to Denver, the place of dreams, with Bruce a tiny baby. Well, no, not the same girl, but remarkably, sometimes disgustingly unchanged inside. Yet so much time had passed, so *much*. It was frightening.

Still, there had been all the good things in that time. She and Bruce and Eric and Gail had somehow found each other and had, with the very minimum of difficulty, formed the two families into one. She had, with Eric's encouragement, begun to write things for sale. They had found this house, big enough to serve their various needs, far enough out of the city to be free of most of the city's problems, giving them a hint of country living with the city's advantages available and easily accessible. They had friends, a few of them true gems. Eric's primary job, engineer with a large company which made electrical equipment, was a good and substantial one. His promotions and raises would have come more frequently had he been willing to accept transfer, but when they had first met, Chandra had warned him that she would never again live away from the mountains.

She had first seen the Rockies at the age of fifteen, while on a trip with her mother, by bus, to visit relatives on the West Coast. The mountains enslaved her and Bobby Burns' words "My heart's in the highlands," said it all. Before coming here to live, she had returned only once, with Les, when he was entering rodeos in the mountain states, but the Rockies remained a physical force. She could feel them, even in Chelsea, Texas. So, as she left Les, girdling herself viciously so that her pregnancy would not be detected during the divorce hearings, while she lived briefly with Mama again because there seemed no other way until she and Bruce grew strong after his birth, Chandra knew where she was going, where she had to go. It had little to do with Denver. Denver was a fine place, so far as cities went, but Denver was just a place to be, where jobs could be had, within easy sight and reach of the mountains—*her* mountains.

Eric had come west at about that same time, in flight, seeking relief in something different from the New York suburbs, where he had known Mona. Mona, with her ambitions of acting, had yearned for California. She and Eric had lived there for almost a year of their brief marriage. When things hadn't immediately fallen into place for Mona in California, she insisted on going back east, then on returning to the West Coast, and she returned to California alone, leaving Eric with Gail, who had been less than two at the time. When she was killed in the crash of a light plane, Eric, who had just managed to finish his first engineering degree in night school, sought work in a new place, because he had to try to escape the painful memories of familiarity.

In all the years since they had known each other, Eric had told Chandra surprisingly, disturbingly little about his first marriage, while she had told him, eventually, most of the sordid, humiliating details about her three years with Les Campbell. It was Eric's favorite sister Betty who had, in short and thoroughly enjoyed visits between New York and Denver over the years, filled in some of the gaps: what a bitch Mona had been, nagging, sulking, blaming Eric and the baby for "holding her back" when she did not achieve overnight fame, totally selfish, and stupid. "She had the looks to be an actress," Betty had said once, rather grudgingly. "I don't think anyone ever denied that. She was the most beautiful woman I've ever seen, but empty." And Mona had been a beauty, dark red hair, lovely, perfectly balanced features, flawless fair complexion, fine, though rather vacant-seeming green eyes, a lush, voluptuous figure. Chandra couldn't help believing, in moments of despair, that Eric still thought of her, dreamed of her. Mona had been dead thirteen years now, but his reticence on the subject of her still seemed threatening. Surely, her desirability, her beauty, could do nothing but increase with time and memory. The mind had a way of sorting, closing out the file on the bad times, treasuring the good.

About her own first marriage, Chandra felt only a grim bitterness now, a vague embarrassment, though, of course, there had been good times with Les. The human animal was such that it could scarcely live through three years without finding some enjoyment. But it had been such a mess, that marriage, such a dismal failure, even before the actual ceremony had been gone through. It seemed to her that Les and Mona had similarities, good looks, total self-absorption, the unswerving capacity to blame someone else for their own failures and shortcomings.

Eric and Chandra were alike, perhaps in too many ways. That old thing about opposites attracting hadn't held true in their case. Sometimes, Chandra more than half wished this were not so. The same things hurt them both, or touched or upset. They were hypersensitive, particularly toward each other. Both had quick, hot, defensive tempers and one's temper, in its brief raging, had the power almost totally to destroy the other. They both had overactive senses of responsibility, and of trying to see a situation from all sides, while desperately needing to feel understood. They were nervous, impatient people, but intolerant of the nerves, the impatience, the moods, of anything they felt to be failure. The difference lay in how they accepted themselves. Chandra chafed constantly, while Eric seemed far more capable of contentment. The similarities should make them understanding of each other, and they did often understand and agree, but all the likenesses seemed to preclude a complementariness in their relationship. For instance, when Chandra was depressed and Eric became aware of it, he was immediately and deeply more depressed. It was not an attention-getting mechanism or anything of the sort, but a very real and disturbing fact. Chandra would then feel that Eric's bad mood was her fault, her responsibility to alter, and, at the same time, be hurt and resentful that he would not or could not help her. Still, overall, theirs was a good marriage, a good life. They could and did share some very fine things.

In trying to view herself, Chandra tended toward the psychological, always trying to analyze reasons and motives. Eric seemed to feel that this was a case of a little knowledge being a dangerous thing, and to be able to accept himself more easily, without fretting. Chandra wondered if this acceptance was real or a cover-up. If it were real, then she couldn't seem to help resenting it a little. She wouldn't wish Eric, or anyone, tortured as she was by constant doubts, fears and insecurities, but how could anyone want to be wholly unaware of what went on inside and why? She patently refused to be convinced that Eric was incapable of thinking seriously about himself, that his mind didn't run in such channels. He was brilliant and sensitive and it just must happen sometimes. How, if Eric never looked within himself, never revealed to her what he saw through such viewings, could they ever truly know each other, fully share life? She was so often self-revealing, laying herself bare to him. It was a thing she couldn't seem to help doing. She had a pressing need to put things, thoughts and feelings, into words, to be understood and, at the same time, to try to clarify them to herself. As time passed and neither of them seemed able to change in this respect, Chandra had begun to feel cheated and afraid. It seemed that while she kept struggling to let Eric into herself, to give him what glimpses she could of her inmost being, he was, deliberately or not, continuing to keep her shut out, denying her the opportunity to progress in knowing him, and stunting the growth of their relationship.

Chandra had, through all her memory, been haunted by the ultimate, ineluctible loneliness of the human being. She felt that an important part of a good marriage was to lessen this inexorable apartness. In the past few years, she had begun to fear this was not going to happen for her with Eric, and the idea made her abysmally sad—and lonely.

Perhaps everyone had to try to settle for less than they had hoped for, in marriage or almost anything else in life, to make adjustments that were not particularly desirable, establish priorities, weigh the good and the bad, come to terms with life. Chandra didn't like trying to believe that, settle for it. This marriage was too important. On the other hand, had she, was she, at almost forty, still trying with such fierce determination to do nothing more than live in a world of romantic dreams?

Everyone had his problems, which didn't make one's own difficulties any the less, but theirs *was* a good marriage, certainly so in comparison with most of the others of which she had any knowledge. Probably everyone was hurt, disillusioned, disappointed when they got down to the nitty-gritty of coming to terms, accepting themselves and their lives. No doubt she had, as with almost everything, expected too much, more than ever could have been.

She nibbled at a cookie, put it down, lit a cigarette and determined to go on with blessing counting.

There was Eric's engineering job, which paid well and with which he was reasonably content, and he had the part-time work, as drafting instructor for a community college class, which he truly liked. At home, he had the studio, where he worked occasionally. He was very good at cartoon drawings and at all kinds of sketching. Chandra wished he could devote more time to that, really use and develop his talent. Eric said he wished so, too, but, for the most part, he seemed more than willing to go along with the status quo. The studio was one of the reasons they had bought this house, the studio for Eric and the office for Chandra, set apart in a wing, relatively isolated from the rest of the house.

Chandra had worked for the ad agency for three years after their marriage. She was good at writing copy, reasonably apt at coming up with the catch phrase or slogan. She still did an occasional bit of work at home for her friend Sheila Summers, with whom she had worked and who now owned the small agency. One day at a luncheon she had been asked to attend, Chandra heard an editor of juvenile books talk about what was needed in the way of new writings in his business. At about that same time, she had come across a brief item in a Sunday supplement, a little-known facet of western history that caught her fancy. During the next several months, she managed time from other things so that she could do research and writing. Eventually, her first juvenile book was finished, sent to an agent and, ultimately sold. People in other parts of the country or world didn't see the American West, either now or historically, with much reality. Chandra Barrie Whitman's books were chiefly concerned with fictional characters, but well-grounded in history. She presented the real life of a cowboy, not romantic claptrap, but true day-to-day ranch life, not fraught with drama, but interesting in its own right. She wrote about prospectors who did not strike it rich, but who came to love the hills they dug in, and stayed on to become good, ordinary citizens of the West. She wrote about a wagon train's journey, not about Indian attacks, but about the grueling tedium, the small daily heroisms of ordinary people under their slightly mad compulsions to wrest new lives from the frontier. She wrote of a cowtown marshal who never wore a gun. The main characters of these books were always young people in their teens. The books' popularity had grown gratifyingly as each new one was released. Just yesterday, at her favorite bookstore, the manager had proudly shown Chandra boxed sets of the books, just in for the Christmas trade. The first juvenile book had been published eight years ago, the sixth was now in process of publication. Very satisfying. Still, Chandra did not want to write juveniles anymore, or at least not for a long time.

The income from those books was good, and as dependable as anything in the publishing business was ever likely to be. It had, with Eric's salary, enabled them to buy this house, to get themselves and the kids as far as Clover Hill, to keep them out of debt during the past few years. Subject matter for new books was virtually limitless. Chandra could, if she were content to do so, go on turning out a book a year, approximately, forever—ad nauseam.

Chandra had always loved writing. She had played with it from the time she *could* write, and, before that, had entertained herself with stories she made up and told to herself—lonely way back then, needing so often to fall back on resources that were purely her own. She disliked those stories about writers and other artists, highly sensitive people, whose families were completely insensitive, without understanding and inferior. Her family, while not necessarily inferior, had been convinced that trying to understand a child was, at the least, silly and a waste of good time. Making stories, and reading other people's, had been a very important and private part of her childhood years. And there had never been anyone with whom to discuss those things. The few times she had tried were disasters: laughter, mild, indulgent ridicule, or just absently, "Why don't you go on outside and play like other kids? You need the air and sunshine and I don't like it when you just mope around in the house with your nose in a book."

She had never dreamed that writing could become anything more than avocation, for which time was guiltily stolen from other things, not until that first juvenile book had come together with such relative ease, not until there had been Eric's warm encouragement and absolute, unwavering faith. He had been the first person with whom she was able fully to share anything she had written, anything she cared about; papers for schoolwork and the ad agency didn't count.

Or, perhaps she *had* dreamed, because before the second juvenile had been released, in that long, bleak desert period between writing, acceptance and publication, when she should have been preparing a third book, she had come to know that she could never be content with doing juveniles alone. She wanted to write adult novels, books that were far more concerned with people than with plots. She tried one, putting together several concepts of characters and parts of story lines that had been floating in her mind for years. This work was a delight, frustrating, painful, frightening at times, but basically a great release. She had to live her people and their experiences and that was often very hard. She was miserably sensitive about everything concerned with the book. It hurt terribly, while bringing immense, though qualified relief. Someone else had written that writing was "an onanistic experience." Those were possibly the truest words Chandra had ever come across.

When it seemed she had done all she could do for the novel, she and Eric had driven all the way downtown one Sunday night, to the post office annex, to mail the manuscript to her agent. Chandra cried all the way home. They couldn't even stop for the celebration drink they had planned because she couldn't stop crying. Eric understood. She was never ready to let the books go, though the juveniles were far easier because they were not nearly so much a part of herself, more things done on the outside.

The novel sold rather quickly for hard-cover publication. Chandra's agent had suggested, meantime, that she might use a pseudonym for the novel, since she was beginning to gain a slight reputation as a writer of juvenile books. She was furious at the suggestion, and deeply hurt. It seemed derogatory of the novel, and an insult to her. Why couldn't one become known, if a reputation were possible, for more than one thing? She knew how actors must feel about being "typed," refused to consider a pseudonym and was upset about it for weeks.

The novel was reasonably successful, for a first novel, had a good paperback sale, and was still rather widely available in paperback, which was no mean achievement when one knew that the sales life of the average paperback was only a few weeks. The "success" was more ashes than gold for Chandra. It was such a long, dreary business, publishing, so long in all the processes, writing, acceptance, the payment of an advance, editing, publication, and twice as long before royalty monies finally began to trickle down to the writer. All the time, the apparent indifference of absolutely everyone except those closest to her, who *had* to care, didn't bother Chandra nearly so much where the juvenile books were concerned. She could be in process of writing a new one and easily stop to go over galleys of the last one being processed. She could go to an autographing of one just released and from there to the library to research one not yet begun. But the novel took everything. The certainty with which she finally came through the whole experience was that she had to do another. She had to do the juveniles. The money they earned was very welcome, the books were good in their field and she was proud of them. And they were *there* for her to write. She had to write the novels for herself. "Why not do just that?" Eric had suggested. "Write them and keep them. Selling, publishing, is such a lousy business for the writer." Chandra appreciated his empathy, was half convinced he was right, if only she could do the work she loved sometimes without feeling guilty—until she received the novel's first fan letter. It was a shocking, beautiful experience. A reader in New England had "just felt I had to write." Chandra was startled, incredulous, deeply happy as she read in the shy, simple letter that this reader had found in her book some of the very things she herself had found, had been trying to convey. It was wonderful. Maybe it was just the call of grease paint or the fire bell or freight-train whistle, but she felt, from that one letter and others like it, that, if she could be the one to hold up a mirror in which readers could recognize a reflection, any reflection at all, if she had that capacity, that talent, then she had an obligation, a duty, to *hold* the mirror when she was able, not to turn it to the wall or to allow only Eric and herself, possibly a few friends, to look. "And," she had told Eric jauntily, "all that pain and suffering that goes into a book ought to be good for some kind of compensation of a material nature. If we were still using the barter system, how many visits to Gail's orthodontist do you think that hard-come-by book would get us? Besides, I think I have to write another. *Do* you see?"

When she had first begun to believe she might make a relatively dependable income from the juveniles, Chandra had been happy to quit her job at the ad agency.

She wanted to be at home with Bruce and Gail. She had felt that both children and both parents had missed a terrible, irreplaceable lot of togetherness. She had worked since her high-school graduation, first to support Les's expensive tastes and ego, to supplement what he might or might not make redoeing, then, trying to support herself and Bruce, she had both worked and attended college. She wanted to do things with and for Bruce and Gail, who were both in school by the time she could afford to leave the advertising business, to be there when Eric came home, to bake bread and cookies, have the laundry and cleaning done during the day. So she had left the agency, done those things and more. The juveniles went on, the first novel, and now a second adult book was ready for the editing process. They found this house. The children grew. She had been a den mother, a room mother, a band mother and the rest of it, and fitted in her writing where she could, resenting, sometimes, when the need to write was most pressing.

Then, when they had been married almost five years, had come their biggest and best blessing. Chandra was pregnant. Both she and Eric wanted another child. Actually, though they were deeply concerned with the problems of over-population, they had wanted two children. Chandra had had a bad time when Bruce was born, and the doctor had told her then that she might never again be able to become pregnant. At that time, bitter, newly divorced from Les, alone though her mother and one sister were entirely too near by, Chandra had thought that never being pregnant would be one of the nicest things that could possibly happen. Years later, loving Eric, loved by him, desperately wanting a child of their love, she had undergone corrective surgery for which the doctors actually held little hope, and almost two years later, when they had begun to give up hope, she was pregnant. They named the baby Thegn, which meant and was pronounced the same as the word thane, which meant, among other definitions, "free-born man."

Thegn would not have a younger brother or sister. After his birth, the obstetrician had said positively not again and Chandra's tubes had been tied. They had discussed adopting. Both of them wanted that and felt it would be good for Thegn, as well as for the prospective child, but, somehow, they had never got round to going through all the paperwork and investigation. Chandra felt guilty about it. The major part of the red tape would, after all, have been up to her, and she just had never got to it.

It seemed that the major part of so many things was, after all, up to her. If she didn't *do* the things, then she had to be the instigator of getting them done, which was, oftentimes, worse. . . . But they had Thegn and Thegn was wonderful, their very own proof positive that miracles could happen.

Yes, miracles. So why did she feel like crying, and cry, so often lately? Was she getting *bored* with her very full life? How the hell was there *time* to be bored? She got up, sniffing impatiently. There wasn't even time to try to understand why she felt as she did, and this was certainly no occasion to give way to shaking, soppy emotions, not with Mama about, literally, to descend on her.

She looked at the clock, putting her dishes into the sink, then looked into the oven, just at the wrong time. The cake was risen beautifully, but not done. Her interference just at this moment would surely make it fall.

Right now, Mama should be in Dallas, changing planes. Chandra and the children would leave for the airport just about the time Mama was leaving Dallas. Let the flights be safe ones, she thought, almost prayerfully. For her own part, she loathed flying, was terrified by it. Mama said it scared her too, but she could always give a wealth of details about what people looked like, wore and said, what was served in the way of food, how she was offered liquor and "let them know right straight" that she didn't hold with that, who she was almost sure the man in the blue suit must have been, some television personality usually. Chandra, on the other hand, froze on planes, after pathetically requesting a double vodka martini, concentrating all her being on the seemingly uncertain sounds of the engines and the queasy feel of the plane in the air. Fear of flying, she thought with a grimace. Okay. Better Mama than me.

Thinking of Mama and vodka martinis, she went absently into the living room and looked rather ruefully at the little bar. Nothing was out on top of it, but it was well-stocked, a rather newly acquired piece of furniture of which they were proud. Mama didn't approve of drinking, not in any form or quantity. When Chandra and Eric decided to marry and Chandra called to tell her, Ethel's sole response had been, "Honey, does he drink?" Not, "I'm glad you've found each other," or "I hope you'll be happy," or "Do you love him?" just, "Honey, does he drink?" Ethel was sure Chandra had been "ruined," "taught things," when she "had to go off so far from all of us." Surely, somebody "taught" her smoking and drinking and suchlike vices. Holding the telephone that night, Chandra's hands had gone cold and sweaty, her eyes filled with tears, and she had said, choking on the words, that Eric did not drink. She meant not excessively, but her exasperation and hurt at the stupid, irrelevant question had been so great that she immediately wished she had said, "Yes, Mama, he's a real lush, but that's about what you think I deserve, isn't it? your divorced, crippled, scandalously living daughter?"

Mama had not been to visit them in this house. She had come only once since their marriage, and that was while they still lived in the Denver apartment. The Whitmans had been five times in the ten years of their marriage to visit Mama in Chelsea. Chandra preferred it that way, even when they had to go by plane, because then the visits could be short, four or five days, a week at most. When Mama made a visit, it was with a kind of dogged determination, "a good long stay and my money's worth." Usually, when Mama began to write that she was thinking of coming, Chandra managed to find time to go to Chelsea for a few days, taking whoever else could also find time to go with her.

At any rate, when Mama had come to visit them in the apartment, they had put away the small amount of liquor in the house on a high shelf in the bedroom closet. After several days, when Chandra had begun to feel suffocated, literally having trouble breathing, she had begun to drink orange juice often—with vodka in it. It wasn't a fair way to behave, not to Mama, and not to herself. She wasn't living wickedly or shamefully, not drinking herself under the table, so she ought to be able to live openly. Which was what she and Eric had discussed at some length this time, with regard to Mama and liquor and the new bar. "If we want a drink," Chandra had said bravely, "or if someone comes in who wants one, we'll just damn well have it. She isn't too old to learn *something* and she can just find out from experience that a drink or two does not turn anyone into a raving maniac." She had stopped then, thought about it and sighed. "It's just plain idiotic that I have to say or think things like that, and then feel guilty about it. I guess I just can't *feel* much freedom; no, I *know* I can't. Thirty-eight years old, for God's sake!"

Now, looking at the new bar, which glowed darkly and faintly, she thought she'd better take a couple of tranquilizers. They weren't tranquilizers, actually, but antidepressants. They never hampered her driving ability—she probably wouldn't be driving anyway. Bruce would want to and that was worse—and maybe they would help in coping with Mama and the airport and traffic. Sometimes, she wished pills *would* hamper something about her. Eric could swallow two aspirin and immediately "feel funny," and all three children were like that. Chandra, on the other hand, had a very high resistance to any kind of drug; probably, she thought guiltily, because, over the past twenty years, she had taken great quantities of so many of them. She suspected that most of the usefulness of this latest antidepressant was as a psychological crutch. It was a very strong and expensive prescription, but seemed to have little real effect, just something to swallow while trying to hope for effect. She could think of the pills, their shape, where the bottle was, and start salivating, making spit to get them down with. Never needed water. And Pavlov had used dogs and food and bells. Still, if she stopped taking the pills abruptly, which she had tried a number of times, she would, in the course of a week or two, become badly depressed, frighteningly despondent. But was that the pills or her dependence? She wished with a sudden desperation that she were writing again, right now, deeply involved in that new novel, shadows and portents of which were already so constantly in her mind. That way, she would be absorbed, freed from the thoughts that were so troubling, so uncertain, so . . .

She shook her head, frowning at herself in the mirror of her bathroom. Then she stopped and really looked; it was a thing she didn't particularly like doing. A woman's face, honestly looking somewhat younger than thirty-eight, a longish, narrow face which couldn't take much more extra weight and look well, blue eyes, long-lashed but ordinary, a reasonably good complexion, especially considering that she'd never been willing to spend any particular time on it, short rather curly brown hair. Her only concession to what she considered as women's bondage to the cosmetic people was that she kept her hair tinted more or less what had been its original darkish brown color. Strands of her hair had begun to fade toward gray fifteen years ago, when she really was too young to be gray. Now, she didn't like the idea of being observed during the fade-out period and rather feared she might be completely gray, if the truth were known. She still wasn't ready for that. Hooked on hair dye, she thought with a grimace. Well, of course that's just what the makers hope for and, outside of the dye, perfume and bath oils, she really didn't make much of a contribution to the livelihoods of such people.

Mama, now—Oh, poor Mama! Chandra laughed at herself and turned away from the mirror. She really is a pretty nice lady, my Mama. Why do I always think of her with exasperation or something? But Mama and cosmetics and clothes were a different story. Vain old thing. Still, I hope I'm as interested in other things as she is in her looks when I'm her age.

The doorbell rang and she started irritably. This morning, while she'd been rushing through housecleaning before time to get Thegn from kindergarten, there'd been a salesman and a religious missionary. She'd been rude to both because they did not want to go away, and she didn't like being rude. Those people had to make a living too, but she resented their ability to summon her and her time by simply pushing a button. There weren't many door-to-door solicitors on Clover Hill, but evidently this was the day for them.

It wasn't a salesman. It was Joyce Crittenden, and Chandra found herself wishing fleetingly that it had been someone she could turn quickly away. Joyce was dear, really, but today was just too hectic.

"Chandra!" Joyce cried, hugging her. "I remembered this was going to be an awful day for you, and I thought I'd see if I can't do something to help. I'm later than I meant to be because I had to have lunch with Hal and a couple of clients. I was afraid you might have already left for the airport. No, no, I'll just put my coat right here. Don't bother about it."

The coat was fur, new to Chandra and very nice, though she couldn't tell one kind of animal skin from another. Joyce and Hal, with their two teen-agers, lived up on the top of Clover Hill, where the native trees grew. The two women had met years before when both their sons were Cub Scouts and Chandra had been their den mother. Joyce was more than a little enamored of the fact that Chandra was a writer. She wanted to write herself—as did so many people when one came down to it—and Joyce liked to collect artistic people as friends. And she always wanted to be helpful. It was a warm, real wish, but it carried something of desperation, so that one felt one *had* to find something for her to do. Joyce was one of those women who stood a little away, wistfully looking on and feeling firmly convinced that almost everyone else's life was more glamorous, smooth, exciting and just generally better than her own.

Chandra said, "Thanks for thinking of me, but I really can't think of a thing just now. Come on in the kitchen. I think there's still some coffee."

"You haven't forgotten our party this week?" Joyce asked almost tensely. "I know it won't be easy for you, with your mother here, but you will come, won't you? You and Eric?"

"We'll try. At least one of us can be there, I think. If we can't, I'll call you, as soon as I know."

"Well," Joyce suggested eagerly, "I can stay with Thegn while you go to the airport. Is he napping?"

"Yes, and I have to wake him right away. But he'll be going. He wouldn't miss meeting Grandma, or a trip to Stapleton. We're picking Gail and Bruce up at the high school. They'll each miss their last class of the day, but that's okay, for special occasions."

"Oh, then the whole family will be there. How nice for your mother!"

"Well, no, not Eric. He has a meeting after work, then he'll go straightaway to teach his class. If things work out right, he should be able to get to the high school in time for most of the program."

"The music program?"

"Yes. Isn't Mike in it?"

"Oh, yes, but just a little. He's nothing like your Bruce, you know. Oh, Chandra, you are so lucky! Such a *talented* family! . . . But will your mother be going to the program?"

"I don't know," said Chandra, taking out cake and casserole and switching off the oven. "We wrote her about it. She may be too tired after the trip. If so, Gail has offered to stay home with her. I really want to be there. This means a lot to Bruce. We all want to hear it."

"I just don't see how you're going to manage it all, but of course you *always* manage. What time is the plane?"

"Three forty-eight. Aren't airlines schedules crazy? Not four o'clock, not three-thirty or even three forty-five, but three forty-eight. If we're lucky all round, if the plane isn't late and the traffic isn't too bad, we could be back here by five-thirty. The program doesn't begin until seven-thirty, so we might even have time for supper. It's ready. All I'll have to do is heat things up."

She glanced round and found Joyce watching her as she hurried from stove to sink. She hated being looked at in that particular kind, pitying way. Her limp was so much worse when she was tired.

"That's a beautiful cake," Joyce said gently. "And you always bake from scratch, don't you? I just can't get over it."

"Not always," Chandra said and heard herself sounding defensive. "I was just sure this one was going to fall."

Joyce smiled fondly, wistfully. "Oh, you always put yourself down. I don't believe a cake of yours *ever* fell. You are always so *together,* Chandra. I don't see how you do it."

All right, don't believe it, Chandra thought. I am *not* together. Can't anyone see I'm falling apart? What you mean is, being a cripple and all. Can't you, can't anyone look at *me*? But she felt angry with herself rather than with Joyce. Chandra was being unfair, hypersensitive again, but all her life it had been such a struggle, trying to make people forget her leg, think of her. *Make* them. Therein lay the whole problem. You didn't *make* people think much of anything. You might, as with advertising, *persuade* them that they needed, must have some specific item, but *making* them *think*, especially when it concerned some preconceived, generalized way of looking at something specific about another person, was another matter entirely. So why did she keep struggling? And why did it matter how others saw her? Because it did, that's all. However, her insecurities were not of Joyce's making.

Joyce was going on effusively, wistfully, as always, "And your whole family! Your children are all so talented and intelligent and good-looking. You and Eric both carry on two jobs. You know, this probably sounds stupid, but I've just come to realize recently that homemaking *is* a job. Women are wrong, putting themselves down, when they say I'm *just* a housewife."

She lit a cigarette and drew on it as Chandra emptied the sink of some soapy water she'd had for wiping up. Then Joyce said, rather diffidently,

"Now please don't get the wrong idea, but what I most envy you is what you and Eric have. The way he looks at you . . . the way his eyes follow you in a group of people. If Hal ever looked at me like that . . . You two have a perfect love, that's plain enough for anyone to see, and so much respect for each other. Eric is so *very* proud of you and of your books, but *you* come first, by far. He's so handsome and you're so pretty, you, the whole family just have *everything!*"

Do we? wondered Chandra and felt guilty and ashamed at her bitterness. Joyce was right, mostly, only . . .

"And he's every bit as artistic as you are, in his way, and just as capable and efficient. Some women like you would have husbands who are just—well—parasites, but I know Eric's not like that. I just feel I'm lucky to know you."

No, thought Chandra morosely, the last thing Eric is is a parasite. He's built far too sturdy a wall around himself to ever be that.

Joyce said eagerly, "What's happening with your books?"

"I got the jacket for the new juvenile since I saw you last. I'll show it to you in a minute. I'd thought I'd have the galley proofs of the novel by now. Since they haven't sent it yet, I think they'll probably wait until after the first of the year. People in the publishing business seem able to take off a lot of time for the holidays."

"You must be just so *thrilled* to have *two* books in the works. Oh, Chandra, if I just had your strength and will power! If I could just *take* the time to write!"

She looked sad and forlorn and tried to cheer herself bravely by telling the names of some of the people who would be coming to her party. Then she said brightly, "Listen, Chandra, will you come to the new writing class I'm taking? I've told the teacher, and everyone, that I know you, and they're *so* eager to have you come and talk to us. I've told you about the class. They'd be so delighted to meet you."

"I could come, I suppose. But, Joyce, I never know what to say to writing classes. They sit there and look at me, and they're thinking: Go ahead, say something authorish. Give us the *answer*. And the only answer I know is Go home and write. If you have to write, it's going to happen, almost in spite of you."

"And you really think that's all there is to it," said Joyce bleakly.

"Well, not *all*, but it's about all I can say. You have to know grammar, things like that, but nobody can *talk* himself into being a writer. You develop an idea; then one day you sit down and start writing. That's a long process and sometimes it's very dreary. There isn't any way I know of to get it done but one word, one *letter* at a time. People want glamor, gratification right away, and there just isn't much of that."

Joyce was sadly thoughtful. Chandra collected trash into a big bag and put it on the back porch.

"Chandra, dear, you really are tired. Isn't there *something* I can help with?"

"I just can't think of a thing, but you're sweet to ask. All I have to do now is wake Thegn and get our clothes changed."

"I want you and your mother to come for lunch one day while she's here. How long is she staying?"

"I don't know. Two or three weeks, I should think."

"How will you *manage*? Oh, but you *always* manage. I suppose she's a big help? Mothers are like that."

"Well, Joyce, I don't know about coming for lunch. Actually, Mama is shy. She's always uneasy about that kind of thing. Maybe that's where my shyness comes from."

"Shy! You are the most unshy, sure person I know. Don't try to kid me. Ask her about coming to the house, will you? I'd really like to do that much."

"Yes, I will. Thank you."

They were in the hall again, Joyce getting into her coat. She looked into a mirror and agonized aloud over her need to lose five pounds.

The postman's jeep was coming along the street. Through the open front door, Chandra saw him putting a large, fat envelope into their oversize mailbox. The damn galleys! she thought. How *can* I work on them with Mama here, and Christmas, and . . . ?

"By the way," Joyce was effusing eagerly, "you remember my new group I told you about? The consciousness-raising group? Chandra, it's just fabulous! I can't tell you! I've *never* realized so strongly how much I've missed, *let* myself miss, as a woman, as a person. You just have to attend with me after the holidays. I know you could get so much from it, and *you* could contribute."

"I don't know, Joyce. I'll have to see how the time goes. Thanks for stopping by."

Hurrying upstairs, she thought. What is all this consciousness-raising and self-actualizing and liberation? Haven't these women been conscious before? Can't they think except in bunches? She shrugged mentally. I suppose I must be liberated. At any rate, there's never time to worry about it. But can't they think without getting into a group? Do they only have an identity in the plural?

2

Thegn was a beautiful child, in all ways. He looked very much like his father, with Eric's golden blond hair and fair skin. His eyes, opened wide now in excitement and anticipation, were large and dark brown like Eric's, giving Thegn's small, narrow face a wistful, questioning, rather startled look. He was a serious, thoughtful child, whose bright smile, because it was rare, was like the sun, breaking through briefly on a cloudy day.

In Thegn's room, having taken his own nap on the floor, was the huge, shaggy, Newfoundland crossbred dog, whom Gail, six years ago, in his puppyhood, had facetiously named Prince Charming. Thegn had learned to walk holding onto him. The great dog was still entirely too puppyish at times, and completely devoted to all of them, though he considered Thegn his very special property.

Thegn said, still drowsy, "Can Charming go with us to meet Grandma?"

The dog was never called anything as commonplace as Prince. It was Charming or the whole name or some other variant, but *never* Prince. They all agreed that Prince would have been an insult, too ordinary entirely. His huge tongue slathered lovingly across Chandra's face as she bent to retrieve Thegn's shoes from under the bed.

"No, he can't go," she said rather harriedly, looking for a tissue. "There won't be room."

"But behind the seat where he always rides. Well, almost always. Look at him, Mommy. He knows we're talking about him. Isn't he sweet?"

"Very sweet. Get dressed. Quick now. I'm sure he wants to go and knows we're talking about him, and just everything, but we'll need the place behind the back seat for Grandma's luggage. Anyway, Grandma doesn't especially like dogs. She wouldn't want him breathing down her neck and licking."

"She's going to *love* Charming," Thegn averred firmly. "Everybody does. Besides, she could be sitting in the front seat and he couldn't reach her."

"No, Thegn. He'll have to stay home this once. Come on now. Hurry up."

Outside, the day had been slowly graying all through its progress, growing more leaden and heavy, so that the great brown smudge of smog that lay over the city below them was less noticeable than if the sky had been clear and bright. The air was still, with a portentous feel, not cold, but chill, with a dampness unusual to the country. It felt like snow, but for a perfect storm, some wind was needed first, to clean and freshen and lighten the air. But one did not wish lightly for wind on Clover Hill, for it often came with a vengeance, roaring down over the great wall of the Front Range and through the trough of the foothills, of which Clover Hill was one.

"I know it's going to snow," said Thegn firmly as Chandra backed her neat little gray Volvo station wagon down the wide driveway.

"You just may be right," she said, maneuvering to the mailbox. "Reach out there, love, and see if you can get all the mail."

Before the attempt, Thegn said, "It's got to be a white Christmas this year, Mommy. It's just got to."

He released his seat belt, opened the window, knelt on the seat, and brought forth the mailbox's contents with great care and concentration. That was another way he was like Eric, Chandra thought, impatience tightening the back of her neck painfully. The infinite patience and care with things and how they were done, a constant, steady, indomitable seeking of perfection. She made a concious effort to relax her jaw, stop gritting her teeth, as he brought forth the mail, piece by piece. She had so little patience. Her aim was always to get things done, not perfectly, perhaps, but finished. Writing was the only thing with which she was really willing to take infinite amounts of time. Eric was occasionally less patient than she, where people were concerned, but with things, accomplishments, he was *so* patient. They had quarreled openly about this difference more than about anything in their lives together.

It was first brought home, jarringly, shortly after their marriage when, on a Saturday, they cleaned the apartment together. He cleaned the bathroom; she did the other five rooms, the laundry, and . . . It was the most beautiful, utterly spotless, germ-free bathroom in the world and Chandra was simply wild with frustration. They had both tried to change, but it was no use, so they carefully planned *not* to do things together around the house anymore.

Taking the mail, she said to Thegn, "Well, you know it's still ten days till Christmas. If it does snow now, it would melt long before then."

"When can we get our Christmas tree?"

"We've told you quite a few times, we'll get it on Friday."

"Look, Mommy! Is this your book? your gallons?"

"Galleys. Yes, I'm afraid it is."

She put all the things on the dash, bank statement, advertisements, a couple of bills, letter from her sister Evelyn in Beaumont, two or three things not immediately identifiable, and the galleys. She had been uneasy about receiving these proofs since the late summer, when she and the editor had discussed, by phone and mail, the editor's suggestions for alterations in the manuscript. This second novel, she had sold as an original paperback. There was less prestige for the writer in such a sale, but more money. If a book was sold first to a hard-cover publisher, tradition dictated that monies from a subsequent paperback sale be divided fifty-fifty between author and publisher, and paperback sales was where most of the money came from. Chandra did not like the editor who had worked on her book. Far worse, she had no respect for the woman and her judgments. She had never had a serious disagreement with an editor, but had begun to anticipate one when this paperback editor wrote that her publishing house never, never had time to let an author go over an edited manuscript before it went to galleys. Chandra supposed they had given her the magnanimous time of two weeks or so to go over the proofs. How was she going to do justice to the book with all the other things that had to go forward? Well, she just would, that's all. Why agonize when there was really no question about that? She could work on it at night while everyone else slept.

"Will Grandma come to my Christmas party and program?" Thegn was wondering. "It's on Friday." They had already discussed this, a number of times.

"Yes, Thegn. I'm sure she won't want to miss it."

Clover Hill was actually a ridge that extended eastward for a little way, from the main wall of the mountains. Twelve years ago, when green belts and other environmental considerations were not mandatory, a developer had bought up the whole hill. He had subdivided it into large lots, quarter acres around the hill's base, with larger plots as it progressed upward. The houses he built had a number of floor plans and varied in price with the elevation. The houses on top—there were only fifteen or twenty of them—were custom-built and very expensive. In the beginning, the Whitmans had wished they could afford one of the top houses. The land up there was nearly level and there were the woods, sparse woods, with small trees, but natural because of the altitude. The house they bought was, however, a little below the natural tree line, and, in time, they came to be glad of that. The woods drew all the children to play in the open spaces up there, and motorcycles and four-wheel-drive-vehicles and snowmobiles were always ranting around on top of the hill. Down the backside, there was a trail, for walking and horseback riding, which drew the vehicle drivers, though it was supposed to be off limits to anything motorized. The lower parts of the hill, as things had turned out, were actually more quiet and private.

The first owners of the Whitman house had done some very nice things in the way of terracing and landscaping, in addition to building on the wing, which now contained Eric's studio and Chandra's office. The wife had dabbled in painting and had wanted her own private sitting room as well as a room in which to work. It was a larger house than Eric and Chandra had dreamed they could afford, but the owners were pressed to sell and they were delighted with it. There were five bedrooms upstairs; on the main floor was a living room, formal dining room, a very large family-kitchen-dining room, plus laundry room, a small maid's room, the two added rooms and an oversize garage. They had had a maid for a while. In fact, they had had several. Ruby was the fourth and she had stayed longest, almost a year. They missed her when she married and still saw her occasionally. When Ruby left, Chandra decided she didn't really need extra help anymore. Ruby had been dear, but somehow, there always seemed to be plenty of work in the house for Chandra, even with her there, and Gail and Bruce were certainly old enough now to take care of themselves and to help out with the common good.

Avoiding three little children in the street, wondering what got into parents, Chandra thought back to the time when they had bought the house. How excited the four of them had been! Could she still feel that kind of happy excitement? She hadn't done for a long time. "We'll never fill it!" they had speculated delightedly about the new house. But of course they had filled it. Thegn had been born; things had accumulated as Gail and Bruce grew into their teens. Chandra often felt now that they were pressed for more storage room.

The truth was that Chandra often wished now for another house. Not necessarily larger; they could manage, actually, with a good deal less space. What she kept fantasizing was a place in the real country, a small ranch maybe, high up in the mountains, not a suburban place, but really rural; a little like where she had grown up, but more isolated, far better because it would be in the Rockies, with pine and aspen trees and a clear little stream, not the rough but basically flat and treeless land of her Texas childhood. In her dreams, there was little pressure of community involvement, no traffic, peace.

Below Clover Hill, there was a small shopping center, a few churches, the elementary school. The little town of Sherman, across the interstate, had begun over a hundred years ago, as a base of supplies for the gold or silver strikes higher up in the mountains. Poor little Sherman, left to sleep when the mines were done, had been inundated by suburban life now. There were a huge shopping mall, a country club, and a dozen housing developments crowding its edges. The busy super highway, after passing through the Sherman area, bored relentlessly and carelessly through the very heart of the mountains, and it made the area particularly desirable for many families. The Whitmans' back yard had a view to the north and eastward, over the metro area, but first and unavoidable was the super highway, arcing immediately below their hill. The house had been advertised as having a "beautiful view" and this was it. False advertising, certainly. The traffic noise was muted, but constant, something one could not forget and which, at its heaviest, could be a deterrent to back-yard conversation. They all preferred the front view, where one could see, across the street and across a side lawn with small trees, the open hillside, stretching up to the sparse beginnings of the woods.

Eric was almost as enamored of the dream of living in the real mountains as was Chandra. At least he said he was. They talked about it often. The family sometimes went camping, or just driving and hiking in the mountains, though it grew harder with every year to find places with any degree of privacy within a day's drive of the city. But their discussions of a real country home always went round in circles: What would Eric do in the way of work if they were away from the city? They all had friends they would miss. The children's recreations were near at hand on Clover Hill, and their schools were rated as some of the best in the state. Neither Chandra nor Eric wanted to be working ranchers, but the sizable piece of land they yearned for would surely have to produce something, in order for them to be able to afford it. They always ended by agreeing that nothing could be done about this dream for some years to come. They agreed. It was just a dream for now, something to be taken out and looked at with fond wistfulness from time to time.

So why, Chandra demanded as she drew the car up near the high school, did the looking hurt her so much? Why couldn't she just leave it alone? Did Eric really want it? Changing houses wouldn't mean changing people. That made her shudder. She didn't *want* to change people. Well, did she? No. They were a basically happy, compatible family, weren't they? Certainly, she would want no other. Maybe what she wanted was just slight variations, little changes that would make so much difference. Minimally changed values for the children, more time for Eric and herself, more time for them all to be at home together, quickly now, before Gail and Bruce would go away from them, more shared interests, Eric's not having to work for and be responsible to a lot of strangers—if only he'd do something with his drawings—more time for her to write without feeling guilty and pressured by all the other things from which she was taking that time . . . But wasn't that exactly what everyone was talking about these days? Family togetherness, self-fulfillment, back to basics, real values. There was nothing unique about her at all, then, except her nagging, inexorable refusal to be satisfied with anything. Other people longed for these same things, or at least felt they should long for them, but, very probably, they didn't cry secretly with the longing and the pain it brought, didn't delude themselves with the thought that a physical move could make all that difference. They had agreed that Clover Hill was not exactly what they wanted, but a step in the right direction. Only . . . what *did* Eric want? Did the things that mattered so much to her really matter that much to him, or did he just say so because he felt he *had* to say so? They had been happy on Clover Hill, seeing Gail and Bruce grow and expand after their release from apartment life. Then there had been the distraction and pure joy of Thegn's birth and growth. Was her nagging, constant dissatisfaction and growing insecurity and uncertainty just another symptom of her age? God, why couldn't she just leave it all alone? Was it the knowing she had reached, approximately, the midpoint of her life, that she was being troubled by all she felt she had missed and now could never have? If she was anything, she was tenacious, persevering. She had always believed that one could have anything one wanted, if one wanted it badly enough. But she had not had some of the things she wanted. What? A different kind of marriage? Well, no, not really that, only . . . Gail and Bruce looked blurry as they ran toward the car from the steps of the school.

Bruce wanted to drive, naturally. Chandra got into the back seat, where she felt safer, giving Gail the front passenger seat. Thegn sat on Gail's lap; he always wanted to be in the front seat if possible. They were a nice group, those three, Chandra thought as they drove away from the school.

Gail had inherited her mother's looks, but in a metamorphosed way. Mona's dark red hair, in the few pictures Chandra had seen, looked very thick and completely straight, falling around her like a dense chestnut curtain. Gail's hair was thick and of the same shade, but it was a curly recalcitrant mop which had to be kept short to be managed. Gail had Mona's very fair skin, but with freckles. She had Mona's eyes, but they were a calm, expressive green, not the cold, almost astringent green Mona's had seemed to be. Gail did not have her mother's figure. Mona had been tall, statuesque and very well endowed. Gail was diminutive, boyish. A few months ago, she had said casually to Chandra, "Do you think this is all there's going to be for me, Mom? In the way of boobs and things?" "Well," Chandra had answered, considering, "you've been having your period for a couple of years. It seems as if physical maturity might be getting on toward being finished for you. What will enlarge your boobs, if you're concerned about it, is having a few kids someday." "Yuk," said Gail and went off to ride her horse.

They boarded the mare, Cherokee, at a nearby stable. The horse was just one of Gail's many "favorite loves." In addition, there were tennis, swimming, bicycling, skiing, painting, her family, friends, the dog and cat, various foods and drinks, the mountains, some things about school, baseball and a good deal more. Certainly, she had inherited nothing of her natural mother's temperament, nor of her stepmother's either. Gail was generally calm, what the kids called together, quick, efficient, able to deal with almost anything or with several things at once, quite mature for her fifteen years. She had far more offers of dates than she had dates. "That serious stuff" just didn't interest her yet, though she had more boys than girls as close friends. She was very good in school, wanted to become a veterinarian "and a good painter on the side." Chandra, whose adolescence had been a time of turmoil and confused pain, envied Gail the warm, blithe, loving way she was passing through her teens. The two of them loved, admired, respected and, best of all, liked each other, Chandra and Gail. This had come as a gratifying and very pleasant surprise for Chandra, who had always got on so badly with her own mother and had taken on another woman's daughter with no little trepidation. Gail, naturally, took their relationship as a matter of course. "It's no big deal, getting along with your mother," Chandra had overheard her saying on the phone recently. "I just don't understand all this generation-gap stuff." She had paused then, laughed a little. "Sure, Sandy, all you have to do is have a neat mom."

Gail said now, as Bruce drove—too fast, Chandra thought—up the access ramp to the highway, "Is this the galleys, Mom?"

"Yes. I don't even want to open them."

"Oh, boy!" said Gail with sympathy. "Wonder where the time for *that* is going to come from?"

"Oh, Mom'll get it done," said Bruce casually. "You know good old Mom always comes through."

It seemed to Chandra that the words were touched with scorn and she bit her tongue to stop a tart, defensive reply. Bruce was placid too, but wholly different from Gail. He was careless, often thankless, tending to use people and take them for granted. Chandra didn't have the patience or empathy with Bruce that she could always seem to find for Gail. The truth was that she hadn't liked him particularly well these past few years. They had been very close, good friends, when he was younger and perhaps that was because he had been more malleable as a small child. Chandra was a manipulator and she knew it. Bruce's irritating ways now reminded her all too often of Les, though she knew that was usually unfair. What she had been most determined to give the boy, from birth, was the right to be himself and to like that person. It seemed, for the most part, that she had succeeded. Bruce was very definitely his own young man, and very distinctly complacent about it. But Bruce could be so much *more* than he apparently was. She should have been able to help him to be so much more. Eric assured her that Bruce was going to be all right, that he would, in time, become an adult with whom they could be friends, but Chandra often had serious doubts.

Bruce was a tall, somewhat overweight seventeen-year-old, who tended toward the gauche. He had inherited his father's looks, with little metamorphosis. His face would be darkly handsome one day, if he ever got rid of the pimples that sprouted more liberally and prominently than the whiskers he had recently begun shaving. He had Les's sleek black hair which, somehow, on Bruce, always looked faintly shaggy, and he had Chandra's blue eyes. In that face, those eyes gave a look of innocence, immaturity. Bruce liked biking and hiking but, otherwise, he was not nearly so much an outdoor person as Gail. His schoolwork was usually a little better than average. His parents, teachers and various test scores agreed that he could do much better. The problem, for Bruce, was application. He loved reading, but on certain very circumscribed subjects. He adored anything mechanical, but usually only so far as taking it apart. Just now, his bedroom ceiling was a veritable web of heavy cord which he had rigged so that, from bed, and with the help of pulleys, he could open and close the doors from his room. He was planning a similar apparatus by which he could spread up the covers on his bed. He loved to plan things, but most of his inventions never got beyond the planning stage, which was something of a relief to the rest of the family. Invention, innovation, possible genius should not be quashed, but Bruce was—well, just plain tiresome about his interests. He took it as a matter of course that everyone else was just as interested and enthralled as he. On the other hand, he could rarely spare a moment for anyone else's concerns. The words churl and oaf came to mind when Bruce's mother thought about him. He was sloppy and awkward, loud and inconsiderate. Those close to him knew that some of Bruce's "cool" was hard won. They knew because he suffered from what Chandra's mother had always called "sick headaches" when he had been trying to be particularly "cool" in the face of worry, apprehension, tiredness or excitement. He would turn pale and blotchy, his head aching blindingly, vomit once or more and finally sleep deeply. Sometimes, they only realized his deep concern about something because of the onset of one of these headaches. Chandra had the same sort of sickness, but surely not from holding back her feelings, trying to be cool? Or maybe she expressed the wrong feelings when she should have . . . But why couldn't Bruce talk about things before they came to have such overwhelming importance?

Looking now at the dark head which almost touched the car's vinyl ceiling, Chandra thought it would not be in the least surprising if Bruce came home from the school's music program with one of his headaches. Music was very important to him and he was good at it. He played several instruments well and might have made music his profession, had he let himself become involved enough to expend all the time and energy on practice. He seemed to want, perhaps expect himself to be able to do things without half trying. If anything took much effort or perseverance, Bruce tended to leave it. Yet, he did care. Why was it so hard for him to admit as much?

One thing to be thankful for—and there *were* many—was the way Bruce and Gail had always got along. They fought sometimes, and were generally nasty to each other, which was considered "the only way to fly" between brother and sister, but there was real, deep love between them. When they were little, seven and five when the parents first married, when they were being tucked in at night, they would call to each other, "I'm glad of you, Bruce." "I'm glad of you, Gail." "Will you be here in the morning?" "I'll be here, will you?" And the parents, holding each other later in their own bed, would, with smiles and sometimes tears, repeat the ritual to each other. "All of us," Chandra had said once in those early days, "have spent too much time in institutions, like offices and nursery schools."

She said now—sharply, she couldn't help it— "Bruce, you don't have to change lanes like this every time we get near another vehicle. There's not that much traffic and we aren't going to a fire."

"He's not driving on the way home, I hope," said Gail, turning a grin to the window.

"I'm a better driver than you'll ever be," said Bruce with a touch of sullenness. Probably, he meant both of them.

"When I can drive," Gail said happily, "I'm going to scare the shi—the stuffings out of you."

"I don't doubt that for a minute," retorted Bruce with some fervor.

"When I'm big and *I* can drive," said Thegn, "I'm going to have a big truck, yellow, just like that one. See it?"

Bruce actually *was* a good driver, Chandra was thinking. Her reluctance to ride with him was, in great part, due to the fact that she was not ready to have him drive, even though he had been driving for over a year now. One of Bruce's pet projects, when he wasn't reading or playing or listening to music or eating or webbing his room with string, was an old jalopy he had bought with savings from a summer service-station job. It was a convertible, topless and in sad shape. It needed all the garage room, and still parts kept spilling over to the kitchen table. Bruce had practically lived with the old car for the first few weeks of its residence, but now his interest had flagged and it seemed the convertible might never be eligible for safety inspection. Eric and Chandra were not particularly enthusiastic about Bruce's having a car of his own and now they were inclined to decide it might never become a real and present problem. But he was a good driver, because he respected and cared for cars. The trouble was, he was never content with just driving, he had to be *handling* the car, changing lanes, utilizing the short turning radius, the quick getaway, the good brakes, adjusting things on the instrument panel.

Eric was the better parent for Bruce. Generally, they got on beautifully. Les would have been a lousy father, playing his childish *macho* games. Eric never lectured or preached at the children, but set his own kind of examples by going on steadily with living. He was more tolerant and willing to accept than Chandra could be. The perfection Eric sought from things, Chandra sought in people, particularly in herself and her family.

"It's the old thing about meat and poison, isn't it?" Eric had said carefully the last time they had discussed Bruce. Words came with such difficulty for him and with such facility for Chandra. Perhaps words were *too* easy for her, spoken before she had put enough thought behind them. "Maybe," he had gone on slowly, "Bruce *is* striving, trying for his own kind of perfection."

"Then I wish he'd let us glimpse the struggle a little," she had said, "talk about it now and then. I wish he wouldn't shut himself behind walls all the time. What have we done to make him feel that anyone in this family has to live like that?"

But she had known the answer suddenly, part of it, and clamped her lips together, not to say more. Eric, too, for whatever reasons, had his own particular need for "cool." But then, didn't everybody? Didn't everyone want...

"It's hard for you too," he had said after a moment, and she looked at him sharply, wanting to make sure she understood. He was always doing that to her, giving her just a hint of his thoughts, seeming never to doubt that she could follow.

He did not go on, and her irritation grew. "Do you mean that I hide behind walls, or that Bruce is hard for me, or what, Eric? I truly am not a mind reader."

"I mean that it's hard for you to ask for—no, to accept help."

"I'm like Bruce. Is that what you're saying?"

"No, Chan, I—oh, I don't know what I'm saying."

Chandra's eyes prickled again as she sat in the car. Was she discouraging him from talking simply by trying to understand? Was she so frightening? And what did she want from Eric? Well, again, it had to do with dreams.

Chandra's father, Luther Barrie, had died when she was eight. She had very little in the way of memories of him. Sometimes, he had yelled and spanked her, for reasons she seldom understood; at other times, he had been indulgently and outrageously permissive, for reasons just as obscure to a child. Later, she knew that most of her treatment had been defiance of her mother. Luther and Ethel were a couple whose marriage seemed to have consisted of one long argument. When they disagreed, which was almost always, Luther would deliberately do something he knew Ethel would not like, and Ethel would sulk for days, sighing, pointing out that she was not well, how much she always had to do, generally playing a martyred role. The child Chandra was a trump card for both parents, a thing they could and did freely use against each other. They had done the same things with the older children, but Chandra, so much younger, had to go through it all alone, feeling always that she was somehow to blame, responsible for the parents' constant unhappiness.

Luther had been a weak man, though physically strong and a constant and hard worker. Mentally, he was simple, probably because of lack of education and severely limited interests. So far as Chandra's memories and the recollections of her sisters went, it seemed that emotionally he had been very nearly deprived, with no empathy for anyone. He might not have been nearly such a steady worker if Ethel hadn't been such a driver and nag. Of course, he might have been different in other ways as well, had Ethel been another person.

It had been Ethel who was responsible for their being able to buy a small place of their own in the early Depression years, her will, her single-minded saving. They ran a few cattle, kept a big garden, and Luther often worked away from home, usually on construction jobs. Chandra recalled his saying things about "hating to have to leave y'all," and having "to make it when and where I can." She felt later that the happiest times of his life, and of her mother's, were the times when Luther was away from home. Ethel ran the place, saw to the children, saved money, and made sure everyone was aware of what a hard life she had. Sometimes, Chandra felt sorry for her father in retrospect. Usually, though, she felt only a residual resentment and contempt. He was a grown man and a father. Why couldn't he do something, *be* something that might have been relevant and worthwhile to his children in their own lives?

Chandra's sisters, Dorothy and Evelyn, had been twenty-one and eighteen when Chandra was born, and her brother Glen was fifteen. Glen had died two years later, in the pickup accident when he was driving Chandra to see Santa Claus in Chelsea. She had no memory of him. According to her mother, Glen had been "the best thing God ever put on earth." Her sisters seemed to have only good recollections of Glen. Chandra couldn't remember her father ever speaking of him. Chandra, as a child, thought of her brother often. She dreamed of him by day, and sometimes at night. If Glen were here, he'd know, he'd understand. Glen would play with me sometimes, and talk to me and help me know how to be good. On the other hand, she sometimes hated him, but these feelings were quickly and guiltily quashed.

Two days after high-school graduation, she had married Les Campbell—he was the only boy about whom she'd ever been really serious—Les with his great ego and craven weaknesses, Chandra with her insecurities and lonely dreams. And they had been so *bad* together, from the very first, Chandra miserable and inarticulate then, Les, going off to his rodeos and other women, cursing drunkenly, bragging for anyone to hear that *he* never tried to hide anything. Chandra knew even then, in her ultranaïve and forlorn youth that, if Les had been a more malleable person, they might have ended by being a carbon copy of her parents.

After the divorce, after she had come to Denver, there had been two or three very brief affairs. They had been sordid, shoddy things, leaving her feeling little more than shame because the men were such leeches or such pompous fools. Each time had been a sellout for her, demeaning, simply because she so desperately needed the nearness of another human body, someone at least slightly older than Bruce. She had tried to hope for little more, and she became more and more convinced that she deserved a little better.

And still, she dreamed of a man, someone so much *more* than any of the men who had come closest to her life. She began trying to form the dream into reality, standards to be met by the man she might someday meet and marry. She tried out various images of the man, thought about the warm, loving family he would come from. They would have to have many things in common, he and she, tastes, ideas, interests. And then there were the really important things: She must be convinced beyond doubt that he loved her, and Bruce, and he must be—well, the nearest she could come to defining the rest of it was something she had read. A woman in a book had said of her man, "He rests me. Just being with him rests me." Chandra yearned for that. If rest were there, in the connotation it had for her, then all the other things would follow, or wouldn't matter.

She and Eric had been attracted from the moment of their meeting. Love had been beautiful and sweet and good for both of them, two hungry people, sitting down to a wholesome, hearty meal. Their sexual relationship was still just as good, and Chandra knew, from the quick, embarrassed confessions of other women, that this was a rare thing after ten years of marriage. They were both grateful, treasuring the relationship as it deserved. Only was Eric feeling as she did? Was he . . .

Eric did not particularly look like any of the men she had dreamed. His family was a close one, in its ways, but his parents were dead, his brothers and sisters still all lived in the New York area. When they had first met, he had still been going through the financial struggle of paying Mona's debts, though she had been dead two years. He had just finished his master's degree in night school, so that he could take a second job as a teacher and it was all he could manage to keep his small daughter and himself from actual want. Chandra had just finished her own bachelor's degree then, and shortly afterward, she got the ad-agency job instead of the secretarial ones that had seen her through school. They knew that their financial situations would begin to improve soon, and besides, when they were together, when they saw their children together, nothing else mattered very much.

But Chandra had refused Eric's first proposal, determined to be realistic this time. "And I love you," she had said, "but there's so much more to marriage than love. Surely you know that too." Maybe she had stifled his romanticism, even that far back, his tender, gentle wish to give? And now she needed it so desperately.

"But with love," he had said, "the rest can be worked out, can't it?"

"Can it, though, Eric? I mean after years. Will we always like to pay the bills together, agree about the kids? Will we—oh, I don't know, darling, I just have to try to feel sure about so many things. I'm just not ready to marry again yet."

So they had lived together, agreeing that this would be the real, acid test. Besides, they had felt incapable of living apart. The relationship had had its complications, with two locquacious children and a disapproving landlady. Living together was not, then, the accepted, almost standard thing it became over the following ten years. After several weeks, Chandra had been ready to agree to marriage. It was not a stumbled-into marriage. She had never felt that, though they had been very lucky in many respects. They had known each other only a few months, after all, not really long enough. Their many compatibilities sometimes, even now, came as small, delicious surprises. But . . .

But, looking back, Chandra thought she at least knew now what she hadn't been able to put into words when they had first discussed marriage. The rest of it, the most important part . . . She had felt, in the beginning, that Eric "rested" her. Now, all she seemed to do was want to put words in his mouth, tell him how to behave, what to think. But had she, was she still, crediting him with thoughts and feelings he had never had? She had believed he could come to know her, that he wanted that; and that she could do the same with him. And she did not know him, that seemed more apparent every day lately, because Eric could not or would not let her know him. He said he believed he did know her, but he seemed to show little indication of it.

When he had asked recently what indication she wanted, Chandra had said, struggling not to cry again, "I want you to hold me when I need holding; let me go my way when that's what I have to do, but don't act as if you're indulging a spoiled little kid. Don't always say 'Whatever you want' the way you do. You don't mean it, and I don't like it. What I want is for you not to have to *ask* what indications I want. That's the whole thing, don't you see? You say you know me. Well, if you do, then you do. Why do I always have to *tell* you?"

But *was* it all a dream, her ideas of a marriage growing in all those ways? Was she still just putting together leftovers of what the father and brother and first husband had *not* been? Was she being completely unfair to Eric, and to herself, in feeling, as she did now, so dismally, that there were great emptinesses in their marriage and that those holes must, somehow, be filled soon? She had not really considered divorce or separation. There were far too many things on the plus side of the marriage, the family, to think for long of dissolution. Besides, she needed Eric, far more, she was afraid, than he needed her. She was a very strong person, so far as things like determination, ability were concerned, but she had never been cut out to be a woman alone, sole adult in a household. The very prospect frightened her. She needed his moral support, his love and encouragement. And they *did* love each other, very deeply—didn't they? So what was she going to do? Go on worrying, gnawing and tearing at what they had until it was ruined, all in the name of things that might never have been possible? Was she doing this out of some dark perversity? Boredom? Had things been going *too* smoothly of recent years? Couldn't she live comfortably without some crisis, some extra dramatics? All of those things might have their peculiar grains of truth, but it didn't feel like perversity, boredom or the need for dramatization that was wringing her insides, making her eyes burn again.

At the end of that talk, Eric had said, miserably, that he didn't think he was able to be what she wanted, needed. That seemed about as final as could be. So what was she going to do, in order to go on feeling that she was growing, a viable person? She didn't really want growth, development, entirely separate and apart from him. But what she wanted, or didn't want had become a moot question, hadn't it? After he said . . . Wasn't it now a question of what she could *have*, not of . . .

"Mommy!" Thegn's yell gave her a violent start. He was skewed around on Gail's lap, looking at her. Gail was trying to see her too.

"What, Thegn?" Chandra was surprised to find that they had almost reached the airport exit. Well, at least for a while she hadn't been criticizing Bruce's driving.

"I called you four times," Thegn said reproachfully.

"All right, I'm sorry. What is it?"

"When can I go see Santa Claus?"

"Next Saturday, Thegn. You know we'll wait until Daddy can be there too."

"You could have asked us that, dummy," said Bruce, "instead of yelling at Mom. Besides, you know the answer. You've talked about it twenty times a day for at least a month."

"Bruce," Chandra said automatically, wearily, "Please don't call people dummy. It's all right, I suppose, among your friends, if you all agree it's all right, but Dad and I have both asked you not to call Thegn that."

"Anyway," said Thegn righteously, "you don't care about Santa. No wonder he never brings you anything when you call people dummy."

"Look at the plane taking off," said Gail pacifically.

"That's not Grandma," said Thegn, excited nonetheless. "Grandma'll be coming *down*."

3

"Your mother wasn't *on* the airplane!" cried Shirley Soderberg, aghast. "Where is she, Chandra?"

The Soderbergs had bought their house on Clover Hill before it was built. It was pure coincidence and good fortune that they were the Whitmans' next-door neighbors. Shirley and Chandra had experienced a warmth, an understanding from their first meeting, though, on the surface, they seemed to have little in common. Shirley and Jim had five children, the oldest in college now. A few years ago, Jim had started his own cement contracting business and Shirley worked with him in her "spare time." Before this, she had held a number of part-time secretarial jobs. She was plump and rosy, with warm brown eyes and medium brown hair, fading to gray. Though the Soderbergs had a number of relatives in the area, Chandra and Shirley thought of each other as sisters. Shirley had hurried in at the Whitmans' back door a few minutes after their hurried arrival back home from the airport.

"Well," said Chandra with a small half-hysterical laugh, "we think she's coming on the next flight. I can tell you it was quite a shock to us, standing there, watching all those people coming off the plane and no Grandma. We went to the main airlines counter to check and they said the connecting flight, between San Antonio and Dallas, was late into Dallas. Mama just didn't make it. They won't tell you, the airlines people won't, if some particular person is or isn't going to be on a particular flight. It's against regulations and I guess I see their point.

Anyway, with all the reservations at this time of year, they wouldn't really know if they'd be able to get her on the next flight."

"And when is that due?"

"Six fifty-two."

"Suppose she's not on that one?"

"Well, I guess we just—keep meeting planes. I'm going to call my sister in San Antonio in a minute, make absolutely sure Mama left there. Want some coffee, Shirley?"

"I do and you could use some. Sit still, I'll bring it. The airport must be extra busy right now."

"It's a madhouse," agreed Chandra, sinking back in her chair and lighting a cigarette. The two women were at home in each other's houses and Shirley's bringing her coffee didn't make Chandra uneasy, as it would have done if Shirley had been almost anyone else.

"But couldn't they have called you from Dallas?" called Shirley from the kitchen, "your mother, or the airlines people, if she'd asked them to?"

"Aunt Shirley," said Thegn from the table where he was eating the supper Chandra had heated up, "could you pour me just a little more milk?"

"I sure could, little monkey boy. Chandra, what about the school music thing?"

"I just can't make it," she said. "There's no way. Bruce and Gail are upstairs changing now. I've told them they can eat at that hamburger place near the high school. We'll drop them off there when we leave in a little while." She accepted her coffee with a rather wan smile of thanks. "We had plenty of time, driving home, to try to plan strategy. Yes, Mama might have tried to call, but her plane was due out of Dallas at about the same time we left the house. She might have tried, but I doubt it. Mama isn't exactly a world traveler and you have to think fast at a time like that. Anyway, she probably considers the lateness of the plane from San Antonio as a personal insult. God, I hope they do get her on the next one. I know she's exhausted. The poor thing will have sighed a million sighs. Oh, Shirley, I did want to go to this thing at school!"

"Is Bruce upset?"

"Bruce? No, I doubt it, but I am."

"What about Eric? Couldn't he meet the next plane?"

"No, he'll be meeting his class about that time. He won't know anything about this mess until he gets to the high school and Thegn and I aren't there. There's no reason why he should know. What could he do?"

Shirley was silent for a moment, until Chandra looked up and met her eyes.

"I'm going to talk to you straight, now, lady, okay? I think he *would* do something, if he knew. He must know how much you've been counting on this thing at the high school. Maybe he could just tell his college kids to conduct a review themselves, or whatever it is they do in the next to last class of a semester. Maybe he could get a stand-in to do a review with them. This reminds me of the time when you first moved out here and Bruce broke his arm. You were trying to get Gail ready to go off to some Scout camp or something, but it was just an hour until Eric got off work and you wouldn't call him or let him be called until you got Bruce to the hospital and it was quitting time for Eric. He was hurt about that; I was there and I saw it. Besides, he once said to me that he can't understand why you have to take so much on yourself, be so damned independent—those last three words are mine. Why not at least call him, give him a chance to help this time if he can take it?"

Chandra was silent for several minutes, turning the hot coffee cup in her hands, staring into its depths. Why had Eric never said such things to her? Well, he had, actually, in both words and actions, but there never seemed any real choice about whether to be independent, to always manage, when things got down to the nitty-gritty like this. She *could* manage, so she did. Sometimes, she felt such an ache just to turn over control of everything, including herself, but nobody, not even Eric, could change things that much for her, change her.

She looked up finally and found Shirley watching her uneasily. They did "talk straight" with each other, but Shirley was worried that she had gone too far this time.

Chandra smiled to let her know it was all right. "For one thing, I wouldn't know where to call him. He's at a dinner meeting and I don't know where it is. For another, my mother would never, *never* let me hear the end of it if *I* wasn't standing in that airport lounge when she comes off the plane."

"Okay," said Shirley, "I give up." Then, more lightly, "And I thought I came over to tell *you* a sad story."

"What's happened to you?"

Shirley shrugged. "What hasn't? For openers, I can't go to the concert either. My brother Joe, who lives in Missouri, you know we've been thinking they might come to spend Christmas with us? Only we didn't expect them before the weekend? Well, they're coming, all right, and, from where he called from an hour ago, it seems they should be here by midnight. The house is a real disaster, as usual. I've just got to stay home and try to do something about it."

"Oh, boy," said Chandra in grim sympathy.

"Wait," cautioned Shirley. "That's not the best, or worst of it. I was working for Jim till about three. I stopped in the store and while I was inside, spending all our money on groceries, somebody smashed my car, really creamed the left front of it."

"Oh, Shirley! Were there witnesses?"

"Not that the police or I could find. There's brown paint all over and maybe they can be found from that, but I'm sure not going to hold my breath. Jim's having a fit about the fit the insurance people are going to have. Of course I called him, first thing. You know old bigmouth Shirley. The cops brought me home. It must have been exciting for the neighborhood. Can you believe, no one in our nice little community would wait around to tell me who hit the car? It's getting bad out here."

"So," said Chandra, considering, "you don't have a car for tonight."

"Jim won't be home in time for anything. Can't be. Busy. God, I tell you, the business needs the work, but I wish it would snow and turn bitterly cold so Jim can be off a while. He's exhausted and so am I. I couldn't go tonight because of the house, but I could have driven the kids and picked them up, yours too, if I had a car. You know David took that wreck of his back to college at Thanksgiving. I came over here, originally, to see about finding rides for at least part of our group."

"They can go early with Gail and Bruce. My best offer."

"No, they'd never be ready, not my bunch. Other people around here will be going."

"Yes. The Sobols?"

"Too many. They'd never have extra room."

"Crittendens," Chandra said triumphantly. "Joyce was here today. She said they'd be going."

Shirley drew a sigh of relief. "I knew you'd come through. I'll go home and call her."

"Shirley, someone ought to stay home and help you. I know Anne will be playing, but Mark or Scott?"

Shirley laughed, rather madly. "You *are* kidding. Both those boys are a total loss. I can get a lot more done with all of them out from under foot."

"Well, maybe Tina would like to go along with Thegn and me to the airport."

"Nope. They're all going to the concert. You've got enough problems. In addition to everything else, you've got a headache, haven't you?"

"Why do you say that?"

"Because you look it, pale and drawn."

"Well, I haven't, not yet at any rate."

Shirley stood up. "I'll get out of here so you can call your sister, and I've got to get on with it. You *will* let me know how this turns out, won't you? We've probably got two of the wildest families in the world. If something ever, just *once,* went smoothly, I'd be scared, wouldn't you?"

Dorothy answered her phone on the second ring and Chandra explained the situation as quickly as she could. "Oh, poor Mama, bless her heart!" cried Dorothy in her warm Texas drawl.

Chandra had been fighting that drawl since she was a small girl, long before she had left Texas. Kids in school had teased *her* about having an accent. It was one of those things from the past that suffocated her, the way it took all the people from back home so very long to get anything said. They had, or claimed to have a good deal of trouble understanding Eric, who spoke very crisply and clearly. When Chandra went back to Texas and talked with strangers, store clerks and the like, they almost invariably said, dragging the words out to infinity, "You a Yankee, aren't you? (or ain't you?)" Anyone from "off somewhere" was a Yankee. There was no point in trying to tell them Westerners were different. Texas talk was, of course, different from other southern drawls. People from the Deep South spoke softly, often mellifluously. The Texas drawl was harder, cruder, and the people seemed to find a special pride in bad grammar and mispronunciation. Chandra found it irksome that, with all the time she had spent on speech improvement, she tended to backslide when listening to or talking with anyone from back home, people with what Eric called "the Texas speech impediment."

Dorothy was saying, "Yes, I put her on the flight out of here, all right. It was a little late leaving, but they thought there'd be plenty of time for her connection. I bought her a magazine, tried to see she'd be comfortable. Oh, bless her old heart! she's going to be worn out and worried plum to death. You call me, Chandra, after that next plane. I just don't know why those airlines people won't tell you *something.*"

"All right, we'll let you know."

"Mom!" bellowed Bruce down the stairs.

"Listen, Chandra," said Dorothy. "I'm glad to have this minute to talk to you. Something's got to be *done* about Mama."

"*Mom!*"

"What's wrong?" she asked into the phone and, covering the mouthpiece, "What, Bruce? I'm on the phone."

"She just oughtn't to live anymore way out there by herself," said Dorothy in rather irritable-sounding consternation. "Evelyn and I have been talking about it. She just can't always manage by herself any more. I'm worried to death about her."

At the same time, Bruce was yelling, "You know those dark blue socks of mine?"

"They're still in the dryer," Chandra called and Bruce did that fast, very loud thing of his that always sounded like falling downstairs and made her cringe. She caught a glimpse of him, going through the hall, nothing on but shorts, long hairy legs flying.

"I was going to write you all about it," Dorothy was saying. "There's no use telling everything on the phone, taking up your money. Evelyn said she'd write you, too, when we saw them a few weeks back."

"Mommy," said Thegn, leaving the table.

"I think there was a letter from Evelyn in today's mail," said Chandra. "I haven't had time yet to read it."

"You ought to read your mail, hon. Might miss something important. The thing is, Mama just needs to live *with* somebody. Evelyn thinks a little apartment close to one of us would do, but you know how Evelyn is. She don't want to take Mama herself, or feel guilty about *not* taking her. And they do live in a pretty small place themselves, Evelyn and Steve. I can't see for my life why they wanted to sell that nice house they had, soon as the kids was grown, but I reckon that's their business."

"*Mommy!*" pulling at her sleeve.

Covering the mouthpiece, Chandra said urgently, "Thegn, I'm trying to talk long distance with Aunt Dorothy. Now you just wait a minute, till I'm through." She was aware of the drawl, creeping back into her edgy voice.

"And of course there's Evelyn's job," Dorothy was saying with some mockery. "Evelyn *works*, you know. You just wait, Mama'll tell you all about that. She don't seem to know *I* work, just because my work's out of our home. Well, *we* can't have her, Tom and me. You know how much I keep our two little grandchildren. I *want* to do that, and I *mean* to do it, help Martha out when I can. They're just babies yet, and they worry Mama when she's around them for long at a time, and Mama worries *me*, just wears me to a frazzle."

"I just want to know if I can give the rest of my milk to Magic," said Thegn, catching Chandra's eye.

Chandra nodded.

"Can I talk to Aunt Dorothy?"

"In a minute, maybe."

"Chandra, is something going on there? I keep having the feeling you're not listening to me."

"I'm listening, Dorothy. What kind of problems has Mama been having?"

"Oh, just a *lot* of things, little things, most of them. I won't go into it on the phone. I'll write you, and you'll have a chance to see for yourself while she's there, forgetful, worse than ever, and feeble at times. You know how her health's been lately. Evelyn and me—well, it just seems to us like you might think about having her to live with you. I mean, I know you work too, but you *are* home all the time, and you've got that good big house. She could be a help to you, times when she's her real self, and she'd like that. Besides, you don't have any real little children around."

Lighting a cigarette, dragging deeply, Chandra said, "Dorothy, she doesn't like Colorado. I don't think she *would* come to live with us, even if we—"

"Oh, that's just a notion she's got, that there's not

any place to be but out there around Chelsea. She'd get over it if she felt *wanted*. I think she's about ready now to be willing to make some kind of a change. Tom does too."

Chandra saw Thegn spill some of the milk as he poured it into a bowl for the big black cat who was rubbing around his legs. He scampered for a wet paper towel, looking guiltily to see if she had seen.

Into the phone, she said, "How is Tom? And Martha and the family?"

"They're all all right. Martha's kids are so excited about Christmas. Makes it nice for us. Tom's working right hard. He says he's got a lot to get done before he retires next year. Tom's right worried over Mama too."

"I'll talk it over with Eric, Dorothy." She wanted to scream. Why *must* she feel so defensive? "A thing like that needs a lot of thinking over, on everyone's part."

"Well, yes, but it's not like it's coming out of the blue or something, Chandra, or it oughtn't to be. We've all known it would come to something like this someday. Mama's not getting any younger, bless her heart, and she can't go on forever. And I'll tell you this just like I told Evelyn, I don't want *my* mama stuck in one of them homes, one of them institutions."

"Can I talk now?" Thegn was leaning against her leg, which ached with the familiar bone pain, dull, but not to be ignored.

"In a minute."

"But I just don't see how we *can* have her," finished Dorothy and waited significantly.

Running downstairs, Gail said worriedly, "Mom, shouldn't I go out and start the car? Look what time it is."

Chandra gestured to her purse where the keys were. Gail yearned to start driving. Starting the car wouldn't really speed them on their way, but she liked doing it.

Into the phone, Chandra said, "Well, do send us a letter about everything. We'll see what—"

"Chandra, we're *here*," said Dorothy with earnest

righteousness. "We try to go out there and see about Mama at least twice a month."

"I know you do, Dorothy, and—"

"I know you're too far to come often, but Evelyn's sure not and they don't see Mama much more often than you do. And neither one of you really knows what it's like, I mean day after day, ordinary things. You just don't have any real notion of what she's like. I—"

"Listen, honey, I'm sorry, but we've just got to leave, right now, or we won't be there when the plane comes in. I've promised Thegn he can talk to you, just for a minute while I get my coat."

"Well, all right, but you let me know, Chandra. I'm just worried to death, about the plane and this other business. But wait! How *are* y'all?"

"Oh, we're fine. Busy. My latest galleys came in today's mail and—"

"Well, y'all take care now, hear? It's real good to talk to you, even if it's a kind of emergency. Say Merry Christmas to everybody for us."

"You, too, Dorothy, and the family," she said, feeling so tired. "Here's Thegn."

Chandra turned and saw Gail in the hall, a horror-stricken expression on her face. "Bruce!" Gail screamed up the stairs.

"What is it?" Chandra cried.

"Your right front tire's flat as a pancake," breathed Gail. "I saw it as soon as I turned on the outside light."

The afternoon flight from Dallas, the first one they had met, had been twenty minutes late. The early-evening one was, of course, on time. Chandra had driven frantically to get back to the airport, but then it took a good deal of time to find a parking place and after that, there was a long way to walk. The plane was in when she and Thegn came into the main lobby of the terminal and its arrival gate was, naturally, at the far end of the longest concourse. A skycap, seeing Chandra limping along, hurrying as best she could, once they had gone through the safety check, offered her an empty wheelchair he was returning to the main lobby. She was slightly embarrassed, as always when anyone noticed the trouble with her leg, but there was also a warm rush of gratitude at his obvious, open concern. He was an elderly black man, with an expressive, friendly face. She refused the offer, thanked him, and was swept by an urge to drop her head on his shoulder and cry. Then, as he was going away, she turned and called him back.

"I don't need the chair, but do come along with us. We're meeting my mother and she's going to be very tired."

Thegn wanted to ride in the wheelchair and Chandra nodded, she and the skycap exchanging smiles.

Mama was there, waiting for them, looking more than a little desperate. All the other arriving passengers had left.

"Oh, honey," she said, exhaustedly hugging Chandra and Thegn, "I have had *such* a time!"

"I know you have, Mama," Chandra said warmly, "and I'm so sorry we're late, but everything's all right now. You're here now and we can get home."

Ethel was surprised by the wheelchair, obviously embarrassed, but pleased. She looked nice, Chandra thought, and told her so. The dark blue dress was virtually unwrinkled, the makeup was good and careful, her blued gray hair had obviously been very recently done. Nice—but so very tired. Chandra wondered if she'd ever leaned her head back in all that time in Dallas, or sat down without a thought for creasing her dress. She was wearing heels too and the seams of her stockings were flawlessly straight. Chandra was glad they had chanced upon the chair.

"Go ahead, Grandma," Thegn was urging. "Ride in it. I did. It's fun."

Smiling self-consciously, moving gingerly, Ethel sat down. "I don't need it, but I reckon I'll do it, since y'all have got the thing here."

They started back toward the baggage area. There would be a service elevator they could use for the wheelchair, and Chandra would be glad not to have the stairs. She could go and bring the car around and get the skycap to carry out the luggage. She loathed always having to think things out like this, partly to make allowances for her leg, but it was an innate part of her life. She always managed well, with a little planning ahead. Worse was when someone else tried to do that. Unless they knew her well, they always tended to try to overcompensate.

"My, Thegn honey, how you have grown!" Ethel was saying as they walked along at either side of her chair.

She insisted on pronouncing his name "Thin." Chandra and the rest of the family, including Thegn, had been correcting her for years, until they'd given up trying. She would say, inevitably, "I just can't remember how to say it. It's a odd name. I never heard of it. Tell me how you say it now."

"Look at all these people," she was saying in tired awe. "I didn't know they was so many people in the world as I've seen today. I tell you, that Dallas place is the worst place I've ever seen, crowded, ever'body rushin' around like chickens with their heads cut off. This don't seem *quite* as bad."

"Well, this time of year is about the busiest, Mama."

"Lordy, don't I know that now! I know one other thing, I'll never try to travel at this time again. I was just a-tellin' one of them stewardesses—right nice little thing, born down close to home, I forget the name of the little place—I was a-tellin' her, I *know* I'm a-goin' to have to wait till well after New Year's before *I* git on a plane agin. I just don't know, Chandra Lynn, how many times I've wished today I'd never of started out, wished I was back at Chelsea, good an' quiet an' peaceful."

"You can get a good rest soon," Chandra said soothingly. "Your flight from San Antonio was late and you couldn't make the connection? Is that what happened?"

"Huh?" asked Ethel, inclining her head. Chandra repeated the question.

"Oh, lands!" groaned Ethel. "It was late a-leavin' San Antone, yes, nearly a hour late. *I* don't know what was wrong. Didn't seem to me like nothin' was, but they just fooled around and fooled around. I'd told Dorothy to go on back home. They wasn't no use for her to just stay around there. You know how she is. She had some appointment or somethin', at two o'clock, I think it was, an' she's just always in a stew, a-tryin' to be the most important somebody in the world. If she *had* of waited, I tell you right now, I'd of got off of that ole plane an' gone back with her.

"It was late to start with, comin' in from Houston, I think they said it was, an' then, when ever'body was all on an' all, they just *wouldn't* start. They told me, before we come to Dallas, that we might not git there in time for me to catch the other plane, an' then we had to wait to *land!* Did you ever hear the like? But the people was awful good to me, I *will* say that. They was a young man come in a car to where that plane come in to Dallas, an' he drove me all around that big ole place, over to where I had to wait for that other plane. I reckon that Dorothy must have told 'em at San Antone that I might maybe need a little help, because this young feller with the car was right there a-waitin' for me. I'd told Dorothy not to say anythin', but I reckon she went ahead and done as she pleased, just like she always does. I didn't hardly know what to say when this total stranger come up and says, 'Miz Barrie, I come to meet you.' "

"I'm glad he was there," said Chandra warmly. "What did you do, all that time you had to wait, then?"

"Huh?"

She repeated.

"Honey, I set. There wasn't anything else *to* do. I walked around a little, but if a body went very far, they had one of them places where they go through your purse an' ever'thin'. I didn't want to fool with that agin, or git lost in that ole place. An', right a-past that checkin' place, I could see they was a bar, right the first thing, so I don't reckon I missed a thing by not a-goin' out there. Dorothy had give me a magazine. It wasn't one I cared a thing about readin', but I've read it, nearly ever' word of it, a-settin' there. An' I worked on my crochet some, when my hands wasn't a-hurtin' too bad."

She still carried the work bag and her purse, though she had relinquished the magazine to Thegn.

"But you know the worst thing, Chandra Lynn? They kep' a-sayin', 'Miz Barrie, we just can't *promise* you you'll git on the *next* plane.' Did you ever hear the like? When I'd been a-settin' there, in all that loud, rushin' mess fur nearly *five hours?*"

Chandra and the skycap exchanged compassionate smiles. His lips formed the words, "Poor old lady," which deepened Chandra's smile, because he looked scarcely younger than Ethel.

She said, "Well, Mama, I know it was bad, and I'm so sorry it happened, but—"

"Huh?"

"Mama, where's your hearing aid?"

Ethel tapped her purse triumphantly. "Oh, I brought it. Don't worry about that. It's right here. I taken it off before we got to the airport in San Antone. Planes an' these awful ole places is so noisy. I can't stand to wear the thing where they's such a racket.

"But what I was a-tellin' you, Chandra Lynn, they *held me back!* Wouldn' let me git on that plane I come here on till *the very last one!* Did you ever hear of 'em not a-meanin' to let a body on? When you've paid for your ticket an' *ever-thin'?*"

Chandra had a fleeting vision of airline authorities using violent physical restraint to keep Ethel back from boarding. She said gently but loudly, "Mama, it's just been a mess. But, you know, those other people had tickets too, reservations for that second flight. Luckily for all of us, someone probably didn't show up, so they had an empty seat they hadn't counted on. They have their jobs to do and—"

"Well," snapped Ethel righteously, "it shore wasn' none of *my* doin' that that plane from San Antone was late. I had my ticket an' all ready, and yet they just made me wait an' *made* me wait before they'd even let me on this other one. Do you know how much these tickets cost?"

They had reached the baggage area. Thegn, leaning on the side of the halted chair and speaking very clearly, said eagerly.

"Grandma, I go to school this year. Did you know that?"

"What is it, honey? You'll have to talk up, good an' loud. Grandma just don't hear very good anymore."

Thegn repeated.

Ethel hugged him. "Yes, I know you've started ot school. You're just goin' to be plum grown before I know it, especially when it's so long between times when we see one another. I just wish your mama an' daddy didn't have to feel like they have to live away off like this. Wouldn' you like it if you lived in Texas, closer to Grandma?"

Chandra said, "Mama, give this nice man your baggage checks and I'll go get the car."

"Huh? Give what?" Ethel looked at the skycap with frank suspicion.

"Let me have your ticket so we can see about getting your suitcases."

"Well, be careful with it," Ethel said dubiously, delving in her purse. "It's got the part for me to go back, you know. I sure wouldn' want to lose it."

She frowned worriedly and stood up when Chandra gave the ticket to the skycap.

"Why don't you just sit here, out of the crowd," Chandra suggested. "Thegn will wait with you, won't you,

Thegn. I'll get the car, he'll bring your bags and we can get out of here."

"I'll sure be glad to do that," Ethel said fervently, "git out, I mean. Is that where the suitcases comes? That thing there?"

Chandra nodded.

"Well, I better try to see about 'em. He won't know . . ."

The skycap, who had started to walk away, looked back and winked at Chandra. She gave him a shrug, a resigned grin and went to get the car.

In the car, when they were finally settled and driving away, Ethel said in a somewhat awed, incredulous voice,

"Chandra Lynn, it's not my business, I know, but did I see you hand that colored man five dollars, or am I a-seein' things?"

"I did, Mama."

"Why, what *for*, honey?"

"He was very helpful and we took a good bit of his time. Besides, I liked him."

"I liked him, too," said Thegn from the back seat. "While we waited for you, Mommy, he told me he's got two grandsons that are twins and they're just my same age. They go to kindergarten too. You know what, Grandma? When we get home to our house, you'll get to meet our dog and cat. They don't know you yet. And we have—"

"Yes, honey," said Ethel absently, but with fervor, "I'll just be mighty glad to git to your house, dog or cat or whatever." She turned back to the matter at hand. "I just don't see what you mean, Chandra Lynn, took his time. It's his job, ain't it, to do such as that? Carry suitcases an' such?"

"Well, yes, but people—"

"Huh?"

Chandra lit a cigarette. "Yes, it's his job, but people with those kinds of jobs usually don't get paid very much in wages. They depend on tips for a good part of their income. Mama, don't you tip people like the man who drove you in the airport car today?"

"No, I never," she said, troubled. "Do you reckon I ought to? I just had never thought about it."

"I'm sure they'd appreciate it, but don't worry—"

"But *five dollars?*"

Chandra could hear the little wheels turning, Mama wondering what they spent for this and that, how they ever expected to get anywhere in the world if they always tried to throw money around as she had just seen. And, any second now, when she could tear her mind away from the five dollars, Mama was going to talk to her very earnestly about smoking. Chandra took a big, hungry, defensive drag from the cigarette and was briefly reprieved as Ethel said,

"Maybe I wrote you about this. They's a colored family livin' out close to our place. I guess that it was last winter they moved to Simmses. You remember where that is? Well, they're just as nice as can be, an' *clean!* Why, you never see a piece of paper nor nothin' a-layin' around the yard there, an' I bet the house is kep' ever' bit as nice."

Thegn began, "My teacher, Miss Cunningham—"

This time, it was Chandra who interrupted him. She didn't like doing it, but she just wasn't ready to have Miss Cunningham discussed yet. She said brightly,

"I hope you had a good supper on the plane, Mama."

"Oh, honey, I couldn' hardly eat a bite. I was just still so tore up about all that, them a-tellin' me I couldn't git on till the last thing an' all."

"I have some things cooked at home," Chandra said. "Or we can stop somewhere for something, if you'd like."

"Huh? Honey, I just can't hear if you don't talk up."

"Put on your hearing aid, okay?" Chandra said mildly.

Hurt, Ethel searched in her purse again. She said, sounding subdued, wounded,

"This thing just don't give the service it ought to. I'm forever a-havin' to put new batteries in it. I wondered if maybe Eric could fix it some way. I know he's good with things like that. They's *bound* to be somethin' the matter with it."

Chandra repeated what she had said about food.

"Oh, no!" cried Ethel, sounding frightened. "*No,* I don't want to stop anywhere to eat. I just want to git somewhere where they's some peace an' quiet. How far is it?"

"About thirty miles."

"*Thirty miles?*"

"Yes, Mama, we've been out there seven years. We've written you and told you. We live right at the foot of the mountains now."

"Oh, them ole mountains! I remember how rough an' cold they looked, from that other time I come here to see you. You an' Eric kep' a-tryin' to git me to go for a ride up in there, but I could remember how scary they was from that time you an' me come through 'em on the bus. You remember that time? You was just a little girl, not much bigger than Thin."

"I remember. I was fifteen, Mama. It was the summer—"

"Well, I thought to myself then, up there on that bus, on them awful scary roads, that if we got down out of there alive, *I*'d not ever go back. You remember, your uncle Horace, out there in Oregon, got it fixed up some way for us to have our bus tickets changed so we could go home another way, and not be in much mountains, through Newbrasky, I think, wasn' it?"

"New Mexico," said Chandra, smiling. The map, outside her home county, was all the same to Mama, a total loss, with one place essentially the same as another, not good. She always came "down" to Colorado.

"Yes, well, some place. But what I was a-sayin', it's none a my business an' I know it, but I just don't see for my life why anybody in their right mind would want to live right up aginst them mountains, nor in 'em. I bet you can't even grow any garden, where you're a-livin' right now."

"Yes, we can."

"Huh?"

"We have a nice garden every summer. We have some fruit trees too, though we are a little high for them."

Ethel was convinced of nothing, and made a small sound to show as much. "I was a havin' fresh new leaf lettuce an' radishes when I left home. I asked one of the Wallace boys to see after things, told his mama she could git him to pick whatever come ready an' she could keep it for herself, but you just can't depend on the kids these days. They just don't have good sense, seems like, most of 'em. I asked Dorothy if her an' Tom couldn' go out home at least once while I'm gone an' see that things is all right, but she just didn' know if they'd have the time or not.

"I'm glad Dorothy's got her job. It's good for her to have somethin' to do, an' she does well at it. She taken me by today an' showed me a house she thinks she's about to sell—big, fine place, we just looked at the outside, you know, the people is still a-livin' in it—but she has to act like it's the most important job a body ever had. I feel right sorry for Tom about it sometimes. *He* works, always has, an' Tom's a good worker an' makes right good money. Dorothy didn't start in to do anything till after Martha married, but the way she acts, a body'd think they wouldn' have a thing if it wasn' for her job."

"It *is* important, Mama. Tom's going to be retiring next year and—"

"Now Evelyn, bless her heart, Evelyn has *always* worked, even when she had them four little young'uns at home. Not that Steve's not a good provider. I like Steve, always have. It's just always been Evelyn's not one to just set an' hold her hands. She's got to be up an' a-doin' somethin', an' she's always felt like she *had* to be a-workin'. An' *she* don't work at just a-stayin' home an' waitin' for the phone to ring. Why, she has to leave home before eight in the mornin' an' don't usually git in much before six. That's why they got that apartment. They're a-buyin' it, you know. I didn't know a body *could* buy an apartment, did you? Before they done it, I mean. Oh, it's a *nice* place! I wish you could see it. I went up there, to Beaumont, you remember? Back in last April, I think it was. It's all air-conditioned, not just air conditioners in the windows, but one of them central ones. An' ever'thin' built in in her kitchen, a dishwasher an' all. She's even got one of them things for trash, you know, that squashes up the cans an' even bottles.

"They sure hated to sell their house, Evelyn an' Steve did, but they just said it seemed like they couldn' keep it up anymore. Steve wasn' a-havin' time to do the yard work, an' it was just too big for them, with all the children off different places. You know what a *good* housekeeper Evelyn's always been, not a thing out of place an' ever'thin' just a-shinin'. She said it seemed like it had to be the house or her job, an' you know she's been with that comp'ny a *long* time. They depend on her, her boss an' them do. She'll git a big retirement pay if she just hangs on long enough.

"I'll tell you this: I'm mighty proud of *all* a my girls, an' their fam'lies too. I think you girls has done mighty well. Dorothy never even got to go to college, an' Evelyn never got to start till she was nearly thirty because she just couldn' do it with all of her children little. An' you've all three got mighty good husbands an' fine children, I can tell you.

"But talkin' about children, you ought to see how foolish Tom an' Dorothy is over them two little grand-young'uns of theirs. I'm glad for 'em. They lost the two babies of theirs, an' then waited so long before Martha was born, an' now these are the only grand ones they'll have. Martha had her tubes tied, did you know that? Dorothy said Mark didn't like it, but they never ask Mark what he wants, the rest of 'em don't. But my! They do spoil them little ones, Tom an' Dorothy do."

To change the subject, Chandra said, "I've been wondering, Mama, did you try to call me from Dallas when you knew you couldn't make that first plane?"

"Huh?"

She repeated. There might or might not be something wrong with the hearing aid, she thought. Mama was as bad as Bruce in her own particular way, about tinkering with things. If anything had a switch or plug, any sort of adjustment, she had to be constantly adjusting, dissatisfied. If the device had a battery, she deeply resented the need to change it. Also, it was hard to know how much of conversation she really missed, and how much of her asking for repetition was her great need for attention. When Chandra had been a child, Mama had asked to have things repeated and had done a great deal of repeating herself, almost as much as now. Just the other night, when they had had the discussion about the bar, Eric had said, grinning, "I'll bet if one of us said 'whiskey' in the bathroom with the door closed, she'd hear it anywhere in the house.' But, poor Mama, like many others, was at heart a very insecure person, and craving people's notice, even of a negative nature. Chandra could be patient and sympathetic now, though she knew that, within a day or two, the repeating, the being told things she already knew, over and over, would become sorely wearing.

Ethel had finally understood the question and was saying, "No, I didn' try to call. I didn' even think of it. I ought to of. You went out there, didn' you, an' met that other plane?"

"Yes," Chandra said lightly, "and we were pretty surprised, weren't we, Thegn, when there was no Grandma?"

"We didn't know *what* happened," said the little boy, still impressed by the experience. "I was afraid you crashed, but Gail said you couldn't all by yourself, without the rest of the plane. And then we—"

"*Who* said?"

"What? Oh, Gail said, and then—"

"Was Gail with you?"

"Yes, Bruce too, and we—"

"Well, I did wonder where the rest of them was tonight. I missed them."

Chandra said, "Eric's working, Mama, teaching at the college, and this is the night for Bruce's music program at school. We wrote you about it and hoped you could go. That's where Bruce and Gail are."

"Oh, yes," Ethel said regretfully. "Don't you tell Brucie, but his program just went clear out of my mind with all of this other. I *wish* I could have heard it. I meant to go when you wrote about it. But do you mean to tell me you drove all this way and then went *home* again, and then back?"

"It's not so far. Eric drives almost this far to his job every day."

"Well, I don't see how the pore boy does it. *He* surely don't want to live so far from his work. Mercy! the gas it must take! But I really did want to hear Brucie play tonight. I never have got to, you know, not with a bunch of others. Are they all all right, the rest of the family?"

"Yes, they're fine."

"An', Chandra Lynn, can you really *afford* to pay so much, for gas an'—things?"

"We have small cars, Mama. They really don't use all that much gas."

"Well, Eric must make mighty good money, that's all I can say. Is this a new car? At the airport, it didn' look to me like the one you come home in that last time."

"It was Eric's car we had then. His is green and just like this one, except that his is three years old, and mine we've had for five years."

"Are y'all *payin'* on two cars?"

"No, Mama, they're both paid for now."

"Well, that's good anyway. This one seems awful small. I guess I just always had it in my mind you'd have big, fancy cars. You know Tom an' Dorothy have bought a big fine one? But what about you, Chandra Lynn? It don't seem like you've hardly said two words. Tell me how you are. At the airport, it looked like—maybe it was imagination an' not seein' you for so long—but it seemed like your limp was right bad."

Chandra lit a cigarette. "I'm fine, Mama, just a little tired. Things have been busy."

"Your leg still hurts you, don't it?"

"Yes, but it's all right."

"Are you a-tryin' to write another book?"

She tried, by mail and phone, to keep her mother posted on the various stages of her various books. She knew it all ran together for Mama, who couldn't remember any of the names of the juvenile books and certainly hadn't thought much of the first novel, but it was something to take up space with, in letters. Ethel took pride in saying something like "my daughter, the author," and she had been duly impressed on the few occasions when Chandra had told her the amount of some recent check for writing work, but she had no idea of the time and energy it took to write a book, or of all that was involved in publishing. When Chandra had mentioned once in a letter that her novel was being looked at by some movie people, Ethel *had* written back rather excitedly to ask when the film might be expected to play in Chelsea.

She began to answer, "No, I'm not writing now, but I have some—"

"How many books have you got now? I can't keep a count. That's somethin', isn' it? So many I can't even keep track."

"Eight, now, though two aren't published yet."

"Well, don't you let me miss out on when a new one's comin' out. That reminds me, they put another piece about your books in last week's Chelsea paper.

Patsy Kelly did. I brought that, an' a piece about Les I thought you'd want to see. It come out several weeks ago, the one about Les. You remember Patsy, don't you? Her maiden name was Hazard. She married Will an' Mary Kelly's youngest boy. Or was it the next to the youngest?"

"I remember Patsy. We were in school together and she came out to see us the last time we came to visit you."

"You were in school together? Is Patsy *your* age?"

"She's a year older, I think."

"Well, maybe I oughtn' to say it, but she don't look it, Chandra Lynn. I was thinkin' she was several years younger. But then, Patsy always looks so nice. She knows how to use makeup an' wear clothes better than about any young person I know. I have always thought a lot of Patsy an' her folks. She said somethin', the last time I talked to her about her brother might come down here to Denver about somethin'. I forgit his name. He's been gone off somewhere from Chelsea for years. Anyway, Patsy put another piece about you an' your books in last week's paper. It's right nice. You'll have to write an' thank her. Did you notice I've had *my* hair cut lately?"

"Yes. It looks very pretty."

"Another thing I thought I noticed about you at the airport, you've put on weight, haven't you? What do you weigh now?"

Chandra could hear the triumphant smile in her voice. Evelyn and Dorothy had always been rather hefty ladies, always agonizing over diets. It had bothered Ethel, all Chandra's adult life, that this third daughter weighed less than she did. Well, she thought, smiling grimly, I guess I'm glad my extra weight can do somebody good.

She answered, "About a hundred and forty-five."

"That much! My, you have put on! You know I never have weighed more than a hundred and forty in my life. It don't make any diff'rence what I eat or anything. I just stay right about the same an' I never have thought about any diet. I noticed while I was there this time that Tom an' Dorothy have got a icebox full of that diet stuff, but I can't tell they're any skinnier. But you needed to put on, Chandra Lynn. It looks good on you. I really think it does. You always used to be just too thin.

"Now, if you could just quit that ole smokin', honey. I do worry so much about it. You never would have started it if you'd of stayed down home around Chelsea. You *know* it's bad for your health. They've proved that. If you don't care about yourself, I do. Besides, you ought to think of how it looks around the baby."

Chandra found herself wanting to reach for another cigarette to light, though she already had one in hand.

"Seeing Mommy smoke doesn't make me want to, Grandma," said Thegn reassuringly. "Mommy and Daddy are both going to quit sometime. They know it's a bad habit but, see, grownups can get bad habits, too. I used to want to smoke, when I was a little kid. I thought it would be neat, but now I know—"

"You *know* better, don't you, honey," said Ethel with feeling. "Well, Grandma's just so glad to hear *that,* anyway. You keep right on a-thinkin' that-a-way."

There was a silence and Chandra wanted to say, "Why have you brought me another clipping about Les?" Mama insisted on keeping her posted on Les and she hated it. And Mama would say, "I know you don't care a thing in the world about him, Chandra Lynn, don't *feel* anything, I mean, but I just thought you'd like to know, and that maybe Brucie would. He *is* his daddy. I'm just tryin' to keep you up on homefolks."

When Bruce had been a tiny baby and he and Chandra were living at home with Ethel, for as brief a time as possible, there had been a night when Les called, telling Ethel he meant to come and talk with Chandra.

"What could I do?" Ethel had asked, near tears. "I didn' know what to say to him on the phone."

"Didn't you just tell him to keep away?"

"Why, no, I couldn' do that."

"But, Mama, I don't *want* to see him! Do *you* want to? You've had so many mean, critical things to say about Les in the past few weeks that I've felt as if I ought to defend him sometimes. The divorce is final now. I don't have anything to say to Les. I hope I never see him again. Don't you know that?"

"Well, yes, Chandra Lynn, and I can't say I blame you, though you've waited a gracious long time to do this, an' with a little tiny baby an' all, but when a body wants to come to a body's house, there *is* such a thing as bein' polite an' I—"

Chandra had dropped the book she'd been reading on the bed, got up and roused the sleeping baby, tears running down her face. "Mama, I'm *afraid* of Les. He's said a lot of things you don't know about, said them to other people, knowing they'd be sure to tell me. For one thing, he's said he means to take Bruce away from me. I don't believe it for a minute. At any rate, he'd never keep him. He might have to earn some regular money for food if he had a baby to support. But I don't want to listen to things like that from him."

"Maybe I can tell him you're gone to bed, don't feel like gittin' up," said Ethel rather desperately. "Don't cry like that. *I* haven't done nothin'. You needn' to git mad at me. *I*'ve known Les Campbell wasn' worth the powder it 'ud take to blow 'im up since away back when you was in high school. *I* never wanted you to go with him in the first place an' all this business lately has nearly worried me to death, I can tell you that. But Les's mama an' me growed up on ranches right next to one another, went to church together an' ever'thin', when we was girls. I've heard a lot of tales about how wild an' no-account Les has turned out, but I can't help but think of Ivy, what a fine, good, Christian girl she was an' what a friend to me, an' I'd think, It ain't Ivy's doin', how he turned out. It was that rotten daddy of Les's, come from around Fort Worth someplace. He wasn' any good either. Now Ivy's a-livin' off there somewhere an' I know all of this divorce business has worried her to death, just like it has me. I don't want it ever to git back to Ivy that I wouldn' even give her boy a glass a lemonade on a hot night."

Ivy! Chandra had wanted to scream. You think about Ivy! Why can't you give me some of that nice, warm, Christian consideration? But she said nothing. She snatched a light blanket and wrapped the fretting baby clumsily, her hands shaking.

"Where are you a-goin'?" cried Ethel sharply.

"To the barn. You can call me when Les has had his lemonade and gone."

"You're a-goin' outside in nothin' but a housecoat an' gown? What if George Tatum was to be outside of his house an' see you?"

The screen door had slammed before anything furthur occurred to Ethel. Then she followed a few steps to call out apprehensively,

"Chandra Lynn, do you think Les might be *dangerous*? You better come back in here, young lady, an' stand behind your mama."

Les hadn't been dangerous, of course, only full of talk, as usual. He had a second wife now, and two children, or was it three? He was a salesman for an automobile agency, a good salesman, no doubt, whenever he chose to show up for work. Mama and other people from around Chelsea said he still talked, when he was drinking, about how Chandra had stolen away his firstborn son. And Mama still saw she got the newspaper clippings.

Ethel broke the silence in the car and her voice made Chandra start. "That thing in the paper about your books? They was a man called me the next day after the paper come out. My name was mentioned too, Patsy usually does that. This man lives over the other side of Chelsea from our place. I forget his name. They just moved, two or three years ago, from Corpus Christi, I think it was. Oh, he just bragged an' bragged about that book of yours *Dawn*. Said how much him an' his wife both liked that one, an' that their kids have read all a your children's books. I told him that he oughtn' to think, from that dedication thing you wrote in that book *Dawn*, he oughtn' to think we ever lived that-a-way, like them people in the book. They was wicked folks, an' you know I don't like that kind of thing. But he was just so full of praise, I was downright embarrassed, didn' know hardly what to say. You say you're not a-writin' anything new?"

"No, I've got two books to work on, getting them ready for publication, before I can have the time to start on something new."

"Huh?"

"No, Mama, I'm not writing anything just now."

"You know, it really does bother me that I didn' try to call you from Dallas. It *does* look like I could of thought about that."

Chandra patted her hand. "Don't worry about it. We very likely wouldn't have been home. We had to leave our house about the time that first plane was taking off from Dallas."

"Did you?"

"Yes, so no one would have been there to answer the phone."

"Here comes our exit, Grandma," said Thegn.

"Your what, honey?"

"Where we get off the highway to go to our house."

"Well, lands! I think it's about time! You do live a long ways from everythin'. Just feel my hands, Thin, see how cold Grandma is."

"Why didn't you say you were cold, Mama? We could have had more heat."

"Law, honey, I've been cold since before I left Chelsea, just a'thinkin' about comin' down here to this ole cold country. Besides, I don't know anything about these little foreign cars—this *is* a foreign, ain't it?—didn' know if you had a heater. Oh, lands, is that a snowflake, right there on the windshield, or just a little bitty chip out of it?"

"It *is* snow!" cried Thegn happily.

Ethel sighed, shivered, pulled her coat closer and folded her arms protectively.

"Did you know about the new car Tom an' Dorothy have got? I believe it's a Ford. Your daddy always used to favor Fords. Tom says it's un-American to buy cars or anything else from them foreign countries, an' I don't know but what Tom's right."

Wednesday

4

Chandra woke dazedly to the violent clanging of the alarm clock. Need for more sleep seemed a palpable thing through her whole body. It had been after three before she slept and was now only a little past five-thirty, still very dark outside. Vaguely, she was aware of the sound of wind, fingering around the corner of the house. She moved closer to Eric in the king-size bed. He was conscious, or partly so. He had moved quickly to turn off the alarm, mumbling something angrily, and now he moved groggily to put an arm around her, warm and solid. Eric could always doze again, after the ringing of the alarm, then wake up again in fifteen minutes or so. He kept the clock set early for that very purpose. If Chandra slept again after the startling clamor, she might not wake for hours. That must not happen today. Mama was here, there was so much to be done today.

She thought dismally of her galleys, of the disturbing letter from her editor, included with them, which had been a part of the reason she had taken so long to fall asleep. But she had always had difficulty sleeping, even as a child. Don't think about the book now, or Mama, or . . . Sleep was such a blessed thing, such a drowsy, dragging need.

When she next woke, Eric was moving about the bedroom, getting dressed. A cup of coffee he had brought for her steamed invitingly on the nightstand.

"Oh, dear," she said grimly and sat up immediately. The lovely lethargy evaporated instantly, to be replaced by the day's inchoate tensions. It had been almost an hour since the ringing of the alarm.

"Everything's under control," Eric said mildly, putting his own coffee cup on the dresser.

He, too, disliked mornings, but needed time for a long wake-up shower, to move into the day with slow deliberation. Usually, Chandra started up, wide awake, at the sound of the clock. Both of them were basically night people, and they had such different ways of beginning to face the day.

The school buses came to Clover Hill before eight. If things went well, Chandra could get most of what had to be done around the house finished by nine, then have almost three hours to work in her office before going to fetch Thegn from kindergarten. Then, she would give the little boy some lunch, do a bit more housework while talking with him about his interests. Thegn still napped most afternoons, which gave her another hour or two in a quiet house. Most of her work outside her office was done after four, when all three children were home and she needed to be more available. They were all helpful around the house, to their individual degrees, and when Chandra was deeply involved in a writing project things could be managed without her, but she was, after all, right there at home, so vulnerable, so on call for interruption, with her own inner compulsion to be so.

Buttoning his shirt now. Eric said calmly, "Just relax a few minutes more. Drink your coffee."

"It's so late," she fretted, still sitting upright in the bed. "I didn't mean to go back to sleep." But she lit a cigarette and leaned back against the headboard. She felt guilty about these moments, but sipped at the coffee, still not quite able to face the morning that waited so inexorably outside the bedroom. "Is everybody up?"

"Not Bruce and Thegn, but I think they're working on it. Mom was downstairs as soon as I went down to make coffee. You know her usual thing about not being able to stay in bed. She's told me, again, about the horrors of her trip yesterday. Gail's up. They're doing breakfast. Let them. You look as if you didn't sleep much."

He had a nice voice, deep but light, with a fine, crisp East Coast accent, even when he still sounded sleepy. His voice could still send little thrills of pleasure down her spine.

She said compulsively, "Mama will go home and tell everybody how she had to take care of us, nobody else to cook breakfast and all that."

Eric said, rather absently as he looked through a drawer, "She enjoys it. She's going to say those things, no matter what you do, isn't she?"

Chandra moved to pull a drape aside. The stiff wind was fast dispersing yesterday's clouds. If they were lucky, it wouldn't turn into a gale, but just blow away most of the city's smog for this day at least. The sun was just coming up in a sparkling sky.

Chandra had told Eric last night, when they finally got to bed, about her phone conversation with Dorothy. It came back now, deeply troubling. They *did* have room for Mama, and she wouldn't be a financial burden, but to live with her, day after day . . . The mixture of love and defiance, guilt and resentment, compulsion and negation made a slight nausea rise up in her throat.

Eric turned and looked at her briefly, then sat down and pulled on his socks. He said reluctantly, "She has a problem, Mom does. I don't like to lay it on you, first thing, but she's going to."

"What is it?" she said, dragging on her cigarette.

"She'd rather sleep downstairs somewhere than in the guest room. Says the stairs hurt her legs, arthritis—authoritis. Besides, she says she never could sleep well on a second floor."

Chandra frowned, standing up wearily to reach for her robe. "I suppose we can make up the couch in what used to be the maid's room, but we use that room for so many things, ironing, sewing, paying bills. Still, it's there, and if she's made up her mind she doesn't want to be upstairs . . ."

Again, the wearing ambivalence. Probably it really was uncomfortable for Mama, in a number of ways, having an upstairs bedroom, when she had always been used to a single-floor house. On the other hand, couldn't she try, just a little, to accommodate herself to someone else's house and way of life? Suppose she were to stay on with them, resisting the guest room. The downstairs bathroom was between the maid's room and Chandra's office. It was an agreed-upon matter, among the family, that no one use that bathroom while Chandra was working. Calls of nature were a necessity and Chandra wanted to be able to take care of these interruptions of her work quickly, without having to wait for someone else to finish with that bathroom. Also, the noises of other people's flushings and the like could be distracting when she needed deep concentration. She couldn't, of course, ask Mama to use an upstairs bathroom if her bedroom were to be right next to the one downstairs. Sometimes, Chandra's working needs seemed, even to herself, picky and childish, but they did exist. And Mama would never understand. Then, too, there was the fact of her liking to work late at night, able to relax about it, knowing everyone else was in bed and she would not likely be disturbed, by telephone or doorbell. Alone on the lower floor, she could feel sure that her typing, moving around, would not distract or disturb anyone else in the house. But with Mama right next door . . .

Chandra wished that Eric would say some of the things she was thinking now, let her know that he understood. Evidently, he was going to leave the whole decision of what to suggest about Mama's future entirely up to her. Last night, when they had briefly discussed the phone conversation with Dorothy, before Eric had fallen quickly into sleep, he had said that, yes, they *could* take Ethel, if she wanted to move in, that he didn't much like the idea, but that if she, Chandra, decided it was necessary, he could go along. Go along! Chandra had wanted to grind her teeth. That *made* it her responsibility, pushed it squarely onto her, alone. Why couldn't he have said something like, "Absolutely not. We'll find a good home for her if she really shouldn't live alone any longer. You just don't need, shouldn't have to have, that additional hassle." Being absolutely honest about it, Chandra knew that if he had said words to that effect, it might only have served to trigger her daughterness, push her further toward a decision to ask Mama to come to them permanently.

In the burgeoning light of the new morning, Chandra believed Eric did understand most of her difficulties, knew the ambiguities she felt about her mother. If only he would put things into words, she wouldn't have to guess about it; she could know that one person in the world understood, really understood. The final decision in this matter of Mama, she supposed, should be rightly hers. This was her mother; she was the one who would, by far, spend the most time at home with her. But if only Eric would verbalize some of the arguments, pro and con, she could know she didn't have to be entirely alone in trying to find a solution.

Reaching for slippers, Chandra's eye fell unhappily on the large envelope of galley proofs where she had finally laid it on the carpet by the bed at three that morning. The letter which the editor had enclosed with the proofs told her that this particular editor was leaving the publishing house. The name of the editor's replacement was given, but the new woman would not be taking over the job until mid-January and the galleys were wanted back in the publisher's hands by January fifth. The letter strongly reminded Chandra of the extra expense involved in making any changes, once the book had been put into proofs and, generally, took her approval of everything for granted. Reading all this, Chandra felt more apprehensive than ever about what might have been done with her book. She had brought the galleys upstairs last night and had read almost a hundred pages, about one fifth of the novel. It wasn't easy to read galley proofs in bed. They were printed on long, limp sheets of newsprint. So far as she had read last night, there were no serious problems, no major corrections to be made on her part, but she had not yet come to the scenes which she and the editor had discussed most, and about which they had disagreed. She must get through the proofs as quickly as possible, to have her feeling that something was going to go very wrong confirmed or negated. Perhaps all her uneasiness was groundless. The business of publishing tended to make a writer paranoid. Still, why had the editor been so insistent that there was not time for her to see the edited manuscript before it went to proofs when the manuscript had been in the publisher's hands for months? She sighed as she spread up the covers and laid the envelope of galleys against her pillow.

"How much did you read last night?" asked Eric, turning from the other window.

"I read quite a lot," she said, "but I haven't come to any of the parts I'm really worried about yet. What will I do, Eric, if she's made some kind of awful mess of it? You read her letter last night. They want these back by the fifth, but if there *are* problems, I don't even have a name of someone to talk to there for another ten days after that."

He said, sounding faintly indulgent, "Well, maybe she hasn't done anything drastic," and went into the bathroom to comb his hair.

Eric was handsome, rather tall, sturdily built, with light, graying hair and dark brown eyes that gave even more expressiveness to his squarish, mobile face. He had had a mustache for most of his adult life and, of recent years, a beard, thick, curly, rather distinguished-looking. His immediate boss frowned upon beards and had finally suggested, very strongly, that Eric shave and keep his hair cut shorter. Eric simply pretended he hadn't understood the suggestion. Chandra was proud of him for that. Yet, in other ways, he did let his boss run and disrupt his life, their lives. Last night he had told her that a sudden need for consultation had arisen, that people would be flying in from Philadelphia and, in this final week before Christmas, he would have to attend meetings before and after his regular working hours, might take a motel room in town for a night or two because there would scarcely be time to drive home and get any sleep. She supposed there was no help for it, but wished he would exhibit more chafing at the situation. He could maintain his identity, individuality quite nicely by little things like keeping the beard. She wished he were a little less resigned and placid about having his holiday time—theirs—interfered with, about her worry over her book, her mother . . . But why, *why* must she be always picking at him, mentally, if not otherwise? What a difficult, contrary, perverse, even mean person she must be to live with! Eric didn't say she was any of those things; he didn't say . . . If only he *would* say more things, even negative ones! At least, she'd have some real, concrete knowledge of just where she stood.

Feeling guilty, annoyed, sad, she moved to meet him at the door to the bathroom. They held each other briefly and kissed. That was good, wonderful, if only he'd say something, *anything* right now. Oh, why did she keep doing this? It's good, but! She disengaged herself, not too gently, and turned away to brush her own hair, feeling the all too familiar prickle of tears behind her lids. What was there for Eric, for anybody, to want to say at this hour of the morning? As usual, she was being unreasonable, wanting the impossible, if only she knew what that might be.

She said, trying for lightness, "I guess we won't have to go to Joyce and Hal's party, if you have to work so much extra time."

For a moment, as he turned to put on his jacket, she had a glimpse of both their faces in the mirror. Hers looked petulant, like a sulky child's, his troubled, perplexed, distracted. The silence, for her, lengthened unbearably. She had, chiefly, just been making conversation. So why couldn't he make some response, anything? Conversation was a two-way thing, back and forth. Why must a simple exchange take so exasperatingly long? Had he even heard?

"When is their party?" he asked finally, sounding apologetic.

She actually did grind her teeth now, as he looked away, and felt ashamed of herself for doing it. Why must she be the one to remember and keep track of such things? He was as much a part of the invitation as she. The things in his life were no more distracting than those in hers. They should be less so, in fact, because during his working hours, all he had to think about was his work. He rarely even attempted to keep tabs on the children's activities or . . . She had never really wanted to go to the Crittendens' party, but it had now taken on inexplicable, disproportionate importance.

"It's Thursday night, tomorrow," she said, hating the sound of her weary, aggrieved voice.

"I have to meet my class that evening," he said, putting things into his pockets. "It's the last one before Christmas and there's a test. If the men from Philadelphia are in town by then, I'm afraid we'll have to have a meeting afterward. But that's no reason why you shouldn't go to the party. It's at their house?"

They had, desultorily, discussed the party two weeks

ago, when the invitation was received. She really didn't care about going, but she could have managed it, amid her various jobs. What she wished was that he could manage more, more time, more thought.

Now she loathed the mock patience in her tone. "They've got a private dining room downtown at the Montview. Joyce is trying to put together all the artists she's managed to collect, mix them together for a Christmas thing..."

"Oh, right. Now I remember. Well, you'd better go. You might meet someone interesting."

Suppose, she thought achingly, he asked me to meet him somewhere for an early dinner, before his class time, just the two of us? Then he could go on with his business, I could drop in on the Crittendens' party for a little while ... If he made a suggestion like that, all on his own, I'd cry, that's what. Oh, for God's sake, why do I try to keep willing ideas, thoughts, feelings, words into his mind? He's a person, a separate person—but *how* separate? What's *wrong* with me? She stepped over beside the bed and swallowed the last of her coffee, cold now, with convulsive gulps.

"I doubt I'll go," she said quietly. "Mama would be hurt if I left her, and she certainly wouldn't have any interest in going."

If only he would say something like, "But think of yourself sometimes. Do what *you* want now and then." She was always giving him leads, hints of what she wished would follow, but the most he seemed able to do was look worried, concerned, uncertain, as he now did.

Chandra left the room and went slowly, reluctantly downstairs. The Crittendens' party was now painfully vital and she still did not care a damn about it.

"Well, *here* she is!" cried Ethel, sounding righteous and indulgent.

The boys were up, eating bacon and eggs. Gail was bustling around, collecting used dishes. Smiling good morning, she took Chandra's coffee cup and refilled it. Gail, far more than any of the others, could be cheery in the early morning.

"I see you still like to stay in the bed of a mornin'," said Ethel triumphantly. "Well, you know me, or you ought to. I just never was one for layin' around. I'd been awake a right long time before I heard your clock go off. I come down as soon as I heard Eric a-movin' around. He was already in here, a-fixin' the coffee. He said you'd gone back to sleep, said you still don't hardly ever git to sleep before two or three o'clock of a mornin'. But that's mostly habit, you know, Chandra Lynn. If you was to go to bed at a decent hour, an' then git right up, first thing of a mornin', you'd soon git so you could have decent nights. *I* always have tried to do it that way. The Lord made the dark time to sleep in. Course I never have slep' what you'd call a lot, but some just has to make do with less than others can git. Now, what do you want for breakfast? I've fixed the children's eggs just the way they wanted 'em an' all. I don't know how they'd of managed if I *hadn'* of got up."

"Sit down, Grandma," urged Gail brightly. "I'll get Mom her toast and juice. She doesn't like to eat breakfast."

Chandra tried for a grateful smile, but then bit her lips when Gail's back was turned. She could just hear Mama back home, "Why, Chandra Lynn don't have to lift a finger. Eric an' them young'uns waits on her hand an' foot. *He* gits up, real early, an' makes coffee an' then takes it to 'er in the bed, an' that little ole Gail . . ."

Bruce was saying smugly, "We fix our own breakfasts lots of times, Grandma."

"Yeah," put in Thegn. "When Mommy's writing, she works all night sometimes."

Chandra wanted badly to defend herself, but nothing she could say, or do, would really change Mama's opinion of her. Ethel was looking pityingly from one poor child to another.

Gail set toast and juice before Chandra and went upstairs to dress.

Thegn began to tell, again, in detail, about his kindergarten's Christmas party and program. "And don't forget to bake cookies, Mommy. Six dozen. How many is that, anyway?"

Ethel put a hand on Chandra's arm and said confidentially and apologetically, "Honey, I just hate to start in a-complainin' nearly the minute I git here, but I'm wonderin' if they ain't someplace down here where I can sleep after this. You've got so *much* room. What about that little room where the ironin' board's set up? They's a ole couch in there that looks to me like it's one a them that makes a bed. Goin' up an' down stairs all the time is hard on my ole legs. *You* ought to understand about how *that* is. A course, a lot of it is from all that settin' I done yesterday, but I want you to just look how my ole knee is swelled this mornin'."

She wanted them all to take note, including Eric, who had just come down. No morning robe and slippers for Ethel. She was completely dressed, including support hose, "the lightweight ones that nobody else don't hardly notice you're a-wearin'." The knee did look painful, swollen and bruised-looking, the old veins standing out prominently.

"Yes, Mama, that surely must hurt. I'm sorry. But you know that maid's room is full of so much junk. We thought you'd be a lot more comfortable in the real guest room. Also, it's more peaceful up there. The kids will be having a lot of company during the holidays, and they might disturb you sometimes, if you're trying to sleep or rest down here. If I work late in my office, that might bother you, too, and Eric's going to be in and out at all hours for a few days."

"Now don't start worryin' about things like that. We can just move a little a that stuff out of there. About all I need is room to sleep an' someplace to put my suitcases and hang up a few clothes. If somethin' you or the children does keeps me awake, I reckon I'm big enough to say so, don't you think? The stairs does hurt my leg. I just don't know how you manage, a-runnin' up an' down all day, though I expect *you* need the exercise. Anyway, I just never have been able to feel easy about sleepin', or tryin' to, on a second storey. I can't help but think of fire an' things such as that. It looks to me like you'd worry yourself to death about it, all of you off up there, doors shut an' all. An' it's not as if you've not got another place for me to sleep. You say that was built to be a maid's room? You ain't got a maid, have you?"

"We had one for a while," Chandra said. Mama had heard all about that, and made her appropriate comments, at the time.

"I remember her," said Thegn. "She used to take care of me sometimes when I was little. Her name was Ruby and she was nice. We still know her, a little bit."

"Well, I guess it'd be all right," said Ethel firmly, "but I wouldn' have some stranger a-livin' in my house an' a-raisin' my little young'uns." Then, lowering her voice, almost whispering, "She was a *colored* girl, wasn' she, Chandra Lynn? Yes, I guess I do remember now."

Thegn's big dark eyes opened wide, his fork paused in midair. "Why, Grandma, are you bigoted?"

"What? That's a funny word for a little boy to be a-usin'. Your Grandma ain't had a awful lot of education, Thin. I don't even know for sure what that word is."

"Nigger-hater," said Bruce around a mouthful of toast, earning a flash of eyes from Eric and an angered gasp from Chandra.

Ethel's face flushed painfully. "A course I'm not that, honey." She spoke only to Thegn. "Grandma's just as broad-minded as the next one when it comes to diff'rent kinds of folks. God made us all, didn' he?" Now she turned, rather defiantly to the table in general. "Why, I've got a whole colored family a-livin' just down the road from me right now, down home, an' they're just as *clean*. You never see a scrap of paper or any kind of trash a-layin' around in their yard, an' I bet they keep their house ever' bit as nice."

Thegn looked a little perplexed, but said confidently, "Good, then you won't be bigoted about my teacher, Miss Cunningham, when you come to our Christmas party."

"What's that, honey? You ought to know by now how Grandma's hearin' is."

"Come on, Thegn," said Bruce, slightly subdued, "let's get ready for school."

"What did he say about his teacher?" asked Ethel as the boys went upstairs.

"Miss Cunningham is black," Chandra said baldly and with sufficient volume.

Ethel couldn't decide where it would be best to look. The flush had faded from her face and now she was a little pale.

Eric said, "Anybody for more coffee?"

Chandra gave him her cup and Ethel, after a moment's silence, decided there could be nothing further to say on the subject. She hit her stride again.

"Well, you sure have got a big fine house. I'm glad to git to see it after all these years, but the payments surely must be high, an' I know one thing, I'd sure hate to have to be the one to try to keep it clean. The heat bills must be somethin' fierce an' it don't ever seem to git warmed up. About the cleanin', as a example, it looks like these windows could stand to be washed. I didn' notice the rest, but in here, they're right streaky."

"We all do our part about trying to keep the house fairly clean," Chandra said, "and the windows will just have to do for now. It's too cold to do the outsides."

"Huh?" asked Ethel, but did not wait for the repeat. "No, Eric, I don't believe I'll drink any more coffee. You know, I just hate to have to be done for special, but this stuff with caffeine just don't agree with me at all. The doctor says I oughtn' ever to drink it. I have to be so careful about my ole stomach an' it just aggravates the life out of me to have to be that-a-way. The next time somebody goes to the store, I'll send after some instant that's had the caffeine took out."

"I got you some, Mama," said Chandra, getting up to look for it.

"Huh?"

"We found it earlier, Mom," said Eric. "Don't you remember, I showed it to you in the cupboard?"

"I'll put on water for another cup," said Chandra, moving to the stove.

"Huh?" she asked, looking miserable. "I hate to always be a-sayin' 'huh', but I just can't seem to hear worth anythin' anymore."

"Where's your hearing aid?" asked Chandra loudly.

"It's up yonder on the dresser where I slep'. I don't usually put it on, the first thing in the mornin'."

Chandra went to the foot of the stairs. "Whoever can hear me, bring Grandma's hearing aid from the guestroom dresser when you come down."

"Okay," called Bruce.

"I'm afraid the baby might drop it if he was to try to bring it," worried Ethel.

"Bruce will get it," said Eric.

"Oh, was he the one answered. Well, all right. Did you say they *is* some instant coffee without no caffeine?"

"Yes, I showed it to you when you first came down and you put water on to boil."

"Oh, well, I guess I just didn' understand. I had Gail to turn off the stove. I thought somebody had put on the teakittle an' forgot about it. I wish I had of known. I've already drunk two cups out of the pot. What do you want for your breakfast, Eric? I reckon Chandra Lynn's forgot about you."

"No, she hasn't, Mom. It's all right. I—"

"Huh?"

"I don't like to eat anything until about ten, when I have a break."

"Well, you ought to eat right when you first git up. It ain't healthy for a body to work right hard on a empty stomach."

Lighting a cigarette and smiling at her, he said loudly, "I'm fine. I couldn't think of doing anything as drastic as eating at this hour of the day."

"Why, this ain't early," said Ethel, fondly returning his smile. "If you'd of growed up in the country, you sure wouldn' think this was early. I don't know where Chandra Lynn come by her night-owl habits, for she sure never got 'em at home. *We* had to git up an' git some work done. I meant to ask you last night, Eric, what kind of a prank are you a-growin' your beard for? I mean, is it a Ole Timers' Day, or somethin' such as that?"

Eric shook his head. "I had the beard the last time we came to see you in Texas, remember? I'm growing it because I want to. I like it."

"Huh? It's like what, did you say?"

Just then, Bruce did his falling-downstairs thing and laid the hearing aid in front of his grandmother as Chandra brought Ethel's coffee.

"Mercy!" cried Ethel, paling. "I thought sure you'd fell, Brucie honey." She stirred cream into her coffee. "That's just a little bit strong, Chandra Lynn. Even without the caffeine, I don't like it real strong." She turned back to Eric. "I was a-wonderin', ever since I decided to come off down here, if you'd look at my hearin' aid for me. I remember how you fixed my TV an' that ole no-account mixer somebody put in the church rummage sale. They's just *bound* to be somethin' wrong with this thing. I'm just forever a-havin' to put new bat'ries in it."

Bruce had brought down case and all. Eric took it. There was a rack built into the case to hold six of the tiny batteries.

"You mentioned last night that you've been having trouble with it," Eric said. "I'm sorry I forgot about it."

"Well, lord-a-mercy, who wouldn' forget things last

97

night," said Ethel and laughed a little. "This place was in a uproar an' all. I *did* tell you, didn' I, how they held me back from gittin' on that plane in Dallas, after I'd set for nearly the whole day? Well, anyway, some of them bat'ries in there is used ones. I brought them for you to look at, too, thought you could might maybe tell somethin' from them. Can't bat'ries be charged up agin or somethin' like that? I don't know the right word."

"Not these, Mom," he said, peering at the contents of the small case. "Your hearing aid is a sealed unit. I don't know that there's much I could do about it. I don't know anything about this kind of thing. Maybe the people you bought it from—"

"Humph!" snorted Ethel contemptuously. "*They* say they ain't nothin' wrong, for fear they might have to be out somethin' on fixin' it. I *know* it ain't a-workin' right. It's just *always* a-needin' another bat'ry, ever' few days. Last night, I couldn' hear worth anything with the thing an' I just put in a new bat'ry when I started to Dorothy's house in San Antone."

"Which of these are the used batteries?"

"I believe it's them three," she said, frowning. "Or, no, maybe them others. I don't remember just how I did decide to put 'em back."

"I'm sorry, Mom, but I just don't see anything I can do. We can find someplace while you're here and get some expert to look at it. If I don't leave right now, I'm going to be caught in the really heavy traffic."

"An' Chandra Lynn told me you drive all that long way, ever' day. I don't see how you can stand it, especially when you've put in a full day's hard work."

Eric left for work and, shortly afterward, the children went off to catch their school bus at the corner. Chandra poured herself one last cup of coffee, rinsed the pot and lit a cigarette. She itched to get busy, but that surely wouldn't seem very friendly and companionable on Mama's first morning. She could sit and talk for a few minutes at least. She'd have to get through the galleys as quickly as possible, in case any big problems turned up, but they could wait a little longer.

"I can make you another cup of coffee, Mama. The water's still almost boiling."

"Oh, no, honey. Even without the caffeine, it just don't set well on my ole stomach. You surely know I don't like to have to have this special stuff bought. It's good of you to remember about gittin' it for me. Dorothy an' Evelyn always does that, too, has me a little jar of coffee an' the kind of crackers I can eat, an' other special little things. I don't even like most of the ole stuff, like this instant, but the doctor always says for me to stay on my diet."

"But you did have some breakfast with the kids, didn't you?"

"Huh? Oh, yes, I eat a little somethin'. Now, Chandra Lynn, they's somethin' I want to tell you, right off. I don't want you to feel like you have to make any kind a fuss over me while I'm here. A body's mother ain't exactly comp'ny. I know you have your work to do—a part of the time—an' I can find plenty to keep me busy. I've brought my crochet to work on. You've got all these books all over the place; I can surely find somethin' I'd want to read. An' I may watch television a little. I've got one or two stories I don't mind watchin' when I ain't busy at somethin' else. I aim to have a good long visit, since I'm down here, so you ain't to think I need watchin' after ever' minute. I aim to help you out with this house. Evelyn said to me, when her an' Steve was out home at Thanksgivin', she said, 'Now, Mama, don't forget, just because Chandra's at home all the time don't mean she don't have to work some at her writin' things.' Well, *I* know that, an' I told 'er so. So, whatever you've *got* to do, you just do, an' don't be forever a-worryin' that I have to be entertained."

"Really," Chandra said gratefully, "I had meant not

to have to work on any writing things while you were here, but I do have those galleys that came yesterday and I'll have to get them finished and returned. I'm afraid the editor may have done some rewriting on her own in parts of the book, and I don't think I can—"

"Eric an' the children sure helps out a lot, don't they? Why Eric just made that coffee this mornin' like he's used to doin' it ever' day, an' that little Gail fried the bacon and made toast like any woman. An' last night, too, when ever'body finally got in, I noticed how they all put their things up an' helped with the dishes an' all."

"Yes, they are helpful," Chandra admitted, feeling defensive now. "But they *should* help. They're quite capable, and they do live in the house, too."

"Yes, but there's a lot wouldn' do it, husbands especially. I never wanted your daddy anywhere about the kitchen till his food was on the table. He was like a bull in a china shop, nearly drove me off a my rocket when he tried to do around the house. An' I just can't hardly git over that little Gail. I mean—well, you're not her real mother, but she *acts* like she don't never think a thing about it."

"I don't guess she does think about it, Mama. *I* hardly think about it. After all, ten years is a long time, two thirds of Gail's life up to now."

"Is it *that* long? Law, the time does fly, don't it? Oh, I do wish y'all would live closer to home so I could see the children more as they're a-growin' up."

"You know," Chandra said, smiling but feeling slightly queasy, "we don't live any farther from you than you do from us."

"Huh? I don't see what you mean, honey."

"Well, that you might spend more time with us, and maybe with Evelyn and Dorothy, too. You're not making a big garden the way you used to. There aren't any cattle to be seen to . . ."

"Oh, well, but I've got a-plenty to do, though. An', you know, there just ain't no place like a body's own home. An' I don't like to take trips either, especially not like that business yesterday where they held me back an' held me back, after *they*'d been the cause of me a-missin' my right plane."

Now she became very grave indeed. "Chandra Lynn, it ain't my business, I know, but do you an' Eric, both of you, really think it's a good thing for little Thin to have a—well, a colored teacher? I know Eric come from back East, an' them people was brought up diff'rent to what we was, what you was, but . . . "

"Mama, Miss Cunningham is a *very* good teacher. You'll like her. Right now, I think she's just about Thegn's favorite person in the whole world."

"An' you don't think he ought to be put into another school, or someplace where . . . ?"

"No. It's a fine school."

"Well . . . " she murmured, looking worried. Then another worrisome matter caught her attention.

"You know, honey, I'd give just anythin' if you could quit that ole smokin'. It's such a *awful* habit. I believe if you'd quit, Eric could stop, too, an' maybe then that would keep all the children from startin'."

"Why do you think Eric would stop if I did, Mama? He smokes more and he's been smoking a lot longer."

"Well, you know it's generally always up to the woman in the fam'ly to set the *good* examples. I just wish you never had of started. To me, it looks ten times worse for a woman to smoke than for a man anyway. An' there *are* the children to think about. A mother—or even a stepmother—always ought to be the very best example she can be."

"Bruce smokes a pipe sometimes lately," said Chandra and despised herself for the bit of childish defiance. Besides, she had played right into Ethel's hand.

"Now, you see there! Just what I've been a-sayin'!

If he hadn't never of seen you with a ole cigarette a-hangin' out a your mouth, he never would of been tempted to start in. A mother has big responsibilities, I can tell you that. Awful big, an' they ought never to be out of her mind. I ought to know. I raised all of you children what you might say alone. Even before your daddy died, he was off an' gone so much of the time."

Searching for a change of subject, Chandra said brightly, "Well, Mama, suppose I work on my book for the two or three days I'll need, then we can all begin really to enjoy Christmastime together. Eric is going to have to be working quite a lot of overtime for a few days. There are one or two parties I may have to show up at, later in the week, one of them tomorrow night, in fact. The kids all have a lot of activities coming up but there won't be much I'll *have* to do, once the galleys are ready to go back. Would you like to do some shopping? We could go on several different days, if you'd like, so it wouldn't be too tiring."

Ethel's eyes brightened, but she said deprecatingly, "Oh, I just don't know about any shoppin'. Things is always so packed with people around here, like that ole airport last night, an' I'd think it would be even worse ever'where, this time of the year. But we might go to a store or two, sometime, just for a little while, if I can stand it. Seems like I git so nervous lately. . . . I made you an' Eric a Christmas present, somethin' for the house, an' I made somethin' for Gail. Has she got a hope chest?"

"No, not exactly, but you know how she loves the pretty things you make. We all do."

"I haven't got anythin' for Brucie an' Thin. Boys is always harder to do an' buy for. Maybe we could go out, just for a little while one day, an' find presents for them. You could help me decide what they might want. I'd thought I might spend about five dollars apiece."

Chandra smiled. "I know they'll like anything you give them. Grandma is a pretty special person around here."

Ethel was pleased. "Well, none of 'em knows but this one Grandma. I guess they'll have to make do. Brucie won't never have a chance to know Les's people, an' didn' you tell me Eric's parents have both been dead a long time?"

"Mr. Whitman died when Eric was ten. His mother worked and her parents took care of Eric and his brothers and sisters. Mrs. Whitman, Ana, died when Thegn was a baby. Don't you remember, she came out to visit us several times, the first years we were married?"

"Yes, I do remember now, you've talked about her. Wasn't she from some foreign country?"

"Her parents came from Poland just after the First World War. Ana was born in Poland, and so were their other children, but Ana was only three when they came to New York. They're a really nice family. I especially like Eric's older sister Betty. She wants us to come for another visit and it is our turn to go there. Maybe we'll do it at Eastertime, before the weather gets too hot. I'd so much rather they came here."

"Why don't you want to go see his folks?"

"Oh, just because it's so rushed and crowded anywhere around New York. I do like seeing them, Betty's family, especially, and I guess it *is* our turn."

Ethel had grown very sober, foreboding was perhaps the better word. She said quietly and very sternly, "You better go, Chandra Lynn. Eric's just been too good to you for you to do anything to keep him from seein' his folks, or doin' anythin' else he might like to do."

Chandra was shocked, an inexplicable physical jolt. Then there was anger, pain. She stood up and gathered the remaining dishes shakily from the table, keeping her face turned away from her mother. What was *that* supposed to mean? Eric had married her, a cripple, a scandalized, divorced woman, with a son already extant? *What* did she mean? Chandra lit a cigarette and turned toward her mother, who was up too, fussing around the kitchen. She spoke quietly, but her troubled eyes held Ethel's, commanding her to listen, to hear.

"Mama, just what does it mean: Eric's been too good to me?"

"Well—why, just what I said, Chandra Lynn. It's the truth, ain't it?"

"Yes, it's the truth, but don't you think I've been good, too, to him and for him? Don't you think marriage, a family, are—mutual things?"

She wanted to go on with it: Is it your idea that one of Eric's "goodnesses" has been letting me "play around with writin' stories," indulging me? Do you have any idea what portion of our income comes from that "playing around"? Was it better of Eric, more magnanimous of him to take on my child than it was generous of me to accept his? Do you think he's "humoring" me because of where we live and—my God, why is this upsetting me so much?

Ethel was saying stiffly, "Why a course you've been good for him, Chandra Lynn. All I was a-sayin' is you're lucky to find a good husband. The good ones seems to git fewer ever' year. I just don't know what the world's comin' to, with the wickedness a-gittin' more ever' day. An' after the way Les was, well, I'm just happy for you is all, an' for Eric an' the children too, a course."

She was running water into the sink, looking flustered and uncomfortable. She said brusquely, "Here, let me wash them dishes. Is there a church around here to go to?"

"Let me show you how the dishwasher works," said Chandra, feeling suddenly exhausted and as if she might begin crying. "Gail's got it half loaded already."

"I don' understan' these newfangled gadgets," said Ethel curtly, "an' I don't know that I want to. What I do want is to be some help to you, an' if they's one thing I *know* I can do, it's wash dishes. I don't believe them washers gits the dishes real clean anyway, do you? I'll just do 'em up right, this onct, at least. What was it you said about a church?"

"There are several churches close by."

"An' which do y'all go to?"

"None of them, Mama."

"Oh, honey," she said with bleak sadness, "that's another example you ought to be a-settin' for them young'uns, an' for Eric, too. *You* wasn't brought up not to go to church."

"If there's one you'd like to go to, one of us will be glad to drive you and pick you up." The surliness of her tone was quite clear to Chandra's own ears.

"Where's the soap?" asked Ethel, then, mournfully, "Just tell me, honey, why you won't go."

Chandra made an effort at placidity. "Mama, we talk about this every time we see each other. I always tell you that it seems to me that so many 'good' church people are hypocrites, that I don't believe in the same kind of God they seem to believe in, that I think how people get together with God, *if* they can do it, is a very personal, private matter. You never want to try to understand or accept the ways I think and I just don't see any point in hashing it all over again."

There was a silence. Chandra walked to the table, put out her cigarette, emptied the overflowing ashtray and dropped it in the dishwater.

Ethel, deeply hurt and concerned, said in subdued tones, "Well, I won't be here long. Maybe if I was to find a good church to go to, all of y'all would come along with me, just the once, to humor a ole woman. Then you might find out you like it an' go agin sometimes at least. I know you think it's none of my business, but I tell you, young folks an' little ones—big 'uns, too, whether they think it or not—needs the guidance of the Lord an' a good church."

Another silence, then she said more lightly, "You show me just where the dishes an' ever'thin' goes an' then git on about your book business. I'll find a-plenty to keep me entertained. You know, I think Eric looks right cute with that ole bushy beard, but when is it he says he's a-goin' to shave it off?"

5

Chandra spent the next half hour rearranging the maid's room, bringing her mother's things downstairs. She couldn't get the old sofa to unfold so that a bed could be made up. That would have to wait for Bruce or Eric, someone with more brute strength than she could muster. Prince Charming the dog and Black Magic the cat followed her closely, getting in the way of everything, as they always did when all the children were away from home. She put them out, finally, into the sunny, breezy back yard and went upstairs one more time, for the galleys.

"I'll do some washin'," announced Ethel as Chandra came down again.

No laundry had to be done that day, though it was, as always, available. Chandra knew her mother's penchant for keeping busy, sympathized with it, so she sighed only a little to herself as she went upstairs again for the dirty clothes.

"Show me how the washer works," said Ethel. "Then I won't have to bother you agin."

Chandra put in clothes, detergent and bleach, pushed the proper buttons, whose uses her mother might have read quite easily, and started the washing machine.

"How many water heaters have you got in this house anyway?" asked Ethel critically.

"Just two, Mama."

"Don't you think you could save some gas or 'lectricity, whatever they use, if you turned 'em down or off when you ain't a-usin' 'em? That water in the kitchen's nearly boilin'. I about scalded my hand."

"They'd use more gas, Mama, if they had to start cold every time."

"Huh?"

"Come in the family room now and let me show you about the remote control for the TV."

Ethel frowned over the gadget, looking helpless, pathetic. "Well, that channel will do for now. I may have to call you if I want to change. You know I never did have no head for machinery. I don't like all this new-fangled stuff people thinks they have to have. Just somethin' else to break down is about all it's good for. I may not have put all the dishes and things where they belong in the kitchen. I hope you can find ever'thin' when you need it."

"I'm sure everything is just fine. Thank you for doing it. Now, I think I'll go and—"

"Did you bring down my crochet?"

"Yes, Mama. All your things are in there now."

"Have you got any sewin' for me to do—buttons off, things like that? That's somethin' I know you never would do if you could help it."

That was certainly true. Chandra had a very strong aversion to mending and had been saving up a basket of it since they had learned Ethel would be coming. She brought it, along with her meager sewing box, and finally escaped into her office.

When she had been reading for perhaps ten minutes, frowning irritably over some utterly stupid corrections of grammar in dialogue, the telephone rang.

"Mrs. Whitman?" said a voice she did not recognize. "My name is Laura Forbes. My daughter Rachel is in kindergarten with your son, and I'm in charge of their Christmas party preparations. I just wanted to make sure your little boy brought home his note for you."

"About the cookies," Chandra said. "Yes, they'll be there."

"Oh, good. You know five-year-olds can't always be depended on to carry notes and remember things."

"Yes, that's true, but I did get the cookie one."

Chandra was trying to go on reading, making sense of the manuscript, while seeming to listen and respond with a modicum of intelligence. Her office door opened and Ethel stood there.

"I didn' know if you'd answered that," she said. "The one in the kitchen was a-ringin'. Law, you've got a lot of phones in this place."

"Uh—Mrs. Whitman," the caller was saying. "I understand you're a writer. The children's teacher told me, and then I have a friend who lives on your street, Muriel Stanford."

"Yes," said Chandra, rather absently.

"Well, I was wondering if we couldn't get together sometime. You see, I have this *marvelous* story about my grandmother. She was a fabulous woman and had so many adventures, funny, sad . . ."

"You should write about her," Chandra said, trying for a tone of interest and encouragement. Everyone, it seemed, had these wonderful ideas for books or stories the minute they heard there was a writer who might be accessible.

"She was really a liberated woman, long before her time. I just haven't been able to get it out of my mind, what a wonderful book her life story would make, since Miss Cunningham told me you write. I've been thinking we might—what do they call it—collaborate? I could be free almost every morning while Rachel is in school."

"Well, I'm pretty busy, Mrs. Forbes, I—"

"Oh, I don't mean right *now*, during the holidays. My goodness, *I* couldn't find the time *now,* but maybe in three weeks or so we could get started. I think it would be *such* fun! What is the usual procedure in an effort like this, about dividing the money, I mean? There'd be a contract between us, of course. My husband is an attorney and he always says *everything* should be down on paper, especially among friends, so there can't be misunderstandings or hard feelings. I'm sure he could—"

"I don't really know what the procedure is," Chandra said coolly. "I've never collaborated, and I'm afraid I have too many other things going just now, even to think of it."

"But it would be such a *good* story, timely and—"

"I'm sure it would, Mrs. Forbes. Why not try writing it yourself?"

Chandra lit a cigarette, feeling, as always, incredulous, amazed, by the sheer gall of people. She looked up questioningly at her mother, who still stood in the doorway.

"Do call me Laura," urged Mrs. Forbes. "The truth is, you know, I've hardly ever talked with a writer before and I'm just so pleased to have the opportunity. As to *my* writing about Grandmother, *I* just would never have the time it would take. I have Rachel and her daddy to look after, and the house. You know what servants are these days. I have a maid now who's just about as good as one can seem to expect to find, but she has to be watched like a child. Why, just the other day, she was putting the electric coffee pot into the dishwasher when I happened to notice, just in time."

Chandra completed the reading of a rather long paragraph in silence.

"How many books have you written?" persisted Laura patronizingly.

"I'm working right now on getting my second novel ready for publication. There are five juveniles out and the sixth is—"

"The *time* that must take!" burbled Laura. "It takes me simply hours just to write a letter. But of course we all have our own special things we can do best. Don't you find that's true? That's why I was so delighted to hear of a real writer right here on Clover Hill. A dear friend of mine is a writer, you know, someone I was in school with, but she's all the way back in Illinois where we came from, so I can't very well work on my idea with her to sell. She sold a book about a trip she and her husband took, all around South America, you know, the living conditions, things like that. I don't know *how* much she made, after the publishing was paid for and such expenses, but I'm sure it was a great deal. If you don't mind my asking, what does it cost you to have your books published?"

"That isn't my problem, Mrs. Forbes," Chandra said curtly. "The publishers take care of publication costs, advertising, distribution and all such things. What you're talking about is called vanity publishing, where an author bears all the costs, just to see her name in print. It's a cruel phrase, vanity publishing, but it's a cruel business. I don't work that way."

"Oh . . . well . . . I see. But then, that just means all the more money for you, doesn't it? I understand, too, from my friend Muriel, who lives quite near you, that you're—uh—handicapped. I think you must be just a wonderful person, to be *doing* something with yourself. So many people with—uh—afflictions—special difficulties, just sit back and take welfare. But then, writing is an easy thing to do, I mean relatively, of course. After all, one just has to sit in a chair . . . "

"That's true," Chandra agreed blandly. The woman was not just ridiculous, she was funny.

"Are all your books available at the library in Sherman?"

"The published ones are."

"There seem to be so many of them. I hadn't realized . . ."

"They're also available for sale. You know a writer doesn't make any money at all unless readers buy."

"Well, yes, I hadn't really thought of it that way. We don't have much time for reading, though. My husband takes law journals and such, but I've always been far too busy for books, so the library would be best for us. We're really very busy. Jeff has a great deal of socializing we must do, in the course of his business, and I have my bridge club. I've taken up golf this past summer.

There just always seems to be something. Tell me, where did you get the ideas for your other books?"

"Various places, Mrs. Forbes. It would depend on which book we were talking about. I'm afraid I really have to get back to work now."

"Yes, of course, I must be keeping you from something. We will meet on Friday at the children's party. We can talk more then about getting together, can't we? Surely, we could work out something. I *am* looking forward to knowing you. I think you must be a rather remarkable woman, and I'm so glad you've been able to find something to do with your time to—well, you know —keep your mind off—other things."

"I'll be sure to remember to have *one* of my maids take care of the cookies for Thegn," said Chandra sweetly and hung up.

She was angry, raging actually, but also smiling, rather in spite of herself. People were absolutely incredible. She was tempted to call Eric and tell him all about Laura Forbes. They could laugh and be flabbergasted together. Also, this was something Shirley mustn't miss. Shirley had said recently, "Living right next door, I get to be a writer, too, in a way; what do you call it? Vicariously? I can get in on most of the crap from agents and editors and publishers and just people generally, and it doesn't cost me a lot, in pain and suffering, or money. Sometimes there are even *good* things. I think I get more good out of those than you do."

Chandra's eye fell on her mother, waiting still in the doorway.

"I didn't know if you had a phone in here," said Ethel. "Was that some important call, from New York or some of them places?"

"No, it was just about cookies for Thegn's Christmas party."

"Would you want me to make them?"

"Yes, Mama, that would be really nice, if you want to do it, but let's leave it for tomorrow. If you make them today, I'm afraid there won't be enough left by Friday. You *will* go with me, won't you, to his program and party? Thegn's been counting on it."

"Huh?"

"Mama, where's your hearing aid?"

"It's still in yonder on the table. I don't need the thing when there's nobody to talk to. Where'd you git all the pictures in here? I meant to ask about that while I was a-lookin' around the house last night."

"Eric did most of them. Aren't they good? I have a lot more on my walls than he has in his studio because I like them so much. He uses the studio for working up things for the class he teaches and for a lot of other things, so I get the cartoons. Gail did that little oil."

Ethel studied the little painting of a litter of kittens. "That's real sweet," she said, smiling fondly, but then frowned as she looked at a cartoon on the wall near the painting. "Is that supposed to be the President? It don't seem hardly right to me to make fun of our country's leaders that-a-way. I never will look at them kind of things in the papers. Still, I guess it's a way for Eric to relax, if that's the way his mind runs, gits him away from *real* work. But it always has seemed to me like a kind of odd thing for a grown man to do, fool around with pencils or Crayolas or whatever it is, a-drawin' things. It makes a real nice little hobby for Gail, though, don't it? Wasn' her real mother a painter or somethin' like that?"

"An actress. At least, she wanted to be an actress." Chandra was trying to read again, with what degree of unobtrusiveness she could manage.

"Was she in any movies?"

"No. She had a few small parts in some plays. Mostly, she was a model."

"She died in a car wreck, did you tell me?"

"No, she was killed in the crash of a small plane."

Ethel shook her head, tsking fervently. "That was after her an' Eric was already separated?"

"Yes, about six months."

"She just run off an' left him, didn' she? With a little tiny baby to raise? Was she a-carryin' on with that feller that had the airplane?"

"I don't know, Mama, but I wouldn't be a bit surprised. I think Mona did quite a lot of—carrying on."

More sympathetic sounds and head shakings. "Well, all I know to say is I can feel for Eric. It reminds me of one of my TV stories, 'Today an' Always.' Do you ever watch that one?"

Ethel moved to the battered old love seat, the first piece of furniture Chandra and Eric had bought together, and sat down.

"You can read with me a-talkin' to you, can't you? I'll go an' leave you alone in a minute, but let me tell you just a little bit about the story. It's plum pitiful what's a-happenin'. Makes a body cry sometimes, the fixes they git in."

The detailing of personalities and events from the television serial took some time. Chandra could only half listen, trying to nod at strategic points and look interested or shocked or saddened. It was the same old situations; thwarted love, pregnancies out of wedlock, various "carryin's on." One thing she had learned as a writer was that there were, really, very few stories to be told.

She was always a little surprised that Mama, who saw real life in such stark blacks and whites, who would not tolerate the presence of real people who behaved as her TV dramatists did, if she had an inkling of such behavior, who had no shred of understanding or acceptance of extenuating circumstances in real life, could take the make-believe so eagerly and sympathetically into home and heart. Ethel's views of Chandra and Eric in their first marriages made an excellent example. She had not known Eric during his marriage to Mona, nor for a long time afterward, so she enjoyed hearing bits and pieces about it, could "feel for Eric," be completely on his side.

But she had been there, gone through, in part, Chandra's divorce from Les. Mental cruelty or incompatibility were not generally accepted grounds for divorce all those years ago. Les's infidelities were no secret from anyone, but having to use them as reason for divorce, having them discussed in court, and thus through Chelsea and the whole county, had made Chandra wait far longer to file for divorce than she would have done, had it been less embarrassing. It had been far more humiliating for her than for Les, and Mama's attitude and, to a lesser degree, the attitudes of her sisters, had seemed somewhat to coincide with Les's, when he said, "If you was a *real* woman, I wouldn' have to go lookin' aroun'." It would have happened, with Les, with any woman. Even in the miserable depths of her degradation, Chandra had known that, but she had felt very little in the way of bolstering, supportiveness from her family: *Everyone* knew, after all, that the woman had the chief responsibility for keeping a marriage together; men, even ones like Les, whom the family had never approved of or liked, were simply weaker, more apt to be fallible by nature. If Chandra had exhibited the proper strength and guile with him, right from the start, he would never have begun to "slip around on her." A bad marriage was one thing, but a lot of women managed to live a lifetime with those; divorce, shaming herself and so the family in front of the world, was an entirely different matter. They had not openly said all these things, and perhaps she was judging them even more harshly than they had seemed to judge her, but they had made her *feel* them, more than half believe she was more culpable than Les.

The big difference for Mama, she realized now, in her situation and Eric's, was that Mona had been the one to leave Eric, Mona had filed suit for a Nevada divorce and, perhaps most important, Mona had been dead for some time before Eric remarried. She, Chandra, could not only not lie in the bed she had made in marrying Les, but she had had the audacity, the shamelessness, to drag it right out in front of the whole world for its unmaking. No one "around home" had known of her pregnancy until after the divorce was final. She and Les had had a grubby little apartment above the movie theater in Chelsea, Les's base of operations as a Casanova and would-be big-time rodeo roper, Chandra's place to come home to after her days as a secretary in the offices of the local gas company. Had her family and friends known she was pregnant, the pressures to "try to make the best you can of a bad business" would have been almost insurmountable. "You've got somebody else to think about now," Mama would have said, "not just yourself, like you always have. A baby needs its daddy, don't make no diff'rence what kind he is. Anyway, bein' a daddy *could* just be the makin' of Les. It wouldn' be the first time a thing like that has happened—a baby an' a *good* wife."

Chandra pulled her thoughts together as Ethel paused significantly in her narrative. She was certainly not getting anywhere with the galleys, and what difference did all that about Les make now? None, of course, except that it was just one indication, a large one, of how she had always felt in the wrong at home, never really loved or approved of—until Eric. Eric was, literally, her salvation. She wished she could talk with him this very minute, try to apologize, explain if she could, her picking and worrying to the bone of every little thing. She was truly sorry. All her concerns and wantings and questionings were making both of them miserable. Being sorry, even miserably so, didn't make all the little troubles and wistfulnesses go away, but if she had two grains of sense, she'd make herself forget or ignore them, lock them away in some airtight, unused compartment of her mind, be content, grateful for all that was good about her life. Leave well enough alone, only . . .

"An' I wanted to ask you," Ethel was saying, "there's a blue shirt in that stuff that needs sewin'. I can't tell if it's Brucie's or Eric's, but you don't have any thread that matches it, an' it's got a big rip."

"Just use whatever there is that comes close," Chandra said absently.

"No, I want you to come an' see what you think. I want to do it the way *you* want it done. It seems to me like, when you go to the store, you might git some thread that color, an' some others too. There's not very much in that sewin' box you got out for me. A body needs to have a big lot of thread if they're a-goin' to mend things up halfway right. I don' see how you can make do without a machine. All this other fine stuff an' gadgets you've got, an' no sewin' machine."

They went into the hall and Chandra said, "How did it get so hot?"

"Oh, I hunted around till I found the heat control. I know a body ought to be savin' with gas an' such, but I was purely a-freezin' to death. Didn' you notice I've had to put on a sweater? Oh, I brought two good sweaters. I knew how cold I'd be, away from home, especially down here right next to them ole mountains."

"Mama, this is an old shirt of Bruce's. It's not going to last more than one or two more wearings and washings. Use the black thread. That will be fine."

"Now, honey, I know I'm a-keepin' you from your work, an' I didn' mean to do that, but since you're out here, show me how to work your dryer. *I* never have give up to have a dryer, you know. Evelyn an' Steve said they'd buy me one last Christmas, if I'd use it. I appreciated it, but I told 'em it would just be a plum waste a money. I like for *my* clothes to hang out an' git the air an' sunshine, an' we've got a-plenty a that out home. Besides, when I git ready to have a thing like a clothes dryer or such-like, I can still buy it for myself. Your daddy wasn't much a man for thinkin' ahead or tryin' to save anythin', but he did have that life insurance, an' I been careful with that money. An' then now, I've got the Social Security an' all. I never aimed for my young'uns to have to take care a me, though I do appreciate it when they think about it.

"Now then, before you go back in your room, show me just onct more how to work that television what-you-may-call-it, an' do you reckon it'll be all right if I turn up the heat just a little tiny bit more?"

Back in her office, finally, Chandra opened a window. The house was stifling. The wind, still no more than a stiff breeze, swept grandly through a bright sky. It was warm for the time of year, regardless of what Mama was suffering, probably well over sixty. Fleetingly, she thought of going down to the stable where Gail's mare was boarded, riding for a while, free in the sun and wind. Impossible, of course, another thing to be put off until another time.

If they really lived in the country . . . Well, what? Would there be more hours in the day, more time to waste or play with? No. Whatever time there was, things would always expand to more than fill it. And, mostly, she was happy with that. She needed pressures to keep her busy, always active at something. She was proud of her ability to deal with several things at once, only . . . Only sometimes she wished she could just drop everything, have a horseback ride, sit silent and stare from the window, lie on the bed with her eyes closed, thinking of practically nothing—and not feel pressured or guilty about doing nothing. She envied people who could do that sort of thing with seemingly clear consciences. The children could do it; Eric could. Well, children ought to be able to. It ought to be an intrinsic part of youth, though she couldn't recall much of such relaxations in her own growing-up days. Working for someone else, as Eric did, was a rigorous business, and she was glad he could relax at home, only—she also resented it. Why?

At any rate, if they really lived in the country, she wouldn't be standing, staring down over an expressway, smelling, albeit faintly today, exhaust fumes, hearing a garbage truck banging along the next street. There would be woods, the sun-warmed, wind-blown scent of evergreens, silence, except for the wind whooshing in the treetops, maybe a stream, a bird. . . . But, even in the country, with all those dreams realized, could she manage with Mama in the house, day after day? Could she ever get *anything* done, finished? And if she did accomplish something, would it really be worthwhile when finally won? Could she just enjoy, even for a little while without the driving need, the dissatisfactions? Could she and Eric . . . would he ever . . . And what were they going to do about Mama? No, what was *she* going to do?

She remembered then that she had not yet read the letter from Evelyn that had come in yesterday's mail. She remembered that Bruce had carried in the mail from the car at some point last night. No doubt the letter was lying with the unpaid bills and unopened ads on the little desk in the maid's room, Mama's room.

Chandra opened her office door furtively and was struck by a new wave of heat. The television set blared from the family room and she moved silently along the hall. She got the small stack of mail and crept back to what was supposed to be her sanctuary. She wouldn't read the letter even now. Evelyn would be offended at that, and probably rightly so, but the letter was going to contain, essentially, what Dorothy had already said on the phone. They, at any rate, had obviously made *their* decision. She dropped the letter, with the rest of the mail, into a desk drawer.

She stood again, for just one more moment, by the open window. Prince Charming gamboled in the sere grass for her benefit, but she was feeling the mountains. She didn't really have to look, though on a day like this, one could see all the way south to Pikes Peak. She didn't have to have a window or a clear sky; the mountains were here, a great soaring wall of complete indifference and absolute security.

When she had first come to live in Denver, alone but for the infant Bruce, the mountains had been everything: the assurance she had never felt from her family, the secure dependability and stability she had never received from a husband. Her feeling for the mountains was so great and so deep, she rarely even tried to express it. She had tried to include some small part of it in her books, because she felt she owed the magnificent country whatever small tribute she could give, in return for all it had given her. Of course, that was ridiculous in a way, because, to the understanding of most people, the mountains gave nothing; simply, they were here, beautiful or ugly, frightening or reassuring, but if one *got* something from them, it was strictly all in one's head. But they *do* give, she thought fervently. They are certainly indifferent, but that's such a great part of their importance, their giving. I can count on their not caring, on that great cosmic indifference, draw on it for whatever I need. They'll never really change; they'll never let me down, or fall short, or be disappointing. I can draw and draw and draw on the mountains, and it's never the slightest drain, nothing I have to repay or feel obligated about. The mountains represent everything that's good, for me. How can I say it? If only I could write it all down! That would be the finest philosophy ever put on paper, if only I could do it. It could, ultimately, say all there is to say about good and dependability, strength, security, beauty, and the mountains would never know or care that it was done. Thoroughly selfless and completely absorbed, simply in being.

She was smiling wistfully and she gave a sad little shrug and looked down into the big wistful eyes of the dog in the back yard. If she could only live far back in the mountains, away from all the distractions of city and suburb, then what? Would her writing be better? Could she be a better person? She truly believed so and believing was, after all, the greater part of the battle. She could take from the mountains—or from her feeling for them, it was all one—in perfect trust and love. Suppose she lived there, in her dream place, all alone . . . ?

The mountains made no demands, brought no guilts or obligations, cared not in the least who or what she was. If it could be like that with people . . . but how selfish, how grasping that was. The mountains, whatever else they might seem, were inanimate, and people, to *be* people, had needs, feelings, personalities, rights to reciprocity. And she wanted to reciprocate—didn't she? If only, sometimes, relationships returned to her the things *she* needed, wanted. Did she make up her mind, before the fact, that the longed-for return would not come, and so blind herself to its varied forms? Was she so afraid, distrustful, certain of disapproval and disappointment that she was constantly and thoroughly insulating herself against all the potential signals, the inchoate reachings-out from others, from Eric? Could she only feel wholly safe, trusting, free, with mountains?

She scrubbed at wet eyes with her knuckles. The questions were too big, too frightening, and she must get on now with something she could handle, the galleys.

She had not turned over many more of the long limp proof sheets before she reached one of the scenes about which she had been concerned. All her fears were justified. The editor had mangled a passage several pages in length. Chandra could hardly bear to read through it. The scene had been cut, added to, "clarified" in places, obfuscated in others, so that she could scarcely recognize it. She was incredulous, physically sick. Tears filled her eyes in spite of all her efforts to be cool, sensible, objective. She could not have said if the tears were compounded more of anger, hurt, outrage, exasperation or simple disbelief.

Sniffling, grinding her teeth, she got the original manuscript from a file cabinet, found the scene and read through it. That served only to increase the churning, sickening clamor of emotions. Furiously, she reached for the phone to call her agent in New York. He would not be in, of course. It was lunchtime in New York. Luncheons and cocktail parties were very important functions for agents and others in the publishing business. Everyone except writers seemed to make all their worthwhile contacts and arrangements at these events.

Peter Curran was, in fact, not in, expected back at two-thirty. Chandra was shaking as she put down her phone. It rang almost immediately.

"Chan?" It was Eric. She was deeply grateful for the sound of his voice. "How's it going there? Are you getting anything done? Anything you *want* to do? I know it doesn't help if I'm interrupting, but I've been thinking about you all morning and I wanted to call and check."

"Oh, Eric," she was all but wailing. "All the cruddy things I was afraid of have been done to the book. I've only just got to the first really bad part, but I can't tell you how she's ruined it."

"Goddamn the woman!" he said with a quiet vehemence that startled her a little and eased things the slightest bit.

She was crying now in earnest, trying not to let him know. "Nothing like this has ever happened with my writing," she said and bit her lip hard, trying to stop its trembling. "I guess I just still can't believe it. She's changed things, dialogue and the way things happen. She's cut vital bits and put in sheer inanities. Thegn could do a better writing job if he knew all his letters. You know how she was always saying or writing in her letters, 'My reader won't understand this,' or 'My reader will be bored,' or 'My reader will need clarification'? What she's done to this part is just a shoddy mess that doesn't even make sense and is nothing like the rest of the writing. It isn't *mine*. It's been all I could do to read through it, and how much worse is it going to get with the other scenes I refused to change?"

"Well, you're not going to stand for it," he said, his low voice harsh with shared anger.

"No. I've already tried to call Peter, just now. He's out for lunch. But when I get him, I don't think he's going to be any real help. I'll have to call the publishing house myself, but, Eric, I don't even know who to talk to there. *She's* gone, that half-witted editor. I showed you her letter last night, that said she was leaving for another job. I hope to God it was because she's been fired."

"Surely Peter can at least give you a name. Or you can look up the contract, call whoever signed it if he has no better suggestion."

"Oh, Eric, it's such a lousy, *lousy* mess!"

"I'll read it tonight. Listen, love, try not to be too upset. You *are* the writer. They can't publish a book with your name on it without your approval."

"Are you sure of that?" she asked grimly and tried a little laugh that came out unsteadily. "I'm not, not at all. It seems to me, from my several years of experience and hard knocks, that publishers can do just about anything they damn well please. There are literally thousands of yearning authors who'd pay *them* to get something published. What the hell do they have to care about one individual writer who's trying to make a living and at the same time have some pride and authenticity in her work?" She was feeling more than a little hysterical now. "They've got the publication date and things all set up. I've never had any real problems with an editor before. I just can't even make a guess what they'll do about this, but I'm afraid they'll—"

"Talk to them," Eric said firmly, and she could imagine the set of his jaw. "Talk to Peter, too, of course. He needs to know what's going on, even if he doesn't do anything. But don't ask him to call them and then get back to you. You know how long that could take, not to mention the possibility of being botched in transit. Get a name and then tell them at the house that you're not going to stand for this. Of course it can be straightened out. It has to be and you'll see that it is. It's your book and they have no right to ruin or even change any part of it without your approval."

"I told you, last summer, when she wouldn't send

me the manuscript before it went to proofs that she was up to something."

"Yes, I know you did. Maybe I'm just naturally an optimist, but I kept hoping you'd be wrong this time."

"One thing they're going to say is how much it costs to make changes in galleys."

"Well, that's damn well not your fault. You had the manuscript in that idiot's hands months before it was due. Be sure to point that out to them."

"She *knew* I'd never approve the edited manuscript. With it already set in galleys, she thinks *I*'ll think I have to let it go." She was being flooded with a wave of anger now, and was glad of its sweeping away some of the other emotions, at least temporarily.

"Obviously that's exactly what was in her mind. Tell them how hard you tried to arrange to see the manuscript. I can get you copies here, of letters or anything you may need."

There was a silence. The most recent wave of anger was ebbing. She felt a terrible need to have him here, physically close, his arms about her, holding her, keeping all the rest of it at a bearable distance. She was frightened of those New York people, always had been, because they had such power to hurt her, through her inextricable deep involvement with everything that was her books.

"What about Mom?" Eric was asking solicitiously. "Is she giving you a hard time?"

"Not right now. She's doing some mending and watching her TV things, I think. She doesn't know about this, and I don't think I want to try to explain any of it to her."

"Should I come home, Chan? Dixon would have a fit, but I could get away for a couple of hours."

She said, trying for lightness, "You'd have to spend half that time driving, and—what could you do?"

"Well—keep Grandma off your back for one thing, while you make the phone calls. Read the stuff for myself. I need to see just what that half-wit has done."

"You don't believe me when I tell you—"

"Of course I believe you. You'd have to see it for yourself too, wouldn't you? To know just what degree of crud it is?"

Only slightly mollified and trembling again, she said bitterly, "I'm not even sure if I can stand to read any further or not. I just can't take this in."

After another moment or two, a few more useless repetitious words, they hung up and Chandra was crying again. She despised the crying. It was exactly what one would expect of a woman who felt she was in any danger whatever of not being able to handle things by any other means. But how in God's name did you stay cool and detached, reasonable and objective about the treatment of something that was like your child, your very self? And why couldn't Eric have...

She left her desk and sat on the worn old love seat, turning sidewise to lean her cheek against its high back. There was a tiny particle of solace in the touch of the rough fabric against her face. She wished desperately that Eric would come home, that he had just shown up without asking her if she wanted him, that he still might come. But he *had* asked, at least there was that much. However, his asking meant she had to refuse, didn't it? "Dixon would have a fit." Why couldn't he have just done it? She wished he would come and make the calls for her. He wouldn't be in constant danger of bawling on the phone. And, after all, they were his books, too, weren't they? In the same sense that he shared her life and the income from them? He could have taken this off her back, *and* Mama as well, just for a little while, so she could go into the darkened bedroom and hide for a time, until the pain and shock had lessened a little.

No, Chandra, be honest. You'd have to *hear* what was said on the phone, not just depend on a repeat of it. Eric's never any good at what he said and I said; he just hits the high spots of a conversation. And if you just tried listening on the bedroom extension, you'd be putting in your two cents' worth every minute. This is your baby, all yours, and you *will* handle it. . . . But when people hurt me like this, I want Eric to *want* to fight for me, at least some of the battle, not think of Dixon's fits, and not for the book, but for *me!* They *can* hurt me by hurting the book and he knows that. I just can't seem *not* to be vulnerable that way. *Why* must I be always on my own? Alone. It's a little as if someone were brutally maligning Thegn. Eric wouldn't just stand by for that, would he? Just tell *me* what phone calls to make and about getting copies of things? I'm alone. I'm *so* lonely for someone who will understand and *do* something.

Are all people always alone in the really important things? I detest those things people are always writing about the super-sensitivity of artists, and their innate and necessary solitariness. But are they true? I'm not that different, am I? I'm not crying for the moon, am I? Oh, Eric, please just come and take care of this, or of me. *Help* me handle it. I just need some real, concrete backing. I'm always afraid, insecure, except sometimes when I'm writing, or making love with you. Sometimes, just now and then, I'm *very* sure of myself at those times. I never really doubt the overall integrity of the books, but I'm so vulnerable where they're concerned. People can never make me doubt the books, but all they have to do is frown, or seem to, to make me have these terrible doubts about myself. And when we make love, almost always, I feel so safe, so trusting with you, except . . . Can't you *know* any of this? Won't anybody ever see how scared and insecure I am about—just everything? I *need* you, Eric. I think I *have* to have somebody. . . .

But, no! Good old Chandra! She can cope with just anything, do a little trick and get it all fixed up—maybe not for herself, but what the hell does that matter, just so other people are comfortable? Chandra will handle it. Watch her! Just watch her!

And suddenly she was remembering something from her very early childhood. Perhaps she had been three.

The cast must have been very recently removed from her injured leg. When that was done, she had had virtually to learn to walk again. Her parents, no doubt because she needed the practice and exercise, would send her for things: "Bring Daddy his shoes," "Git Mama the spool of thread." There had been people at the house at this time she remembered, and she was sent to fetch something. "Watch her, now just watch her!" she had heard the grownups whisper to one another as she hobbled painfully out of the room. She had realized then, with a painful physical shock, how ugly her scarred, twisted leg was, how different was her walk from anyone else's. At that age, she hadn't known the word freak, but she had known what it felt like to be one. No doubt, the whispers had been, in great part, admiration for what she had accomplished, but it hadn't seemed so to her. The trouble was that her mother often used those words, spoken in anger and derision, "Chandra Lynn, you're a-goin' to spill that milk if you don't be careful. Now watch 'er! Look at that mess! Watch 'er, watch 'er!"

Chandra jerked herself erect on the old love seat, scrubbing fiercely at her wet face, pushing damp hair away from where it plastered her cheek. All right! Watch her, then! See Chandra Barrie Whitman stand up to the New York publishing world! . . . God, Chandra, you always will rise to the bait, won't you? And what if you didn't, just once? What if you waited, let somebody else do it, or just let it go? *Let* them? They wouldn't. Not anybody. And I won't have this book ruined. Maybe the things I care most about will never be worth anyone else's rising to, but it's important to *me!* Maybe *I*'ll never be important enough to anyone else that they'll want to take care of things, of me. Maybe they'll *never* think of what I need, without having to be told. But *I*, the things I care about, have to have some importance to me—well, don't they?

Stop it! Oh, God, just stop it! Wash your face. Pull yourself together, because, for damn sure, nobody is going to do that for you. There *is* something to be done, so take care of it, protect the book. There is just not time and energy for all this half-assed analysis on a broken-down old love seat. I don't know why I haven't called the Salvation Army to come get the damned old thing years ago.

Ethel was occupying the downstairs bathroom. "Chandra Lynn?" she called when Chandra, having momentarily forgotten her presence in the house, tried the closed door.

"I'll be out in just a minute, honey. I went ahead an' hung them sheets out on the clothes line. They was lookin' right dingy from bein' dried in the dryer all the time. I'm a-tryin' to warm up my ole hands now, with some warm water. Them sheets'll likely be froze in a minute, but it'll be good for 'em to have the airin'. This ole authoritis in my hands is nearly a-killin' me from the cold out there. I've folded up that first load of clothes, but I don't know where any of 'em goes. I laid 'em on the stair steps. Maybe you'd want to put 'em up while you're a-waitin' for me to git out a your way in here. Huh? Did you say somethin' honey?"

"No, Mama," the words were very nearly a shriek.

"Well, I'm a-dryin' right now." Ethel laughed a little. "I can't think why I locked the door when I come in here, just to wash my hands. Just bein' in a strange house, I guess. I can't turn the lock till my hands is good an' dry, for they're so stiff. Don't you think it's awful cold in here?"

Chandra fled for the stairs.

6

In her office again, in far better control now, waiting for the long New York lunch hour to be over, Chandra skimmed quickly through the rest of the galleys. As she had feared, every major scene where the editor had suggested changes—some of them already rewritten by Chandra herself—had been hacked to pieces, reworked almost beyond recognition. The feeling of physical sickness was rising strongly in her again when Ethel opened the door without warning, to ask what she had intended doing about lunch.

"My God!" Chandra muttered, horrified with herself. "I was forgetting all about picking up Thegn at school."

"Huh?"

Then she had to wait while Ethel, pretending reluctance to go along for the ride, combed her hair and fixed up her face. She kept up a monologue about how she "Wasn' one a them people that has to be always on the go," didn't like "to be a-jumpin' in some car ever' few minutes."

Chandra was unusually glad to see the little boy come running from the school steps. Such a surge of warmth and love swept through her at the sight of the tousled blond hair, the grave, sweet face, that for a moment she feared tears again.

"I waited and waited," Thegn remonstrated mildly.

"I know, honey, I'm sorry."

"We learned a new song today. It's not about Christmas. Miss Cunningham said we needed to get our minds off Christmas for just a few minutes. It's like this: 'Little Ducky Duddle went wading in a puddle, Went wading in a puddle quite small. He said, "It doesn't matter, How much I splash and splatter, I'm only a ducky after all." ' "

"That's nice," said Chandra. "Can I sing it with you?"

Ethel was impatient, she had other things to say, but they sang "Ducky Duddle" all the short distance home.

In the kitchen, she put sandwich makings out and made one for Thegn.

"Mama," she said, "I bought this luncheon meat for you. It doesn't have spices or anything."

"It's awful sweet of you to remember about things

like that, honey. Most of them special things like that just don't seem to have no taste atall though. You know, it's awful when a body has to give in to their stomachs, eat things they don't even like because of 'em. So much stuff just don't agree with me, an' it seems to git worse ever' year. You don't never use that other room in yonder?"

"The dining room? Yes, we use it when we have a lot of people. Would you like to eat in there?"

"Mercy, no! I was just a-wonderin'. Seems like you don't *need* about half of this house. I had four children an' always made do all right with just five rooms."

"What can I get you to drink?"

"Oh, just some milk, maybe, if you got it to spare. But I'll git it. You ain't got to wait on me."

"Well, I'm not going to eat right now. As soon as the coffee's ready, I'll take a cup into the office. I've got a phone call or two to make."

"Not a-goin' to eat! Why you didn' have a thing for breakfast. I seen you throw that toast away. Don't you think you drink too much a that ole coffee, Chandra Lynn? *I* know it ain't good for you."

"Thegn, my love," Chandra said lightly, tousling his hair even more, "can I get you something else?"

"No," he said. "Won't the people you call be eating their lunch?"

"No, because they're in New York. It's a different time there."

"New York!" said Ethel, her eyes widening as if Chandra had mentioned phoning to another planet. "You're a-fixin' to call New York City?"

"Yes, Mama. I have to talk with my agent and with the publishers of the new book."

"You must pay a fortune in phone bills. What in the world do you have to *call* about? Couldn' you just send them a letter? *Postage* is high enough."

"No, I can't send a letter," she said, suddenly furious again, and trying not to let it show. What had happened to her book was none of Mama's doing, after all. She knew it was a mistake to try to go into it with Mama, but she wanted, needed to share her outrage, so she tried to explain what had happened while waiting for the coffee to be ready.

"Well," said Ethel, looking very sober as she made herself a sandwich with the spiced luncheon meat, "ain't a editor *supposed* to work on a book? I thought that was their job."

"Yes, they're supposed to work on a book, but they aren't supposed to *write* it. She made a lot of suggestions, and I used most of them, even some I thought were unnecessary. I don't *like* having my books edited; I doubt that any good writer does, but I think I'm very reasonable about it. I have never had a serious problem with an editor and I just will not *have* this."

"Well, Chandra Lynn, I know I don't know much about it, an' it's none a my business, but if I was you, I wouldn' git too smart an' high-handed with any a them people. I know you. I know how you can git carried away about some little thing an' plum fergit to show good sense. Why, what if they was to say, if you're a-goin' to be that-a-way, they just won't print the book? Where would you be at then?"

"Thegn," Chandra said, pouring coffee with a shaking hand, "when you've finished eating, go and get ready for your nap. I'll come up for a few minutes before you're asleep. I want to hear about what else went on at school today."

"Can Charming have his nap with me?"

"Of course he can. He always does."

"This morning, Grandma said him and Magic ought to stay outside all the time."

"*He* and Magic," Chandra corrected, already turning toward her mother. She could feel that her eyes were flashing and she put down the coffee cup, not to spill it.

"The dog and cat *live* here, Mama. *We* live here. Our animals come inside whenever we let them. They can get into bed with us if we choose, or anything else. It's *their* home too."

She switched off the coffee maker, picked up her cup, and when she turned from the counter, Ethel was gone.

"Grandma went in her room," Thegn said in consternation. "Maybe she was crying. Mommy, are you crying, too?"

"No," she said and turned back for a moment, unnecessarily, to the counter. "Everything's all right. Finish your lunch. I'll make my calls and see you in a few minutes."

"When you come upstairs, could you explain why Grandma doesn't like Charming? *He* likes *her*."

Chandra kissed the top of his head. "Yes. We'll talk about it."

Perhaps Peter Curran had tried to reach her while she was out, picking up Thegn, but she doubted it. Peter wasn't particularly known for returning calls. She placed the call again and told him, as quickly and dispassionately as she could, why she was calling. All the bad emotions were still there, but strangely, she was feeling somewhat better about the whole thing. She read Peter a few of the worst paragraphs from the galleys, then what were supposed to be, basically, the same paragraphs from her original manuscript.

"So what she's done," Peter said, sounding incredulous, "is *write* some of your book."

"Exactly, and an eight-year-old could have made a better job of it."

Peter laughed. Chandra wished she could reach across the miles and strangle him.

"I have never had this experience before. None of my clients has."

"Neither have I," she said grimly, but things were getting easier. She didn't know why and wasn't about to try to go into understanding it. "So what do I do?"

"Well, talk to them over there, I suppose."

"*She's* gone, Barbara Liscombe. Her replacement is to be a Ruth Courtney."

"Yes, I know Ruth. She's a fine person."

"But, Peter, she isn't starting work there until the middle of January. I'm told these galleys are to be back at the publisher's by the fifth. Who—whom—do I talk to?"

"I think it's a lucky thing for all of us that the Liscombe woman is gone. Surely, you can work better with someone else, almost anyone. But, you know, I don't know anyone really well at that house anymore. They've got a lot of new people in lately. Your guess would be about as good as mine as to who to call. You know their scheduling will be getting pretty tight now. Isn't the book due for release in April? And it *is* expensive to change galleys."

Chandra held her breath to keep from screaming at him: Can't you see how she's carved up my book? Ruined it? Damn you to hell, what am I paying you 10 percent for? Just so you can get a chuckle out of my unusual experiences? Can't you, ever, just once, *talk* as if you're on my side? Why is it just a general principle of the trade for everybody else in publishing to put writers down every time they turn around? *I* haven't made this mess!

If she began to talk like that, she'd get incoherent, maybe hysterical. In which case, in a few days, Peter would send her an eminently sensible letter—from his point of view—saying she mustn't get paranoid and hypersensitive, that he had only been pointing out the concrete facts.

She paid Peter 10 percent because she had to have someone in New York representing her books. An agent had the connections, not only for initial sales of books, but for movie and foreign rights and other things, which most writers could never hope to have or would want to be bothered with. Chandra felt that, over the years, she and Peter had become reasonably good friends, but *outside* their business relationship. She just could never seem to deal with the business in a business-like manner. Sometimes, she liked Peter—but not often.

His voice on the phone was going on pleasantly. "Otherwise, I'm glad you called. *I* have some good news. In yesterday's mail, we had a letter from England, with an offer for *Dawn* and for the fourth juvenile—I think it's the fourth. The agency we use in England is on the ball. They've found a German publisher who wants to translate *Dawn,* and the British publisher who's done the other juveniles wants this one. Hold on, I'll find the letter and tell you what the offers are."

Chandra's first thought was, You wouldn't have called me, you bastard; *you*'d have made do with a letter. Never do anything to lead a writer to think that anything *good* about her books should warrant a long-distance phone call. But she was pleased. In fact, she might eventually become elated. It was especially good news about the novel, her first adult novel, and the first thing she had written to be translated into a foreign language.

When she had finished talking with Peter, she looked up the signature on the contract for *Season of the Wolf.* It had been signed by the president of the company. She placed a person-to-person call to him, feeling actually a little giddy with optimism now. Her high was not detracted from by the fact that he had just returned from lunch and seemed quite willing to talk with her. While she waited briefly for the secretary to put him on, she wished she had not gone through all that bad time about Eric earlier, that he could know how well she now felt things were going to go, and about the foreign sales. She would call him, and she must tell Shirley.

Quickly, to the publisher, she outlined what had happened. "I know you won't be the one to handle this," she finished, "but I really didn't have any other name, anyone I could contact immediately. I think you can understand that I'm very upset and I want to expedite the corrections that must be made as quickly as possible. I know the schedule is getting tight now, but Miss Liscombe had the manuscript in her hands for months before my deadline on the book. I can't let the book be published with my name on it when parts of it are so obviously not mine."

"I'll have my chief editor call you about it," he said. "Today."

No apologies, of course, no sympathy for her poor mangled book and feelings, but his voice was not patronizing or derisive as had been some of the voices she had heard from the publishing world. He sounded businesslike, perhaps even mildly concerned.

She thanked him and hung up, feeling vaguely deflated, very tired, but almost content. Maybe they would handle it as she wanted. Maybe the problem was, after all, not insurmountable. Standing up from her desk, she smiled a little shakily, feeling foolish over all she had been suffering such a short time ago.

She went upstairs for fifteen minutes with Thegn, Prince Charming and Black Magic, then came down to try to make her peace with Mama.

Ethel was sitting in the family room, looking forlorn as she leafed desultorily through a magazine.

"Mama, I'm sorry I hurt you," Chandra said gently, putting a hand on the thin old shoulder. "But you know, we really do have to go on with our lives."

"I just never have thought animals belonged in the house," Ethel said dolefully, looking as if she might cry again. "But you're right. It's your house, an' not my business a bit what you do with it. I'm so used to bein' in my own place, doin' as I please. I oughtn' to of come."

"Oh, now, that's just nonsense. You know how much we've all been looking forward to Christmas with Grandma. People can't always agree; we mustn't expect it of each other. Maybe you'd like to take a nap now? I need to get as much more reading done as I can before Thegn wakes up and the others come home."

"Huh?"

Chandra repeated the salient parts of what she had said.

Ethel said bleakly, "I don't never sleep in the daytime. It always makes me feel bad. I'll just set here by myself a while, then go git them clothes in off a the line. What part of 'em do you want ironed?"

Chandra said gaily, "I hardly iron anything anymore. Come on, Mama, let's be friends. I got some good news from New York. They're going to publish another of my children's books in England and *Dawn*, the first adult novel, is going to be translated and published in Germany. Also, I think we're going to be able to work out the problems with the new book."

"Germany!" said Ethel with sudden warmth. "Well, now that's somethin', ain't it?" She sobered quickly and said severely, "I hope you wasn't smart-alecky with them about that other business, after them a-bein' so nice to you."

Chandra made two quick calls, one to Eric, who sounded harried and preoccupied, but was warm in his pleasure and relieved that she was feeling better, and one to Shirley who, after hearing Chandra's news, announced the estimate for having her car repaired. Then she was able to work for almost an hour before the phone rang again. It was Sheila Summers calling, from the ad agency where Chandra had used to work.

"I suppose you're busy," said Sheila in her usual tart manner. "I won't keep you because I am, too. Will you have dinner with me Saturday night? There's a lot I need to talk about. Well, not a lot, but I expect I'll find a lot to say."

"Oh, Sheila, I'm sorry, but I don't think I can. Eric's going to have to work a lot of overtime, right through the weekend, it looks like, and my mother's with us—"

"For Chrissake, Chandra, can't your mother entertain herself for one evening?"

Sheila had no patience with family situations, but the two women had always liked and respected each other deeply. Chandra heard the doorbell ring as she began:

"The kids have a lot of parties and things at this time of year. I don't know exactly what—"

"Oh, you are so *damned* domestic," snapped Sheila. "Two of your kids are practically grown. Can't they ever fend for themselves, even for a few hours? I've *got* to see somebody, and it has to be Saturday night, because I'm tied up every minute until then and I'm taking a plane for St. Louis early on Sunday morning."

The doorbell hadn't rung again. Surely Mama had answered it, or maybe Thegn was up.

She said harriedly, "If it's about some work, I just can't take on anything more until—"

"Goddamn it, it's not about some work. I'm leaving Brian, *that*'s what it's about. *Now* will you take it seriously?"

Brian was Sheila's third husband. Chandra liked him.

"Oh, Sheila, I'm so sorry. Do you need anything? I mean, before Saturday? I could—"

"Well, I'm not sorry," said Sheila curtly. "The sonofabitch! Marriage is for the birds. Just ask me. I'm a real expert."

"Would you want to talk with Eric, too? He likes you both very much and sometimes he can come up with a different perspective, about other people that—"

"I love Eric dearly," said Sheila shortly. "I should have taken him away from you years ago. Then, maybe I'd be in decent shape, but the *last* thing I want right now is the shoulder of *any* goddamn man to cry on. What I want, mostly, I guess, is to try to get some of the venom out of my system, get more than a little drunk. Will you come or not? Vernon's at eight?"

"Well, I'll try. I'll call you if I absolutely can't make it. Sheila, are you—all right?"

Ethel opened the office door and stood there, making some indecipherable gestures.

"God's sake, of course I'm all right. Are you still really naïve enough to think that a woman *has* to be all torn up every time some fucking man turns around? I just want somebody to listen to me rave for a couple of hours when I can fit it in, that's all. You're soppy and sappy and romantic and sometimes just plain dumb, but you can listen. Now I've got a client waiting—two clients." She hung up.

Ethel said, almost whispering, "They's a hippie girl at the door, Chandra Lynn, a-askin' for Eric. That doorbell woke me up right out of a sound sleep on the sofa in yonder. Like to a scared the water out of me."

Ethel had closed the front door, leaving the girl outside. Chandra opened it. She was wearing tight jeans and a baggy, disreputable shirt. She had golden brown hair, thick and long and very straight, shining in the sun, and being whipped about her by the wind. Her figure, under loose shirt and tight pants, was lush. Her face was beautiful and she had big lovely hazel eyes. She was perhaps twenty, looking very young and vulnerable and —what?—uncomfortable? Sad?

"I'm Mrs. Whitman. Can I help you?"

"Oh, well—uh—I asked for *Mr.* Whitman."

"I'm sorry. He's at work, won't be home for several hours."

A stronger gust of wind covered the girl's face completely in the beautiful shining hair. She pushed it aside with both hands.

"Would you like to come in, out of the wind?"

"Well, yeah, okay. Just for a minute."

Chandra closed the door. Ethel was standing in the family room doorway, peering avidly.

"Come into my office," Chandra said. "I've left papers on the desk and the door and window open. I'm afraid things may be blowing all over the place."

She closed that door firmly, without looking back toward her mother.

The girl laughed a little, nervously. "You're a writer, aren't you? I know that because he talks about you all the time. Eric does."

"He does?"

"Yeah, well, see, I'm in his drafting class. My name's Candace Miller, Candy. He goes out with us sometimes, for coffee or beer, after class, you know. It gives us a chance to talk to him because he doesn't have regular office hours, like the full-time professors. And he's told us you're a writer. He's really proud of you—and his kids. He's a swell guy, really neat. I guess you think it's funny, strange, I mean, for a girl to be majoring in engineering."

"No, Candy, I think it's perfectly normal, if that's the kind of work you want to do."

"Well, a lot of people think it's strange—like my folks do—and there are only three other girls besides me in Eric's—Mr. Whitman's—drafting class. Mechanical engineering is my thing. I just love to take things apart and put them back together again, especially cars. I want to design new cars someday—you know, with good fuel economy and hardly any bad emission, but with good looks and enough power and everything. Detroit just won't get with it."

Candy cleared her throat and for a moment Chandra was afraid she was going to start crying.

She said quickly, lightly, "Our son Bruce could probably use your advice. He's been working on fixing up an old car for months."

"Yeah, I know, he's told us about that, too. He really loves to talk about his family. I mean, he doesn't do it all the time, so it gets, like, boring, but just sometimes, when some of us go out together for a little while after class, he tells us little things. I never knew a man that did that, seemed so—openly proud about his family and all like that. See, I'm an orphan, so I guess I don't know an awful lot about different kinds of people. My aunt and uncle raised me. They don't like kids and they don't like each other, and they don't like much of anything that's going on these days. They're just—well, you know, bitchy, a couple of old drags. I work through breakfast and lunch hour at this crummy restaurant, and sometimes I help my uncle out so he can take a break on this night job he has, so I can only take one or two evening classes at a time. It must be really neat to be in a family where people really like each other and are, you know, interested. You must all have a neat life."

"As a matter of fact, Candy, it is pretty neat most of the time. Would you like to sit down?"

She perched momentarily on the edge of the love seat, but then stood up again. "These are his cartoons, aren't they? Eric's? Sometimes, he draws something really kooky on the board at school to illustrate things. Most of the time, he's serious in class, but sometimes, he's really funny."

She moved slowly around the room, studying the pictures, giggling appreciatively.

"Did you need to talk with Eric about something that has to do with the class?"

Candy glanced round at her with—what?—fear?

"I guess you must think I've got quite a nerve, just showing up here like this. What I did, I looked up his name in the phone book and found the address. This is a really nice neighborhood."

There was a little silence before she went on, studiously gazing at one of the cartoons, which Chandra felt she wasn't seeing at all.

"Uh, yeah, I did need to see him about—about class. It's a test we took. No, not a test. He only gives one test a semester and we won't be having that until tomorrow night, but we have these projects. We don't have regular tests in his class. We just have to draw things, and like that. It seemed pretty important to me to—to find out some things, about this project, and I felt like taking a nice ride out this way, so I thought I'd just take a chance on Eric's being home and . . ."

"Well, I'm sorry," Chandra said and meant it. "With a drafting project, I'd be absolutely no help."

There was something haunting about the girl. Was she somehow familiar? Or was it just the haunted expression that kept showing up in those lovely eyes?

"Well, yeah," said Candy, smiling and making a disparaging little gesture. "If it's not your thing—I mean a person's thing—it just doesn't, well, turn them on."

"You'll be having your class tomorrow night. You can talk with Eric then."

"Sure. Right."

"I'll walk out with you. I think the postman came by a few minutes ago."

Candy said, as if suddenly recalling something, "Do you know some people named Smithfield? I think they must live around here somewhere."

"Yes, I know who they are, though we don't know them well. They live on top of the hill in a dark brick house with green trim."

"I used to know this guy, Jim Smithfield, we went all through grade school and junior high together. His dad made a lot of money and they moved out here because they didn't want Jim to go to the crummy high school we had to go to in town. I wonder if he'd remember me."

"I think Jim's in college," said Chandra. "I don't know if he'd be home for his holiday yet."

"Oh, sure. Jim would be going to college. He was a good football player and all the time, even when we were little kids, he always said he was going to be a doctor. I'll bet he is, too. I'll bet he's going to some real fancy college back East, or maybe in California. Since I'm so close by, maybe I'll just go and ask about him. It would really be neat to see him again after all this time."

"I'm sure you can find the house. Their name would be on the mailbox."

Candy chattered as they walked slowly out toward the street, about the house, the neighborhood, the weather. Then she suddenly broke off in midsentence, stopped walking and said hesitantly, "Eric never said anything about you—I mean, he never told us you . . ."

"Have a limp?" Chandra said easily. "You can say that to me. I know about it."

Candy stared for an instant, then laughed delightedly. "Hey, wow, man, that's really cool. I mean, a lot of people couldn't hack it like that. You're really neat."

"Thank you," Chandra said, smiling. "Is that your car?"

A little Volkswagen sat at the curb, old and battered, painted a bright yellow with round black spots all over and small bug antennae on each front fender.

"Yeah," said Candy with a fond proud smile. "I painted it myself, souped up the engine too. It's a great little car, can do just about anything a jeep or something like that can do. I can do just about anything with or for The Bug, except, sometimes, pay for gas. Well—uh—thanks a lot, Mrs. Whitman. Sorry I bothered you, but it was really nice meeting you. I'll talk to Eric at school tomorrow."

Chandra carried the mail inside. Ethel was waiting in the hall.

"Who in the world *was* that?"

"One of Eric's students."

"Do they come here all the time? Are they all hippies like that one? My land, the way children dress these days! Now a nice pants suit is one thing, but that stuff she had on looked like it was picked out of somebody's rag bag. And that straight, stringy hair all over the place! Ain't you about through with your readin' for today? What was you a-thinkin' about fixin' for supper?"

"I have most of the supper all ready. It's in the freezer. I'll stop in just a few minutes, Mama. Gail and Bruce will be home soon and Thegn will be waking up. I just want to get my papers in order and have a look at the mail."

"Nothin' there for me, I guess." Ethel laughed a little, to let it be known she was being facetious, but she was also very curious about the mail.

Mama needn't have wasted her curiosity on the mail, Chandra thought absently, as she flipped through the envelopes and dropped several things into her waste basket. There were several Christmas cards, and she'd readily share them. A few were even from people Mama would know. As she opened her desk drawer to drop in the rest of the things for later perusal, two things from yesterday's mail caught her eye, Evelyn's letter and another letter-size envelope that hadn't been readily identifiable when Thegn took it from the mailbox on their way to the airport. She picked up this envelope and could feel there were small, rectangular hard things inside. Credit cards? No, tickets of some kind. The return address read "Bill Hazzard, Reicher Ranch, P. O. Box 83, Plains Haven, Texas." Bill Hazzard. There was familiarity in the name, but she couldn't place it.

The envelope contained two tickets for something called the Holiday Stampede, and were for the matinee performance on the following Saturday. There was also a note and the latest clipping from the Chelsea paper about Chandra's books. She had read about the Holiday Stampede, a newly organized rodeo, premiering in Denver this year, but who would be sending them tickets? The note read:

Dear Chandra,
    You won't remember me. I was way older and ahead of you in school. Patsy Kelly is my sister and you used to be good friends with her. I still get the old home town paper.
    Have worked at this ranch for the past fifteen years. We raise rodeo stock and are the stock contractors for this Holiday Stampede in Denver. I will be there all week, overseeing our stock. Thought you and your husband might

want to see a performance. These are box seats. The ranch gets a box for the whole week, but the Saturday performance might be the best. The last one is on Saturday evening and you can change these afternoon tickets if you want to.

I would like to see you again and meet your husband. If you want to get in touch with me, I'll be staying at the Fortunata Motel, room 216. Hope to see you.
Bill Hazzard

Chandra remembered Patsy's big brother now, big, good-looking in a rough, craggy sort of way, and rather obnoxious. She had liked rodeos once, but three years with the boastful, insufferable Les, who had been so certain he would someday be roping champion of the world, and had hardly ever earned a dime, had turned her former enjoyment and excitement to loathing. Well, that was no fault of Bill Hazzard's and the obnoxiousness she remembered was probably due to the fact that her clearest memories of him were of when he had been seventeen or eighteen, a generally obnoxious age.

It was thoughtful of him to send the tickets. Eric would probably be working, not that she wanted to go anyway. Maybe Gail and Bruce would want to use the tickets. If not, certainly they could find someone else who would want to go. If she could only remember it at a convenient time, she would call Bill at the motel and thank him. No doubt, he wouldn't be in now. She suspected he might have sent the motel information because he would like an invitation to supper, but she didn't think she'd be able to manage that.

She opened the desk drawer to drop in the tickets and her eye fell once more on Evelyn's letter. Finally, she opened it. It was mostly about Mama, less emotional and defensive than Dorothy had been on the phone, but then Evelyn and Chandra could, most of the time, afford to be less emotional and defensive than Dorothy, who lived only sixty miles from Chelsea and did her best to look in on Mama twice a month. Dorothy was truly an exemplary daughter, despite her complaints and bickerings with their mother, and Mama was always so hard on Dorothy.

There were no really specific facts from either of the sisters about just why Mama ought to move away from the home place, but Chandra could readily see that their point had grounds. So what was she going to do? Could they live together, perhaps for years and years, she and Mama and the rest of the Whitmans? Would she, Chandra, be able to maintain a shred of identity, of sanity, with Mama in permanent residence? Identity was all in one's own head, of course. No one else *let* one have or *took* away one's identity. But Mama, meaning only what she considered well, had come very near to destroying her a number of times already, and she had been here less than twenty-four hours.

What if she posed this problem to Shirley and Sheila? She had never been much inclined to share her serious decisions with others, except Eric, but it made her smile, imagining the conflicting reactions she'd get from those two. The prospect was interesting. Maybe she could see some new and different light on the matter out of the very conflict.

She put the book galleys and her notes into an envelope, wincing at the thought of having to go back to work on them, but she'd take them up to bed later. It was well past five in New York now, and no chief editor had called, but her feeling about the whole matter was so much improved now. Tomorrow, the call would come and it would all be put right somehow. Hope springs eternal, she thought to herself a little grimly, but it was pleasant to feel optimistic about something, anything, in the publishing world.

She turned to leave the office, then caught sight of Evelyn's letter, lying on her desk. She had just finished tearing it into very small pieces and dropping them into her waste basket when Ethel opened her door again.

7

Eric, Chandra and Ethel sat together in the family room. Eric had just come down from seeing Thegn to bed. Gail was next door with her friend Anne Soderberg; Bruce and a friend of his were in the garage. Fire crackled softly on the hearth. The dishwasher had just finished its cycle in the kitchen.

Chandra was knitting. She found it relaxing when there was nothing else that had to be done, and she could never sit still without something to do.

"That's a right pretty color of yarn, Chandra Lynn," said Ethel comfortably.

She smiled. "I'm a little surprised it hasn't faded. I've been working on this sweater for a long time."

"You say it's for Gail? That'll go right nice with her colorin'. She's a right pretty little thing, Gail is, but don't you think it's about time you let her wear just a little bit of makeup?"

"I'm not stopping her, Mama. She just doesn't care about things like that."

"Well, I know times change, an' people's ways, but it don't seem to me like a little somethin' artificial can hurt if it helps a body's looks. Just a little lipstick, maybe? I guess she takes after you in that. You wouldn' hardly wear lipstick nor nothin' like that, even when all the rest a the girls was a-doin' it an' I was willin' for you to."

"I didn't like to start wearing bras either," Chandra recalled drily. "I'd be right in fashion now."

Ethel glanced embarrassedly at Eric. He was looking through the newspaper, but listening, smiling faintly behind the sheets.

Chandra hadn't liked the advent of bras or much of

anything else about her burgeoning maturity, because of the family's reactions. Her mother's attitude toward almost anything physical was secretive, embarrassed, slightly proud, but also vaguely as if it were obscene. Chandra had felt gross, ashamed.

Ethel said, "I'm a-crochetin' this afghan for Sally's baby. She expects in Feb'uary."

Sally was one of Evelyn's daughters. Ethel had already reminded Chandra about the baby, told her about the afghan at least three times. Really, Chandra thought, poor Mama had so relatively little to talk about that, after a day or two, her conversation had to be made up, in part at least of repetitions. Chandra was feeling rather mellow tonight, less tense than usual.

Supper had been ready when Eric came home. The table talk had been mostly the children's, but Eric had been eager to know if there had been further developments about the book. She had rather wished they could wait for this talk until they were alone together in their room but she had liked telling them all about the foreign sales. Even Bruce had looked pleased, a little surprised, vaguely impressed. Eric's face, his eyes, had glowed with pride and pleasure. He had said almost nothing, but held up his water glass in a toast, in which the children had joined. Ethel had looked around at this, perplexedly.

Chandra had been suddenly determined to get *some* response from her mother. I'm still just a little kid, she thought tolerantly, trying to win praise and approval from my mommy.

She had said, looking at Ethel, "I really am awfully pleased, especially about the German sale. A thing like this can be enjoyed several times, because everything in the book business takes so long. I can be pleased about it now, because the arrangements are being made. I'll be awfully happy to have copies of the book, when it's done, in another year or two and, of course, the money will be very enjoyable, whenever we get it."

To her satisfaction, Ethel's eyes widened and her face lit up. Ethel said, in an awed tone, "Do you mean they're a-goin' to *pay* you?"

Chandra subsided very immediately. So much for trying to boast to my mommy, she thought, but she could smile as she caught the twinkle in Eric's eyes.

Bruce said, in his usual head-on, unsubtle fashion, "What do you think, Grandma? That she just does all that for nothing? It's a lot of work, writing a book."

Chandra gave him a grateful look. She had never before been really sure if Bruce himself realized that fact or not.

"Oh, I know she works," Ethel said comfortably, "though today ain't seemed like much of a example. Seems to me like she talks on the phone a lot, too. Did I tell y'all about the big fine new car Evelyn an' Steve has bought?"

While the supper things were being cleared away, Eric went into Chandra's office and read the passages she had indicated, first in the galleys, then in her copy of the original manuscript. He always followed her books avidly during their planning and writing, so he knew this one quite well already.

He came from the office and stood in the kitchen doorway, his face dark with anger. Chandra could see some of the hurt and incredulity she had felt in the depths of his brown eyes. She closed and turned on the dishwasher and, without interrupting Ethel's monologue about the doings of some neighbors down home in Chelsea, went to stand close to him.

"Jesus Christ!" he muttered fiercely and took her in his arms. "How could anybody have the audacity to call that mess writing? That's not *your* book, those parts she's 'fixed up.' It's criminal."

His outrage felt good to Chandra. His arms felt wonderful. She raised her eyes to his and was deeply touched to see tears glistening there.

She said firmly, "They're not going to get away with

147

it. I have a feeling—maybe it's just stupid optimism—but I think, now, that it's all going to be okay."

He cleared his throat huskily. They were talking softly, under Ethel's talk, Chandra glancing her way often to reassure her that they were listening.

Eric said, "What I'm wondering is if they've *got* the original manuscript anymore. In some of those scenes she's been at, it looks to me as if she's literally cut it to pieces."

"Well, we can make them copies of the pages they'll need for the corrections. You said you'd get them at the office."

"Make them pay for the goddam copies," he said adamantly.

"Oh, Eric, it's not really *their* fault either. It's all Barbara's doing, and she's gone now, damn her. If they don't give me a hard time about making the corrections that have to be made in all those pages, we can surely furnish copies." She kissed him gratefully. "Would you just go light the fire now? Let's just have a nice evening. I don't feel nearly as bad now as when I made that first horrible discovery, or confirmation. If I can just make myself read through the rest of what she's done and arrange to have it made right . . ."

She wished she need not feel defensive of the publishers, need not be the one to be giving reassurance to Eric, but that was her doing, and none of theirs. She really did feel so much better about the book, and about most things in general. She didn't know why. Surely the news of the foreign sale had helped. For now, she just wanted to take her feelings at face value and enjoy them, no analyzing or questions.

It was pleasant, sitting here in the quiet house, knitting, hearing Eric rustling the newspaper and the snap of a branch in the fire. Evidently, Ethel was feeling somewhat that way, too.

She said, "This is a right nice room. I like it. I don't see, though, what you need with that other livin' room, or the special dinin' room either. Do you ever use 'em?"

Eric half-folded the paper, saying to Chandra, "Did you read Pittman's article about mass transit?"

"No," she said. "Let me see."

He gave her the paper and said to Ethel, "Sure, Mom, we use those other rooms. It's nice to have rooms the whole family can really live in, and others for company. The living room and dining room stay clean most of the time. The furniture and carpets don't take a beating in there, and the kids can still enjoy the house."

Ethel preened visibly, delighting in his undivided attention. He had brought home several packs of new batteries for her hearing aid, had sorted the used ones from the case and thrown them away. She had put herself happily and entirely in his hands regarding the matter, though Chandra knew she was likely to rescue the discarded batteries from the kitchen waste basket if she remembered them tomorrow. She would have so much to tell everyone "down home" about how knowledgeable and thoughtful Eric was.

Ethel said, smiling at him, "Where is it that Brucie and Gail have gone? I didn't quite hear all they was a-sayin'."

The children's plans for the evening had been discussed at the supper table, but Eric repeated them for her.

"Don't seem like I've hardly seen 'em," said Ethel tolerantly, "but I reckon young'uns thinks their doin's is important."

"There'll be plenty of time to see them," Eric said comfortably.

He and Chandra talked then, a very little, about the problems of mass transit and smog. Ethel had no interest whatever in things that did not involve her personally or had no connection with people and things very familiar to her. She fidgeted and looked aggrieved, left out.

Finally, she said, almost coquettishly, "Eric, don't you think Chandra Lynn's a pretty name?"

"Yes," he answered immediately and smiled at his wife, who disliked her name. "And so is she, beautiful."

"You know it was her brother Glen give her the name of Chandra."

Ethel had told Eric all about this each time she had seen him over the past ten years, but Eric was kind, and could be a most gratifying listener.

"Oh, Glen *did* love his little baby sister," Ethel said, and her eyes were bright with tears. "He was the *best* boy! You know, so many boys, especially when they're teen-agers, is so smart-mouthed and big for their britches that a body can't hardly stand to live with 'em, but Glen wasn' never like that, not a bit. Poor little thing didn' hardly have time to be. Luther, my husband, had to be off an' gone so much of the time, to find payin' work in them hard years, that Glen had to be the man at home a whole lot of the time. An', oh, he could do it, too! He could manage most ever'thin' around our place by the time he was twelve or thirteen, an' he was always the sweetest thing. The girls, Dorothy an' Evelyn, just didn' hardly know what they did think about havin' a baby sister after so long a time, but Glen, he was just tickled plum to death, an' he wanted her named Chandra. It was a word he'd come acrost in some book, an' he said it meant moon in one a them languages they speak off in India. Bless Glen's heart, he did so love to read, an' he didn' hardly ever have time for it. I put the Lynn with Chandra. I thought it was a real pretty name, an' it wasn' near so common back then as it is now. That tickled Glen too, because it rhymed with his name. He was named Luther Glen, after his daddy. Oh, he *did* love that baby. He was just all the time a-tutorin' with 'er an' a-pettin' 'er. An' Chandra Lynn, she just thought the sun rose an' set in her big brother, from the time she first begin to notice things. I guess you just don' remember him atall, do you, honey?"

Chandra shook her head, wishing the subject could be changed. Why did she feel so self-conscious and guilty when Mama talked about Glen? And Mama was *going* to talk about Glen. There was never any sidetracking her on this subject. Chandra wished she *could* remember her brother. She fervently hoped he had really been the wonderful person she imagined and about whom she had a great feeling of loss for the not knowing. Of course, one must always take into account Mama's own imagination, wishful thinking, the polishing of memories of her only son, dead now these thirty-six years.

"You know, Eric, he had taken Chandra Lynn to see Santy in Chelsea when they had that awful wreck. It was just about this time of the year, a few days earlier, the fourteenth day of December. She was just old enough, that year, to be interested in ole Santy Claus. Knowin' how Glen was, I expect he got more enjoyment out of it than the baby did. He just loved to take her places an' show her off, an' do things for 'er. He was as gen'rous an' good a brother as anybody ever had.

"We'd been a-havin' a mistin' rain that day. I remember it like it happened this mornin'. Luther was off a-workin' someplace—Lubbock or one of them Mexican-name places. Dorothy an' Evelyn was both married an' gone from home by then, but they was a-comin' for Christmas, so we could all be together agin. That rain started in a-freezin', after Glen left for town. It don't hardly ever git that cold up in our part of Texas, but it was one a them northers had come through. When Glen started in to come home, why they was ice had froze on the bridge over Santy Fe Creek. You recollect where that's at, don't you, Eric? Not two mile from our house. They was a neighbor of ours, Johnny Tate—he's dead now—was a-drivin' behind Glen an' seen it all. My boy just lost control a that ole pickup truck. He wasn' a-drivin' too fast nor nothin' like that. He never was reckless. It was just that ice, an' a-comin' on it sudden, you know."

Ethel sniffed, stifling a sob, and wiped at her eyes

with the baby afghan. Chandra was looking down at the newspaper beside her, but not reading.

Eric said gently, "Why don't I get us all some coffee?"

"No, honey," said Ethel gratefully, her voice still unsteady. "I can't have nothin' like that after night this-a-way. Even that ole awful-tastin' stuff with the caffeine took out keeps me awake if I drink it late."

"Maybe some tea then?"

"No, I don't believe I want anythin' atall. You go ahead if you want to, you an' Chandra Lynn. An' I tell you this, I just think you're the sweetest thing in the world for doin' around the house the way you do, an' a-waitin' on yourself. I'm afraid Chandra Lynn don't half appreciate you. Most men don't even know where the kitchen's at in their own homes, let alone to fix an' do the way you do. Course I wasn' raised up to think a man ought to *have* to do such things, after he's put in a hard day's work, nor I didn' *think* I'd taught my girls any such ways."

"I don't work very hard," said Eric casually. "And I do live here. I'd be pretty stupid if I couldn't take care of myself, don't you think?"

"Well," said Ethel, with yet one more meaningful look at her daughter, "they's a mighty lot a men wouldn' never see it that way, I can tell you that."

Eric looked the offer of coffee at Chandra and she shook her head. What she really felt like having was a vodka collins, but she simply didn't have guts enough to make use of the bar in Mama's presence. She wished Eric would, literally, break the ice about that, but they really didn't drink often, and he came back after a moment with only his cup of coffee.

Ethel had not been distracted and she was ready to go on sadly. "Dr. Baker, our good ole doctor that we'd used for years—brought all four a my children into the world—he's been dead now, twenty years, I guess it is— he said after that that poor little ole Glen never suffered, never felt a thing. He was killed instant, an' that's the Lord's mercy, I reckon, if it had to happen. An' the baby, we didn' know for days an' days if she was a-goin' to live or not. Oh, it was a awful time, me at home by myself when the word come, an' it was the next mornin' before Luther or the girls could git there, with the roads so bad. I can tell you, *that* wasn' no happy Christmas."

Chandra was swept by bleakness. She had always known that Mama, probably the rest of them too, wished that she had died instead of Glen. She could understand it: He was almost grown, Bruce's age, someone who had already established his personality and place, while she had been a baby, still virtually an unknown entity. But it was a heavy burden to be the survivor and feel guilty about it. Eric was looking at her with love and understanding and she had to turn her eyes to her knitting after an instant.

"An' then," Ethel was going on heavily, "Chandra Lynn had to be in the hospital all that long time, an' they thought for the longest that she might not never be able to walk agin. They said if it hadn' of happened when she was so little, she *wouldn'* ever have been so she could start to walkin'. I don't know what we'd of done through all that if it hadn' of been for my daddy.

"I guess you've heard all about this before, but my daddy was a *fine* man. He had a freight-haulin' business out there around Chelsea, started it back when they used to have to use wagons. He paid for Glen's funeral an' all, an' the baby's hospital bills. We paid 'im back later, a course, but right at that time, we didn' have nothin'. An' then he set up that trust fund for her, five thousand dollars, with the understandin' that it was to be used for her to go to college, or, if she didn' go on to school, she could have all that money when she come to be twenty-one. Daddy couldn' do such as that for all a his grandchildren—he had sixteen of 'em, I believe it was—but the rest understood, my brothers and sister did,

I mean, that Chandra Lynn might maybe need some special help, an' that Daddy wanted to see she'd be took care of.

"Oh, we took 'er around to doctors for the longest time, a-tryin' to see if they wasn' somethin' more could be done. We went to Dallas an' Houston, an' even plum to New Orleens onct, but they always said—"

"Excuse me," Chandra broke in stiffly. "I'm going up to check on Thegn." She was painfully conscious of her limp as she walked quickly out of the room.

She sat down for a few minutes in her own bedroom, so that maybe Mama would get finished talking about her as if she wasn't there. That damned five thousand dollars, she thought wryly. The importance that money had had for her mother! It had been a big factor for Les too. He had yearned over it, all during their marriage, accusing her almost daily of deliberately withholding what was his by rights, as her husband. And her approaching twenty-first birthday had been a factor in the timing of her divorce.

Chandra couldn't remember her grandpa either, but she was truly grateful to him. The money hadn't come to nearly as much of a fortune as Mama liked to believe, even with having accrued interest for eighteen years, but it had saved her life, bought her freedom. The very words "five thousand dollars" made Mama's mouth water, and she had told Chandra almost every day of her growing-up years how lucky she was, how rich she was going to be at such an early age, how she must be ready to accept the counsel and guidance of those older and wiser in the use of such a fortune.

Chandra knew just how Mama's story went on. Downstairs, she would be filling in the years, again, for Eric, telling him a little about Luther, how he had been a good man, in his way, but with no head for business, little willingness to give thought to tomorrow. And they had paid off things and begun to save, through Ethel's constant nagging and scrimping, though she wouldn't put it quite that way, of course. The Barrie place had been paid off when Luther died, and then there was his life insurance money. Once Chandra left home, Ethel had been able to begin adding to her savings again. She sold the produce of the place, vegetables, milk, eggs, a few beeves each year, and she had her Social Security money. Probably, she would proudly quote for Eric's benefit, the exact figure of her savings account, and he would look duly impressed.

Saving was almost a frenzy with Ethel and, in her own right, she had reason to be proud. Her life had never been an easy one, though she had created most of its strictures herself and, by her own standards, she had done well.

Chandra most wanted to avoid the part of the repetitious story that concerned her father's death. She had such guilts about that, too. She knew the guilt—and the bitterness—were unfounded, but knowing and making the feelings go away were such very different things.

She had very little in the way of real memories of her father, but she remembered the circumstances surrounding his death with painful clarity.

Luther had been home for two weeks or so, between construction jobs, and he had been ill, some sort of stomach trouble, for which Ethel dosed him, often and harshly, with his total cooperation. Ethel, who would never learn to drive because "I'm just too nervous an' it ain't ladylike," had got a ride with some neighbors to a church meeting one night. Chandra was not taken along because she had a cold. Besides, she had to get to bed early; the school bus came shortly after seven in the morning. She went to bed, and Daddy went to take a hot bath in the recently installed bathroom, saying he thought the heat and steam might make him feel better.

When she was just falling asleep, Chandra heard a strange, heavy thud. Listening, and hearing nothing further, she got up after a few minutes and called to him at the bathroom door. There was no sound at all. Her eight-year-old heart began to thud with apprehension.

The door was not locked. She opened it a crack and, in the steam and the dim light from a dangling bulb, saw him, lying on his side, naked and still wet, on the bathroom floor. After what seemed for her an age of terror, he groaned and became conscious, but only just. In a weak, vague voice, he said that he was very sick, that she'd better run to the neighbors for help. There was no telephone.

In her nightgown and bare feet, she ran the short distance to the nearest neighbor. It was raining. Running frantically through the downpour, Chandra remembered how she had heard all those times that it had been raining the time Glen died. This was a violent early-spring storm, with daggers of lightning and great splitting roars of thunder.

The neighbors came back with her. Somebody brought Mama. An ambulance came and took her daddy to the hospital. Someone said Dorothy and Evelyn should be called. Chandra went to sleep at the neighbors'. What people mostly wanted, it seemed, was to forget about her. All she was, was in the way. She lay awake a long while in the unaccustomed bed, hearing the storm finally move on, not knowing what might happen, but terribly frightened of whatever it was to be—and guilty.

It was a long time later before she knew or understood the real details: that her father had been suffering from an intestinal obstruction, which finally closed his bowel completely, that surgery successfully remedied this problem, but that his body, weakened by harsh medicines and systemic infection, could not survive the pneumonia which followed the operation.

At the time, she knew that he was moved from the small hospital in Chelsea to San Antonio. Dorothy lived in San Antonio; Mama went to stay there, and Evelyn came from Beaumont to be there too. The big hospital wouldn't allow little children in, and her daddy was too sick to see her anyway. The best thing she, Chandra, could do, was to stay with Aunt Mamie in Chelsea, keep on going to school and, above all, be very quiet and *good*.

Aunt Mamie, Chandra's great-aunt, actually, was a crotchety old maiden lady, who had never once in her life thought of a child as a person. She said, on the rare occasions when she did anything but nag about Chandra's table manners or other bad habits: "What are you a-cryin' about? Don't you know you can't help nobody that-away? No, you *don't* feel sick! There's enough worries around here. You ain't to cause any *more* trouble."

Chandra's daddy died after four days in the San Antonio hospital. They told her about that: "Now you'll have to be strong for your Mama's sake, an' just as *good* as you can be." She hadn't gone to the funeral because her cold had grown much worse. She had a fever. She was glad about not going—though guilty. She was afraid of seeing her daddy dead—or anybody.

Finally, they were all back home, Mama, Dorothy and Tom, Evelyn and Steve and their children. The church women had prepared a meal. Aunt Mamie and another old lady brought Chandra home. She was frightened and quiet, still feeling very sick, but she was glad to be home again, to see the niece and nephew who were nearer to her age than her own siblings. She rushed up to Evelyn, who was holding the new baby Chandra had not yet seen. She looked on the sweet sleeping infant with excited awe and love, while Evelyn was receiving the commiserations of one of the church ladies. Then Chandra cried, far more loudly than she had meant to, "Oh, Evelyn! Can I hold the baby?"

Evelyn seemed scarcely aware of her, but Aunt Mamie rushed across the room, grabbed her arm and hauled her painfully away. "Can't you never hush up?" she whispered fiercely. "Don't you know your daddy's dead? It ain't Christian to holler an' carry on like that in the middle of bereavement. Sometimes, I'd swear you ain't got good sense. An' you stay plum away from that baby. It's apt to git your cold. Go on in yonder an' git in the bed. Your fever's a-comin' up agin. I wonder just how much more trouble you *can* cause."

Chandra lay there miserably, as small as she could make herself, alone, hearing the muted voices from other rooms of the house. Glen died and Daddy died, she thought. If I got too close to the baby, will he die? Oh, I don't want him to be dead, or Daddy, or Glen. I'll be *so* good after this, all my life. *I* should die, but I don't know what it's like, except awful scary. I wish Aunt Mamie and Mama and the rest didn't have to feel so sorry I'm alive.

Standing up miserably in her own bedroom, the now-Chandra, grown up in body so long ago, wondered bleakly why it took the emotions so unconscionably long to catch up with physical growth, or if they ever could. She looked in on Thegn, tucking his covers unnecessarily, gently kissing the warm soft little-boy cheek, then she stood by the hall window a few moments, looking up at the starry night sky. She reached out for the feeling of the mountains and it was there. All right, Chandra, those things from the past that hurt so much aren't going to change. Mama, who brings them back so often and so vividly, isn't going to change. But *you've* changed and you can go on changing, growing. Things have, actually, turned out rather well for you, partly *because* of you. And there's Eric. Oh, why was I feeling so miserable about him today? I love him. God, how I love him, and if he can't be exactly what I want, whatever that is, it doesn't change my love for him, nor his for me. I've never in my life been sure of the love of another adult.

She wanted not to go downstairs again, simply to get ready for bed and lie there, quiet and alone, knowing he would come. Mama, of course, would be offended if she didn't at least show up to say good night.

When she came back into the family room, Ethel was saying critically, but with indulgence, "Well, you're sure not a ole man, like one a them prophets in the Bible or like that, an' you're not one a these young kids a-tryin' to look dif'rent just because they knows it aggravates the life out of their elders that's got more sense. It just looks odd to me, an' I know it ain't my business, for a man like you to have a beard. But at least it's clean."

8

When the household was in bed, Chandra found, to her surprise and pleasure, that she had somehow regained the feeling of relative peace and stillness. She and Eric made love and it was good—truly making love—as it almost always was between them. On this night, Eric took the initiative and that made it all doubly good. Chandra often felt that she initiated intercourse too often, intercourse of any kind. Tonight, she was not the one in control, the one who *had* to be in control. For so many years, she had felt frightened, unsafe, terribly threatened unless she could believe herself in control of herself and, basically, of any situation. But, in their beautiful, unique sexual relationship, she was no longer concerned about the brief, blissful oblivion, of expressing herself, consciously or not, in whatever words or movements followed from her total trust and enjoyment. Was Eric still guarding himself at these times of joy and true togetherness? She feared he was. Why could she not let him know, and he let her know, that there was complete safety for them both, here in each others' arms, everything else briefly locked outside their bedroom door, so that they had only to think about renewing, reaffirming themselves and their love in these truest moments of togetherness? She was more aware during their love-making than, perhaps, at any other time, of his individuality, his separateness as a person, his beautiful unique selfness, yet they blended so perfectly with one another. In the physical act of intercourse, in the emotional makeup of the act for them, she felt, more than any other situation, that they truly could and did complete each other. It was such a wonderful, restful, sacred thing, this complementariness, the very essence of what she seemed to be yearning for in everything else in their lives together.

Steeped in this renewal, she could be more charitable, at least for a time. Eric's reticences, his reluctances and hesitations, were understandable. His family, though seemingly loving and caring for one another, had no tendency or willingness to discuss or even express their deepest feelings, or to talk about their most serious problems. Competence, coping, were important to Eric. One handled one's own difficulties, deep emotions, doubts, worries, even joys, or, if these things could not be handled, dispatched, one tried not to think about them at any time they could be avoided. And then there had been Mona in his life. Though he spoke of her so rarely, Chandra thought she knew how deeply Mona had hurt him. He had, perhaps, been ready and willing to give himself freely and with abandon at the age of twenty-two, when he had first known and married Mona. He would have loved her completely, or not at all; Eric was that kind of person. Not only had Mona scorned and destroyed his inchoate love and trust of her, she had, surely, made him have serious and painful doubts about himself, his judgments, the things within him in which he had thought he could believe. So he had learned carefulness, guardedness, in the most painful way and those things did not pass off easily, even over a period of many years.

But Chandra, too, had had some of those same experiences. Her family was less honest, less communicative in ways that counted, harder on themselves and each other than Eric's would ever have dreamed of being. She had been just as romantically and foolishly in love with Les Campbell at one time as Eric could possibly have been with Mona. Yet she had come through those things, those years, so differently, with this achingly growing need to be truly present, at last, known as deeply as possible to one other person. Eric would always listen to her, to the expressions of her thoughts and feelings, her attempted self-revelations, with interest and concern, with great love, perhaps with understanding, but he did not seem able to respond in the ways she needed. Except for her own conviction that he did care about the things she tried to express from the depths of her inner self, she had no proof that he thought about them, remembered them, heard her bring them to him, laying herself bare, utterly vulnerable to him and his reactions. And it seemed now, after ten years together, that Eric was never going to be able to open himself to her, to tell her, freely and spontaneously, his deepest, most private thoughts and feelings, truly to share himself.

This was not a wanting to own, a desire for complete possession on Chandra's part. She had the greatest respect for the privacy of one's inner self. What she wanted, couldn't seem to stop reaching for with a helpless longing that seemed to bring only hurt, confusion, disappointment to them both, was the sharing, the seeking to understand, the yearning truly to know. People need *not* always be alone and lonely within themselves. Chandra was convinced of that, chiefly because she, with all her hangups and repressions, could keep seeking, wanting to know another as fully as he could let her, could keep wanting, needing, to reveal her inner being—her soul?

Still, if she could finally believe and accept that Eric could not give what she craved, or completely receive what she tried to give, then everything would be simpler, easier, for everyone but her. If she could say, and mean it, it's just another dream that *can't* come true . . . But she could not seem to do that. Sometimes, she thought it was working, but then she always came back to the contention that if she could do it, want it, then it must be within many other people, the same basic wish, need, ability. She could never believe she was so different, so unique, that the workings of her mind were totally a one-of-a-kind matter. Eric was as intelligent as she, more so in many ways, and perhaps he was even more sensitive. She couldn't stop believing that, in the carefully guarded depths of him, he *had* to have some of the same wants and needs. Surely they were universal, those needs to reach out, to recognize and be recognized by at least one other human being?

But perhaps not. Perhaps she was simply flinging herself again and again at the stone wall of a wishful dream, making demands, pleadings which Eric was simply not capable of answering in the ways—whatever they were—for which she longed. But, no, she just couldn't believe that. All right, don't believe it, but do leave him alone, and yourself. Leave your shared love alone. They are wondrous things, Eric and your shared love. You want certainties, well, you have at least that one, he loves you. Many people go through a lifetime without being fortunate enough to have that surety, the true love of another human being. You have it. If he can't be, or is not yet willing to be, responsive in the ways you think you want, ways you can recognize, that does not detract from the love you know he has for you. Don't let it detract from yours. Hold the precious things you have together gently, with awe, protect and cherish them. . . . But I want to keep growing, growing *with* him. Maybe it's just my childish need for expressed love and approval, but I'm so afraid I can't keep growing, mentally and emotionally, without having someone share the process. Then *you* share, but don't keep trying to force Eric to be *like* you. He's certainly not stultifying, he never will; he's not the sort of person who could do that, no matter how inviting the prospect may seem at times. If he can't or won't look analytically into the depths of himself, bring what he finds there to the surface and share it, then, in many ways, he's fortunate, isn't he? But I feel he's making us miss something, complete togetherness. Maybe some intricacies, some machinations, are better missed; maybe they should even be avoided. But I don't believe that. Then don't believe it; show some tolerance for yourself, for what you can or cannot think and believe, but give Eric the same break, acceptance.

Chandra did not think these things as she lay with her husband. They made only a small shadow in a remote corner of her mind, and that tiny place of darkness could not, for this little time, at least, darken, mar or chill the warmth of them, together. As they lay there, quiet now, gently holding each other in tenderness and fulfillment, she wondered, only fleetingly and with a faint smile, if Eric fantasized during love-making. He would be uneasy if she asked such a question and it was, quite probably, one of those things that was better undiscussed. She did, sometimes. Long ago, she had felt such fantasies to be a secret, rather shameful aberration. Then she had found, through reading, that she was not at all unique in this either. It was infinitely good to be an individual but, in some things, it was also very comforting to find human similarities. Most women fantasized during sex, the books had told her. Chandra's fantasies had to do, chiefly, with time and place. Sometimes, she thought of a male character in one of her books, but the man making love to her, the body and the mind, were never *not* Eric. Smiling more broadly, she supposed that fantasizing took the place of, as many books suggested, actually moving the physical place and circumstances of intercourse. After all, even a thing of such perfect beauty needed some variety if it was to go on being so exquisite. Neither of them cared much for experimenting with strange positions, or for performing the act in unusual places. The privacy and comfort of their bedroom was quite enough. Yet something that was so often repeated, that must already have occurred a thousand times since they had met, could not just be relatively ignored, taken for granted, and expected to survive in all its glory. Sometimes, they imagined, pretended things together, such as that they were a couple of teen-agers, making out in the back seat of a car. That was fun, and it made her feel almost certain that Eric, too, often did some imagining on his own. Still, for herself, when they came to the ultimate moments, it was always the now-Eric to whom she clung, unfettered, slightly delirious, utterly safe.

He opened his eyes and said drowsily, "Is something funny?"

"I was just thinking," she said, "that I'm glad we don't have to fuck under the kitchen table or on the garage roof."

"I guess I'm glad about that, too," he said with feeling, smiling back at her.

"There are a lot of things to be glad about," she said softly.

Languorously, she got up and went into the bathroom. When she returned, after a few moments, he lighted cigarettes for both of them and they sat, leaning back against the headboard of the bed.

"I really ought to want to stop smoking," mused Chandra without conviction.

"Me, too," he said, but with no more authority. "Ethel's been counseling you about it, I suppose?"

"Oh, yes, but her kind of therapy only makes me wild for the next cigarette. Eric, did she talk about me when I came upstairs this evening? I mean, not just things like that I was there when Glen died. Did she say things about *me*?"

He frowned a little, trying to recall. "Well, let's see. She told me all the things she's always told me, about your dad, your great inheritance. She got round to Les eventually. I think you were still out of the room then, how she'd warned you not to marry him and all that."

"She never really did, you know. None of them ever said anything like that. If they had, before the fact, I suppose I'd certainly have gone ahead with it. But I was so scared and uncertain, those last few days before the wedding! I think if I'd had someone to talk with, *really* talk with, I might have avoided those years with Les.

Still, it was the thing to do then, get married as soon as you got out of high school, or before, and I wanted so much to get away from home, to start having what I thought would be *some* control over my own life. God, what sappy innocents most of us are at eighteen! And no one can tell us anything, even if they truly try. But you haven't told me if she said anything about *me*."

"She said Les was mean to you, a tramp. That's all I can think of."

Chandra smiled grimly. "Well, I suppose that's something. If any of them had said even that much, directly to me, at the time, I'd probably have been so dissolved in gratitude, I'd never have got out of Texas. All I ever heard from them, if you don't count eavesdropping, was that it was a scandalous mess, but that I probably could have straightened it out, or at least made the best of it, if I'd really tried. You know, I've just now realized something. I think that because I *was* able to walk after the accident, have some sort of 'normal' life, even excel at a few things, I was even less a person to them than another child would have been. For them, it must have been rather like living with a clever monkey. And I believe it's still like that for Mama, maybe for my sisters, too. Chandra Lynn may never walk again, but, look! She's mastered it. Watch her! You've got trouble with your marriage, Chandra? Do a little trick and fix it up. You want to play around with writing? Well, that's nothing anyone couldn't do; just learn a slightly different routine, flick your magic wand, do another little trick."

Eric put his arm around her and said gently, with a tentative smile, "Well, just see you mind what kind of tricks you turn."

She looked away from him as her eyes prickled with tears. Lightly *was* the way to handle it, of course, but she wished he could have said, in their privacy, something like, "They've always been bastards to you." It wouldn't make any difference for the past; nothing could change that, and it wouldn't make any change in the way

Mama and the others saw her now. It would only say that he did understand, and *that* was where the importance lay.

After a moment, she said, quite levelly, "Sheila's leaving Brian. She called this afternoon."

"God," he said wearily. "Do we know why?"

"No, not exactly, not yet. But I suspect it has to do with her liberatedness. You know our Sheila. Brian was probably trying to squelch her somehow."

"Brian wouldn't try to squelch a cockroach."

"We know that, and some people would say Sheila never deserved him anyway, but she is—*searching* so, Eric. I think I do understand that."

"Well, so far now she's searched through three husbands and a lot of other men on the side. People respect her, as a person and as a businesswoman. If they don't respect her ability and acumen, they damn well respect her mouth. Just what is it she's searching for?"

"For—for Sheila, maybe," Chandra said sadly. "I don't understand this part, but she seems to be one of those women for whom any relationship with any man has to become a battle of the sexes. I never have understood why that has to be, on either side. It must be just one more basic insecurity, I suppose, but men and women are just *people,* after all. They've been brainwashed, acculturated, to believe in a lot of fundamental differences, and they're not there at all, I think, except for the physical ones. If they begin to suspect all those differences may not really exist, it seems to frighten people like Sheila. She's not really sure where she stands then, so she starts fighting, because that's a response, in herself and her men, that she can handle. It seems to me that the women who are really most concerned with being liberated, the really pilly ones like Sheila, are the ones most in bondage, and making most of their own bonds.

"Look at what editors, most especially women editors, are clamoring for for the fiction market. Anything that can't be immediately classified as science fiction or high adventure or the like, they have to call a 'woman's book.' "

"Sometimes it seems," he said thoughtfully, putting out his cigarette, "that those people who are knowledgeable, who are supposed to be, believe men read fiction only for illusion. But fictional romance can be escapist, illusionary, too."

"Exactly, and that's an insult to both sexes. Men *can* look at reality, and women also like adventure. It's the need to categorize, of course. Now we have that marvelous classification of books called 'historical romance.' You know how hard Barbara Liscombe has tried to make my novel fall in there, what she pleasantly called 'historical novels without history.' You know how furious she got in that one phone conversation we had last summer when she accused me of writing for myself, not the market, and I told her that's exactly what I do. Anything, books, readers, are so much easier to handle if you can classify them, sort them and put them in boxes. The *last* thing you want, or will recognize, especially if you're trying to sell something, is any sizable minority that fits none, or all of the above.

"A lot of things and people *don't* give women their due, but now, so many want to swing to the other extreme. Look at commercials; look at the real 'women's books.' They make women sex symbols still, which most women scream that they want to get away from, but they also make them the most absolute heroes the world has ever seen. Those women are all-knowing and they can handle anything with one hand tied behind their backs. And the men are just a bunch of saps, who haven't known about the right deodorant, or how to make love, or *anything* until some dame *helps* them toward right thinking. I don't see how anyone with any sense, of either sex, can steep themselves in that kind of stuff and feel—enlightened."

Putting out her cigarette, she felt self-conscious. Here she was, on another soapbox, and Eric was saying nothing. And just what was *she* saying? How significant was this to the way she had been feeling and thinking about their relationship? She'd have to try to understand that, sometime. She turned to find him looking at her with interest, but why couldn't he *say* things? Agree or disagree? Perhaps she was just too verbal to be a good conversationalist, making it more of a monologue than a conversation. Maybe, if she allowed longer periods of silence, he would express himself. She had tried that, though, many times and, usually, nothing at all had come of it, had come from him. She felt stiff and embarrassed now, a little foolish as she slid down to lie in bed as she said brightly,

"I haven't had a chance to ask about your overtime. Are you going to have to do it?"

"Three engineers are flying in from Philadelphia in the morning. We'll be working on this consultation, three of us from here, with them, while we try to keep on with our other projects. I think they'll be leaving by the first of next week, then maybe I can take comp time for the days right around Christmas. As long as they're here, though, I'm going to have to spend a lot of extra time in the office. I won't miss meeting with my class, but there's only the one more session before the holiday break. I don't know just how we're going to work around the other things, but I think maybe I'll stay in town tomorrow night. I'll call you tomorrow, as soon as I know. We'll probably have a meeting after I've finished at school, and it could last all night. I'll have to let you know where I'll be staying. I forgot to check about a reservation somewhere, and I've even forgotten where the Philadelphia people are staying. I'm sorry about this, Chandra. I don't like it either."

He was still sitting up, against his pillows. She knew this was because, if he lay down, he would be almost immediately asleep. He had told her that, before they met, he had gone through long periods of insomnia. Since that time, however, he always seemed to sleep easily and quickly. Chandra was glad that something about being with her made him comfortable, able to sleep, but sometimes she resented it. She also knew that he could sleep, not just for needed rest, but as an escape, and she could not help feeling, now and then, that it was this latter reason that made him leave her so quickly.

Sleep had rarely come easily to Chandra. She lay awake to plan books, to worry or to rejoice. Sleep was a thing to be wooed and courted, crept up on, tricked into coming. She invented games to lull her mind, to lure sleep. She read, watched television, listened to the radio. None of these things ever seemed to disturb Eric; at least there was that to be glad of. Over the years, she had tried all the pills, drinking heavily, everything. Sleep induced by drugs was not satisfactory for her and she required such strong dosages that she felt groggy and useless all the next day. Nothing was effective after three or four usages, but seemed to take on the opposite effect, making her more wide awake and restless than ever. Anyway, Eric simply seemed to require more sleep than she could get by with. But sometimes, when she had been lying wakeful for hours while he snored blithely, she could not help feeling angry, cheated, deserted. The feelings were totally unreasonable, of course, as were so many other things.

They both enjoyed and treasured their time alone together at night. Having had two children in the house from the very beginning of their relationship had made these hours or minutes doubly precious from the very start. Sometimes, they read together, one reading aloud to the other, but Eric, no matter how intent he might be on the subject of book or conversation, always had to sit up, to fend off sleep. Chandra was grateful for his effort now. She felt an especial need for his companionship after the sort of day this had been, and tomorrow night, he probably would be away. She always missed him so on the rare occasions when he had to stay in town, as if they hadn't already spent ten years of nights together.

Looking up at him now, she could see new lines of tiredness in his face. His job was one of heavy responsibilities and he did work at it seriously and with great concentration. He would not be the wonderful person he was if he did not feel he owed himself to his work. Chandra understood that, because she was in almost total agreement with it. . . . If only he could be a little less —single-minded.

He bent and kissed her lightly on the mouth. "I love you."

"And I love you."

"Will you go to the Crittendens' party tomorrow night?"

"Well, maybe I will, just for a little while. It seems so important to Joyce, and I really think I can cope better with things here, with Mama, if I'm away for a little now and then. She's going to be hurt if I leave her."

"I hope you'll go, though; if it's something you want to do."

"She makes me feel so guilty, Eric, about absolutely everything."

"I wish you could get away from that," he said earnestly. "You have nothing to be guilty about, nothing. People shouldn't spend their lives building up debts against their children the way she has. But the debts, the believing they're there, is her problem, not yours."

Chandra liked that because he, not she, had said it, and it was something to think about.

"You're right, I know," she said, "but knowing and doing and feeling can be such very different things when everything is so involved and ambiguous. It has to do with my whole life, my whole self-image, I suppose, the way I've seen that image reflected back from other people. Eric, I just don't see how I can have her live with us, how *we* can. I just can't seem to stop what she can do to me at close range. I know it's up to me, but Mama is so very present, so ubiquitous, when she's anywhere nearby. She just walks into my office a dozen times a day. Knocking just doesn't exist, not on *my* door, and she'd be cut to the quick if I asked her to do it. She'd be right in the middle of *all* family discussions. She'd be guiding the children, trying to teach them all kinds of precepts that we couldn't go along with, doing all she possibly could to make *them* feel guilty and full of self-doubt. She wouldn't *know* she was doing that, couldn't possibly see it as harmful, but there'd be no discussing it with her. She'd just have her feelings hurt and be ten times more righteous for that. I don't think she'd bother Bruce or Gail too much. I hope they're beyond her, but she *would* trouble Thegn and I just couldn't bear to see that happening. I've been thinking we could offer to help pay for a little apartment for her somewhere. She could well afford it if she sold the home place, but her savings give her such satisfaction and security, and God knows, she's earned them. I wouldn't mind the expense, would you?"

"No, but do you think she'd do it? Where would it be?"

"Well, Evelyn's thinking along those same lines. She wrote that maybe Mama could come to Beaumont, be near her and Steve, though not in the same building or anything so drastic as that. It would be a very difficult transition, *if* it were to happen. Mama's never been good at adapting, not to anything. If she were really to consider it, maybe she'd want to choose San Antonio, because it's nearer home. She knows the town, a little, and she's so used to depending on Tom and Dorothy. They really have been so good to her, all these years, and I don't think she realizes the half of it. By rights, it's past time Evelyn or I took some of the responsibility."

"But, do you think she'd ever, under any circumstances, be willing to live here, in Colorado?"

"Well, I can't imagine that she would, right now, but if she were to get started moving toward something different, a new idea, who knows? I don't want any of us to try to take away any independence she doesn't want to give up. After all, she is a grown woman and still of sound mind. I think Dorothy badly wants to see her settled with Evelyn or with us, so Dorothy won't have to feel that there *is* any responsibility anymore, and I can certainly see it from her point of view. If *I* could choose, I guess I'd want to see Mama go into a nice home somewhere. It wouldn't have to mean giving up everything for her. Some of those places have sort of efficiency apartments, where people can do their own cooking and everything they want to do for themselves. She'd still have all her crafts work and a lot of other things in the way of recreation and entertainment. She'd almost *have* to make some friends, all the things she'd have in common with the other people there, or with some of them, at least. In a regular apartment, I'm afraid she'd never get to know anyone except whichever daughter she was near. It would be quite a load for one of us to carry, and for our family. I suppose I'm being totally selfish."

She wished he'd say no, the idea was eminently sensible. Instead he said, "Maybe she'd consider moving to some little place in Chelsea. She knows plenty of people there and she wouldn't be living alone out in the country. She'd still be dependent on Dorothy, maybe even more than she is now, but it could be a start, don't you think? Maybe after a year or so in an apartment there, she'd be willing to live in a home, or at least in another town."

Chandra smiled in warm gratitude. Obviously he had been giving some thought to the matter and was not going to leave her alone with it.

"That's the best idea yet, though poor Dorothy wouldn't think much of it. Could we talk to Mama about it, when the time seems right? We could just mention that maybe it's time she started thinking about selling the place, getting something smaller, with closer neighbors. She really does put so much more credence in anything you say. I can talk till I turn blue and she'll never think of me as anything but a little kid, but you can say two words and she'll listen, think about it. *Will* you talk with her about this?"

He grinned ruefully. "I guess I could try, if she'll stop staring at my beard and put on that damned hearing aid."

He sorted his pillows and lay down. Smiling, Chandra turned out the lamp.

"No galley reading?" Eric asked, surprised.

"I just can't tonight," she said, sighing comfortably and snuggling against him. "I feel too happy, too peaceable, to try to deal with any more of Barbara's botchings now."

"Good," he said, yawning. "You know, I'm beginning to think you're right. Someone from the publishing house will call tomorrow and it will all get straightened out. I hope you have a really good night."

"I was thinking," Chandra said, not quite able yet to let go of their closeness, "in the course of the day, while I was trying to think, among other things, about what, if anything, we might do about Mama, well, I got thinking, again, of the place we might have, sometime, up in the mountains."

He put an arm around her. "I wish we could do it now," he said softly, "forget all the ifs and buts and just start looking for the place. You'd certainly work, you'd work anywhere, but I just don't know what I'd do away from the city. It just seems we're not ready yet to be able to manage on one income, never mind that that one gets better every year. I'd make a hell of a rancher, Chan. I'm still not really sure which end of a cow is which unless I can see some horns."

"Maybe you could teach." They'd gone over it all so many times. She felt very tired now, and sadly wistful.

"Yes, I could, and I'd like doing that, full time, but the place we've always talked about wouldn't have a college town that nearby, would it?"

"If everything else about it could be resolved, we'd

only *look* at places with a college town near enough. But, Eric—you're an artist, too. I know you could sell some of your drawings, if it really mattered to you."

"If selling mattered, or the place mattered?" he asked quietly.

"Well, either, both. You really are a fine artist, in your own right."

"I suppose I'm selfish," he said slowly, "and a coward. I'm afraid I'm pretty well caught up in the nine-to-five routine. I'm not at all sure I'd be worthwhile, trying to live the—unstructured life that getting away from that would mean. Also, I don't really *want* to try to sell any drawings. I don't think, frankly, I could take the kind of crap over them that you have to take over your books. I do them for my own pleasure and satisfaction. Really, I don't even want people looking at them, other than the people I care about. I don't like to think of strangers considering them as a commodity. They might not understand."

"My God," she said tenderly, "don't you think *I* can understand? I was saying, just before, about the accusatory, derisive way Barbara asked me if I write for *myself*."

"Yes, I know you can understand. That's the only reason I'm saying it."

"But it's quite a—luxury, in a way, isn't it? Just to do those very good things for yourself?"

"It is. But I *can* do that. I'm sorry. I know that's wholly selfish. We've talked like this before, about your writing. You feel compelled to try to sell, after all the time and effort it takes to do a book. Drawing and painting don't take anything like that much of my time, and blood, but even if I could spend full-time on them, I don't know if I could bring myself to try to sell. They're awfully—personal things, my pictures, and I know you can understand all about that, too. I told you I'm a coward. Furthermore, I don't think most people *deserve* a look at my pictures, any more than I think they deserve your books. I just can't like the idea of making people a gift of —part of myself, and having my face slapped, or worse, in return."

"But, Eric, it's not all like that. There *is* a satisfaction in holding a printed book of mine in my hand, at last, and think of the fan letters."

"Well, yes, but I guess it's something I'm not ready to try to face yet. I can't promise that I ever will be ready. I *want* the country place, and I like the idea of our being two artists together, the kinds of freedom that sort of life would bring, but . . ."

"Well, suppose you didn't work? Away from home, I mean. We could manage on what I can earn, especially with Bruce and Gail so nearly grown up. We won't have all their college expenses, because we've agreed, and they know it, that they'll have to work and pay for a part of that education."

"That's true."

"And we certainly could do with a smaller house and fewer of the gadgets Mama talks about."

"Yes."

"Well, would you mind being a—a housewife—househusband? If I had the time for just writing, and you could look after everything else . . ."

"I think I wouldn't mind that at all, but you would."

"I would? Why?"

"Because you're that concerned about what other people think, that's why. When people said, 'What does your husband do?' would you be happy saying, 'He's a housewife'? And you'd feel guilty about all the wife and mother things you weren't doing, even if I was handling most of them. Even if it was my only job. Other people's opinions wouldn't bother me, except for yours. But the thing with me is that I'm afraid I *need* structure, to have to be somewhere, doing some special thing at some certain time. Some people are self-starters and others, maybe, are just born timeclock-punchers. I know how much you hate that. I'm trying to learn to feel differently, to *be* different, and maybe I can, eventually. We can certainly begin looking for the place, anytime you like, and see how things go from there."

She knew he was right about her feelings concerning his taking over the household, but maybe her concepts could change, too, given time. Maybe she could, somehow, learn to relax a little, not to mind so much about so many things. At least he wasn't the kind of man who was always making a conscious, concerted effort to be "masculine." He would never say, or think, *I'm* the man, *I'm* chief wage-earner. You play around at whatever you like, but see that the dishes are done and don't try to be head of household. The possibility of an almost complete role change was not threatening to him. He really *could* be a housewife, in perfect equanimity—if he could only stop striving for such absolute perfection and get on with the jobs in hand. It would be Chandra who would be concerned, worried about this sort of role-playing, about how others saw it. And she *would* feel such guilt about not doing everything that it would probably interfere with the work she did do. Some things about her, she thought uncomfortably, Eric knew almost too well.

She said, rather tersely, "Well, the kids are awfully happy here. They'd hate a shake-up like that."

"*We* have to live our life," he said quietly. "The kids will grow up and go away and have their own lives. It's important for us to be satisfied with where we are and what we're doing. I've said this to you before: Your writing is the most important thing in our lives. It's *not* our lives, it's not you or me or the kids, but it's part of all of us, and it's the most important *thing*. You know I don't mean the money, though your income has been better than mine for three years running now. The writing is something you do because you *have* to. It's not just a job, and particularly so since you've made a start with the novels. If you think you could write better somehow in the country, if you *want* to be there, then we'll—"

"I appreciate what you're saying," she said tensely,

"but don't you see, you're putting it all on me, my decision, my responsibility, what *I* want?"

"Yes, I do see that. I'm sorry. I can see that you don't like it, don't want it to be this way, but I just don't see how it can be otherwise. I want the best situation for you, and for your writing, because it's so much a part of you, of all of us, especially of me."

"I don't want you to feel you have to sacrifice—"

"Chandra, I don't feel that. Can't you take my word for it, for anything?"

They lay silent for a time, his arm around her, her head on his shoulder, tears pricking at her eyes again. Then she started slightly, recalling the immediate present.

"Will you be staying in town Friday night, too?"

He had already begun to slip toward sleep and said drowsily, "I just don't know yet, darling."

"It's when we've said we'll get the Christmas tree. We all want you around for that and Thegn is certainly not going to forget the promise. Also, we were all going with him for his talk with Santa on Saturday."

"Well," he said slowly, considering, "suppose I try to get home about the usual time on Friday and we'll do both things that evening, okay? Thegn can see Santa and then we'll get the tree. Everyone can stay up late because their holiday vacation will have begun. We should be able to get most of the decorating done. I know I'll be working Saturday, probably Sunday as well, but I don't want to be responsible for postponing the real start of Christmastime here at home. Will that do, do you think?"

"I think so," she said and hugged him. "Have a good night, darling."

"You too," he said, turning, so that now she snuggled against his back. "An extra special good one."

His breathing quickly slowed and deepened. Chandra lay still, enjoying the unusual lethargy she was feeling. Then she remembered one more thing.

"Oh. Eric?"

"Mmm?"

"Candy was here today, Candy—Miller, is it?"

"Who?" drowsily, as if he couldn't care less.

"She's in your drafting class."

"Candy? What was she doing here?" He stretched, turned slightly, drawing back momentarily from sleep.

"She said she needed to talk to you, about a project or something."

He stretched, yawning.

"I was a little surprised. This is the first time a student has sought you out at home since we moved out here."

"Candy's rather a sad case. She needs a lot of attention and she does have problems."

"She told me a little about her family."

"She did? She must have been here a while. I'm sorry about your time."

"Not long, really. Now that I think of it, I'm surprised Mama didn't think to mention it to you. She was so appalled by Candy's hippiness. I felt sorry for her, for Candy. There was something so sad—haunted—about her, just a glimpse I kept getting now and then. I'm glad I remembered to mention it, because now you can tell her I told you she was here. I think she's a person who —needs to be remembered."

"Yes, all right, I will," he murmured, the words blurring together. "Good night."

"Good night, love."

Chandra lay still, holding her own drowsiness to her gently. It was such a pleasant surprise. Candy certainly had a crush on Eric. Poor little girl. Suppose she knew he had fallen asleep while trying to talk about her? Chandra hoped she would find someone really to love, someday soon, someone who would find a way to dispel that pathetic look from those lovely hazel eyes. She thought, for only a fleeting instant, of Eric's having some involvement with Candy, aside from drafting instructor and, perhaps, confidant, a passing friend in need.

Eric was someone people liked to confide in. His innate warmth and caring radiated to people almost as soon as they met him, and he was often taken advantage of, as was Chandra. They were sought out particularly by two kinds of people, those who seemed convinced they hadn't sense enough to direct their own lives, like Mama and, at the other extreme, those who themselves lacked direction, were sure that one or both Whitmans had all the answers, were "so together," had the "perfect marriage." So many people saw only what they expected to see, what they wanted to see.

At any rate, she thought sleepily, unfaithfulness on Eric's part was one thing about which she would never worry. He was tremendously attractive to other women, but the very idea of "playing around" seemed a thing almost beyond his ken. She hardly knew the meaning of jealousy, *of* Eric, or *from* him. It had occurred to Chandra from time to time over the years that *she* could be capable of an affair. The thought had come at times when she was feeling misunderstood, aggrieved, downtrodden, alone. But there had never been another man who interested her in that way, who tempted her, even slightly, not since Eric. A shared bed, they both felt, was not a thing to be jumped into and out of lightly. To make love in the beautiful, mutually satisfying way they shared was, surely, not a thing that could happen easily on one-night stands, casually, and it was the only way either of them wanted sex to be. Poor Sheila and all the men and women like her, who looked for all the wrong things in all the wrong ways and places . . .

Drifting comfortably, Chandra remembered something from a book she had been reading recently, "A writer lives many lives." Maybe that was why the idea of an affair had never really interested her, because she had all those people in her books to live for. And, evidently, there was at least one other writer who wrote as she did, *living* his novels. So, in that way, she had far more experiences than other people ever had the chance for. It was a blessing, a kind of miracle at times. It was also a curse, needing all her strength and sanity at times. But everything was mixed, wasn't it?

The point she was trying to come to, without letting go of the dear, warm drowsiness, was that she mustn't expect everything. That really had to stop. Wanting was fine, trying to have was a part of what made life interesting, worthwhile. But she could not have complete happiness for more than surprised, fleeting instants. There would always be things in Eric, in everything and everyone, especially herself, that she could wish were different. Often, there was no harm in trying gently to change those things, but perfection would not come, not in more than tiny bits and pieces. Live with that, make the most of it. Be tolerant of others and of yourself, particularly within yourself, because no one else can possibly do *that* thing better than you can.

She snuggled against Eric's back and slept.

Thursday

9

Chandra arrived at the club a little past nine. The Crittendens had hired a large room for cocktails, a late supper and dancing.

"We can go on as late as we like," Joyce told her happily as they met near the door. Joyce was always most content when "mixing" people.

Chandra knew some of the guests at sight, but no one well. There had been a time when she had longed to know other writers, real ones, not the yearners, but, among those she had met, she had found little common ground.

She was placed, for supper, at a small table for four. There was a young man, perhaps twenty-five, who had sold a few articles to national magazines, another man, in his sixties, who had several articles and a few how-to books published, and a woman, thirtyish, who did book reviews for local newspapers and had had a few sales of articles on a national level. These table companions were very locquacious, each trying openly to keep the conversation on himself, his writing. The young man asked, with a show of modesty and a desire for advice, about the marketing of magazine articles but, clearly, this was just an excuse for detailing of his various experiences with the sale of his own articles. The older man and the woman vied to give him advice, setting forth at length, what they had done and how they had gone about doing it.

At one point, the older man turned a chilly smile on Chandra. "I know who you are," he said, accusingly? defensively?

Chandra felt, as she often did with other writers that, because she did fiction, she was supposed to be something less than they. Or was it just that any writer, for the sake of his own ego, has to put other writers in their place? She believed there must be those, content enough with their own work, secure enough, not to have to put other writers down, to be able to talk with relish and interest of things outside their work. The trouble was, she had never found them.

The others at her table began to drop the names of magazines and editors, fast and furious, rather like three contending hailstorms, Chandra thought wryly. The older hands were using the guise to advise the relative neophyte—who had, after all, asked for it—where and to whom to send specific kinds of articles. Something so many writers, even after they had become "professionals," always seemed to be striving for was THE ANSWER. And there really was no answer, no fail-safe solution to selling anything. There were as many things to write as there were people writing, and marketing seemed to be, ultimately, a mystery, a question of having the right piece in the right place at the right time, a complicated, partly serendipitous conundrum to everyone concerned.

Chandra wished Eric were with her. They could have discussed people and conversations later. That was a part of such gatherings for them, sometimes the only really interesting part. She had never really wanted to come here alone, wished now, glumly, that she were shut in her office or bedroom at home, working on her galleys. However, getting out of the house had become more and more important during the course of this day.

Her unusually restful night had ended toward morning, when she had had one of those ridiculous and terrifying dreams which had troubled her in recent months. In the dream, she was a tiny, almost microscopic being, dashing about and chittering insanely, trying to accomplish a multitude of unclear but vital tasks. Then a vacuum cleaner, enormous, gigantic in comparison with her own minute size, was roaring and gulping toward her. Screaming, she tried to hide under the cushions of the living-room sofa. The faceless person operating the vacuum could not see her or hear her shrieks. All anyone else would ever notice was whether or not she had completed the things she had to do. The vacuum's huge, sucking upholstery brush came inexorably closer.

She woke gasping, her face wet with tears of fright. Eric was leaning above her, grasping her shoulders.

"Chandra? Chan? Are you all right? What is it?"

"Just a—a dream," she gulped, breathing unevenly, still crying.

After a little, she told him about it, because putting it into words seemed to make it less fearsome. She must have had almost this same dream a dozen times recently.

"It sounds like some animated cartoon character in a TV commercial," Eric muttered sleepily. Then feeling her stiffen, "You know, you really don't have to feel that way."

"What way?" she asked tensely.

"Well, like all we care about you is what you can *do*. *You* are pretty important around here. Can you get back to sleep? What time is it? Can you see?"

It was a few minutes before four. Chandra could not sleep again. Her palms, her whole body kept sweating nervously. She was hot or cold by turns, feeling vaguely ill. When Eric's breathing had, very quickly, grown quiet and deep again, she slipped out of bed, put on robe and slippers and, carrying the envelope of galleys, went down to her office. She felt lonely, abandoned, but what did she want? expect? He had got right at the crux of the dream, hadn't he? She couldn't expect him to lose almost two hours of sleep just because she was wide awake, could she? The best thing to do with this time, now that she had it, was to use it, with gratitude, for some uninterrupted work. Once she became absorbed in her book, all the other confusing things would fade far into the background. She wished she were done with these galleys, with Christmas, with Mama, so that she could begin working on the new novel that kept growing in her mind. That would solve almost all her problems, writing again, at least for a time.

She made coffee, creeping about the house in fear of Ethel's waking, read a respectable number of pages, and was back in the kitchen, being the good wife and mother, before Mama got there.

"Honey, was you in that office all night?" Ethel asked solicitously. "I heard you a-comin' out a there just after I woke up this last time. I was awake a lot in the night. I nearly got up several times, but I didn't want to wake anybody else up. You know I just don't sleep good here. I believe it's somethin' about the air. An' I just freeze all the time."

"Isn't your electric blanket working, Mama?"

"Well, yes, but I don't like to have them things on, except to warm up the bed. It's a waste of 'lectricity an' I can't help but be a little afraid to just leave 'em on when I'm asleep. Don't you think we could turn up the heat, just a little? OO! just looky out there, how cold it looks."

When Bruce came down, he complained loudly about the hotness of the house. Gail threw a significant look at the grandmother and said to him softly, "She's freezing. I almost got sick when I opened my bedroom door and got hit by the heat."

Chandra brought up the subject of her going out that evening when the family was all downstairs, at the various stages of their breakfasts.

"Sure," said Gail easily, "we'll be here to see Thegn gets to bed, and to stay with Grandma."

"Nobody has to see I get to bed," Thegn told her righteously. "I'm not a baby. I can tell time and know when to go to bed. Tomorrow's our party and things. I have to get a good night's sleep."

"You mean," said Ethel wonderingly to Chandra, "you're aimin' to drive clear to town just for supper with some people?"

"Mama, we said we'd go before we knew exactly when you'd be coming. Eric can't be there now, because of these people from Philadelphia, but I really feel I ought to show up, just for a little while."

"I'd better be going," said Eric, standing up, gathering his things, bending to kiss her cheek.

Chandra wished irritably he would *say* something to Mama in her behalf. "Chandra doesn't get out nearly enough. Don't bug her about this." But why must she always feel that someone else had to take her part? She was a big girl, wasn't she? Why couldn't she just go ahead and do her thing and feel all right about it?

After the children were off to their bus, Ethel said dubiously, "Do you go to parties an' such without Eric most of the time? It's not my business, I know, but it does seem to me like that's not a very good sign, Chandra Lynn. Yes, I know he's got to be a-workin'. That can't be helped. A body that's got a boss has got to do like he's told if he aims to keep his job, but don't you reckon Eric would feel better, about just ever'thin', for knowin' you're safe here at home an' a-waitin' for him? If I was you, I wouldn' drive around no big town by myself after night for nothin' in this world."

"Mama, if you'd rather I didn't go . . ."

"Oh, no, now, it ain't me. I've told you, I don't want to be treated like I was comp'ny. It's you I'm a-tryin' to think of. I can manage, an' I'm glad I'm here to see to the young'uns while you're off an' gone. I aim to be *some* use. What time do you reckon you'll be home?"

"After midnight, maybe. You just go to bed at your regular time and don't worry."

"Huh?"

Chandra repeated.

"Midnight! Ain't that a awful late time for somebody to be out that's got a work an' a school day the next mornin'? What kind of a doin's is it, anyway, that don't start till nine o'clock of a night? Well, I may *go* to bed. Seems like I don't never feel rested, down here in this country—nor warm—but I know I won't sleep a wink till you come in, an' maybe not then. I know Eric can't help it that he has to work late, but I don' think I can rest easy in this place without a man in the house. All them stories a body hears about when people's crowded together this-a-way. . . . Well, don't you reckon we ought to git started on them cookies for Thin's party? He was a-askin' about 'em agin this mornin', bless his heart. Seemed like it pleased him that his grandma's a-goin' to make 'em. What kind do you want me to make?"

Chandra had to stay in the kitchen during the mixing of the cooky batter. Rather than looking around for herself, at cannisters, spice rack and refrigerator, Ethel had constantly to be told and shown where to find the various ingredients. She also questioned the recipe.

"Do you mean you think it *ought* to have that much butter? That many eggs? I always cut down on some of what they call for like that. It don' make a bit of diff'rence in the world in the taste, especially for little children, an' you've got to buy ever'thin'."

And, when the batter was finally ready, "Chandra Lynn, see if I've got that oven set right. That stove's got so many gadgets, I can't hardly tell a thing about it. Now, what size do you reckon the cookies ought to be? The recipe says to drop by teaspoonfuls, but if I make little bitty ole ones like that, I'll be a-droppin' all day."

With two sheets of cookies finally in the oven, Chandra went upstairs to set the bedrooms to rights. Ten minutes later, Ethel called her down again.

"You reckon them are done?" she said, dubiously peering into the oven.

"Mama, you've baked a million cookies," said Chandra, trying to keep her voice reasonable. "You don't need me to tell you when they're done."

"Well, I wisht you wouldn' git huffy. I just want to do to suit you."

They went to the supermarket after picking up Thegn at school. Ethel kept up a constant detailing of how she disliked shopping, especially for groceries, and a constant dirge on prices, and how various ones compared, unfavorably, with "what we have to pay out home."

When they turned into the driveway at home, Shirley Soderberg came hurrying over.

"All of you, come and have lunch with me," she said warmly, after being introduced to Ethel. "It's not much, but I have it just about ready and I'm all alone. Our visitors are out sightseeing today."

Earlier, Chandra and Thegn had suggested buying lunch at a drive-in, but Ethel had said she was not hungry, that it seemed wasteful to buy food when a body wasn't hungry, that she never had liked to eat out and, besides, they had a whole car full of groceries. Now, before she could speak, Chandra said gratefully.

"We'd like that, Shirley. I've been wanting you to meet Mama. Maybe she can tell you those things you need to know about crocheting. Just give me a few minutes to put some of these things away."

Shirley came into the house with them and distracted Ethel while Chandra and Thegn worked on the groceries. Chandra went into the downstairs bathroom after a few minutes, and Ethel followed, opening the door without invitation.

"She lives right over there in that next house?" she asked, almost whispering. "Seems like a right nice woman. Says she's got a crochet pattern she can't git figgered out. But what I come in here to ask," she peered disparagingly at Chandra's rather aged pants suit, "was, are you a-goin' to wear—*that?*"

She had asked the same question before they had left the house earlier, also being dubious about Chandra's hair—"You don't never roll it up nor anything?"—and lack of makeup.

Chandra said now, tolerantly, "Yes, Mama, we're only going next door."

"Well, I thought *I* might change my dress, an' I've got to do somethin' about this stringy hair. If I don' have it fixed ever' week, it just gets to lookin' till I can't stand it. Chandra Lynn, it don't hurt for a body to fix up a little sometime."

"You do whatever you like," Chandra said, smiling. "We'll wait for you." She edged past her to get back into the hall.

When the two of them were briefly alone in the Soderberg kitchen, Shirley said, grinning, "I think she's just dear, your mommy, changing her clothes and fixing up her face to come to my house, but you remember now, Chandra Lynn, that I've got a mommy, too. I know they have entirely different personalities for daughters than for most other people. Hey, it's such great news about your foreign sales. Do you think we might sneak a quick before-lunch screwdriver to celebrate?"

"I'd better not," said Chandra, smiling ruefully. "If I start this early, I won't get any work at all done this afternoon."

Quickly, she went over the situation about the galleys, and Shirley briefly outlined some difficulties she was having with her visiting sister-in-law. They sympathized, hurriedly, with each other, and found things to laugh about in their various problems.

Ethel did a good deal of talking, through lunch, to an honestly attentive Shirley and, when the meal was over, Shirley said briskly,

"Now, Chandra, if you and Thegn are not interested in crochet patterns and have other things to do you may be excused. I've got Mom Barrie here and I'm not letting her get away until I get the hang of that pattern I've been trying to figure out for months."

Chandra said, "Well, Mama, maybe I will go and get to work. Will that be all right?"

Ethel said expansively, "Why, honey, I reckon I can git back next door all right. If Miz . . ."

"Just Shirley," said Shirley.

"If Shirley needs some help, maybe I can show her about her pattern. First, I'll help to at least git these dishes in the sink." She turned back. "Unless you need me to do somethin' over at the house right now, that is."

Chandra said mischievously, "I just thought you might be ready to take your nap now."

"Why, Chandra Lynn, you know I don't never bat a eye toward no sleep in the daytime."

"It's always so hot in here, Mommy," Thegn complained rather querulously as they came back into the house.

"Grandma's very cold-natured, Thegn. We have to think of her while she's here. Close your bedroom door and open a window a little."

"Why is she always cold?"

Chandra wanted to say "Because she expects to be and it gets attention," but she explained, a little, about how older people's blood circulation sometimes slowed down a bit.

Thegn wanted to discuss several things but, finally, he went upstairs and she settled down in her office. Ethel would be unlikely to stay long at Shirley's but, for now, the house seemed blessedly empty and quiet. Bless dear, good Shirley.

The phone rang. It was Joyce, reminding her again of tonight's gathering.

Then Chandra placed a call for the chief editor at her publishing house, who just might have tried to call while she was out. There was some difficulty and delay in reaching the woman but, when she finally came on, she seemed amenable, in a cool way, to what Chandra insisted must be done about her book. She would take a set of galleys home to read over the weekend, said the editor, also the correspondence file on the book. By then, Chandra would have finished going over her own set of proofs and they could discuss more precisely the corrections and changes that were to be made.

Shortly after Chandra had hung up, feeling pleased and, again, a little deflated, Eric called.

"I tried to get you about an hour ago," he said questioningly.

She told him where they had been, then about her satisfactory talk with the editor.

"Have you found any more places where Barbara's rewritten?"

"Yes, I couldn't get back to sleep this morning, so I came down and got quite a lot of reading done. I found another mess that involves about three galley pages."

"God, I hope that'll be the last of her handiwork!"

"There are still a couple of scenes to come that I'm concerned about, but at least they won't be such an awful shock, now that I'm expecting the worst."

Chandra heard the back door slam. Ethel was home.

"I wanted to let you know I'll be staying at the Knights Rest Motel," Eric was saying. "That's Knights with a K, room eight. Here's the phone number."

"What kind of place is the Knights Rest?" she asked, laughing.

"I'm not at all sure," he said rather unhappily and gave her the address. "Everything in town is full up. It's that rodeo or whatever it is they're having. This place is on the edge of town and doesn't sound like much, but I'll be spending most of my time with the Philadelphia people. *They*'ve got a suite at the downtown Ramada."

He gave her those numbers and Chandra said,

"You've just reminded me of something I forgot to tell you. Have you got a minute?"

She told him about the note and rodeo tickets from Bill Hazzard.

"That was a nice thing to do," said Eric, sounding abstracted. "Would you like to go?"

Ethel had opened the office door and was standing there.

Chandra said, "No. Maybe if things were less busy. You've never seen a rodeo, have you?"

"No, but things aren't getting any simpler here as the day progresses. I know I'm going to be working Saturday, darling. I'll have to."

"I know," she said, trying to convey by her tone that it was all right, she understood. "The kids can find something to do with the tickets, I'm sure. I hope I can remember to call and thank Bill. No point trying now. He'd be at the matinee show."

"But you are going to the Crittendens' thing?"

"Yes, I guess I will."

"Good. Enjoy. I'll see you tomorrow around suppertime."

"I love you, Eric."

"And I love you, very much."

Ethel came in, smiling complacently, as Chandra put down the phone.

"Well, I think we got her pattern figgered out. She sure is a nice woman, your neighbor. Just seemed like home folks, right off, an', law! She must be able to git the work done! Five children, helps her husband at *his* work, an' has got five extry people in the house till after

Christmas—or is it just four? Did you know she used to work in the beauty shop before she married? She offered, all on her own, mind you, to fix up my hair for me, prob'ly Saturday, she said. I aim to go to church somewhere, an' I couldn' do it, stringy as my ole hair's a-gittin' now."

"Oh, Mama, she really is awfully busy. I could—"

"Well," said Ethel snappishly, "I'm just a-tellin' you she offered. I sure never asked her to do anythin'." Then, with relish, "You just go ahead with your readin'. I want to set down here just a minute an' tell you what she was a-tellin' me about *her* mother."

Chandra saw to the preparation and cleanup of an early supper. The children complained and snapped at one another, as they always seemed to do when she was going out. Ethel worried about many things.

"You're not a-goin' out with your hair still wet," she demanded when Chandra came downstairs, freshly showered and wearing a long simple dress with a few bits of jewelry.

"It'll be dry by the time I get there," she said, trying not to snap herself. "It always looks best just after it's washed."

"Honey, it's so *cold* out there. You'll git your death of cold."

"My heater works, Mama. Everything will be fine."

"Well, you're ready, then?"

"Yes, just as soon as I find my keys. I've left Eric's numbers by the kitchen phone, and a number where you can reach me."

"Ain't you a-fergittin' your makeup?"

At Chandra's table now, at the Crittendens' supper party, there was a brief pause in the talk of the other writers, while waiters cleared away other dishes and served dessert.

"And do you write?" the other woman asked Chandra, seeming only now to be fully aware of her existence.

"Oh, she certainly does," said the elderly man quickly, and with more than a hint of condescension. "This is the juvenile writer Joyce was talking to us about earlier. Aren't you a neighbor of Joyce and Hal's, Ms. . . . ."

"Whitman," she said, "Chandra Barrie Whitman."

They had all introduced themselves when they were ready to sit down. The woman, whose name was Carol Smythe, said tolerantly,

"And do you have children of your own?"

"Yes, three."

"Gracious!" cried the young man effusively, "how do you find the time to write *anything?*"

"Oh, juvenile books are easy for one who is used to children," said the older man. "Don't you find that so?"

"It does help, I think, to live with kids," Chandra said. "I have a couple of adult novels as well, though. The second will be released in the spring."

"*I've* been working on a novel," said the young man, "and finding it extremely difficult."

"If I were you," confided Ms. Smythe, nodding at him eagerly. "I wouldn't spend too much time and worry over it. With nonfiction, the type of articles you've been talking about, one always knows exactly where one stands. A novel is such a—well, such an unauthentic, trumped-up piece of writing, and you know, *all* fiction is just simply going by the boards these days. What was it I read somewhere just the other day? Eighty or 90 percent of everything published now is nonfiction. People just don't *want* fiction anymore. The market certainly bears that out. Don't you find it *very* hard to sell, Ms.—uh—Barrie?"

"No," said Chandra placidly, "I haven't run into any problems that couldn't be worked out."

"You must have a very good agent," said the older man rather curtly.

"Or good books," suggested Chandra innocently.

Ms. Smythe said firmly, "*I* certainly have found *my* attempts at selling a fiction piece or two discouraging.

Though I suppose there will always be *some* little-old-lady types among the reading public who need a bit of romance and the like, and just are *not* ready for facts, the *truth*."

The two men were nodding ready agreement. Chandra thought their gall and condescension monumental but, rather than being put in her place, as she felt sure she was meant to be, she found them funny, in an insufferable but pathetic kind of way. She thought, And *I* couldn't write nonfiction, with everything laid out for me, all cut and dried, with no options whatever. A novel, a good one, demands research, authenticity, and it also calls for absolutely all that a writer can give, from and of himself, fidelity to many characters, an interesting, credible story with which readers can identify . . . She wouldn't say these things to these people. They didn't deserve her confidences and convictions. Why did nonfiction writers always treat the dealers in fiction as if they were not-very-bright children, playing their simple little games of making up, of course, not-very-clever stories? She couldn't quite squelch a smile as she admitted to herself that her ego was no less large and vulnerable than theirs.

"I do understand," the young man was saying, "that all fiction, whatever there is of it, is soon going to be done entirely as original paperbacks, because hard-cover publication is getting so expensive and people just aren't buying hard-cover fiction."

Chandra agreed. "My second novel is an original paperback."

"But," asked Ms. Smythe carefully, "don't you find that rather—cheapening?"

"It actually means more money for me," said Chandra, deliberately misunderstanding. "When a book is published in hard-cover first, you know, the writer has to split all the later paperback royalties with the hard-cover publisher."

"Actually, I meant—in the way of reviews and the

like. Most book reviewers won't *look* at an original paperback. I know I don't."

"Perhaps that's your loss," said Chandra ingenuously. "A great many readers seem to look at them."

The older man cleared his throat and announced, *"I* have never attempted a novel. I like to think I know my limitations, and the field where I belong—fields, I should say. Mr. Gruinwald here admits he's having problems with the novel he's working on. And you haven't attempted a novel, Ms. Smythe?"

"Just a few short stories," she admitted rather reluctantly. "I've been so busy with *real* writing since before I finished journalism school, that I couldn't possibly have found the time for anything like a book, *if* I'd wanted to. I can't imagine myself spending months, years maybe, messing about with all those uncertainties like character and emotion. *I*'m out to put the truth on paper. No offense, of course—uh—Sandra."

"Yes, quite," said the older man quickly. "So you and I, Ms. Smythe, have never done a novel. Mr. Gruinwald is still in the attempting stages. So you, Ms.—ah—Mumble—are the only one among the four of us, thus far, to have that accomplishment. Tell us, Ms.—Mumble—what is it really like to write a novel?"

Chandra had once believed that such a question could only come from a nonwriter, that anyone who was himself a writer, of anything, would know there was no answer that could be put into a few words or sentences. But writers were, after all, just other people, and these three, particularly the old man, smirking at her tolerantly, were humoring her, just for a moment, as Bruce or Gail might graciously ask Thegn's opinion about something where his judgment mattered not at all. They didn't give a damn about what she had to say, wouldn't really hear if she said anything, but, having become aware of her, felt she should be included, however briefly, in the supper conversation. I'm always an outsider, she thought, but this time the thought brought no feeling of isolation or aloneness. She had no wish to be included with these three, in anything. For the first time during the evening, they were all three looking at her, waiting for her to speak. Well, she had an answer for them.

"What is it like to write a novel?" she mused soberly, turning a spoonful of strawberry mousse and staring at it intently. "That's very hard to answer, you know. I guess the nearest I can come is to say that it's very much like taking a strong, long-acting but not wholly satisfactory laxative."

She put a spoonful of mousse into her mouth and gazed around at them guilelessly. The elderly man looked shocked, offended. Ms. Smythe's hand went to her mouth. Mr. Gruinwald guffawed, then looked sorely embarrassed.

Placidly, Chandra ate her dessert. After an awkward moment, the conversation resumed around her, but no further attempt was made to draw her into it. And no wonder, she thought, feeling just a little ashamed of herself. Any person had his arrogances—petty or not— and when she deliberately pricked another's pomposity, she was only displaying her own, wasn't she? Still, it had been fun.

When the small supper tables and the chair were cleared away, there was dancing. Chandra couldn't dance, but the party became more enjoyable now. In a corner, she joined a small group—assorted, but not of Joyce's planned mixing—and they discussed current world problems and politics until she suddenly discovered it was past midnight. She went to find Joyce and Hal, to thank them and say good night.

"Oh, Chandra, won't you stay just a little longer?" said Joyce solicitously. "We'll probably be leaving soon, and one car can follow the other out to Clover Hill. I don't like to think of your driving around alone. We're so sorry Eric couldn't be here tonight."

"I'll be fine," Chandra assured her. "It really was a very nice party."

"Well," Joyce said dubiously, "be sure you lock all your doors and stay on the main, well-lighted streets."

"Okay, Mother," said Chandra, laughing.

Joyce laughed too, and hugged her. "Well, now you do need looking after. I'm just not used to seeing you out on your own, away from that dear, handsome husband of yours."

When Chandra took her car keys from their compartment in her purse, she drew out a slip of paper along with them. When she was in the car, doors duly locked, she kept the dome light on to see what the paper was. It contained the name, address, room and telephone number of Eric's motel. She had copied it to leave by the kitchen phone at home and dropped the original into her purse.

She began to smile. The Knights Rest Motel was no more than a mile from here. Surely, Eric's meeting was over by now. Room eight would be on the ground floor, if the motel had more than one floor. He would be very tired. She'd just drive past and, if there was no light in his room, would leave him undisturbed. She hoped, rather excitedly, that he would be still awake. It would be fun to be with him, even for a few minutes, in some unusual place and circumstances. She thought wistfully of spending the night with him in town. No, that would necessitate a phone call home. No matter what Mama's claims were, she would be asleep now, and the entire household would be aroused, probably frightened by the telephone.

Just a few minutes then. If Eric were still dressed, and if the Knights Rest had a lounge or restaurant, maybe they could have a drink or a cup of coffee, almost as if they were not a couple who had spent almost every night of the past ten years together.

It was a seedy little place, with no bar or restaurant. The office looked empty and there was a "No Vacancy" sign. She could drive all the way around the single-story building. The room numbers were hard to see because practically all the lights were out, so she watched for Eric's green car. When she found it, she stopped across the drive, there being no more parking spaces next to the building. Her heart gave a happy little lift, like a kid going to a tryst, she thought. There was a light in room eight.

Chandra locked her car and crossed the drive. Then, just at the back of Eric's car, she stopped abruptly, in midstride, so that it hurt her lame leg. She didn't notice the heavy twinge of pain. She leaned her right hand against Eric's car and stood still, frozen, staring. Just beside his car—she had been about to walk between the two of them—was parked the little Volkswagen, yellow with black spots and the bug antenna. Cindy—no, Candy. Candy what? Candy . . . Candy . . .

As quickly as she could, stumbling a little, she re-crossed the asphalt drive, unlocked her car, dropped the keys, picked them up in stiff fingers, got in and drove away from the Knights Rest Motel. She was numb, dazed. What *was* the girl's last name? . . . Candy . . . Oh, what the *hell* does that matter? It matters because I can't—mustn't—*won't* think of—of him now. I have to get home first. I have to—but then she was thinking. Eric! Oh, Eric, how could you? Why? I've trusted you. I've always been so sure . . .

She pulled the car to the side of the street, trembling badly, tears blinding her.

After a time, perhaps five minutes, perhaps thirty, she began to mop at her face, coming alive again to now, to where she was, on a city street at almost one o'clock in the morning. She must leave this place, make ready for the drive home . . . *our* home, *our* children. Oh, God! All right, Chandra, stop it! You've got to . . . suddenly the girl's name flashed into her mind, along with an image of Candy Miller herself. It was Mona she reminded me of. That's why I kept thinking there was something familiar . . . The coloring is different and I think there's more—depth in the eyes, but the face, the figure . . . oh, damn her to hell! No, damn *him* . . .

Gulping, clenching her lip between her teeth to try to stop further tears, she glared down at her sodden handkerchief and saw a smudge of dirt. Then she saw that most of her right hand was dirty. Where had that come from? This wondering was abstracted as other thoughts, other questions and imaginings tried to force the barrier she was building in her mind, but, she made herself try to remember about the dirt, almost unable to bear the pain which, seeming to begin in her chest, was spreading and gripping her whole body. Eric—no. I *will* not think. The dirt . . . I must have leaned against his car when I saw . . . She wrenched open the glove compartment, found some cleaning towelettes and scrubbed at her hand until the flesh was raw. She might have gone on and on with this—a cleansing ritual?—but there was a tap at her window and she started so violently that there was fresh and different pain through all her nerves.

A policeman was standing there, his car drawn to the curb behind hers.

"Trouble, ma'am?" he asked when she had lowered the window a little.

"I—I was just—no, no trouble."

"I'm afraid this is not a very safe place to park," he said, sounding apologetic.

He looked so young. It seemed almost everyone looked so young these days. Was that why . . . ?

"I know," she said. "I was just about to drive on." Her voice sounded choked, cold, unreal.

"You seem pale, ma'am. If you're sick or . . ."

"I'm all right, thank you."

"Maybe you've had a little much to drink and really shouldn't be driving?"

"No," she said. The desperation now to be away from him, from everyone and everything, making the word sound false in her own ears. "I've come from a party, but the last drink I had was at least two hours ago. I'll take your test or whatever, if you . . . I'm not drunk."

"That's okay," he said. "But just remember not to park in a neighborhood like this at this time of night. The service station there on the corner was held up earlier tonight. You just never can tell what you might get into. Could I see your driver's license and registration?"

It all seemed to take an unconscionable time. He handed back her cards and said, in a friendly, chatty way,

"I noticed your address. That's out around Sherman someplace, isn't it? A cousin of mine lives out there. Some really nice neighborhoods."

"Yes," Chandra said, starting the car. And her bitterness would not be held back. "Utter perfection."

In her driving mirror, she saw the young policeman shrug quizzically as she pulled away.

Friday

10

Chandra awoke a few minutes after six. She had slept for perhaps two hours and her head ached fiercely from the liquor that had made the sleep possible. When she had finally got home, at around two in the morning, the light had gone on in Ethel's room. Mama would have to make a point of making sure Chandra knew she was still, or again awake, but, thank God, she had not come out of her room.

Chandra, feeling numb again, yet inwardly trembling with the things she must not yet feel, made a quick stop at the bar in the living room. She took a glass and bottle upstairs. After carefully putting away her clothes and changing into nightgown and slippers, she found she could not stay in the bedroom. Eric was too present, his things on the dresser and in the bathroom, his clothes in the closet, memories, reminders of him saturating the room and everything in it. Last night, not much more than twenty-four hours ago, they had lain together in this big bed, sharing the thing she had believed so precious to them both, so unique, so . . . Then he had got up, gone into the city, spent time at his office, at the college, at his meeting, and then the Knights Rest. But had there been a meeting? Were there really consultants from Philadelphia? How many other times had there been for him, at the Knights Rest or other places like it? She was so *damned* naïve. In spite of all her years of trying to become mature, even faintly sophisticated, realistic, she was still such a child, so stupidly trusting and vulnerable. Why? Partly because she had so wanted to feel she could utterly trust someone. Eric . . .

She went and looked in on Thegn, sleeping, with the black cat draped across the foot of his bed. His face was so like his father's in the dim light that came in from the hall. The pain she was trying so hard to stifle came near to bursting out in a scream of mixed acceptance and denial.

She controlled herself with tense difficulty and managed to close the little boy's door soundlessly. Dazedly, she went back to their bedroom and put on her robe. It was a pink, fleecy robe that Thegn still liked to stroke. Thegn had given it to her for Christmas last year, but of course Eric had been the one who . . . She poured some more whiskey into the glass, drank until her throat closed, wandered, ghost-like into the hall again.

She was scared now. Unwilling or unable to face what truly frightened her, she felt as she had sometimes felt as a child, that there was Something, some not-quite-known, terrible, fearsome Thing, Out There, a palpable Presence, lurking, waiting, to slip in and catch them, the people she loved and herself, to destroy them wholly, inexorably, horribly. A long time ago, she had decided this awful fear was a natural dread of the unknown and, in far greater part, a product of her own guilt, of the conviction that she did not *deserve* happiness, security, even short-lived feelings of contentment or safety. The analysis, right or wrong, had seemed to help to push the specter away. She had felt its presence less and less often, and not at all since before Thegn was born. Then, she had been frightened that her joy at the prospect of having the baby, *their* child, was too great, could never be realized without some terrible penalty. That was more than five years ago. Thegn had arrived, whole and healthy. She had believed herself to have gained greatly in confidence and security. Their lives had gone along as smoothly as most people's. She had written a great deal in those five years and her work was moderately successful. She could, yesterday, even consider the possibility of living with Mama. And the cornerstone of her shy, gradually unfolding confidence, her very being, had been Eric's love. When she had thought of that, the very bedrock upon which she was gradually finding and building herself, a biblical phrase had sometimes come to mind, "Underneath are the everlasting arms." He was like that for her. Eric had meant that. Well, all this only proved that one *couldn't* depend on anyone but oneself, because tonight, this very moment perhaps, he was . . .

Very quietly, and with a frightened compulsiveness, Chandra checked on the others. Bruce was snoring lightly, hulking very large in his rumpled bed, with his back to the hall light.

Gail lay on her stomach, a heavy skein of hair falling over her cheek. Chandra's terror deepened as, holding her own breath, she crept into the room, certain, for a heart-stopping moment, that the girl was not breathing. Gail stirred, making a soft, protesting sound. Chandra, her heart banging now, fled the room.

Glass in hand, she wandered the house then, like a lost soul. No lights. She groped her way slowly, in darkness, like a wraith, frightened, yearning, but not belonging. The family room where, tomorrow—no, today —they would begin the Christmas decorating; the table where they had shared so many meals, so much conversation, so much of each other; the kitchen which, after two years of planning and consideration, they had had remodeled, exactly to suit her wishes; her office; Eric's studio. Eric . . . None of this had really been hers, after all, not in the deep, total ways she had believed. While she was here, in these rooms, working, living, trying to believe and hope for even more and better things for them in the future, how long had he been . . .

Back upstairs, fumbling and awkward, Chandra moved a few of her things, including the glass and bottle, into the guest room. Carefully, sternly, she kept her eyes away from the great empty expanse of their king-size bed. But how long had it *really* been empty?

The guest-room bed was made up, from Ethel's one night of residence there. Chandra was relieved about that, out of all proportion for, suddenly, she found herself completely exhausted. She could never have mustered the strength to find and put on linens. She dragged herself out to turn off the hall light, closed the door and sank, feeling only half conscious for the moment, into the bed.

The refilled glass on the nightstand was close at hand. She raised herself, drank again, then sank back. Sometime later, sighing wearily, she got up and crept back to the other bedroom for the alarm clock. She had brought her galleys into the guest room earlier, but there would be no reading tonight. Angrily, she pushed the envelope far back under the bed, into utter darkness. How could any book, even her own, matter now? Had anything *ever* mattered, really? Had there ever been, and was there now, anything actually worth the struggle of living?

She got up, yet again, all but strangled by the awful Presence that waited to destroy. She pulled the drapes more tightly closed and, swaying now, holding herself tightly under control, went downstairs, in darkness, to check that all the doors were locked.

Back in bed, leaning to place her glass carefully on the table, she noted that the time was near three-thirty. An hour and a half since she had got home? Why wasn't she feeling drunk? Why couldn't she have even that? She looked at the bottle, gauging what she had drunk, she who had hardly ever, before this, been able to choke down straight whiskey. That's enough. More than enough. Relax. Give it a chance. She turned off the lamp and lay there, rigidly, feeling dizzy, sick, but not sleepy nor relaxed. Outside, she could imagine, could all but hear, feel, stealthy, evil claws. Spasmodically, desperately, she groped for the lamp, almost upsetting the bottle.

With the light on again, making a little island of comparative safety, she got up and secreted the bottle in a dresser drawer, thinking Mama might come up here and see it in the morning. I'm not ready for that, either. Then, to her surprise, she was laughing softly to herself. Then she was crying, and after that, she was in the bathroom, vomiting, painfully trying to keep everything silent.

The crying would not stop. Back in the guest room she forced down the liquor that remained in the glass and then lay down, hugging the extra pillow, desperately needing the bit of comfort and tiny solace the pillow's nearness, its touch could give. That way, she finally slept.

There was no need to be waking up at six o'clock. That had been her first thought as she roused unwillingly. Last night, earlier this morning, she had set the alarm for seven, because with Eric away from home . . . With Eric away . . .

She flung herself out of bed and stood trembling, dizzy, sick, scarcely able to breathe as the night came back in an overwhelming wave. After a few moments, she was able to move, soundlessly, downstairs. With only a dim light on, she put last night's glass into the dishwasher and made coffee. If Mama got up and came in here now, she simply wouldn't be able to bear it. She would begin screaming and never be able to stop, or would do something else even more unseemly, whatever that could be. She worked as quickly and quietly as possible, with trembling hands and her whole body feeling stiff, jerky, as if it were being worked by strings.

When the coffee was on and she was waiting for it,

she stood rigid, feeling awkward and shy, an intruder here, in her own house. Then she thought fiercely, I don't have to do this, stay in this room and dread Mama. She got a cup, unplugged the coffee pot and carried it upstairs. The guest room had become a kind of friendly sanctuary, with the lamp burning beside the bed, the bed in which only she, and others passing through, had slept.

She got into the bed, shivering with cold, and had a cigarette. Then the coffee was done, the pot seeming to wink its light mockingly at her. All right, Chandra, she told herself determinedly. Face this. You know you can't hide. It's Here. As she poured coffee, with shaking hands, it seemed she could feel the Thing, waiting to get in.

Grimly, she took her cigarettes, lighter, ashtray and cup of coffee to the chair by the window, and opened the drapes. It was very dark, stars and moon having fled before the unfulfilled dawn. Or perhaps it was cloudy. At any rate, she thought with weary firm determination, there is nothing Out There. If it were light, you could see the Soderbergs' house, and the mountains. But you know the mountains are there, they . . . but, no, thinking of the mountains won't help with this. Still, there's nothing horrible out there. It's in here.

People these days, for the most part, seemed to feel that "unfaithfulness" didn't carry the meaning it had once had. In most states, mental cruelty, irreconcilable differences, incompatibility were the chief reasons for divorce. Les, confronted with accusations of a few of his many ruttings, had said airily, "You're just not woman enough for me, Chandra. If you was, I wouldn' always have to hunt around like I do." But, after the first shock of finding out, and aside from the humiliation with people they both knew, she had, very early, stopped caring what Les did. He had wanted no more from sex than the quick satisfaction of a repetitive need which, with him, was purely physical. Nothing accompanied that, no commitments, no emotions which lasted more than a few minutes. Eric was different . . . She had *believed* Eric to be different.

People were not hung up on sexual fidelity anymore. Oh, weren't they? Suppose *people* found their husband, whom they had come to trust so deeply in this way, at a seedy little motel, with a girl student's car parked snugly beside his, a girl student who reminded her, his wife, of his first wife, who had held him, she believed, so thoroughly in thrall. *Had* Mona meant as much to Eric, hurt him as deeply, as she, Chandra, had always believed? That had been almost entirely guesswork on her part, undue, perhaps undeserved romanticizing. There was so much about Eric she knew she did not know. Now, of course, she knew there was far more than she had dreamed.

But had she, with her yearning to know, her niggling and nattering and picking at things, large and small, her asking for explanations, clarifications, understanding of him and of herself—had she driven him . . .? "No!" she said aloud, fiercely. I will *not* blame myself. Not this time. No doubt, some of the responsibility is mine, but I'm not going to make a big production, not even in the deepest parts of my mind, not now, of finding it and taking it on.

What would Sheila do in this situation? Chandra smiled wanly. With Sheila, the situation would be reversed. Sheila liked to believe herself a fully freed and free spirit, in mind and body. She had no patience with men, husbands or otherwise, who showed any indications of "possessiveness," who sought to deny or restrain any passing whim. Sheila searched for things in bed, as well as everywhere else. She said she wanted fulfillment, in the way Les had wanted it, but whether Sheila knew it or not, Chandra was convinced she also sought self-actualization, identity, all those things the libbers talked about so glibly but, in short, she sought for love shared, for Sheila. And Chandra had sought those things, had believed, up to midnight last night, that she had found a greater measure, with respect to bedding, than most people were ever fortunate enough to know. A great part of what she had believed she—they—had had, was based upon the conviction that Eric got, essentially, what she got from their relationship, that it was as near as they two could come to total sharing.

Obviously, that had not been true. If it had been, he could never have betrayed their love. She remembered her smug thoughts, lying in their bed on Wednesday night, idle thoughts that *she* might be capable of an affair, but not Eric. Never Eric. Another self-deception. One more impossible dream. The idea and all that went with it now shattered, Chandra knew once more her own devastating, ineluctable aloneness. Just how much of all she had thought they shared, of Eric's presence to her, had been deception, by him, or by her own dogged blindness, her yearning dreams? Did he love her at all? Had he ever? Had he wanted Thegn, even half as much as she had? Did he care anything about her writing? Where they lived? Her constant, damned soul-searchings and attempts to find, to *be* herself, to come to terms? Just how long ago had these—other things begun for him? Just how long had she, stupidly deceived, participated in the living of lies?

Chandra gulped, biting her lip very hard. No crying. Absolutely none. There's the day to be got through, Thegn's kindergarten party, Mama's ubiquitousness, the other children, other people, the book . . . an endless succession of other people, other things. She ground her teeth resenting it all with something that scarcely differed from hate.

She looked out of the window again, drawing deeply on another cigarette. A lambent grayness was coming over everything, no real light yet, but she could separate the shape of the Soderberg house now from the surrounding darkness, and she was glad of even that little. The light was coming.

Suppose this happened to Shirley. Suppose Shirley found out that Jim was—what? Sleeping around? Well, Shirley had a lot of fortitude, self-confidence, a good overall perspective on life and on herself. Didn't she? How much, really, could you ever, ever know about the inner workings of any other person? Maybe Shirley *had* been through something like this. They were confidantes, she and Shirley, to a great degree, yet each had a deep and careful reserve when it came to the very, very personal things. They had always been in total agreement that women who eagerly and freely discussed the bedroom were, at the least, worthy of slight contempt and pity. If she could talk to Shirley about this, though . . . but she couldn't, ever, to anyone. It hurt too much. She might shatter into a million pieces, even making the attempt.

That evening, such a few days ago, that hectic evening of trips to the airport and the high school music program, Shirley had said that Eric had said something about wishing she, Chandra, didn't feel she had to take so much on herself. How much did he talk to other people about her, when he almost never discussed her *with* her? There was what Shirley had said and Joyce's wistful comments about his pride in and love for her. And Candy had said he talked about his family, about her. Had she been just too much the manager, too bossy? Was she so busy coping that she had missed things, things she should have heard and seen and felt? But no! she thought fiercely, no blame for me, not now, *that*'s one thing I'm *not* going to try to handle, not yet, if ever.

Shirley, if it happened to her, would find ways of living with it. She and Jim cared deeply for each other—didn't they? They had the children, a shared life . . . Shirley could, perhaps, help her to find some perspective, some sense in trying to select priorities and come to terms with what was and what had to be. But Chandra knew she would not discuss this, no matter how much, how desperately, she felt the need for help. There had been one person once, up until last night—which now seemed so very long ago—one with whom she had believed she could, almost freely, talk about her deepest hurts or greatest joys. Could she ever face Eric with *this?* Could she ever fully face it, bear it herself?

How could he? Oh, God! She had *believed,* had been, for the first time in her life, where it came to another adult, secure, so certain of his love, and he had . . . And that girl! She had actually had the nerve to come here, to *their* house, and Chandra, stupid, trusting, empathetic Chandra, had felt *sorry* for her! Something in her eyes . . . Something indeed!

All right, just stop this! There's all the rest of your life for flagellation, self-pity, bitterness and the rest of it. What about now, this minute, this day? How are you going to go downstairs and start facing things and people? And what *are* the priorities? You think you can't face him with this, but can you go on living with him?

She was shuddering violently, gripping the empty coffee cup desperately with both hands, for here, finally, was the embodiment of her terror. It was not a shadowy, dreadfully half-imagined Thing outside. This time, it was the stark, abject terror of contemplating life without Eric. But, she thought with fierce determination, define *without.* Is it physical absence only? No! No, I can't think anymore now, can't make any decisions. Right now, I think I never want to see him again, but I know that won't be true for always, even when he's . . . Yet, if I can't trust him—and how could I ever, possibly, do that again?—then nothing we've had, nothing I've *thought* we've had, can ever be again. Without those things, without working toward those things, seeking them together, *wanting,* hoping for them, is there *anything?* No wonder I've felt so troubled lately, as if we were growing apart, rather than together, as if I'd never be able, really to know him. No wonder he's said he can't be what I wanted. If I have to live without the things I've thought were most important *in* living, the closeness, the coming more and more together, the growing, individually and with each other, *can* I live? Do I *want* to live? Is there any reason to live?

Of course. There are the children. But Bruce and Gail are almost grown. Thegn would get along. I'm not at all indispensable. . . . The writing, then. Oh, God, no! Nothing matters as much as—as I thought *I* mattered to him. So much for *your* importance, your complacence about—

She started violently, the coffee cup catapulting from her tense hands to smash against the wall, as the alarm, which she had forgot to shut off, rang stridently in the silent house.

11

Chandra moved like an automaton through the day. At times, she was very nearly able to put the previous night out of her mind. Thegn's school party was a noisy, joyous success. As soon as she had come from her room, Ethel announced that she didn't feel well. "I guess it's from not gittin' hardly any sleep last night. Oh, I knew when you come in, Chandra Lynn. Wasn't it nearly two o'clock?" She also repeated mournfully that, while she liked little children, bunches of them together made her so nervous, but she went along to the kindergarten. She made herself pleasant and agreeable to the teacher and other mothers, though every time she was near Chandra, she sighed in a pained, long-suffering way, whispering that her head ached and the noise was wearing her out.

Chandra joined the children's celebrating in a feverish, frenetic way that made her popular as organizer, arbiter, leader of games. Miss Cunningham, the teacher, smiled on her in rather surprised gratitude.

When Laura Forbes, who had called her about the

cookies and the life story of her grandmother, cornered her as the party was breaking up, Chandra said with brittle gaiety,

"I don't see how I can possibly get together with you about your book idea anytime soon, Laura. You see, as soon as the holidays are over, I must start on sessions with my business manager, planning tax shelters, you know. The only way I could fit in time for another story idea would be to give up the daily visits of my analyst, or going to the hairdresser. Besides everything else, my basement maid has quit this week. So you see I really . . ."

She drifted away, letting other people come between them, seeing Laura Forbes first look taken aback, then bewildered, then indignant.

After the party, Chandra drove to a large drugstore. She had brought an old prescription for sleeping pills to be refilled. Perhaps they would work again, for a night or two.

"Let's just have lunch here," she said brightly, "while we're waiting for my prescription."

"Yeah!" said Thegn eagerly. "Could I get a sundae?"

"Why, I'm not a bit hungry," protested Ethel wearily. "We just had them cookies an' all. Did you see that the ones we brought was all eat, an' some of the others wasn't? But le's just git on home, Chandra Lynn. I don't care a thing about eatin' out. Never have."

"Mama, Thegn's so keyed up, he's not going to be able to nap for hours, and we have to wait for the medicine. Besides, I don't *want* to go home yet."

"What kind of medicine is it you're a-gittin'? Didn' I say, the first thing this mornin', that you looked peaked?"

They settled into a booth, Chandra giving the fidgeting little boy a hug. She lit a cigarette and drew on it deeply. Her head ached dismally, but it was not A Headache, the kind that could devastate her for days. She thought almost wistfully of that kind of headache, from which she had suffered periodically since adolescence. If one of those came, she could, would have to, give herself to its all-encompassing pain, forget, for a time, everything else. But the headache she had now was only wearing, debilitating, a residual effect of the bottle in the guest-room dresser drawer, and of . . .

She answered her mother coolly and with a twinge of guilt, "The prescription's for sleeping pills. Lately, I haven't—"

"Huh? What kind of pills did you say?"

"Sleeping pills, Mama."

Ethel frowned in disapproval of a number of things, fanning ostentatiously at the cigarette smoke which wasn't coming within two feet of her face.

"Law," she said, sighing lugubriously, "if I run for a pill ever' time *I* can't sleep . . . It's the hours you keep, Chandra Lynn. If you'd try to git yourself into good habits over such things as when you go to bed . . . My land, I just can't hardly imagine what you was a-doin', out by yourself till two o'clock of a mornin'. I was just so uneasy, all last night, I couldn' hardly lay still. It seemed like you never *would* git home. I was worried to death. An' I don't hold with no kind of pills. These drugs is mighty dangerous things, I can tell you that. A body starts in with 'em, they can turn into a reg'lar dope fein', nearly before they know it."

Ethel picked up a menu the waitress had just laid before her. "I bet they don't have a thing here I'm supposed to eat. You know how my ole stomach is. It's already tied up in knots from all that noise an' all."

Delving into her purse, she said petulantly, "I expect I'd do well to take one or two of my stomach pills before I even think about orderin' anythin'. Can't they even bring a body a glass of water? Lordy mercy! Will you look at what they charge for just any little thing?"

"It's our treat, Mama. Don't worry about the prices."

"You know, Chandra Lynn, it's none of my business, but it does seem to me like you *ought* to worry about prices, sometimes anyhow. You just spend an' spend, like money grows on trees, an' Eric a-workin' overtime an' so hard, just to try to keep things a-goin'."

The waitress returned and Ethel, reluctantly, ordered a sizable meal.

When they reached home, they waved to Shirley, who was shaking a rug at her own back door.

"Good party, Thegn?" she called.

He nodded hard, grinning broadly.

"Come over later and tell us about it. Tina said the first grade's party wasn't worth a damn this year. Those are her words, not mine."

Ethel hadn't caught this last. As they went into the house, she was saying, "She's just the nicest person. Did I tell you she offered to set my hair for me? When I was over there yesterday, a-helpin' 'er with that crochet pattern, she just said, out a the blue, you know, 'Why I'll be *glad* to fix up your hair for you on Saturday, just any time you're ready.' Did you know she used to work in a beauty shop before she married? She had complimented me on how my hair looked nice, though it don'. It's been nearly a week now since anythin' was done to it, an' it's a-gittin' so stringy I can't hardly stand the stuff."

"Mama, I would have tried to do your hair, or Gail would have."

Ethel gave a significant glance at Chandra's short, curly hair, which rarely got more than a shampoo and a quick brushing.

"Yes, I had thought about that. You used to roll up my hair for me, ever' week, when you was a girl, but I didn' allow you'd want to fool with it now. You, an' Gail, too, it seems like you think that somethin' like a body a-tryin' to pretty up a little is such a waste of time, just silly or somethin'. Your neighbor offered, just out a the blue, an' I thought I'd git 'er to do it, for I'm still a-hopin' we can all go to church together on Sunday, an' I sure wouldn' want to be seen out anywhere with my ole hair in the mess it'll be in by then if I don' have somethin' done with it."

"Mommy," said Thegn, "can I call up Kevin Bailey?"

"Take your nap first."

"Lands, yes, honey," said Ethel with feeling. "You ought to be wore plum out from all a that partyin'. Your Grandma is."

"But you liked the party, didn't you, Grandma? It was fun, wasn't it?" His brown eyes sparkled.

"Oh, yes, it was right nice. But, you know, that teacher was a surprise to me. I didn' know she was a-goin' to be a—a—"

"A black," supplemented Thegn, nodding in quick understanding. "Oh, yes, she always has been, and we told you about that before. Mommy, can't I stay up today? I don't need to rest for school because it's over for Christmas. Besides, I'm getting too old for naps."

"No, at least rest this afternoon," said Chandra. "Then you can stay up as late as you like tonight. We'll be going out tonight, after Daddy gets home, to get the tree and see Santa. After that, we can start getting the house decorated."

Reluctant still, but not unhappy, Thegn started slowly up the stairs, bemused with the very nearness of Christmas. He looked back from partway up to call, "Thank you for the cookies, Grandma. They were delicious."

"What did he say?" asked Ethel as he disappeared.

Chandra told her.

"Well, now ain't that sweet?" she murmured, smiling gently, looking a little bemused herself, for a moment. "An' such big words he can use. Do you reckon he really knows what such as that means? He's just awful considert, ain't he, for somebody so young, an' especially for bein' a boy. He does take after his daddy, don't he?

"You know, I am right tired myself. I think I'll just

215

take off some a my things, put on my bathrobe—it's nice an' warm—an' just lay down here for a little while." She indicated the family-room sofa. "Do you reckon anybody's liable to come in for a while, or anything?"

"Rest in your room, why don't you, Mama?" said Chandra in a mixture of solicitude and irritation.

Ethel looked dubious, a little hurt. "Well, at home, I generally always do my restin' in the livin' room."

"But if you go in there and close your door, the telephone or doorbell won't wake you if they—"

"Oh, honey, I don't have no notion of sleepin'. I don't never sleep in the daytime, just can't do it, never have been able to. But I guess I might go in there an' lay down a few minutes. I've had the headache all day, from not hardly sleepin' last night, an' now my ole stomach's a-actin' up so. That food a person gits, out someplace, just ain't pure. They put in all that chemical, you know, to make it stretch further, an' at them prices! It ain't near as good as what a body can fix at home. Well, maybe I will go in my room a while, though I do believe it's the coldest place in the house. I don't like to lay down in any room with the door shut though. That always has made me uneasy. Just look out there. Don't it look like snow agin?"

"It does look like we might get something. But it would be rain, or else it will have to turn a lot colder. It's too warm now for snow."

"Warm! Law, it don't seem warm to me. . . . I'll just take a magazine or two to look through. Unless, that is, I can do somethin' to help you out. What are you a-goin' to do? Oughtn' you to rest a little?"

"No, I want to get back to work on the galleys. You go ahead and have a good rest."

"How much more of that have you got to do? Seems like it takes a awful lot of time."

"I want to have them ready to mail back by Monday. By the way, Mama, you know we'll be going out again this evening."

"Out where? What for?" she sounded indignant.

They had discussed the plans yesterday morning, and this morning as well, but Chandra detailed them again for her.

"Well, I just may not go," said Ethel bleakly. "You know, crowds an' all just makes me so nervous, I can't hardly stand it." They had been through this before, too. "It wouldn' hurt your feelin's, would it, or Eric's or the children's, if I was to just stay home, by myself, this ev'nin'?"

"No, Mama, that will be fine, if it's what you decide you want to do. Maybe you'll be more ready for it, though, after you've rested a while. I'm going to work now, until Thegn gets up."

And she did work, somewhat to her surprise. Almost, she was able to lose herself in the book. She came upon another destroyed scene and felt almost nothing about that, either, as she checked the original manuscript and made her notes. It was well over an hour before the phone rang.

"Hello?"

"Hi, love. How are you? How's everything going at home?"

Somehow, the sound of his voice was a shock, sending a sharp thrill of pain through her. Had she expected, subconsciously, that she might never hear it again? No, she had just tried not to think about it, about anything.

"Everything's all right, Eric." She loathed the heavy, aggrieved sound of her voice.

"Was the Crittendens' party any good?"

"It was all right."

"And Thegn's school thing? How did that go?"

She told him a bit about the children's program and party, sounding too bright now, a little wild. How could he be so calm and cool and—ordinary? How long had he been deceiving her in all these ways?

"And how is—your work going?" she finally ended

lamely, feeling self-conscious as she always did when it seemed she had been talking too much, feeling hollow and flattened, except for the spark of pain and anger in her that would have blazed up, had there not been an almost utter void around it for this moment.

She heard Ethel's door open; after a moment, heard her voice and Thegn's in the hall.

Eric was saying pleasantly, "Actually, it's not going badly. I know we'll be here tomorrow, maybe a part of Sunday, but we'll certainly be finished before the weekend's completely over. Then I'm taking off until after Christmas. I've told Dixon. I don't mean I've asked him. It's all arranged. I'm trying now to get other things here in the office squared away. . . . I miss you, Chan. I don't think you really know how much I hate times like last night." He laughed, sounding young, shy, innocent. "It's got to the point where I don't sleep well away from my own bed, away from you."

Now the spark in her had fuel. Her eyes burned. Her hand shook, holding the telephone. Christ, how did he *dare?* She could not speak, though her mouth was a little open in a kind of silent shriek.

"I should be able to get home a little before six," he was saying. "It feels as if I've been away for weeks. I was thinking we might all go out for supper, before we see Santa and choose a tree. . . . Chan? Do you want to do that?"

"Yes, Eric, all right." Dull, lifeless tone, and the terrible weary hopelessness crushing down upon her.

"Darling?" slow, puzzled, worried-sounding word. "You're not at all all right. What's wrong? Is it the book or . . ."

"I am *fine*, Eric," she cried fiercely. "Whatever *could* be wrong? We'll all be ready to go out when you get home. I'm sure it will all be just delightful, the perfect picture of the diligent, hard-pressed businessman, trying to give his demanding family a little holiday treat, a bit of his oh-so-valuable time, a—"

"Chandra—?"

"Oh!" she cried brokenly and slammed down the phone as the scalding tears began.

Ethel averred that going out at all was a total surprise to her and that she had heard nothing about Eric's invitation to dinner, though they were all ready when he came home. Ethel had spent a good deal of time, with Gail's dubious but willing advice, in choosing what she would wear, in fussing over the condition of her hair, the rightness of her makeup, but when Eric came in, she was arch and heavily playful. She said she had meant to be the one to prepare the supper that night, at home, that she guessed Eric was just afraid of her cooking. She mentioned that she didn't usually like to eat out, but not in the complaining, derogatory way she had kept bringing the fact up to Chandra. She said she guessed if her son-in-law said that everybody in the house was to go and eat out, she'd just better get her coat and did he think it was going to snow?

Eric's welcome home from the children had been far more boisterous than usual. School was out now, they were all a little giddy over the true beginning of the holidays and, when he told them that, after working through most of the weekend, he, too, would be at home until after Christmas, they were delighted, each of them coming up, almost immediately, with three separate projects on which he might occupy at least some of his time at home.

He had come in smiling, but with a tentative look in his eyes for Chandra. She could barely tolerate his warm kiss and hug, standing still for only an instant, stiff and cold, almost overwhelmed by the urge to grab his beard and pull it out by the roots as it tickled her cheek. She did not follow when he went upstairs for a few moments, as she would have done at another time, eager for a moment alone with him, a private word about the condition of the home front or something else they could share.

His eyes followed her through the evening, perplexed, questioning, the hurt and disappointment growing in their expressive depths as the hours passed. Ethel and the children carried most of the conversation, apparently noticing nothing but their own interests of the moment.

Ethel spoke mostly to Eric. She simpered, almost gushed over him, even to the point of asking him to order for her because she "didn' understand about such fancy stuff to eat, and some of it wrote in a foreign language even." Now and then, she threw a small smile at Chandra that seemed to hold triumph. "See what a fine man you've got," the smiles seemed to say; "see how good he is to his mother-in-law, how much he thinks of her."

You vain, pathetic, foolish old lady, Chandra thought wearily. Don't you think we ever go out to eat when you're not here? Don't you know he's doing this for me? But *why* is he doing it for me? Has he taken us all out to eat every time after he's . . . is it an expiation, some sort of atonement? Does it soothe his conscience, a steak or an omelet?

For the most part, Chandra felt only the dull emptiness that closed off the greater part of her anger, bewilderment, pain. A part of her went through the evening with that feverish brightness which flared, from time to time, into a rather strident, aggressive desperation. The rest of her ached for this time of supposed, shared family happiness to be over, yearned for physical aloneness, for respite from pretending. For the children, she thought grimly. She supposed that was why, if they ever thought about it, her parents had felt they had to keep on with *their* marriage. I will *not* make *my* children responsible for a mess like that, she thought. But neither can I, right now, at Christmastime, bring about some great scene or a separation. I can't even face *him* with it, not yet.

Occasionally, Eric's eyes managed to catch hers, and there was urgency in his look, confusion, pleading. How many times, she thought, the embers inside her sparking for a brief fierce instant, has that look of his made *me* feel guilty, responsible, placatory, ashamed? How many times have I apologized, been jolly and lighthearted when I didn't feel that way at all, to cheer him, to reassure him, to try to keep *him* from feeling depressed? Oh, Eric Whitman, you sonofabitch! You *bastard!* How long have you used me, tricked me like this? You're a weakling, a soppy coward and a shameless exploiter. If you were anything else, *you*'d bring this up, have it out in the open between us, you'd be at least honest, for God's sake. Or are you, who I've been trying so *damned* hard to know, one of those men who thinks he can have, is entitled to have, two whole separate lives? When we finally get down to this thing, are you going to try to tell me that Candy— and others?—mean nothing, or that you can love two women at once? God, how I hate you! Loathe you! If you look at me just once more like that, in that oh-so-wounded way, I swear, I'll scratch your eyes out!

She wanted the anger, clung to it when it flared. It made a temporary barrier against all the other feelings.

They came home, finally, with what they all agreed was the most beautiful Christmas tree they had ever had. Bruce and Gail had brought the decorations down earlier from the attic. Two friends of Gail's and one of Bruce's arrived, and all went to work eagerly, Eric standing guard so that Thegn would be sure to have his share of the decorating, among the busy, bossy adolescents.

Chandra brought out cookies, which she had made the week before and hidden away for this occasion. Gail hinted rather plaintively about having one of the fruitcakes she had helped to make, weeks before, on a Saturday, but Chandra, smiling her bright, false smile, said they had not ripened enough just yet and that most were meant as gifts for friends anyway. Only yesterday, when she knew Mama was safely in the bathtub, she had re-soaked the fruitcakes' cloth wrappings in wine. Yesterday, when she hadn't known, hadn't dreamed of ever suspecting . . .

"Look!" cried Thegn joyously. "It's started to snow!"

Ethel, sitting close to the fire, hugged herself with imagined cold as she peered from the big window with its drapes drawn back. Nevertheless, she looked as happy as Chandra had ever seen her. The young people deferred to her occasionally, asking advice about the position of ornaments, and Thegn, stepping back now and then, to survey the tree, leaned against the arm of her chair, patted her wrinkled, veined hand absently.

"You know, Chandra Lynn, I told you we ought to have washed these windows," she still worried above the other noise in the room. "Look at them smudges that big ole dog has made on that one. I'm a-goin' to do that tomorrow. I can at least git the insides cleaned up. I'd do it right now if it didn' make me colder just to think about it."

"You can't, Grandma," said Bruce, rather patronizingly. "We've got a wreath and other stuff we're going to put on that window."

"Well, this is y'all's doin's, I know, but it just seems like to me it would be better to *start* with a clean window."

"Just don't tell anyone about the smudges," said Eric, smiling at her. "Then no one else will notice them."

Going unnoticed into the kitchen, Chandra filled a glass half full of orange juice. Stealthily, and hating her stealth, she went into the very dimly lit living room, to finish filling the glass with vodka. She stayed there long enough to drink a good deal of it. Then Bruce was calling,

"Hey, Mom, where are you? We're ready for the star."

"Hurry, Mommy!" cried Thegn in urgent delight.

Chandra went back, stood by the table at the opposite end of the large room from the tree, smiling, thinking miserably, "How can it *be* Christmas? How does time just keep going on, so heartlessly? She felt utterly alone, bereft, shivering on the edge of the others' warmth and laughter.

Eric held a high stepladder as Thegn climbed up, proudly holding the star. When he had very carefully affixed it—just as perfectly as Eric would have done—amidst advice and applause, he came down and went soberly to the main light switch. As Bruce plugged in the Christmas tree lights, Thegn turned off the room's other illumination and Chandra, with hands that would not be steady, lit the candles which stood ready on the table. It was a tradition the family had started on their first Christmas together. Once the tree lights were up, all further decoration was carried on by their illumination, the fire and candlelight.

"Is there any more coffee?" asked Bruce's friend, Bob Lyons, after the proper moments of appreciation.

"I'll make some," answered Chandra, taking up a candle and her glass. It seemed to her that her pleasant, eager voice came from a great distance.

In the kitchen, she stumbled over the great, furry, black form of Prince Charming, where he lay, panting gently, at a good vantage point for keeping an eye on the entire family room. The stumbling hurt her leg, and she couldn't stop a guilty, apologetic glance over her shoulder to see if anyone had been watching.

The dog got up happily, gave her hand a couple of very wet licks, almost making her drop the candle, and went into the room, tail waving. He looked around delightedly from face to face and settled on Eric, to whom he went gravely, then stood up, placing his huge front paws on Eric's shoulders.

"You kids," Eric mock complained as he struggled with the dog, who was now delirious with his attention, "have been promising me for years that this animal is going, someday, to grow up, in mind as well as in body. Just when do you think I can expect that to happen?"

"He's just happy for Christmas, Daddy," squealed Thegn. "Could I have a ride on your back? It's been a real long time."

"You're getting to be a real heavy person," grunted

Eric, still not extricated from the happy dog. "Anyway, I can only deal with one thing at a time."

How much, wondered Chandra, cleaning the coffee pot, does my lameness, being a cripple, that ugly scar, the way my leg is twisted, have to do with this, with his not loving me? Maybe he never did love me, really, just felt sorry for me, and . . . Oh, for God's sake, Chandra! That has got to be the absolute *height* of whining, maudlin self-pity! Just get hold of yourself. This is not the time . . . Ah, but it never is, is it? Someone else has always got to be thought of, something else done. You're the last person, the *very last* . . .

She drained her glass, filled the coffee basket. This was going to empty the can. It surprised her to have one of Bruce's friends turn out to be a "coffee fiend." Bruce himself never touched the stuff. Surely, there was another can in the storage cupboard. Or had she, of all things, forgot to get coffee on her last big grocery-buying outing?

It's *never* the time for me, her bitter thoughts went on inexorably. What I want or think or feel always has to wait until something else is taken care of, until someone else's needs or demands or expectations are satisfied, till whatever it was I wanted or thought or felt is forgotten or doesn't matter worth a damn anymore. Well, with *this*, there's going to come a time when I can't keep hold of myself, can't keep thinking about anyone or anything else. And whose doing is it, anyway, that I've always had to wait, be last, push myself into the background? It's my own doing, of course, mostly: Be thoughtful of others, Chandra, be considerate, self-effacing, be *good*. Well, by God, other people have rarely enough done as much for me. But maybe a time is coming when they'll have to, when I'll *make* them. . . . But not now. Not yet. I can't start screaming and asserting myself and letting myself shatter when it's Christmas and—

"Chandra?"

His soft voice startled her so that she dropped the half-filled coffee pot into the sink, wrenching away from his tentative hand as if it held hot coals against her arm.

"Chan, tell me what's gone wrong, for God's sake. This afternoon I—"

"*Nothing* is *wrong*, Eric!" Her voice was as low as his, but somehow the words were a scream. "I—I'm afraid we're running out of coffee."

She refilled the pot and put it together, plugged it in. The kids had put more Christmas music on the stereo. They were arguing, bantering good-naturedly, laughing, singing along with the carols. Thegn's shrill and off-key but fervent voice rose blissfully.

"Let's go upstairs," Eric said firmly. "Things will be fine down here without us. No one will even notice we've gone. I want you to tell me—"

"I'm going to have to borrow coffee from Shirley. There won't be enough for breakfast."

"Have you checked the supply cupboard?"

"Eric, you're worse than Mama. I *am* a little more than two years old."

He looked at her steadily for a moment in the flickering light, the hurt deep in his eyes, but anger beginning to spark there, to overlay everything else. Good. If he finally got angry, he'd leave her alone. She knew his temper and his fierce pride. Damn him! Those things she *did* know.

"I'll go over to Soderbergs," he offered quietly, but the pleading, bewildered tone had left his voice.

"I *want* to go," she shot at him in that almost-whispered cry. "I want out of here for just a few minutes. Is that a whole hell of a lot to ask? Can't you just let me alone?"

12

She allowed herself gratefully to be drawn into the warmth, bustle and noise of the Soderberg house. David, their eldest, had come home from college that day, and they, too, were in the first throes of decorating. There were seven Soderbergs, plus Shirley's brother, his wife and two children, a parrot, two small dogs, a large cat and a guinea pig.

"You're jumping out of the frying pan into the fire," Jim had greeted her after she had knocked several times, very loudly, at the back door.

"I've been wanting you to meet Gary and Ruth," said Shirley warmly. "It's not every sister of Gary's that lives next door to a famous writer."

"I've read your book *Dawn*," said Ruth, gushing only a little. "I liked it, very much, and isn't it funny, I'd never even made the connection between that book and Shirley's writing neighbor."

Chandra sat there for almost an hour. Jim put a glass into her hand and she drank. At some point, he refilled the glass. She had no idea what she was swallowing. She smiled her wooden smile, made absent responses when she realized she was being spoken to directly, but had only a minimum consciousness of where she was, what was going on around her.

"Let's all get together, sometime before you leave," she said to Ruth as she stood up, finally, unsteadily, to leave. "I guess I should have got back, a long time ago, to my own madhouse." Her voice, though she raised it, seemed all but lost in the happy babble. She *felt* lost.

Shirley caught up with her as she went hurriedly toward the back door.

"Chan? Don't you want the coffee?"

"Oh!" She laughed, but forced herself to stop that because it was so nearly tears.

"Are you all right?"

Shirley was trying to look at her closely. She turned away a little, pulling on her coat, hiding her face.

"Sure. I'm fine."

They were in the kitchen, where it was a little quieter.

Shirley said, "I had already decided we ought to try

to get these two bunches together soon. How about Sunday afternoon? All of you come over here. We can cook out on the grill; no matter that we can't eat outside."

"I don't know," Chandra said vaguely, trying to get her mind together. "Eric may be working . . ."

"Well, it would be a shame to do it without him, but it could turn out that he'd be the lucky one. Think it over and, if you want to do it, let me know what part of the meal you'd like to provide. I've got a giant ham that just might go around. You can let me know what you've decided when I do your mother's hair."

"Shirley, you're dear to offer to do that for her, but you—"

"And she's a dear lady, though I *can* see how she's got kind of a special talent for wearing a daughter down. It'll take me two shakes to do her hair, and I don't mind a bit, so let's hear no more about it. I mean to ask her to come over here for the operation, if our stress level isn't abnormally high, give you a few minutes to yourself."

"I have to go out tomorrow night," said Chandra, abruptly recalling Sheila. "I haven't told Mama yet. I don't know if Eric will be home or not, but I doubt it, and I can't seem to remember what the kids' plans are right now."

"Well, don't look so harried," said capable, coping Shirley. "Here's what to do. Tell Grandma I can't do her hair until the evening. She can come over here and sit under my dryer. Now that I think of it, Jim and Gary and *some* of these kids are going to that Holiday Stampede thing tomorrow night, so things *might* be almost peaceful here. That will give your mother something a little different to do, besides staying around with your kids, though I do get the very definite impression that she can raise quite a bit of sand over a little bit of differentness, eh? Let Thegn stay here if the older ones are going out."

"Shirley, thank you. You're really kind of marvelous."

"I know," said Shirley, clapping her shoulder and laughing. "Isn't it just almost more than you can stand?

But, listen, is Eric okay? Jim saw him when they both came home tonight. He said he really looked beat and, believe me, if Jim notices, things have to be getting pretty serious."

"He—he's going to have to work through the weekend, but then he'll be home until after Christmas. Yes, he's tired I'm sure. I really better go. Good night, and thanks again, for everything."

"Isn't this snow something?" exulted Shirley at the back door. "Couldn't have come at a more perfect time, though it isn't supposed to last long. I saw most of the evening news, though I still don't quite know how that happened. They say this will clear out tonight and it's going to be very cold, then warm up quite a lot before the next front comes through in a couple of days. I'd be willing to bet we get one of our good old chinook winds, so better batten the hatches. Actually, I hope the streets stay fairly clear for a few days more at least. I've really hardly started on my damned Christmas shopping. I don't know why I can never get anything organized. By the way, did you hear about the cops being called up to the top of the hill earlier this evening?"

"No. What happened this time?"

"Oh, just kids, messing around with jeeps or trail bikes on that back road up there again. I *think* our kids reported that one of them was someone David's age, just home from college, too, but I forget the name. You know, that's no more than an old washed-out trail where it's so steep, going down the back side of the hill. I'm just afraid that someone's going to have to be killed up there before they find a way to stop them messing around like that. Well, good night, and Merry Christmas."

Back in her own house, Chandra's aching eyes darted quickly around the dim family room.

"Grandma went to bed," announced Bruce, catching sight of her. "And Dad's upstairs, getting rid of Thegn. It's okay if we have popcorn, isn't it? And are there some more cookies?"

"We'll make the popcorn," Gail assured her. "Someone came by while you were gone."

"You sure were over there a long time," noted Bruce. "Who came by?"

"I don't know," said Gail. "They just wanted to see Dad, I guess. It's so dark with no electricity on that I didn't get a real look. They only stayed a minute, I think. We've been pretty busy. Look at what we've done in the living room, okay?"

Turning from putting her coat away, Chandra took a candle and glanced wearily into the living room. "It's looking beautiful," she said. "Try to keep the noise level down, will you? Grandma's not far away, trying to sleep. And don't be up too late."

When she finally got to the stairs, Eric was sitting there, on a lower step.

"Thegn's in bed," he said.

"I'll go up and say good night."

"He may be asleep already. You were gone quite a while." And now he was looking stubborn, determined, righteous. "I want you to tell me what the hell has happened, Chandra. Come in the studio, or your office. Is it something I've done that—"

"Do you *object* to my looking in on Thegn?" She spat the words and went past him, up the stairs.

But her last glimpse of his face stayed before her eyes. He *was* tired, wan and exhausted-looking. Why in hell should I notice that, she thought angrily, or care? He was probably kept awake all last night by . . . Turning to glare back at him, she found that he had gone, walking wearily along the hall with his candle, toward his studio.

Before going to Thegn's room, she paused to swallow two sleeping pills. All that stuff about not mixing barbiturates and alcohol had never been applicable to her system. She wished it was.

"Thegn?" she almost whispered, opening his door very quietly.

"Come and talk to me, Mommy," he murmured,

sounding warm and sleepy. "We could have the light on if you want to."

"No, we don't need the light."

She walked around Prince Charming, already asleep, but opening one eye and giving his tail a single drowsy wag, set the candle on the dresser and sat down on the edge of Thegn's bed.

"I'll just stay a minute. It's been quite a day, hasn't it?"

"Oh, Mommy, it's been the *best* day," he said with a happy little wiggle. "It's almost gooder'n Christmas. Is it still snowing outside?"

"Yes, but not much now. I'm afraid this storm is about over, but there's still plenty of time for more before Christmas."

"You know what? I think Santa Claus had onions for supper."

"Do you? Well, I suppose Santa likes onions as much as the next guy."

Thegn giggled. "Daddy said that too. But, Mommy, some of the kids at school say there isn't a real Santa. I know those at the stores are really just helpers, dressed up like Santa does, and they take him messages about what kids tell them, but *they* say there isn't at *all*."

"Then where do they suppose all those gifts come from?"

"I don't know," Thegn sighed happily. "They don't seem to have any answers about that, and I'm not going to worry about it. Daddy thinks I shouldn't."

"Fine," she said, hugging him. "Now you'd better get to sleep."

"Why doesn't Grandma like to go to restaurants?"

"Oh, because she just isn't used to going out to eat. That's nothing to worry about either."

"Well, then, why does she always say she can't eat things, or isn't hungry, and then she eats more than just about anybody?"

"Well, because—because that's just how Grandma is. I'm going to go to bed now."

"Did Daddy or anybody tell you some people came while you were over at Aunt Shirley's?"

"Gail mentioned it, but she didn't know who it was."

"Well, Daddy answered the doorbell, with his candle and I went with him. All those others, Bruce and Gail and them were making a lot of noise and they didn't care who came. We know her, Daddy does, she's a girl from his class at the college. Her name is Candy. I never knew anybody named Candy before, did you? But she's nice, and pretty. There was a boy with her, a big boy, you know, like from the college too. I think maybe he lives around here, but I don't know. She talked to Daddy for a few minutes and the boy went out and waited in his car. They went in Daddy's studio and talked for just a little while. I was putting some things in the dining room so I saw her when she came out. I thought maybe she was crying, but you can't tell, with candles. Daddy gave her one of his cartoons, for a Christmas present, you know, but I don't know which one. I forgot to ask him."

Chandra's pain was so great and terrible that she did not know what she said, or how she left the child. In the guest room, she undressed automatically, with cold, stiff, shaking hands, scarcely conscious of the tears that gushed from her eyes. How could they? How *dared* they meet here in *her* house, with Mama and the children and the children's friends . . . ? That's it. Get angry. *Stay* so furious that you can't think, can't feel . . . Just two nights ago, I was thinking, poor Candy, she has a crush on him and he falls asleep while trying to talk about her. Oh, God, what a *nerve* that man has! How I despise him!

Finally, she grew quieter, the sleeping pills beginning to cast a blessed haze over everything. She mopped her face with a large handkerchief, Eric's. She flung it from her and pulled the covers close, shivering. Please God, let the pills work tonight, she thought dully, grasping at the growing drowsiness. Let something stop all this, even for a little while. But she lay there rigidly, her ears straining nervously for the muting sounds of the house. Just when she was beginning to relax, almost in spite of herself, with the little tense starts and twitchings that sometimes presaged falling into deep sleep, there was a soft knock. She did not respond, but Eric opened the door. I want locks, she thought miserably, locks on everything.

"Why are you sleeping in here?" he asked. But, no, it wasn't a question, it was a demand.

Wearily, she raised herself on an elbow, trembling. "I don't feel well," she said, the words curt but a little blurry. "I want to be by myself. I guess it's the only way *to* be, for me, isn't it, really?"

"Chandra, what is it?" He actually sounded desperate. "Isn't there anything I can say, or do, that will—"

"Yes!" she said fiercely, and now she was, truly, very nearly screaming. *"Get out!"*

"Look, I'm sorry," he said coldly. "Whatever it is, I'm sorry as hell. Can't we—"

"You always try that," she flashed. " 'Whatever it is, I'm sorry.' A blanket apology, in that goddamn virtuous tone. And, no, we can't. Whatever you were going to say, we can't. And we *never* can, not ever again. You *know* what's wrong, Eric Whitman, and what's more to the point, *I* know what's wrong, finally. Now get out of here! At least have the decency to let me have a little privacy. God knows, you've kept *yours* all these years."

She was not crying. Her hot, dry eyes shot sparks at him through the dimness and her fists beat a furious tattoo against her pillow. Eric stood there, holding the candle, staring at her, looking hurt, bewildered, angry. She had never dreamed, Chandra thought blurrily, what a propensity the man had for acting, playing the aggrieved innocent. Just how much else about him was false? Slowly, looking so very deeply troubled, he left, closing the door with angry firmness.

Weeping again now, furious with the tears, she

blew out her candle. Then, she lifted herself once more from the pillow and groped in the nightstand drawer with cold, shaking fingers, she found and opened the bottle, swallowed another sleeping pill.

Saturday

13

Chandra slept heavily until Thegn came into the guest room to wake her. It was almost nine o'clock.

"Grandma was worried about you," said the little boy, looking very worried himself. "I couldn't find you in your room and I didn't know what happened. Gail said maybe you were sleeping in here. Why are you?"

"Because," she spoke slowly because thinking quickly was impossible just now, "because Daddy had to get up so early this morning. I wasn't feeling well last night and I wanted to sleep late if I could."

Thegn, still looking quizzical, said, "Bruce is still in bed, too, but Grandma thinks he's just lazy."

Chandra's head ached as it had the day before, only worse. The sleeping pills left more of a hangover than liquor, but she *had* slept.

"Eric was up a way before daylight," announced Ethel righteously as she came downstairs. "Bless his heart, just like it was a reg'lar workin' day an' not Saturday atall. I heard him in here, a-doin' around, an' I got right up, but he wouldn't eat a bite a breakfast, just coffee. That ain't healthy. I can't help a-thinkin', an' I know it ain't my business, but if you was to git up with him, ever' mornin' an' cook him somethin', he'd git to where he'd want to eat right. He said he'd be home tonight. Said it might be right late, but he'd be here. He looked right bad, Chandra Lynn, like maybe he hadn't slep' any."

Chandra sat smoking, a cup of coffee before her on the table. The bright sun outside the open drapes hurt her eyes. Last night's snow lay in bright, glistening swatches, much of it already melted in the warmth of the sun and a mild westerly breeze.

"Is it okay," asked Gail, "if I go to Laurie's when I've finished my clean-up chores? She's got a sewing project for Christmas presents and I said I'd help with finishing it up."

"All right," said Chandra. "What had you thought about doing this evening?"

"Well—staying home. Maybe I might wrap some gifts. Some of the kids might come by, I guess."

"I'm going into town to have dinner with Sheila, you know."

"Yes, I remember. I'll be here tonight with Thegn all right, no problem. I'll come back from Laurie's by six."

"Huh?" said Ethel to Chandra. "You say you're a-goin' where?"

"To meet Sheila Summers, Mama. I used to work with her at the ad agency. I've told you I'd be having dinner with her tonight. She's leaving town tomorrow, to be away for a while."

Gail went upstairs and the vacuum cleaner started. Thegn, after dreamily surveying the Christmas tree for a few more moments, drifted upstairs too.

Ethel sat down across the table, surveying her daughter with troubled eyes. "Chandra Lynn, do you reckon you ought to be a-goin' off agin tonight? I mean, a man likes to find his wife at home when he gits in, especially if he's a-workin' extry hours."

"It will probably be nearly morning when Eric gets home, Mama. By the way, Shirley said to tell you that she'd like you to come over there this evening to have your hair done. Part of her family will be out for the evening and she wants you to meet her sister-in-law and visit with them for a while."

Ethel looked hurt, doleful. "Well, I don't know that I'll do that. *I* don't like the idy of leavin' the children alone so much. Anyway, I gener'ly always have my hair set in the afternoon. That way, it gits good an' dry by night."

"Shirley has a dryer," said Chandra.

"Oh. . . . Well, I don't know. I'd always ruther stay at home, or wherever it is that I'm a-callin' home at the time. But, you know, I was a-goin' to say, you don't look right to me, either, pale an' all. If you've really got your mind made up to go off to town, agin, you'd sure do well to put on at least a *little* makeup this time.

"My! that was a fancy place Eric taken us to eat last night. I never seen anything *like* the prices. A body can eat so much cheaper at home, even with groceries a-costin' what they do nowadays. Well, if you're a-goin' off agin, tell me what you want fixed for supper. Git somethin' out of the freezer, if that needs to be done. I'd *like* to fix up somethin' that's a favert of Eric's, just in case he *does* git home to eat."

Bruce came pounding down the stairs, making both women wince. He looked sullen.

"I don't see why Gail has to start with all that noise so early, and be so damn bright and cheery about it besides."

Ethel looked meaningfully at Chandra, who sat still,

feeling limp and tired. Then the older woman sighed and said to Bruce.

"You want Grandma to cook you some breakfast, honey?"

"Just a couple of eggs, maybe, and some bacon, or sausage, it doesn't matter which," he answered rather grandly.

"What are your plans for the day?" Chandra asked him, lighting another cigarette.

"I'm going to work on my car, Mom," said Bruce, offended. She should have known. He launched into a lengthy, detailed description of what he meant to do and who would probably drop by, to help or look on.

Chandra, not really listening, put in when he paused for breath, "And what about tonight? Did you want to go out or anything?"

He sighed. "Mom, I'm just *telling* you. I'm going to have that car running in a couple of days maybe. I'm going to be working on it *all* the time. Dad said he'd help if he gets through with his job before I've got her in shape. I sure would appreciate that. He knows more about mechanics than any of the guys that come around here; *almost* as much as me."

"Well, don't start on the car this morning until you've done a couple of hours of house duty. Your room first and then—"

"Ah, gee, Mom, *today?* I mean it's holidays and you know how much I've been counting on getting the car in shape."

"Today," she said firmly, wearily.

"Well, gosh!" he said, deeply aggrieved. "There *are* three women in the house, and I don't see why I have to—"

"There aren't three women in your room, Bruce. It's a mess. And I'd like you to get all the trash together, from all over the house, and get it out."

"Well, damn! Couldn't Gail do my share this once, or you?"

"Gail wants to do other things too, later in the day, besides cleaning. I'm going to be working on my galleys."

"Oh, sure!" he said hotly. "It's just fine and dandy if *you* skip your share."

"Bruce, we've been through this so many times. I'm not arguing, or trying to explain to you again."

"Well, shit! Some holiday!"

"Yes, isn't it?" she flashed at him fiercely and left the table.

She began to gather extra Christmas decorations, strewn through the house. She was putting them into a box when Ethel stood in front of her, looking outraged and determined.

"Chandra Lynn, I'll clean up this house. I could have done the most of it yesterday, or *we* could. We ought to of. I believe in children a-helpin' out, but it don't seem like to me it's their place, especially boys, when—"

"Mama, you clean," said Chandra levelly. "You do just exactly what you like—about everything. I'm going into my office in just a minute. While I'm in there, working, I don't want the vacuum run at that end of the house. I'll clean that part when I'm *through* working. And if anyone, *anyone*, comes into my office without being invited, without having the courtesy to knock first, they'd best be warned that there will be consequences."

Ethel stared for a moment, anger, bewilderment and hurt brimming in the tears that had come to her eyes. Chandra turned and left her standing there.

At the foot of the stairs, she met Gail, carrying an armload of laundry.

"Bruce is doing his injured male dignity thing again," said Gail dryly, with a little grim smile. "I told him it's not a bit manly to just try to goof off every Saturday like he does."

Chandra smiled wanly. "That must have made all kinds of difference."

Gail laughed. "Yeah, and you know *what* kind."

"Where's Thegn?"

"Picking up his room and telling Prince Charming about Santa Claus. Listen, Mom, do you want me to stay here today and baby-sit Thegn and Grandma *and* Brucie? Laurie could probably come over here and it would be all the same to me."

"We haven't got a sewing machine."

"Oh, that's okay. She's ready to do the handwork on her stuff, the part she really loathes. Maybe Grandma would want to help with some of it. That would be really neat. In fact, everything would be great if only it didn't have to be so hot in here."

"Gail, if you could do that, stay home, I'd just appreciate the hell out of it. Look, try not to let any vacuuming get done down here toward the office, okay? I'll do this part of the house sometime later. I mean to be finished going over the galleys before I go out tonight."

She turned away down the hall.

"Mom?" Gail followed a few hesitant steps, lowering her voice, her face deeply concerned. "Is it really bad?"

"Is what bad? The galleys? I—"

"Listen, I know things like this are private, and that parents don't always get along, just like no other two people always get along, but I know you're sleeping in the guest room, and you look—really down. If there's anything I could do, or if—if you'd just like somebody to talk to . . ."

Chandra wanted to hug her, but feared a sympathetic touch would destroy the tight control she was just managing to hold.

"It will pass." Her voice sounded cold because she was trying so hard not to let it tremble. "Don't worry about it."

"You know Robin Murray?" Gail looked very upset now. "Her folks are getting divorced. They had a big family discussion about it the night before last. Robin told me yesterday. She's just about wiped out. Isn't that a shitty thing to do, right at Christmastime?"

"It is," said Chandra stiffly. "I'm sorry to hear it."

Gail walked past her and stuffed clothes into the washing machine.

"I wanted to ask you if Robin can stay here sometimes during the holidays, if she wants to. One thing she says is that it just doesn't feel like her house is her home anymore. She has to choose the parent she wants to stay with. That's the way they handle it when kids are past a certain age. What a *lousy* thing to have to do."

"Ask her anytime you like." Chandra's voice sounded brittle.

"Good. I'll call her right away."

Closing her office door, Chandra found her hands shaking again. She wished she'd brought another cup of coffee, but wouldn't go back for it.

The phone began ringing right away. She didn't pick up her extension. The calls would be for one of the young people. Gail would answer. It went on ringing, often, through the morning. No one came to Chandra's door. She read doggedly, sometimes having to reread an entire scene to be sure she was making proper sense of it. She came upon another passage that had been slaughtered by the editor, and was almost grateful for it. Anger and hurt over that was now a welcome distraction.

She felt so very tired, battered and bruised, inside and out, dull pain in more than her head. She was beaten. No, defeated. What was the point of anything? But she went on with the book. The very thought of having nothing to do, nothing that needed concentration of the greater part of her mind, was terrifying.

She opened a desk drawer for a fresh pencil and saw the rodeo tickets lying there, with Bill Hazzard's note. I should have given them to someone, she thought abstractedly, should have called to thank him.

She went on feverishly, making notes for the passage which must be corrected. Then there was the roar of the vacuum cleaner, coming implacably down the hall toward her door, wrenching her thoughts almost painfully away from absorption in the book. There was a quick tap at her door and Gail slipped in quickly, closing it behind her.

"It's Granny," she said apologetically, rather grimly. "I'm sorry, but I just couldn't stop her. She says we ought to get all the house done today because it's not Christian to do work like that on Sunday. I tried to tell her we could do this part tonight while you're out, but she said Dad might be home by that time and *he* shouldn't have to be bothered with a lot of noise and house cleaning. Geez!"

"It's all right," Chandra said wearily. "Thanks for trying."

"You haven't heard it all yet. She plans to 'straighten up' Dad's studio, clean it real good."

"Well, let her. She's hard to stop when she's got her mind made up to be helpful."

"But, Mom! He'll have a fit."

"I know he will, but he may as well just accept some of her services, as the rest of us have to."

Gail stood there frowning for a moment, then she grinned resignedly. "You know, a lot of times she doesn't hear just because she doesn't want to. I went on trying to tell her things like that Dad doesn't want anyone else fooling around in his studio and that the vacuum would bug you, and she just acted as if she didn't know anyone was talking to her, just turned it on and headed down the hall. Anyway, we've got the rest of the house pretty much taken care of. Laurie's come, and Grandma said she'd help us with the sewing after lunch. She seemed to hear about that all right, and seemed pleased we asked. Thegn's gone over to Billy Halverson's. He called first to see if it was okay. I told him to be home by noon, all right?"

"Yes. Thank you. I think there are plenty of sandwich things for lunch."

"Yeah, we'll find them. Bruce, the martyr, finally got out to the garage."

The phone rang again and Gail sprang to pick it up, saying, "Sorry, Mom. It's really been going strong this morning. Hello? . . . Oh, sure, Ms. Summers, right here."

Gail left the room. Holding the phone on its long cord while she confirmed the dinner date with Sheila, Chandra crossed the room and locked the door. There *was* a lock here. Why hadn't she started using it long ago? When she had hung up and gone back to her work, it was difficult to keep any sense of continuity in the book with the vacuum cleaner bumping peremptorily against wall and door.

After a time of relative quiet, when she was able to become almost wholly absorbed in her work again, there was a rattling of the door knob, followed by a sharp knock.

"Chandra Lynn?" Ethel's voice sounded worried, frightened.

Chandra crossed quickly, resignedly and opened the door, holding a sheaf of galley sheets.

"My land, that scared me to death for a minute!" said Ethel, laughing a little in relief. "I don't know why it give me such a funny feelin' but it did. I never noticed this door a-stickin' that-a-way before this, an' I couldn' hear a sound from in here. Law, this room's just full a smoke, honey. It's a wonder to me you don't choke to death in here."

She was right. Chandra hadn't thought to open a window, had become almost oblivious to the overheatedness of the house.

"I've cleaned up Eric's room in there some. I didn't throw anything away nor nothin' like that, though it seemed to me like that needed to be done. I just stacked things together some, an' like that, so I could dust."

He *would* have a fit, Chandra thought, and found a tiny glint of pleasure in that.

"I wanted to tell you," Ethel was saying, "Gail an'

her friend have got stuff out on the table for lunch. I don't know yet what I'm a-goin' to eat this time. All a that special lunch meat you bought me is gone. Thin has brought another little boy home with him. I've called Brucie an' *his* friend to come in out a the garage, though they ain't come yet. You come an' have somethin'. Don't it git awful expensive a-feedin' so many of the children's friends so much of the time?"

"I don't want to eat now, Mama. There's not an awful lot of work left on this book and I want to go on reading. Don't worry about the boys in the garage. Maybe they're involved with something they can't leave just now. We can all eat as we're ready and look after ourselves."

"Well, it seems to me like a meal is somethin' to set down to, all together. Children, an' other people too, ought to know that. The ones a-doin' the fixin' oughtn' to have to be on call all the day long. I've promised them girls to help with some of that sewin'."

"I'm glad you're going to do that for them and I know they'll appreciate it. Just go ahead with lunch and don't worry about the rest of us. Each person can get his own. We have to do it that way on a Saturday sometimes."

"Huh?"

Chandra repeated. She was gripping the proofs in both hands now and they were getting badly wrinkled.

"Well, I didn' want young'uns a-snackin' an' a-messin' in the kitchen the whole day long. I aim to fix a real good supper an' they oughtn' to ruin their appetites. An', if you'll just go on an' eat you a bite, I'll clean in here a little while the vacuum's right here handy."

"No, Mama," she said tensely. "I'm going to go on working now."

Ethel was staring again, dolefully, as Chandra closed the door.

A little later, Thegn knocked and she admitted him. His friend Billy could stay for the afternoon if it was all right. He didn't have to take a *nap,* did he? Billy never took naps anymore and thought they were sissy. They wanted to play trucks in the back yard. Grandma said it was too cold to be out, but it was really warm now, all the snow gone.

Chandra approved the requests, and asked that he consult Gail during the rest of the afternoon, provided there were no really large problems. As Thegn was leaving happily, she heard Ethel, calling again at the garage door.

"Brucie, honey, you come in right now if you want any lunch. I want to git these things put away an' the kitchen cleaned up."

After a few minutes, Bruce did indeed come in. He slammed the door from the garage. He crashed shut the door to the downstairs bathroom and turned the taps in there wide open. Then there was Gail's bossy voice in the hall.

"Brucie, we all agreed, years ago, not to use that bathroom while Mom's working."

"Grandma uses it," yelled Bruce as loud as he possibly could. "If you call me Brucie just one more time, I'll cream your snotty face. I got to wash up, don't I? Jesus Christ, I just had breakfast a little while ago, and now I've got to eat lunch, *right now!* Mark went home because he thought he wouldn't be welcome. *I'm* not welcome in this damn house today."

"You'd better stop," Gail had begun when Chandra flung open her door.

When she was in the hall, she also threw open the bathroom door.

"If either of you yells one more word here," she said ominously, coldly. *"I'm* going to start yelling."

"Well, gosh," said Gail, hurt, "I was only trying to protect you."

"Protect me somewhere else, please, away from the office door. Bruce, don't come out of there until you've cleaned the grease out of that wash basin. Get some cleanser. You'll need it."

"I have to come out to get the cleanser," he said angrily. "I don't see any in here. Besides, Grandma said lunch—"

"I don't care about lunch," she almost screamed. "Clean it up."

The phone rang as she went back to her desk. After a moment, Thegn called through the closed door, "Mommy, it's Daddy on the phone."

"Yes?" she said coldly, hearing the click as the kitchen phone was hung up smartly.

"I just wanted to let you know," Eric's voice was cool, tentative, "that I can't get home until very late tonight. We'll have supper somewhere and then we're going to try to get this all finished, so it will probably be well past midnight."

"That's too bad, Eric," she said nastily. "Mama meant to see to it you had a decent meal at home for a change tonight."

"Chandra, now listen—"

"If you're going to be that late, you'd probably better just *sleep* in town, don't you think?"

There was a pause. When he spoke, it was clear that he was making an effort at a reasonable tone. She despised his reasonableness.

"Look, if you think it's important, I'll be there for supper. I can always come back afterward."

"If *I* think it's important! Why would I think that? I won't be here myself. I'm going into town to meet Sheila. I don't suppose that had crossed your mind since I first mentioned it."

"Meet *me*," he said quickly. "Come early and have a drink with me somewhere before you see Sheila."

If only he had made a suggestion like that a few days ago! How she would have jumped at it, with gratitude and love! What a fool she would have been!

"You were just talking about making a heroic effort to be home for supper. Don't patronize me, Eric Whitman. I don't care what you do."

Another pause, then he said coldly, "No, I won't be home for supper. Just now, I'm not at all sure I'll *be* home. I want to know what in hell is wrong with you."

"It's quite possible that *I* won't be home either," she said hotly. "And nothing is wrong with *me*, Eric. I've thought all my life that a lot of things were wrong with me, and they still are, but it seems that, compared with some people, I'm in pretty good shape. At least I've always tried to be honest. If you should decide not to come home at all, I'm sure we'd muddle through, somehow."

She put down the phone gently. She was not crying this time, and not angry. She wished it were otherwise. She ached inside, desperately, and knew that she could not work anymore now, that she must get out of the house as quickly as possible, seek some distraction new to her tormented mind. Opening a desk drawer to put away her notes, she saw the rodeo tickets again, snatched them, put them in the pocket of her robe, and went upstairs to dress.

14

"Take your coat off, Chandra," boomed Bill Hazzard jovially. "Put it on the empty seat there. One thing we got here today is plenty of room. Too bad your husband couldn't make it, but, lord, gal, I'm glad to see you. You ain't changed that much since back in Chelsea, you know that?"

Bill was a big man, tall with large bones and bulging muscles, handsome in a rugged heavy way, with sleek black hair and quick observant brown eyes. Three other people were in the box, two cowboy friends of Bill's, who were through, as far as this particular rodeo was concerned, and the girl friend of one of them. Chandra hadn't caught their names. She scarcely heard as Bill recalled for them some old times in Chelsea. She didn't take off her coat. She felt cold with an inner chill that might never be warmed again. She did hold out the soft drink Bill had bought and shoved into her hand, so that liquor could be added to it from a pocket flask. Even the announcer's voice, blaring from the public-address system, the yelling of the crowd around her as a saddle bronc rider was thrown in the arena, the blast of the timing horn, seemed distant, dulled, diminished. I want to be part of something, she cried out within herself. I feel now as if I'm not really alive, as if, maybe, I don't exist at all.

But she felt the whisky in her drink. She had eaten nothing since last night—if she had eaten then, she couldn't remember. The drink hit hard, warming her insides with a welcome heat, but doing little yet to dispel the awful feeling of separateness.

"You say your mama's here for a visit?" Bill was saying. "I remember Miss Ethel real well. Fine lady. What does she think of this country out here? Don't like it? Well, I reckon that's understandable in a Texan, ain't it? Too cold for the ole soul? Yeah, me, too. You know, I heard it was down to eight degrees last night, though it's warmed up mighty fast, over fifty when I got here a while ago. The weather folks say there's another storm on the way, maybe git here by Monday. I sure hope we git the stock loaded out an' well on their way back to Texas before it hits, or we may not git back to the ranch for Christmas. I do admire this country though. No, it ain't my first time here. I been through this town several times, stayed a night or two from time to time. Been deer an' elk huntin' out in the western part of the state nearly ever' year for, le's see, about the last ten years. *That's* some country! Takes a lot of acres to feed a cow, though. I tell you, honey, it's just *real* good to see you. I'd of called or got in touch with you a long time back, if I'd of just remembered you lived here an' could of recollected your last name. I'll have to write ole Patsy, quick as I git back home, tell her I've seen you."

He leaned nearer, adding to the contents of her paper cup again, then turned to do the same for the others.

"I tell you what, Bud," he said to one of the cowboys, "this fancy dude bottle's near about empty. You got another one? Oh, fine, fine! Just keep the sonsabitches comin'. Now I want y'all to watch this here. This here is about the rankest bull ever come down the pike. A stock contractor can go through a whole lifetime of breedin' an' not see no ranker bull than this here ole forty-four."

Chandra looked at the arena, wondering what had happened to the time. Or had they changed the sequence of events since she had sat through all those rodeos so many years ago? She had arrived late, after the parading of the colors, then there had been saddle bronc riding. After that, there should have been some roping events, the bareback riding . . .

She had lied to them at home, saying that when Sheila had called, it had been to ask her to spend the afternoon as well as the evening in town. Ethel had looked at her with compressed lips and a disapproving frown.

"She's a good friend," Chandra had said, sounding defensive, a little hysterical in her own ears. "She's having some serious personal problems and—"

"Well, it ain't my business I know," Ethel had said shortly, "but it don't seem to me like ever'thin' around *here* is just as nice as pie. A body wants to do what they can to help out their friends, but that don't mean things around their own home can just be forgot, like they've quit bein' there."

"Oh, Grandma," Gail had said with a placating smile, "we can handle things around here for one afternoon and evening. You and me, together, ought to be able to take care of just about anything."

Ethel had turned back to the lunch clean-up, slightly mollified, perhaps, but still muttering ominously. Chandra had hurried away from the hurt, quizzical look of her daughter's incisive green eyes.

Now she looked at her watch. It really was past

four o'clock. What had she missed, completely missed?

"You ain't said two words," Bill was saying, leaning toward her again. "It is a right good performance an' I'm glad you didn't miss it, but tell me about your family. Besides ole Harry, I mean. Got a passel of young'uns, have you?"

"Harry?" asked Chandra dazedly.

Her body was suddenly and deeply stirred by his nearness, his touch against her arm. She *could* feel something, something more than the deep cold, hurt and anger. Thank God there was still warmth somewhere. She shifted a little, but did not move away from Bill.

He was laughing. "Oh, I know it ain't Harry. Your husband. I feel shame to admit it, but I've plum forgot his name."

"I think I've forgot it, too," she said lightly, "but we do have three kids at home."

"I've got four," said Bill. "Oldest boy's married and got me a grandchild on the way. Lord, that's hard to swaller. Don't feel no ways old enough to be a grandpa. Course he married young, like I did."

"Yes, didn't we all?" she agreed, laughing. "Is your wife from around Chelsea? Someone I'd know?"

"No, she come from out around Amarillo, an' she ain't my wife no more, ain't been for nearly five years. Yeah, we just couldn' hack it together no longer. She never did like ranch life, Alice didn't, so she found her a dude from Fort Worth owns a goddam shoestore, if you can swaller that one. . . . I've missed the kids. Missed 'em a lot. They come for a while, summers, that is, if they ain't got nothin' better to do. But the oldest boy, the married one, he don't live but about fifty miles from me now, so we're gittin' to know one another again now, a little." Bill laughed, shrugged, but there was a sadness in his eyes. "Mostly, what I know from him so far is, 'Dad can you let me have a little money?' An' what he knows from me is, 'Son, I didn' have nobody to lend to me an' you can just carry on the same way.' Hell,

I'd help him, time come he really needed it, but if he's old enough to git himself a wife an' kid, he's old enough to *think* he's got to make it on his own."

The crowd screamed and Bill yelled with them, cheering a girl barrel racer. When had the bull riding ended? Chandra wondered. She smiled, deciding not to worry anymore over what she might have missed. Bill handed her a newly purchased soft drink. She sipped some of it quickly, so that liquor could be added.

"Listen," he said, leaning to her confidentially again, "what are you doin' when this shindig is over? I mean, you ain't got to go straight home, have you? Or report in so you won't turn into a punkin or like that?"

"I'm meeting a friend for dinner," she said, then smiling in reply to his raised eyebrows, "a girl friend."

"Why, Miss Chandra," he said mildly, "I never thought no other kind. What time?"

"What?"

"Honey, you're gittin' confused. Better have a drink. What I say is, what time are you supposed to meet this here girl friend?"

"Oh. Eight o'clock."

"Fine, just fine. Le's you an' me go some place quieter when this is over an' talk about Chelsea an' all like that. I got to be back here a little before eight, so that'll work out just right. I don't always just set rared back in a box, you know. There's times I have to work, but I could have me some supper after this, you know, an' you could eat or not, whatever suits you. Maybe you know of some place that's a little bit quiet an' not too far from here. Any place I been all week's been noisier'n the inside of a hay bailer, all these cowboys an' such-like riffraff takin' over the town."

Chandra led in her car, and Bill followed in an old battered blue pickup. She felt almost happy now, almost peaceful. It was hours and hours before she would have to go home and take up the real thoughts and feelings again. Now, she wanted only to be calm—no matter that it was a rather giddy, fuzzy calm—and let herself be taken along with whatever events might bring. He was very real, Bill Hazzard—and what a coincidence that Hazzard was his name—real, warm, honest, alive, the largest thing in her life for these moments.

"You ever hear anything about ole Les?" he asked casually, when they were seated in a booth with drinks before them.

"Well," she said carelessly, "Mama tries to keep me posted. I really don't know exactly why. When she came, a few days ago, she brought me a clipping about him from the Chelsea paper. I don't *care* about ole Les, Bill."

"Oh, well, no, I didn' mean to say I thought you did. I saw that piece in the paper, too, about some car-sellin' award or the like, wasn't it? It was in the same paper where Patsy'd wrote that piece about your books. I remember thinkin' it was a kind of a coincidence there'd be pieces about both of you in the same paper. No, what I'd meant to say was, ole Les was a right good roper. I seen him work from time to time. He had a real fine horse, too."

"Yes," Chandra said grimly. "The damn horse literally ate us out of house and home."

"Yes, but with that horse—I remember it was a good, chunky little bay—an' with the ability it looked like to me he had, Les might have really got somewhere if he hadn' been so stuck on hisself, always worryin' about if his hat was on straight an' how many pretty little gals might have their eyes on him, things like that. I knew Les a lot better'n I knew you, back in Chelsea. Him an' me was closer in age, for one reason. But I was right sorry when I heard you two was gittin' married. Les ain't got mind enough but for one thing: hisself. I knew he didn' deserve no *good* wife, nor couldn' keep one for long. I expect he made your life some miserable."

"Yes, but that's all a long time in the past."

The waitress came to take their orders.

"Lemme have a big thick T-bone, honey. Just pass it over the fire, right quick. I want to see blood. French fried, salad with Thousand Island. Miss Chandra, ma'am?"

She ordered a steak sandwich, thinking that if she wanted to go on drinking and stay conscious, she'd have to eat something, thinking she'd rather stay with Bill than meet Sheila.

"I'm glad you're havin' some food," he was saying. "It's seemed like to me you're kind of peaked. Not that it ain't becomin'. Like I said before, you don't hardly look changed a bit from way back when I remember you at Chelsea, in high school, an' what change there is, is all for the better."

"Bill," she said slowly, "what's it like to—play around?"

"Huh?" He set down his glass, looked at her sharply, then away. Chandra had to laugh a little then, because the big craggy face was actually blushing.

"Oh," said Bill, grinning sheepishly. "Oh, I see. You're still thinkin' about ole Lester. Well, it's—all right, sometimes, I guess."

"I'm not talking about Les. I'm just thinking of people in general. Were you, for instance, always—faithful to your wife?"

The courage of liquor, Chandra thought and rather grimly took another large swallow of her drink.

Bill chewed a match stick thoughtfully. "You know, I hadn' hardly expected this subject to come up."

"Can't old friends from Chelsea be honest with each other? Discuss what interests them? I—I'm a writer, you know. I need to know about—experiences, feelings. It's just that I wonder how men really see that kind of thing. I've never felt, with anyone else, that I could just—ask. I feel—comfortable with you. Do you mind?"

"Mind? Hell, no. You just took me by surprise is all. I wouldn' be satisfied if you felt anything *but* comfortable.

Le's see now, the question . . . oh, yeah, me an' Alice. Well, no—in the way women always means it—no, I wasn't always faithful. Neither was Alice."

"The way women always mean it," she repeated carefully. "Is there a difference? Do men mean something else than women do when they say faithful?"

"Well, yes. At least that's been my experience. You see, when a woman says faithful, she means one woman—her. When a man says it, he can mean one—well, one love."

"And do all men see it that way?"

"I don't know, Chandra. I couldn' begin to say about *all*. A lot that I know do, I guess, but it takes all kinds, as the feller says."

"But you and—and Alice, you were married a long time . . ."

"Nearly fifteen years before we split," he said, leaning to light her cigarette with another match, then chewing on the stem of that one.

"And all that time, you both . . . ?"

"Oh, no, not all that time. I had ideas, like all kids does, about ever'thin' bein' sweet dreams forever, crap like that. An' Alice, she did, too. But things, real livin', ain't never like that."

"Never," she said stonily.

"Not that I've heard tell of, honey. Any two people together'll fight, you know, or git tired of one another, or maybe just bored after a while. Now I don't mean to say that ever'body fools around. I guess there's some don't, from bein' too prissy, or from lackin' the chances, or because they're honest-to-God convinced that that's not the way to do. Maybe they take their separate roads some other way, like she's all wrapped up in the kids an' her church doin's, an' he thinks about his job an' watchin' football on the TV. But, you know, the time just does pass when the bed's the big thing in two people's life. Nothin' can be so important an' last over all them years. People—adjusts to that, or else they're plum fools. At least, that's been my experience an' what I've heard from a lot of other men. Alice knew, after a while, that I slipped once in a while. I knew she did. The thing was, with this Fort Worth shoemaker, she decided she *loved* him. She was all hot to start in all over agin, with the dreams an' such-like. Do you see, atall, what it is I'm tryin' to say?"

"Yes," she said quietly and drained her glass.

The food arrived. Bill ate in silence for a time, still seeming discomfited, then he said jovially.

"What kind of work is it your husband does?"

"He's an electrical engineer and he—teaches a college class in drafting two evenings a week."

"Now that sounds like a feller to be proud of. He come from around here, did he?"

"No. He's from New York."

Bill chewed thoughtfully and said, "There was a time, way back, when I thought I wanted to go to college, study, what is it they call it, animal husbandry? My ole daddy was pure death on education, an' he was right, in my case, anyway. I see now that tryin' to git any more booklearnin' into me would have been like poundin' sand in a rat hole. But I can learn from experience, an' that's what I've done, all these years. I've got it pretty good, down where I work, an' I like the work, that's the important thing, so far as I'm concerned. But I'm buyin' into the business. I won't never own no great big share, but I'm a little partner. It's a good business, raisin' rodeo stock, if a person likes that kind of thing."

They talked about that for a time. Bill finished his meal and ordered pie.

"You ain't finished half that sandwich," he said with concern. "I hope you don't always eat this light."

Chandra laughed. "You can see I don't, can't you, from the weight I'm carrying?"

"Looks just right to me."

"Bill . . . I—I've never done this before. Could . . . ?"

"Ain't done what, hon?"

255

His hand reached across to cover hers where it fidgeted nervously with a damp paper napkin on the tabletop. It was a big, warm, strong hand, with black hair standing up all over the back of it, even along the tops of the fingers. Chandra looked at it hard as it covered her own hand, which felt cold and clammy and small.

"You want us to go someplace else together?" Bill asked softly, and held her eyes for a moment before she could look away. "We both got a couple of hours yet, before we have to be someplace else. My place, the place where I'm stayin', ain't a mile from here. I'd be pleased, Chandra, honored, if you want to come."

She felt herself flushing, then the blood seemed to drain from her face.

"I—don't know," she said, barely audibly. "I want to, but I—have to think about it."

"It don't do to think too much," he said gently and she shivered. "You want some coffee while you're thinkin'?"

"Could you just order me another drink, please," she said miserably and stood up. "I'll be back in just a minute."

In the grubby, cold, smelly ladies' room, she stared at herself in the mirror. I want to go. I *need* somebody. This is more than I can stand alone. He doesn't have to know anything about reasons, he doesn't care *why* I'd be doing it. He doesn't believe in too much thinking. He's kind, warm, strong, not just the strength that comes from big muscles. It would be good with him. For a few minutes I could . . .

She was seeing nothing in the mirror, no answers. Dazedly, she went into a cubicle and sat there, staring in revulsion at her scarred, disfigured thigh. If he noticed and said something pitying, or even kind . . . If he noticed and made a careful point of saying nothing . . .

After a time, she returned slowly to the booth, feeling small and shy and ashamed. She swallowed almost half her drink, feeling him waiting, understanding.

She said in despair, almost whispering, "I can't."

His eyes were gentle, thoughtful, not in the least angry. "I've been thinkin', too. There's a country-western song—prob'ly you don't care for that kind of music, but it was popular a while back—but this girl sings about 'Help me make it through the night.' It seems like to me that maybe you need somethin' like that. I ain't *got* to go back to the rodeo. I've got a kind of a ramrod out there could handle things, long's I'm there, early in the mornin', to see to the loadin' an' all. It would be just the one night. You understand that, I guess, after the way I been shootin' my mouth off. I'd like to sleep with you. I like to think you'd like it, too. But it don't have to be that. Or it could be that *an'* other things. Like if you just need somebody to stay with, or maybe to talk to . . .?"

"Bill, I just—can't," she whispered shakily. "You're awfully kind and—understanding, but I guess I'm just not as far along with this as I'd thought. I want to, honestly, but I just—can't. Not yet."

"It's all right, hon," he said gently, and now he took both her cold hands and held them, chafing them a little in his big rough palms and fingers.

"I—I'm sorry."

"Hell, you ain't got to apologize, Chandra. I'm sorry, too, but sometimes things click, sometimes they don't. Just do me one favor, all right?"

She nodded, mute with misery and embarrassment.

"Don't have no more to drink for a while, not when you've got to drive somewhere to meet that girl friend. No, now wait, you'll have to make that two favors. Don't cry neither. I purely never know what to do with a cryin' woman, an' I don't aim to have it. You hear me, little girl? Now, here, drink some of this coffee. I'm goin' to pay the bill an' git on the road."

Obediently, she took a sip of the coffee from the cup he held. Then she laughed shakily.

"Oh, Bill, I can't drink this. It's saturated with sugar."

"I don't know about your saturated, but your sugar's what makes it worth the drinkin'."

He picked up her glass and drained it, resting a hand on her shoulder.

"Sometime when I'm up this way again, fixin' to go huntin' or like that, I'll give you a call. I'm glad you made it to the rodeo. It's been good to see you an', whatever this is now, I know it'll work out for the best. You just wait an' see if it don't."

"Bill . . . thank you . . ."

"Ah, hell," he said with a small disparaging shrug as he turned away. "You finish that coffee now, hear?"

Sunday

15

When Chandra woke, early on Sunday morning, she found she had little memory of Saturday night. She had listened to Sheila dully, responded somehow, through an interminable dinner for which neither of them had any appetite. They had stayed on at the quiet restaurant, literally for hours, slowly sipping drinks after most of the food had gone back, untouched to the kitchen. They stayed because neither of them wanted to go anywhere else badly enough to move, both of them feeling a weary, resigned inertia.

Sheila had asked once if she felt all right. Chandra, shrugging, said she had had better days, but that what she was feeling now was mostly from drinking too much. Yet, almost immediately, they had each ordered another drink. Chandra drank carefully, slowly, just enough to keep the veneer of careless numbness, functioning in a hazy, not unpleasant dimness of mind.

Later, Sheila said irritably, "Well, what is it you've

got on *your* mind? Come on, out with it. I can certainly tell something's got you down."

"It's just—a lot of things," Chandra began casually and found herself going on with it, trying to make everything seem normal, for Sheila. "It's holiday time. I always seem to get to a point around this time of year, when I think I just can't go through with the rest of it. But that passes. At least, it always has."

Sheila nodded in weary sympathy. "*I* sure couldn't hack it, three kids *and* Grandma, in addition to a husband. But I suppose it *will* pass for you and you'll manage. You always do. You're quite a gal, you know that, don't you? I'd give quite a lot to have your— abilities, your self-sufficiency. Of course you know I wouldn't be saying such things if I weren't at least slightly drunk, but that doesn't make them any the less true. We've known each other a long time, and it seems to me that nothing, absolutely nothing is too much for you, more than you can handle."

You know me! Chandra thought bitterly, wanting to shriek at her. Well, the façade must be pretty damned good. God, I wish I wasn't so inured to living behind it, that someone could see, could know. I need help. I need someone just to listen and *be* there for me, even for just a little while. I wish I'd gone with Bill. But, no, I got up the courage to try the confiding bit. I started trying that years ago, with Eric, and look what that's got me.

Sheila was saying, "So what would *you* do—about Brian?"

"Oh, Sheila, I don't have any answers to that." Her voice sounded too desperate. She took another sip of the fresh drink.

"But, think about it. If you were me, wouldn't you be leaving him?"

"I can't be you," she said more steadily. "Maybe, if I were in your place, I'd have tried not to get so— involved with Brian from the beginning, but now—well, yes, if I were you, I suppose I'd leave him."

"You're right, of course. I should have known better than to make any real commitments, or to let him think I was making any, especially so soon after Randy. But it was all the problems with Randy that made me turn to Brian in the first place. Randy was such a bastard and he made Brian seem like—whatever the hell it was I was looking for. *Is* there something in the female makeup that *makes* us always run for a man? I tell you, this marriage crap is for the birds—nothing. Thank God, I'm about past the time of life when the question of kids can enter into all the rest of it. I've often been in a dither over that: shall I or shan't I? And Brian wanted a kid. That's been part—just a small part—of our difficulties. Actually, of course, what he really wanted was just more strings on me."

Sheila sipped her own drink and said pensively, "And you're also right that we couldn't change places, you and me. We think too differently, and you'd never do anything really foolish, would you?"

"You thought I was foolish to marry Eric, remember?"

Sheila smiled thinly. "Ever think I might have been just a tad jealous? Also, I thought you could have had a good career in the ad business, that you were already stuck with one kid and shouldn't take on any more domestic crap, for your own sake. But you knew what you were doing after all, didn't you? Or maybe it was mostly just dumb luck. You and Eric were a couple of moon calves over each other from the first, and the wonder to me is that it seems to have lasted. You've got a good one, as marriages go, and you've also managed to find your own fulfillment, your writing. Sometimes, I'm so envious of how your life has gone since those first years that I really resent you."

Chandra drew on a cigarette and said glumly, "Most of the time while I was getting through college, I thought I might like to go into some kind of counseling work."

"You'd probably have been pretty good at it," Sheila said, rather grudgingly.

"What I'd do," she said slowly, the words slurring only faintly, "is I'd get a client into my office, lock the door, get a quick once-over from him about what his problems were, and then I'd say, 'Is *that* all? You're tearing yourself apart over *those* little things? Just wait till you hear *my* problems.'"

Sheila laughed. The subtle request, plea, was lost on her. She went on talking, repeating things about how impossible and unreasonable Brian was, stifling her, how she'd surely lose her mind if she didn't get out of this town, away from business and nonbusiness matters, at least for a few days. She had a brother and his family in St. Louis; she hadn't seen them for years. Going there was at least a temporary solution. Hardly anyone, particularly Brian, would know where she was.

And Chandra, who had led people to believe she never had any serious problems, could cope with anything, sat there feeling as if she were breaking apart inside, convinced she could do nothing but go on sitting and trying to listen. After all, when she left here, she'd have to go back home, wouldn't she?

It was almost one o'clock when she did finally reach home. Gail and her friend Laurie were still up, watching a late movie on television.

"We're keeping it quiet down here for Grandma," Gail assured her mother. "She spent a couple of hours over at Soderbergs this evening and I think she had a good time. She went to bed about ten. Thegn and I said we'd go to church with her tomorrow and we all picked out a church together, from the phone book. Bruce said he might go, too. Anyhow, somebody'll have to drive us there and pick us up. I can't wait until *I* can start driving. Did you notice that we got more presents wrapped?"

Chandra looked dully at the sparkling Christmas tree with its growing pile of packages.

"So, generally, things have been okay around here?" she asked, trying for lightness.

"Sure," said Gail, and the two girls showed her the sewing feats they had accomplished with Ethel's help.

"She did this lace on the collar of my little sister's dress," said Laurie with admiration. "I'd never have thought of it, and couldn't possibly have made it, if I had thought of it. And she did it so *fast*. Isn't it just beautiful?"

"Grandma really seemed happy, working on this stuff, Mom, maybe happier than I've seen her since she got here. We kept telling her she didn't have to do so much of it, but she really wanted to. She liked acting like we couldn't have got anywhere without her, and we sort of liked acting as if she was right. Oh, and Dad called about ten. He says they're going to finish up the job now, if it takes all night. Those people from Philadelphia have made reservations on an eleven-o'clock flight in the morning. Thegn got his Christmas sock out and Grandma did some little repairs on it. He went to bed pretty early, Thegn did, and so did Bruce. Good grief, I was about to forget the *big* news. Bruce actually had his car's engine running late this afternoon. Man, you'd have thought we were going through a rocket count-down or something for a while there. Things were that tense. But it runs and sounds good, lots of roars and splutters and backfires, you know. You can still smell the exhaust all through the house. Bruce and Mark Soderberg got so excited and bemused, they forgot about opening the garage door, so I had to run out and do that when we began to choke in here."

"The weather people," put in Laurie, "say there's a big storm on the way. Lots of wind for us first, before the front comes through, then at least four inches of new snow tomorrow night."

"Won't that be neat?" said Gail happily, "with all of us home and almost ready for Christmas? Oh, by the way, Mom, don't forget about taking Granny shopping in a day or two. I don't know what she's said to you, but she's counting on it. Hey, Mom? You look really tired. Can I get you something, or do anything?"

Chandra went up to bed. She poured some whiskey from the bottle in the guest-room dresser and swallowed two sleeping pills. After tonight, she supposed, the pills would lose all efficacy for making her sleep. The effect might last longer if she used them only every other night, but she would take no chances with this night. She must get through each day, each night, as it came. She would not give up the near certainty of sleep, oblivion for this night for a possibility on the morrow.

After a few tense moments in bed, she got up again, put on her robe and looked in on Thegn and Bruce. From the top of the stairs, she could hear a murmur of sound from the television set and, now and then, the two girls, speaking quietly. Almost, she went down to make sure Mama was all right. The fear was on her again, the feeling that if she didn't keep a constant watch, something dreadful was going to happen. Tonight, though, after a short breathless time, the terror was mercifully quelled by an overwhelming drowsiness.

She came awake with an almost painful start, groping for the lamp. It was five-thirty, five-thirty on a Sunday morning in December, just a few days before Christmas. Her head throbbed miserably and there was the telltale tension, beginning between her shoulders and working up to a dull ache in the back of her neck. Four hours of sleep or less. *Why* did she have to wake up, with this tense wide-awake feeling that certainly promised no further sleep? She strained her ears tensely. The house was silent, but something had surely wakened her. Then she knew, as surely as if she'd seen it. Eric had come home. He had opened the guest-room door and stood there, the dim hall light behind him, and there had been tears in his eyes, his face unutterably weary, his shoulders stooped a little with his exhaustion.

Chandra felt a flood of warmth and love for him, at the same time loathing herself for her softness and vulnerability. But, somehow, he didn't understand, didn't know she knew, didn't know he was killing everything inside her, everything that mattered between them.

Then she flung herself out of bed, furious with herself because she wanted to forgive him. Tears of despair flooded from her eyes. Her body ached with the need to hold and be held. And now she knew for certain that this day's headache was not merely the result of drugs and alcohol. This was going to be one of The Headaches. She reached out for it as the portentous stiffness ached at the base of her skull. If it had been a concrete thing, she might have hugged it to her breast. It would mean release, that she could, legitimately, stop trying, for anything, could lie hidden and cowering in her bed, with the understanding of all the family and herself, could be alone with the pain and with scarcely thought enough left over for anything else.

From long experience, she knew she had a few hours before it became very nearly unbearable. From her purse, she took two pain capsules and swallowed them. The pills never stopped these headaches, but they did push the pain away a little so that she could, but only just, live with it. Also, if she didn't take the medication now, she might not be able to keep it down later. Another time, she would have tried desperately to go back to sleep, in the hope that the headache would be tricked into stillness. But going back to bed on this morning was useless. She was terribly restless, violently nervous. With hardly a sound, she went downstairs.

The coffee was still hot, though the pot had been unplugged. So he had come home. How dared *he* look at *her* with tears! But she couldn't help remembering other nights when he had had to work late. She would usually sleep, but only lightly, and when she heard his car, she would go down and put on the coffee, often find something for him to eat. They would sit together and go over the day, laughing over one thing, sighing over another, feeling they had been apart for ages, glad and grateful for any time the two of them could be alone together. But *had* he felt those things? Had he, perhaps, come home, not from working late, but from a meeting with some other woman? Was anything about him real, true, honest? Had he ever . . . ?

She took the coffee pot into her office, where she was able to maintain a reasonable concentration on the galleys until it began to grow light ouside. The wind was gusting up rather strongly, but, so far, the sky was clear, the dawn light sparkling.

Suddenly, she could bear the sleeping house no longer. She went upstairs, dressed quickly in jeans and an old shirt and came down again. She had dropped the pain capsules back into her purse. Her head ached sickeningly now, when she bent or moved suddenly. She went outside, with no idea of where she would go or what she would do. If the headache came on really hard, she had her wallet with identification, credit cards, a little money. She could spend a day or two at a motel. Yes, maybe that's what she should do. Just call them later and say she was all right, but would be away for a while, thinking. They'd manage all right, if they had to.

The day was fine, warm for the season, but with a stiffening breeze rising out of the west, in opposition to the sun. Eric's car was parked beside hers on the wide part of the drive, outside the garage door. Chandra knew now what she wanted to do, quickly, before the headache got worse. She would go down to the stable where Gail's mare was boarded and have a ride. She loved horseback riding and had done it with a fair amount of regularity all last summer and fall. Because of the weakness of her bad leg, mounting and dismounting could be a problem, but she always managed. Oh, yes, I always manage, and the thought was bitter gall in her throat. Still, a ride in this early morning would be nice. She would go up to the top of the hill, to the nearest woods, maybe come down the back side, along that trail where the kids were always getting into trouble with their jeeps and motor bikes. Coming back to the stable that way would make a ride of six or seven miles. If she still had the strength and the courage after that, she would go to a motel.

She parked by the stable, locked her purse in the car and went inside. The elderly stableman looked surprised at seeing anyone at this hour, but he was pleasant and garrulous.

"It's been a while since I've seen you, ma'am. Your pretty daughter was down here a few days back, to pay a visit to the mare, but I've not seen much of the Whitman family lately. Busy, I expect, just like we all are. You've picked a fine time for a ride, or as fine a time as a person's likely to find at this time of year."

He was saddling the little blond mare while Chandra fondled her warm soft muzzle.

"Warm today, ain't it, for the season? But don't be took in. It's too warm, you know. Fixin' up for a cold spell an' it looks like we got one a them ole chinook winds comin' before the cold can git through. Weather people say snow tonight an' I think this may be one time when they've hit 'er on the nose. It *feels* stormy this mornin'. The horses are showin' it, too. But I reckon I don't have to give you no weather warnin'. You folks have been around these parts long enough to know about such things. Apt to be a passel a wind today, though."

"I don't think I'll be gone long, Mr. Mapes," Chandra said as he led Cherokee to a mounting block. "Maybe a couple of hours or so."

"Well, you'd best keep a good tight rein on this lady to begin with," he counseled. "She's been gittin' plenty of exercise, runnin' loose out in our pasture, but look at that friskin'. She's glad to be rode agin."

Cherokee was gentle and not a young animal. In fact, Gail was now trying to find a way to get a more spirited horse without giving up her beloved Cherokee.

Gail, like most people, didn't relish weighing one good thing against another and having to make a choice, sorting priorities. And, if a choice were to be made, Gail would always settle on keeping the old, the familiar, the dependent, because she could not bear letting anything, anyone down. Chandra felt there was some significance in that thought for herself, but she did not see it immediately and refused to delve further.

Cherokee was certainly eager to go but, once they had started uphill, she slowed quickly enough to a sedate pace. Chandra stayed at least two blocks away from the Whitmans' street as they climbed up.

I didn't do it. The thought kept hammering at her mind as the pain in her head hammered at her body. I could have gone with Bill. I wanted to, but I didn't. Come now, Chandra, that was mostly because of your old stupid dread of having anyone see your scars. But it wasn't only that. Then it was being afraid you'd break down completely, with a little warmth and closeness to another person, and not be able to put yourself back together again. But it was partly that I thought I couldn't really go through with it with someone else. Not after Eric and I . . . But Eric has done it. *He* seems to have managed quite nicely, even to the extent of behaving as if he's the injured party in this whole filthy affair. And what would it have mattered, to anyone, who could have known, if I'd gone with Bill? Maybe it would have released some tensions, temporarily. At the least, it would have been a new experience for me, screwing around as a married woman. But I can't believe what Bill, and other people say, that it's just naturally like that. Some people *are* monogamous, because they want it that way. Because they're afraid to try anything else? No, because they're building on the monogamy and what it means to them. Building what? Well, what I *thought* we were building, only Eric wasn't. He doesn't care. How long has he not cared?

The strengthening wind pulled at her short hair. Why hadn't she thought to bring a scarf? They were almost at the top of Clover Hill now, getting into the scattered low trees. Though the wind was somewhat diffused on the ground, it was beginning to roar and rant up above, bending the treetops far over to the eastward. Another two blocks and they would be into the green-belt area, away from any houses.

The ache in Chandra's head was creeping around, from back to front, settling grindingly into her left temple and eye. She had had these headaches from time to time since adolescence. The kindly old family doctor in Chelsea had, when his various suggested remedies had no effect, said delicately that they probably had to do with her "coming into womanhood," and would very likely pass when those physiological changes were finished. He had made the same prediction about the severe cramps she had had for two or three days every month, and those had, to some degree, abated after she had had Bruce.

But the headaches kept coming. She had been to many doctors. Eric had made her see specialists. Some of these medical men seemed interested, even concerned, but then they seemed actually angry with her when their theories were disproved and their remedies did not work. The only thing she had found to do about the headaches was to take the codeine, which made the worst of the pain just bearable, and wait them out. Usually they lasted three or four days, if they were just Headaches. If they were Sick Headaches, they were usually of shorter duration but much more severe and included drastic vomiting and endless retching when there was nothing more to be vomited. The various doctors had told her a great deal about what the headaches were not. They did not result from a brain tumor or unusual brain waves; they were not migraine or cluster headaches. Perhaps they were a result of muscle spasms, brought on by tension, one had suggested rather lamely. If that were the case, he said, she should try to avoid tensions. She was, another doctor had said, seeming to feel that she should take pride in and comfort from the fact, one of 5 percent of the entire population of the country who had no desirable response to anything he prescribed. For the most part, the medical men seemed to come to feel, in the end, that the headaches were probably all in her mind. Perhaps, since they always came back to the strong codeine capsules as being the only thing that had any effect at all, she was simply hooked on it, perhaps inventing the headaches so she could keep being supplied with the capsules. A few of them had seen her in the throes of one of the headaches, pinched, haggard, drained of color, but maybe the mind could do that, too. So much, throughout her life, had been just in her mind, not real or valid at all.

Chandra began to cry helplessly. She knew she couldn't go away now, to an impersonal motel. She would turn Cherokee toward home in a minute, when she had regained some semblance of control, stop there, let someone else return the mare to the stable and bring home her car. She had to get to bed, the pain was becoming all-pervading. But her bed had to be near people who cared, even a little.

She had ridden across the rather flattened top of the hill now. The mare, choosing her own way for the most part, had started on the steep trail down the back side. Some of Friday night's snow still lay here, in patches of slush, and, as far as Chandra could see with her blurred eyes, the trail looked slippery with mud. The mare's footing was precarious, the trail very steep here, with an almost sheer drop at its right side. Trying to dry her eyes, she looked for a place where there was room safely to turn the mare. She couldn't possibly manage, today, to go on down this way and around the long way back to the stable.

Abruptly, Cherokee stopped on her own, sliding a little, and Chandra had to grab the saddle to keep from falling. The pain in her head jarred sickeningly with the jolt. The mare was snuffling, flinging her head, frightened. Chandra, feeling afraid now, feeling that the horrible and feared Thing was very near, looked down at the ground immediately in front of the mare. The mud had been thrown up out of the pre-existing ruts and she could see that a vehicle, a car? had gone over the edge. It must have happened, from the looks of the ground, just after the snow had begun on Friday night.

Firmly, trying not to let a tremor pass through her hands or voice, she forced Cherokee a step nearer the edge. She dared not dismount in this steep slippery footing, and she needed the height of the horse's back to see over the brush.

The small car lay there, amid crushed brush, almost a hundred feet below the trail. From its path, she thought it must have rolled completely at least once. It was muddy, partially obscured by scrub, but she could clearly see the crumpled left front fender: symmetrical spots and a broken bug antenna.

She sat there for what seemed a very long time, steadying and soothing the restive mare without really being aware of her. "I can do everything for The Bug except buy gas sometimes." She, Candy, had been at their house on Friday night, perhaps at the very moment when Shirley was saying, "I'm afraid somebody's going to have to be killed up there before they find a way to stop it." And, on Thursday night, this car had sat so flagrantly beside Eric's at the Knights Rest Motel.

Chandra remembered stories of people, trapped for days after an automobile accident. Stroking the mare's neck reassuringly, she called out hoarsely, "Hello." Then, louder, her voice sounding raucous and strange in the wind-tossed woods, "Is anyone there?"

She was shaking, having to force herself to keep looking while holding the mare firmly. She was terrified by the thought of a skeletal hand extended from one of the smashed windows, or a waving lock of that lovely straight blond hair. After horror-filled, interminable moments, she let Cherokee draw back, turned her carefully and rode slowly back the way she had come.

16

When she pulled her car into the driveway at home again, it was not quite nine o'clock. Bruce was out front in his bathrobe, looking for the newspaper.

"Geez, Mom," he said, shocked, "you just now coming home?"

"No. I was here last night. I've just been out for a ride on Cherokee."

Her head pounded with relentless fierceness, but she hurried up to him, hugged him and, standing on tiptoe, kissed his downy cheek. Her joy at being home could, for a moment, almost eclipse the pain. She wanted to be here, with all of them.

Bruce, slightly embarrassed by the demonstrativeness, said, as they went into the house, "Did you know I got my car running yesterday? I mean to have her ready for safety inspection before Christmas."

"You'd better hurry then," she said pleasantly. "There aren't many days left. And, Bruce, have you bought any Christmas presents?"

"Well, no, but I guess I'll get around to it."

"Please do," she said gently. "It really *is* more blessed to give than to receive, you know, and the rest of us just can't help feeling a little hurt when you never want to spend the time and money *and* thought for sharing in the giving."

"Yeah, well, I'll get back to my car this afternoon. Once it's in shape, then I'll have time to think about other things. Me and Gail and the brat are going to church with Grandma this morning. Can we use your car?"

She gave him the keys and was pleasantly surprised when he also took her coat to put it away.

"Well, Chandra Lynn, where have you been *now?*" Ethel greeted her. "Gail said you come in again after midnight last night. I heard you, a course, but didn' know exactly what time it was. We thought you was still upstairs in the bed asleep."

At the stable, Mr. Mapes had given Chandra a cup of water with which she had swallowed more pain capsules. Moving very carefully now, she poured herself coffee, sat down at the table and lit a cigarette.

"I've been for a ride on Gail's mare, Mama."

"Oh, good," said Gail. "She sure needs the exercise. How is she this morning?"

"Fine. She was asking about you."

"I meant to go riding this afternoon. I really did, but the wind's coming up pretty bad, isn't it?"

"It's at least a small gale already."

"You better eat somethin' for sure this mornin', young lady," decreed Ethel. "Out half the night a-galivantin', an' then off an' gone again this mornin', without nobody a-havin' the least idy where you're at. At least a-ridin' around on a horse ought to of made you hungry."

Somehow, the words did not, for a change, chafe or seem badgering. Chandra had fleeting memories of those times in high school when she had had those terribly painful cramps—or a headache like this. How wonderfully good it had been then, to get home, finally, tell Mama what ailed her and go to bed, safe in the knowledge that, for a little time, she need not really think, need not do anything except rest and try to feel better.

"Why didn't you leave us a note, Mom?" Gail was asking.

"I guess I just—didn't think of it," she said vaguely. "I'm sorry."

"Eat some of this toast," Ethel was ordering. "Git that down an' you'll maybe want a egg or somethin'."

From her symptoms, Chandra was afraid this was going to be one of the headaches with vomiting, but she obediently picked up the slice of hot toast and nibbled at it.

Thegn was saying, "Daddy left us a note on the

kitchen bulletin board and I could read it, mostly. It said, 'Home after five and to bed.' We been quiet so he can sleep. Dad writes nice and clear."

"We're a-goin' to church this mornin', me an' all three of the children. You better come along with us."

"I can't, Mama. I'm afraid I'm getting a very bad headache and I still have to finish—"

"You ain't got to tell me you've got the headache, child. It's that, what you used to git when you was a girl sometimes. I don't see why they ain't been some cure found for that in all these years. Do you go to the doctor about it? What I do for the headache is take a aspirin or two an' just keep a-goin'. I know, though, they's some can't do that. You *look* like you've got the headache, peaked an' all peenched up, but I've seen it a-comin'. Ain't I tried to git you to slow down, sleep at decent hours? It's all a this night life, Chandra Lynn. A body's got to try to git some sleep an' rest sometimes, in the night, when the good Lord meant it to be. An' it wouldn' surprise me a bit if them sleepin' pills didn' have somethin' to do with you a-gittin' this headache right now. Anyway, I *have* seen somethin' like this a-comin' on, but I thought if you still felt like goin' out a horse ridin' in that ole cold wind, maybe you might could manage to come to church too."

"Where's Laurie, Gail?" asked Chandra, trying to swallow morsels of toast.

"She had to go home as soon as we got up. You know, this afternoon is when Jean and Pat Sellars are having the Christmas party at their house. Bruce and I are both invited."

"Yes, I remember."

"Well, when I talked to Robin Murray yesterday, about staying here some of the time, she said she might come home with me after this party. Will that be okay?"

"Yes, I suppose it is, if everybody is willing to fend for himself."

"Oh, sure," said Gail breezily.

274

"I'm not going to bother with any party today," said Bruce. "I'll be working on my car."

"You'd better not," said Gail, "if Mom's got one of her headaches. It sure was noisy yesterday."

"I can push it outside today. It's going to be warm and right in front of the garage, it's kind of sheltered from the wind. Okay, Mom?" He looked a little desperate.

"Yes, all right."

"Mommy," said Thegn, "we still got to buy presents for Magic and Prince Charming."

"We'll try and get that done tomorrow."

"Will you feel better tomorrow?"

"I certainly hope so."

"And Grandma hasn't had her shopping spree yet," said Gail, then rather grimly, "and neither has Brucie."

Bruce gave her a glare and was about to speak when Ethel said,

"Now don't worry your Mama about such as my shoppin' spree when she ain't a-feelin' good."

"I could take you shopping, Granny," offered Bruce, suddenly amiable again. "Maybe look around a little bit myself."

"Oh, honey, I know you could. I know you're a real good driver an' all like that, but you an' me might not know which stores to go to for certain things. I expect I'd better wait till your Mama can go along and if"—sigh—"that don't git done, well, a body just don't always git *ever*thin' they expect."

"Daddy would go with you, Grandma," offered Thegn. "He's real neat when he doesn't have to go to work. He knows what's in all the stores, and he wouldn't want you to miss going shopping, especially if it's to buy Christmas presents."

They all laughed, except for Ethel, who had missed the last words and had to have them repeated.

"Well, all three of y'all better git dressed in a hurry," she said, still smiling fondly over Thegn. "We don't want to be late to a new church an' all."

Ethel herself was already dressed, complete with hose and low-heeled dress shoes. She only lacked her make-up and the combing out of her curled hair.

Chandra sat on at the table, looking through the paper, feeling, through her pain, a strange peace and comfort. She felt she knew now what she wanted, what she could and could not have. Surely, the girl was dead. And she could feel sadness about that, so beautiful, so young, but *her* life would go on and, already, she was trying, rather groggily, to put the pieces together again. Ethel's voice startled her.

"That neighbor of yours, Shirley—is that it? I never can remember names—she's the nicest person. I guess you know I went over there a little while last night, for her to set my hair an' dry it. It never got plum dry under that thing. She thought it did, so I didn' tell her no diff'rent. She said for me to be sure an' call this mornin' when I was ready for it to be combed out. I hate to do that..."

"I'll comb it, Mama, if you think you can trust me."

"Trust you? Why, you used to do up my hair all the time, when you was a girl in high school. You fixed your own right pretty then, too, when you cared a little somethin' more than people does nowadays about their looks. Trust you? I don't know what you mean, a-sayin' a thing like that, Chandra Lynn."

She brought her comb, brush and a box for the hairpins. Chandra took down the thinning, blued gray hair and combed it out gently.

"Oughtn' you to git back in the bed?" asked Ethel, turning to face her after approving her hair in a mirror.

"Yes, I mean to, in a little while. I think I can finish reading my galleys, once I get into a good position where I can lie still."

"You'd better try to git some rest," snapped Ethel, but the concern was there, in her eyes. "Them don't *have* to be done today."

"I told the editor I'd mail them tomorrow. I hate to

miss a deadline or go back on my word. I never have done that in the writing business."

"Well," murmured Ethel dubiously, then she said with more interest, "They's just a whole lot left a that roast I cooked yesterday, you nor Eric a-bein' here to help eat last night. Wouldn' it be all right if we had that for Sunday dinner, with some veg'tables an' a salad?"

"That would be fine, Mama."

"I expect you'll say you ain't hungry. I know you never used to could eat much when you had one a them headaches, but, I tell you this, good eatin' habits is important too. They even say that on the television. I believe if you'd just git yourself reg'lated right an' quit that ole smokin', you'd be a whole lot healthier an' so would the rest of this fam'ly."

"Mama, could you just sort of—take over today? I'm afraid I'm going to have to stay in bed and try to get rid of this—"

"Take over! Why, honey, don't you know that all I want to do while I'm here is be some help? No, I won't *take over,* for it's y'all's house, but I'll help all I can. Now, Chandra Lynn, it's not my business, I know, but Thin's mentioned that you've moved out of your room with Eric. Honey, is somethin' awful wrong?"

"No, Mama," she said slowly. "I knew Eric would need his sleep, with all the extra work, and we have been keeping pretty different hours. It will be—all right now, I think."

The wind worried at the house, buffeting and slamming, flinging coarse dust as high as the upstairs windows. Chandra, her vision blurred now by pain, saw by the alarm clock that the churchgoers would probably be back home in another twenty minutes or so. She sighed, fumbling as she straightened the last few galley sheets and put them in place. She was through with them. If she felt strong enough to get up and move around without being totally wiped out by the unrelenting pain in her head, she would get them ready to mail, sometime during this day. She needed to get some Christmas gifts wrapped, too, in fact, she had thought of doing that before coming back to bed, but their gifts were hidden in the big closet in—their room, and she hadn't wanted to wake Eric, hadn't felt like facing him again just yet. Then, without her having heard a sound except for the noise of the wind, Eric was standing in the open door to the guest room.

"Hi," he said guardedly.

"Hello, Eric." Her voice was noncommittal.

He moved a few steps into the room. "You look lousy."

"Thanks. You'd make a first-rate diplomat." She tried to smile, but it wouldn't happen.

"I only meant—"

"Yes, I know. It's all right. You look absolutely exhausted yourself."

"Headache?"

"Yes, but I've just finished with these galleys."

"Are you vomiting this time?"

"I did, just once. Maybe that's all of that."

"I'll bring a basin so you won't have to—"

"It's all right. I'd really rather not talk about it."

He looked around the room uncomfortably and his eyes fell on the publisher's envelope again. "Did you *have* to do the galleys? They could have waited an extra day or two, after all that's happened with this book."

"I thought I did. I'd said I'd get them mailed tomorrow."

"I'll wrap them for you, then, shall I?"

"I'd appreciate that." She couldn't quite meet his eyes and he kept trying.

"Have you got all your notes in here?" he asked. "And what about copies of the original manuscript pages?"

"Everything's there. I had two copies of the original in my files, so I just sent pages from one of those."

"Do you think that's a good idea? Wouldn't it be better if you had two complete copies? I could take these into the office this afternoon and—"

"No, please don't do that. Someone would find you there and they'd come up with some job or consultation that just had to be done. This will be fine, for this once. I—I meant to get some of our gifts wrapped today as well."

"I'll do that," he said. Then he came and knelt beside the bed, kissing her gently. She held onto his hand.

"Is there anything else I can do for you? Get you?" His voice was still wary, as was hers.

"Well, maybe get yourself some coffee, or go back to bed. You really do look pretty awful, you know."

"Why is the house so quiet? I don't think I've ever heard this house so still in the daytime. Or is it just that the damned wind's so noisy?"

"Mama and all the kids have gone to church. I'm afraid they'll be home soon."

He frowned quizzically. "They have? How did that happen?"

"I'm not at all sure, but I suppose no permanent harm will come of it. Is your job really finished?"

"Yes. How was Sheila?"

He sat on a chair near the bed, still looking uneasy, uncertain.

Surely, Chandra thought, it was just the one night, one girl, one time. That's not so terrible, I suppose. I can live with that, if only it doesn't happen . . . She closed her eyes. That seemed to ease the pain a tiny amount and she didn't have to try to keep avoiding his eyes.

She said, snapping herself back to the present, "She has left Brian. I suppose she's in St. Louis by now, to spend the holidays with her brother's family. When she gets back, she's looking for something big, you know, really important, to go on with. God knows what she's going to come up with next."

Eric sighed, shaking his head.

She rolled over, propping herself on her elbows, and reached for a cigarette.

"Probably, you should just try to sleep," he said, but he lit the cigarette and moved the galley envelope off the bed "But—wouldn't our room be a better place to try sleeping? It's quieter, farther from the stairs . . ."

"I—I think I'll just stay in here. . . . Eric, I want to tell you something. You remember I told you about Bill Hazzard, those rodeo tickets he sent us?"

He frowned, trying to recall, looking so weary that she closed her eyes again.

"Vaguely," he said. "It was several days ago, wasn't it?"

"Yes, but the tickets were for yesterday afternoon's performance. I went to the rodeo before meeting Sheila. Then I went with Bill for supper."

She didn't go on. What else had she meant to say, anyway? She waited, eyes closed, letting the sort of silence she hated drag on interminably.

"If it—helped, I'm glad you went," Eric said finally, quietly. "It seems that, in spite of the headache, you are feeling better in some way that I really don't understand. At least we're talking again. That's a relief for me. I hope it is to you. I also hope that, sometime, when you can, you'll tell me . . ." He floundered into silence again, but then said more brightly, "Chan, I've been thinking, a lot, about the place we'd like to find in the back country. Let's start looking, as soon after Christmas as we can. I am ready, if you are."

"Eric, it hasn't had anything to do with that, it's—"

"That's all I've been able to think of, when I've had a few minutes here and there to try to understand whatever it is that's happened these past few days. It's the only—answer I could find. We did talk about it, on that last night before I really got into this consultation. But I really mean what I'm saying about the place in the mountains. I've given it a lot of thought and it feels like the right thing. I'll find things to do, some kind of job, or maybe get more serious about cartoons and painting. If that's *not* what's been wrong, though, I wish you could tell me. You surely know by now that I'm no good at guessing games. I want, more than anything else, not to hurt you, not ever. I know your mother is driving you nuts. I think I've got a pretty good idea of what having your book slaughtered like that must feel like, and then there's all the kids' stuff and the holidays. But I've gone wrong somewhere, for you, and I don't know what to do about it. I want to try to make it right if I can."

Her eyes had filled with tears and she spoke through trembling lips. "You honestly don't know?"

"Honestly, I don't, Chandra, but it must be pretty bad."

Then, without her realization that he had moved, he was holding her. After a moment of stiffness, she lay still in his arms, feeling his warmth, his strength . . . his love?

"I—I can't talk about it yet."

"I'm sorry. I know you're feeling rotten and this is not the time . . . but how can I set about trying to make it right, if I don't know what it is?"

"Eric, please, just be here. I don't mean in this room or . . ."

"Yes, I'm here," he said gently. "Can I get a couple of your pills for you?"

"I've already taken enough," she said through her tears. "Besides, I think they'd come right back up again."

"I'll bring a basin. You don't need to have to get up and maybe try to wait for one of the kids to get out of the bathroom."

When he came back, he touched her hand very gently and she opened her eyes for a brief moment.

He said, "We have quite a lot of time before I go back to work a week from tomorrow. There'll be time to talk, if you want it, and I'll honestly try to participate, really make it a two-way thing. I mean it, truly, about the country place. I've always thought it would be nice, but I've had a lot of scruples and doubts, too. Now, I think I want it as much as you always have. Try to sleep now, all right? I love you, Chandra. I'll try to keep things in the house as quiet as possible."

When would he talk about it? she wondered groggily. Perhaps he never would; perhaps *she* never would. But it was over; she was sure of that. He just couldn't be that much of an actor. Perhaps it had been some sort of accident, one of those odd coincidences, a sudden flaring of passion . . .

Behind closed lids, Chandra could see the little car again, lying battered in the brush. She would never have believed she could be so calm about it, about doing nothing. She could call someone and report having seen the car, without giving her name or any other information. But, really, there was no point in that. The thing had surely happened on Friday night, from the look of the tracks. Either the girl had been taken out soon after that, dead or alive, or she was certainly dead now. Friday night's temperature, after the snow cleared out, had been near zero. Exposure . . . But how can I be so cool about it? she asked herself in drugged wonder, so cold? Because I know now, finally, some of the things I truly want in life and, among the first, is to try to forget that Candy Miller ever existed.

All I've done, all my life, in the face of real threats, is cower and whimper and feel guilty and responsible. Maybe that hasn't shown on the outside—look at the way Sheila and so many other people see me—but it's how I've been, inside. This time, I'm standing up for myself, for what's important to me, Chandra Lynn Barrie Whitman, and I'm doing it by doing nothing.

The other things I want . . . this house, the children, holiday time, even Mama. I want what I can have of peace and happiness, of not feeling guilty, deceived. I want to be *real,* to myself, then I can be me with anyone else and not feel stiff and self-conscious and—

yes—ashamed of who and what I am. And, more than all those other things put together, I want Eric. I can't bear the thought of living without him. I can't give him up, and I won't. She was grinding her teeth in desperate determination. Finally, she began to relax. Oh, Eric, Eric, I need you! I love you! With tears still wet on her face, she fell into a shallow, unrestful sleep.

Monday

17

She was only partially conscious of the passing of time. Sometimes she slept, fitfully or deeply and when, on Monday evening, the terrible pain in her head began reluctantly to withdraw, there were great swatches of time during the past thirty-six hours for which she could not account. When she woke, with a clearer mind, to darkness outside and a quiet house, it took a long time to decide if it were Sunday night or some other time. She remembered what seemed hours of vomiting, then retching on emptiness, and the pain, but, in great part, dreams seemed more clear than reality. Many times, she had seen Eric, standing on the rough hillside above Candy Miller's crumpled car, crying, alone in the roaring wind. She had seen her children, looking at her with sad, questioning, haunted eyes. She had dreamed herself alone, looking at Eric across a great gulf, his back to her, Candy's long fair hair streaming over his shoulder, the sound of his laughter coming to her faintly. There had been the vacuum cleaner dream again, many times, herself, tiny and screaming, unseen, unheard, by anyone. And then there was a dream of the five of them, she and Eric and the children, in a lovely place of evergreen trees and a laughing stream, and they were happy, free of fear, guilt, recrimination. But this was followed by a dream of Mama, pointing an accusing finger, saying balefully, "I just don't know about you, Chandra Lynn, how you come to be the selfish, hard person you are. I know you wasn' raised to be that-a-way."

For what she was certain of reality, there had been the normal sounds of the house, Thegn's laughter, the dog barking, Bruce doing his thing on the stairs, the telephone ringing and, outside, the wind roaring and whining. Often, someone had been in the room with her, Gail coming to whisper the question, "Can I do something Mom, anything at all?" Thegn saying, rather desperately, "But I *have* to kiss Mommy good night." Ethel, "Chandra Lynn, you must try to eat just a little bite now. You asleep, honey?" Then, in the hall, with the guest-room door still partially open, "Well, I'm sure glad you've called a doctor. I guess it ain't my business, but it's seemed like to me it ought to of been done hours ago. Seems to me like, bad as she looks, she ought to be in a hospital right now. I tell you this, Eric, I'm just worried plum to death." And Eric, Eric must have been there almost all the time, however long it had been.

Ethel's overheard words had terrified Chandra beyond all reason. She felt as if she were choking. "Eric, I don't want to be in a hospital. Please! I just want to be here, at home. I'll be better soon. I know I will."

Then the gentle reassurance of his warm, strong hands, holding her cold, listless ones. "All right, Chan, no hospital, I promise. Dr. Greer is coming here to have a look at you, that's all."

"But he won't. Doctors never make house calls anymore. I can't go to his office, it hurts too much. I'd rather die than try to get up and go anywhere."

"He's coming here. I've talked to him."

And later, after a time of fuzziness, the doctor saying in a far-away voice, "A shot of demerol. It'll help you sleep. I want you in my office, young woman, for tests, as soon as you feel up to it."

More dreams: Chandra being looked over by a group of men, as if she were an animal being offered for sale—or slaughter? Bill Hazzard was the only one she recognized. Each of them winced and drew back when he saw her scarred, twisted leg. "But I'm just as worthwhile as any other person. I didn't *want* Glen to die or . . ." She tried to scream at them as they faded into mist.

Reality: Eric, setting up a rickety old cot beside the guest-room bed. "Eric, don't sleep there. You'll be so uncomfortable. Please lie here, with me, and hold me." "I'll stay here for a little while, darling, until you're sleeping again. The cot will be fine for me and you'll have a better chance of a good sleep alone."

Dream: Chandra, surrounded by policemen, huge distorted figures scowling, accusing. "Failure to report an accident," great, booming voices whose echoes went on forever. She was crying. "But it's my *life,* don't you see," she tried to explain.

Then Eric was holding her. Was this real or not? She clung to him, trembling, fearing his disappearance. "It's all right, Chan. Darling, it's all right. Rest now." "Eric, don't leave me!" "No, I won't—ever." "I will try to fight for what I want, what I *have* to have, and I won't feel guilty about any more things, not any. I can do it, I *can*. Why does it seem so wrong, just because I'm the one who's doing it?" "Try not to cry so, love. It can't do anything but make you feel worse." "But tell me, why do *I* always have to be wrong?" "But you're not. You almost never are. You've put yourself through so much hell without any real cause. Everything really is all right. Please, just try to rest." "Why couldn't you have said things like that to me before when they could have counted? Now, you don't know. You don't have any idea what I've done. You'd hate me if you knew, but I can't help that. I *will* look after my interests, what's most important to me. You—" "Chandra, darling, I'm sorry. I just can't understand what you're saying when you're crying so. Here, try to swallow one of these pills Dr. Greer left. You have to rest. Just relax and try to rest." "But don't go, Eric, please . . ." "No I'm here." Finally, quieter now, "What time is it?" He moved to look, she clinging to him fearfully, "Just before five." "What day?" "Monday, Monday morning." "The children . . . ?" "They're asleep. Everyone's fine. Everything's all right. How's the headache? A little better now? Is there anything I can do for you, anything at all?" "Don't ask me for reassurance, Eric, not now. I'm not at all sure I can give it, ever again." His hand, gentle on her hair, her face; sleep, coming blessedly.

She lay in the darkened room now, knowing that it must be Monday evening, hearing faint sounds of dishes and talk from downstairs, trying to separate the real from the nightmare of the past hours. The pain was gone. She moved her head cautiously and there was only the stiff soreness in head and neck, a stiffness, also, in the muscles of her abdomen, an aching in her throat. She felt an inner trembling, a terrible weakness but, strangely, an emptiness, calm and peace. She had come through something more than the illness, something about which she would not think now. She was whole again, more or less, in her home, with her family nearby. The family, too, was whole. Eric had been here all the time, going through this thing with her, as much as he could, holding her, close. She had not been alone. She was convinced that his nearness, his painful yearning to help, had been very real. Whatever feeling he had for Candy Miller was superficial, surely. Now she, Chandra, only had to put back the pieces of her life that had shattered last Thursday night. She would try, never again to think of the Knights Rest Motel. All that was over. With her eyes closed, she could see again the crumpled car, looking very small and battered in the ravine. Thirty-six hours more had passed since she'd actually seen it. And it was over, ended. Eric no longer had a choice. By doing nothing, she had surely won. God, fate, whatever it was, was on her side for a change, for the time it mattered most in her . . . Only, what choice would he have made, ultimately, *if* he'd had one?

She writhed in renewed misery, and this pain was not in her head, could not be got at with drugs. She would have to live with it, with this pain, this question. She *could* live with it. On the surface, their life, their marriage, was whole. She had her priorities straight now. She knew, with whatever she might consider his failings and shortcomings to be, precisely how much Eric meant to her. She could walk away—or ride away—and leave that car, not knowing, never wanting to know . . .

Slowly, carefully, feeling very frail, she got out of bed. Dizzy and trembling, she crossed the hall to the bathroom. When she came out, Eric was there, putting an arm about her, half carrying her back to bed, pulling the covers snugly around her shoulders.

"How are you?"

She smiled wanly, holding onto his hand for a moment. "I'm all right now."

"Are you? Really?"

"Yes. It doesn't hurt anymore. Now I'm just—tired."

"I should think you would be. We've just finished supper. Could you eat anything at all? It would make us all very happy."

Ethel had "strengthinin' broth" ready. She ate a little of that, with some crackers and tea.

"What I'd really like," she confided to Eric, "is a cup of very strong coffee."

He smiled, shaking his head. "No, not now. I think that would just about finish off your mother. Maybe later I can sneak you a cup."

Each of them came, one at a time, into the dimly

lit guest room, to talk to her briefly. They seemed awed, still a little frightened. Chandra felt she was coming back slowly, from a far dark place. She was weak, weary, quiet.

After Thegn was in bed, Eric came back to sit with her.

"I should have a shower," she murmured.

"That can wait till morning. Will you please, come back to our room now?"

"When I have to get up again. Now, I just want to—lie here."

"All right. Is there anything else you want? The coffee, maybe?"

"No, I guess not, just yet. Eric, could you—talk to me? Just about anything. I want to be quiet, but I need to hear someone's voice—your voice."

She felt puzzled, vaguely curious, about the rather smug grin that spread over his tired face. He held her eyes for a moment, prolonging whatever he had to say, whatever it was that seemed to please him so much.

"There *are* a couple of things you might want to know about, I guess. You had a couple of calls today from New York. One was from Ms.—Bartleson—is it? The new editor you've got yourself at the publishing house. She read the galleys over the weekend, and the correspondence file about SEASON OF THE WOLF between you and Liscombe. She said to please send her copies of the original manuscript pages where you want changes made, and that she thought all of it could be arranged to your satisfaction. She didn't mention the cost of changing galleys or anything like that. In fact, I got the feeling she might be someone we'd both like. I told her the galleys and manuscript pages were already on their way and that you'd call her after the holidays to see if everything is working out."

Chandra sighed and lay back limply. She had been optimistic about working things out with the book and now, after the terrible few days between her discovery of its mangling, the assurance was more than a little anticlimactic, though she was relieved. Eric was still looking smug, an expression he rarely wore.

"What else?" she asked, wanly meeting his smile.

"Barbara Liscombe called."

"She *what?*"

"She wanted to know if you wouldn't like to 'come over' with her to the new publisher she's working for."

"That's—that's—incredible!" murmured Chandra fiercely.

"It is indeed, but I just told her I didn't know. I said you'd call her back as soon as you were feeling better, and talk about it. I thought it would do you both good for you to be the one who tells her off."

"Yes," she said grimly, "that will be a great pleasure for me."

The room was silent for long minutes, till she said wistfully, "But, Eric, please go on talking to me, just about anything."

He smiled diffidently, made a small deprecating gesture. "I'm not much good at just talking, but I guess you know that by now. When you ask me like this, I seem to just—go blank. I wish I wasn't like that. But I'll try. Will you mind if I smoke?"

"Give me a cigarette, too"

"Are you sure you ought to . . . ? Okay, sorry."

A night light dispelled the immediate shadows. Chandra lay back on her pillows, her eyes closed, except when she looked at the ashtray in her hand.

"Well, let's see," Eric began valiantly. "I guess Bruce told you the latest on his car. I've worked on it some with him this afternoon. He's really sticking with the job this time. I think he actually might be able to get it past safety inspection in another day or two.

"I suppose they told you, too, that he drove Gail and Ethel to the shopping center this morning, when you were finally resting better. Mom thought she had to wait for you to go with her, but we told her you might not be feeling up to that time. She had to buy gifts for the boys, so she decided she could do it with Gail, and I've been led to believe that Bruce did some quick shopping of his own, though he hasn't brought down any wrapped packages that I know of. Gail and Grandma wrapped her things, and Thegn and I did most of the ones from our closet. Thegn's having a lot of fun this year, sharing secrets. Bruce mailed your galleys while they were out. Ethel just couldn't get over how many people were out, doing things, when it was snowing. I don't think she really believes yet, that she did it herself. We got about a dozen Christmas cards in the mail. The postman didn't get by here until nearly five."

He leaned to tap ash from his cigarette. Chandra opened her eyes and they looked at each other for a moment. Eric smiled quizzically, saying he was a poor conversationalist and knew it. Chandra's return smile was warm, appreciative. Love for him filled the still, empty spaces in her, welled up into her eyes. His hand covered one of hers and she let her eyes close again.

"They—we've all been worried about you," he said softly. "It's been all I could manage to stop Mom from staying up here with you. But—I wanted to do that. She's been up and down the stairs all the time, with hardly a word about her authoritis. I'm afraid she's probably saving all that for you to hear. Really, she's been great. I think she's felt—well, more worthwhile, needed, important, these past couple of days.

"We had a talk last night, Ethel and I, after the doctor had been here. She's already been thinking of putting her place up for sale, and says she wouldn't even consider living with any of her young'uns. She knows some old lady in Chelsea who rents out part of her house since her husband died. Ethel says she's been studying about taking that, if she decides to move. She's afraid the daughters won't want the home place sold. I told her it's her place and she ought to do with it what she thinks best. She seemed to like hearing that, a lot."

He put out his cigarette and there was a long silence. Finally, Chandra opened her eyes and drank some ice water. She had a terrible thrist that, seemingly, could never be assuaged.

After a time, Eric said awkwardly, "You must know, too, that it's been snowing almost steadily since about the middle of last night. First we had some really fierce winds, then things calmed down, after the front passed through, and it's beautiful out, seven or eight inches of snow, lying smooth and even and pretty. I haven't enjoyed a day at home so much in a long time, once you were sleeping and really resting.

"I've spent some time in the studio, working on special cards to go with our presents. That is, I worked on them, once I'd found most of the stuff I needed. Did you know Mom got in there and 'straightened up'? I've been thinking that, once we're living in the real country, maybe I'll have more time and can make all the cards we send out. I'd like doing that. I've always wanted to, you know, and I suppose something commercial might even come out of it.

"Chan, I've talked to the kids about our moving. It's a kind of panicky thing for Bruce and Gail, but they understand we have our own lives to plan too, and they'll be all right. What Thegn wants to know is if he can have more animals of his own if we live in the country, and if we could have one of those houses like he's studied about, in Holland or somewhere, where the stable's part of the house, with Cherokee, maybe a cow and a couple of goats in residence. He says people who live in houses like that always have goats."

Another long silence. The sound of something on television came very faintly up from the family room. Otherwise, the house was very still. The sound of a car, passing slowly along the snowy street outside seemed very remote.

Eric said stiffly, "We don't have any extra people in the house tonight. I've asked the kids to try to cut down on that some, at least for overnight guests. Sometimes, it's seemed to me that this house had become an outpost of the Salvation Army or something. They're watching some Christmas special down there now, Gail and Bruce and Grandma."

He got up and went to the window, holding back the drapes so she could see, too, if she cared to look. "It's stopped snowing and beginning to clear. It's going to be a beautiful Christmas, Chan."

"Yes," she said softly.

"Are you ready for some more sleep now?"

"No, I just feel that I want to be—quiet. But, please, can you keep talking?"

He sat down again and, after some time, said slowly, apologetically, "I just can't seem to think of things that are—original or anything. I'm sorry. . . . I'll tell you, if you like, about something that has been on my mind a good deal for the past several days. If you'd rather not hear about somebody else's problems now, just say so, okay?"

Chandra nodded, shifting a little on the pillows. Without opening her eyes, she reached out to him. He took her hand in both of his, leaned forward and kissed her cheek gently. Then there was another silence.

"Whose troubles, Eric?"

"Candy's, Candy Miller. You remember the girl you said came here on—Wednesday, was it?"

Chandra stiffened. It took a tremendous effort not to snatch her hand away from his, not to open her eyes and search his face in the dimness.

"Yes, it was Wednesday." Her voice was barely more than a whisper, toneless, but with a terrible tension.

"She asked to talk to me on Thursday night after class. I didn't have much time. No time, really, because all those other people were waiting for me back at the office. She asked a couple of questions about their semester project, the drafting project, you know. They were dumb questions and Candy's always done well in class. I could tell that wasn't really what she wanted to talk about. I finally had to tell her I couldn't stay any longer, that if she came up against some real problem with her work, we could discuss it later. She was very worried, upset, I could see that, but I really couldn't think what else I could do about it.

"We finished up at the office around midnight, or rather we stopped working for the day, and I went to that motel where I'd told you I'd be staying. I can't even remember the name of the place now. I had a reservation and when I went in to pick up my key and register, there was Candy. It seems her uncle is night manager there—she's lived with an aunt and uncle since her parents died, years ago—and she'd come in so he could take a break or something. She started crying, right there behind the registration desk, saying something about its being the will of God that I'd come in, things like that, because I was the only person in the world she felt she could talk to, and could she come to my room when her uncle got back. I had blueprints and things to go over, and hadn't been counting on much sleep anyway.

"My room was at the back of the place. When she came, she brought her car around to park it back there. It's a VW with a kooky paint job she's done herself and nobody could miss it after seeing it once. She wanted her folks to think she'd gone home. They seem to be a suspicious lot, the aunt and uncle, and with reason it seems but—Chandra, is something wrong?"

"No." Her voice sounded stifled, choked.

"You look paler again. Maybe it's just the light. Won't you try to sleep some more now?"

"No, Eric. Please, keep talking. Tell me . . ."

He lit another cigarette. She wanted one badly, but lay painfully tense, not daring to open her eyes.

"The thing she felt she couldn't talk about with anyone was that she was pregnant. She wasn't sure who by, and didn't care about that. She said there had been a lot of boys, over the years. She said she'd always felt so alone and, since she'd been old enough, sex had eased those feelings for her, for a little while at a time. She'd managed to get birth-control pills without here family's finding out but sometimes, she said, she forgot about taking them regularly. She wanted an abortion. In fact, she had arranged for one. The appointment was for today, but she was scared, mixed up, with all the feelings anyone would have to have, about whether or not she had the right to destroy life, whether or not this was what she really wanted."

"God!" Chandra gasped. "Oh, my God!"

"Chandra? Darling, I'm sorry. This is no time for me to be—"

"Eric, you don't know . . ." her voice was desperate, angry-sounding. She looked for an instant, a terrible time, at his troubled face, then turned away from him, lying on her side, facing darkness. Her clenched fists pushed so hard against her mouth that her lip began to bleed. "Go *on,* Eric!"

He spoke reluctantly. "She said she had to talk to some adult, that she had this idea I was the most secure, self-assured adult she knew. I—I didn't know any *right* things to say to her. My God, how could I? Mostly, I listened and she talked, clarifying things a little in her own mind, maybe. I hope so. She cried, a lot. She said she hadn't even been able to cry about it before. She must have been there about two hours. When she finally left, she still wasn't sure about whether or not she'd keep the appointment. Then, Friday night—you were over at Soderbergs—she stopped by to tell me about her car, and that she'd—Chandra, what's wrong?"

He had stood up and was leaning over her, trying to see her face, feeling the teneseness of her body.

"Cold," she gasped with the tears burning here face. "Eric, hold me! What about—about her car and—the rest of it?"

"Look," he said tenderly, taking her in his arms as she still lay facing away from him, "you always have this—interest in other people, compassion for them, but this is not the time. You don't need to be trying to take on other people's worries. I remember you said, that night after Candy'd come to the house, that you felt sorry for her, something you'd seen in her eyes, but I shouldn't have begun this now. What is it, Chan? Is the headache coming back? Are you—"

"For God's sake, tell me!" The words were a whisperced scream. "What about her car?"

He said, sounding bewildered, almost angry, "She'd wrecked her car, up on top of the hill. You know that old trail up there, where kids are always fooling around."

Chandra tried desperately not to let him know she was crying, tensing her body further so that it would not be shaken by sobs.

Eric went on, miserably knowing how little he knew, "When she'd first come out here last week, she remembered a boy she'd known through a lot of years of school in the city. His family moved out here some time ago. I don't know the name, but they live on top of the hill. That first day, the boy's mother told Candy he'd be home on Thursday, from some eastern college. Since she'd thought of him again, Candy said, it got to be really important that she see him, just for the sake of old friendships, so she drove out late Friday afternoon. She also meant to stop here and tell me she'd decided to go through with the abortion, but she went up the hill first. This boy mentioned that the police had been around a little earlier, to chase some kids off that old trail. They drove up to look at it, in her car, and she bet him that crazy little Volkswagen could—Chandra, are you crying?"

"Oh, Eric, I don't know," she said desolately. "I can't tell you anything now. Please! Just finish this."

"Well, her car started sliding up there in the mud, where the trail is steepest—it had started snowing by then—and she lost control of it. They both jumped out and, somehow, weren't hurt. The car went over the edge, it rolled and . . . They went back to his house, got his car and—God, it's scary to think about, her condition and . . . but she seemed all right here, sort of wild, the way people can get when they've been really frightened or they're desperate or . . . but she said she was going to stick to her decision, keep the appointment, go through with the abortion. We talked for a few minutes in the studio and I gave her one of the old cartoons that she liked, a Christmas present. Her appointment was for today and I asked her to call, because—well, there just doesn't seem to be anybody else who—Chan, please don't cry."

"Oh, Eric, you don't know . . ."

"I'm afraid you're all too right about that, but I do know that you're not doing yourself any good. Do you want to tell me? I *want* to understand, you know."

"I can't. Not now. Maybe never. Just—stay with me. I think I'll be all right soon. Really all right."

After a long time, the wrenching weeping began to subside. There was a soft tap at the door and Eric sat up as Bruce opened it.

"Dad," said Bruce, almost whispering, "could you come down for just a minute and give me your advice about fuel pumps? There's this catalog—"

"Bruce, damn it," began Eric, but Chandra put in quickly,

"Go ahead. It's all right." Her voice was hoarse now, from crying and weakness.

"You're sure . . . ?"

"Yes, darling, I'm sure."

A few moments after they'd gone, she got slowly out of bed, trembling and dizzy. In robe and slippers, she looked in on Thegn. He was sleeping deeply, with the cat beside him and Prince Charming seeming to be stretched over all available space on the floor. Chandra moved slowly, trying not to make a sound, half afraid to take deep breaths, only now completely terrified by the abyss from whose depths she had been saved. I thought

I could do it. I *was* doing it, but it would always have been a ghost, the very worst in my closet of skeletons.

She went into their room, moving very softly, feeling she had been given back, without deserving it, her right to be there. She sat on the edge of the king-size bed, begging him silently for forgiveness.

Some time later, Gail and Ethel came up to say good night, couldn't find her at first because she had not turned on any lights. Then Eric came, urging her to lie down.

"I want to have a shower first," she said, speaking very softly.

Eric frowned.

"Huh?" demanded Ethel. "Do what? You'd better not be a-doin' a thing in the world, Chandra Lynn, but lay yourself down in that bed. You're still as white as a sheet. I can tell you right now, young lady, you've had me worried plum to death. I've got the headache now myself, so bad I can't see straight from all a the worryin'. An' has any of 'em told you what the weather man's a-sayin'? He said right now, not five minutes ago, that it ain't but ten degrees an' might git plum below zero before the night's over, since it's a-clearin' up. I can tell you this, I'm a-freezin' to death. I reckon I'll *have* to leave that 'lectric blanket on all night tonight. I know I won't sleep a wink for worryin' the things a-goin' to start a fire or the like, but at least maybe I can git warm. You git yourself to bed now."

She took the few steps, kissed Chandra brusquely on the cheek and departed.

"Everything's all right now, Mom," Eric called after her. "We'll all be getting back to normal in the morning."

"Well, I don't know that that's a *good* thing," she said and went away, muttering.

Chandra said meekly, "I just have to have a shower. I feel so—dirty."

"I could come and stay in there with you," offered Gail.

"No," said Eric, catching Chandra's pleading look. "I'll be here, right outside the door. She can call me if she feels dizzy or anything."

Chandra stood up cautiously as the phone rang. Gail sprang for the bedside extension.

"Dad," she said, covering the mouthpiece, "it's for you. Some female."

With a steadying hand on the bathroom door, Chandra looked back at him. "If it's Candy, would you—maybe she doesn't have a good place to spend Christmas."

When she came from her shower, Eric was lying on the bed. It had been freshly changed and made up. Maybe Gail had done it, but, no, that symmetrical perfection could only be Eric's. He smiled at her tentatively. His face looked almost as ravaged as her own had in the brief glimpses she had had in the mirror. Her body yearned over him in deep love and concern. For the first time in her life, it seemed, she was experiencing true calm and peace and the desire to give herself, fully, thoroughly and in all ways, in love to another person, to Eric. These feelings were real now, not just the shadows she had once tried to believe were reality because of her own resignation and determination to have them because she believed they should be there.

"How do you feel?" he asked and yawned.

"I'm okay," she said, going to the window. "Oh, it's so beautiful out there. See the moon?"

She could feel the mountains out there, nearby, standing silent under their cover of sparkling whiteness. She would always need the feeling of the mountains, always rely on it, but it was what was in this house, this room, inside herself that mattered most. It was strange, she couldn't help thinking, that she really felt so little guilt over what she had done, had meant to do or not do about the car. I can stand up for myself, for what's mine. I guess I needed to know I had that in me, but, God, it's a frightening thing. But worse, so much worse, are the things I've thought about Eric, when all along he was only . . .

"Was it Candy on the phone?"

She sat on the side of the bed and lit a cigarette.

"She's all right," Eric said tiredly. "They did the surgery this morning and let her come home in the late afternoon. She hadn't called earlier because she didn't want to take a chance of her aunt or uncle overhearing. She's decided to go to California, right away, maybe the day after tomorrow if she feels up to it. She's got a couple of cousins there and feels sure she can borrow money for a bus ticket. She's been working part-time as a waitress and she had some money saved, but it's taken that for the doctor and the hospital. Her mind seems to be easy about the abortion. In fact, she seems far more upset over totaling that crazy little car.

"Chan, it was a very generous and kind idea, but—I hope you won't mind—I didn't mention Christmas here to Candy. I feel sorrier than I can tell you for her but— want this time for us, all of us, together. We have to think of ourselves sometimes."

She glanced round at him. His eyes were warm, tender. She stared, unseeing, at the closed door to the hall.

"Oh, Eric, it's been such an—awful time."

"But it's over now. Isn't it?"

"Yes, thank God, it's over now. And somehow, in spite of me, in spite of all the wrong things I thought and did and didn't do, it's come out all right and it's over. There never *was* anything, really, but I thought, I was so sure . . . I don't know if I can ever talk about it, tell you. Can you, please, for now, forgive me, believe that I'm so very sorry, without knowing . . . ?"

"A blanket apology?" he said softly.

Her head snapped round to face him, but he was smiling gently and there was no malice in him.

He sat up, took her cigarette, drew on it deeply and

put it out in the ashtray. He threw back his ever-so-neatly spread covers, turned out the lamp, drew her down beside him and covered them both.

"Never mind trying to talk now. Can it be enough that we're here, together, the way we belong? You don't have to tell me anything. Maybe someday you can, but that will be soon enough, won't it? I love you."

"Oh, and I love you," she whispered, holding him with all her strength. "So much..."

She could hear that he was smiling again when he next spoke. "All right. I apologize in advance for having to say this. I know it irritates the hell out of you so often, but I really *have* to say it this time. Can we get some sleep now?"

"All right, Eric," she murmured.

And this time, snuggled against his back, she slept before he did.

ROMANCE...ADVENTURE... DANGER!

DAUGHTERS OF THE SOUTHWIND
by Aola Vandergriff (92-042, $2.25)

The three McCleod sisters were beautiful, virtuous and bound to a dream — the dream of finding a new life in the untamed promise of the West. Their adventures in search of that dream provide the dimensions for this action-packed romantic bestseller.

DAUGHTERS OF THE WILD COUNTRY
by Aola Vandergriff (82-583, $2.25)

High in the North Country, three beautiful women begin new lives in a world where nature is raw, men are rough, and love, when it comes, shines like a gold nugget. Tamsen, Arab, and McCleod now find themselves in Russian Alaska, where power, money and human life are the playthings of a displaced, decadent aristocracy in this lusty novel ripe with love, passion, spirit and adventure.

DAUGHTERS OF THE FAR ISLANDS
by Aola Vandergriff (81-929, $2.50)

Beneath the beauty of Hawaii, like the hot lava bubbling in the volcano's crater, trouble seethes in Paradise. The daughters are destined to be caught in the turmoil between Americans who want annexation of the islands and native Hawaiians who want to keep their country. And in their own family, danger looms ... and threatens to engulf them all!

THE KINGDOM
by Ronald S. Joseph (81-467, $2.50)

To build the Lantana, the 2½ million acre ranch that men will come to call "The Kingdom." Joel Trevor and his descendants must fight for their outsized dream against Mexicans, rustlers, and carpetbaggers. In this first book of an epic trilogy of Texas, the Trevors make THE KINGDOM a mighty legend — first with cattle and barbwire, then with oil.

ROMANCE...PASSION...ADVENTURE...

LILIANE
by Annabel Erwin (91-219, $2.50)
The bestselling romantic novel of a beautiful woman swept by the storms of history from the embattled France of Napoleon to Virginia where violence simmered beneath the surface of slavery-dependent plantation life.

FLEUR
by Rachel Delauney (82-656, $2.25)
Young Fleur was beauty and innocence unguarded—on a plantation where men knew only greed, cruelty and lust. Garland was the only man Fleur could ever love but he was her slave, a man she owned—a man she burned to possess but could not have!

WARNER BOOKS
P.O. Box 690
New York, N.Y. 10019

Please send me the books I have selected. Enclose check or money order only, no cash please. Plus 50¢ per order and 20¢ per copy to cover postage and handling. N.Y. State and California residents add applicable sales tax.

Please allow 4 weeks for delivery.

_____ Please send me your free mail order catalog

_____ Please send me your free Romance books catalog

Name_____

Address_____

City_____

State_____Zip_____

Handle with Care

Tana Reiff

A Pacemaker® *WorkTales* Book

FEARON/JANUS
Belmont, California

Simon & Schuster Supplementary Education Group

WorkTales

A Robot Instead
The Easy Way
Change Order
Fighting Words
The Rip-Offs
The Right Type
The Saw that Talked
Handle with Care
The Road to Somewhere
Help When Needed

Cover illustration: Margaret Sanfilippo
Interior illustration: James Balkovek

Copyright © 1992 by Fearon/Janus, 500 Harbor Boulevard, Belmont, California 94002. All rights reserved. No part of this book may be reproduced by any means, transmitted, or translated into a machine language without written permission from the publisher.

ISBN 0-8224-7151-5
Library of Congress Catalog Card Number: 91-70783
Printed in the United States of America
1. 9 8 7 6 5 4 3 2